# WORLD MADE BY HAND

JAMES
HOWARD
KUNSTLER

# WORLD MADE BY HAND

Atlantic Monthly Press
New York

*Published simultaneously in Canada*
*Printed in the United States of America*

FIRST EDITION

ISBN-10: 0-87113-978-2
ISBN-13: 978-0-87113-978-8

Atlantic Monthly Press
an imprint of Grove/Atlantic, Inc.
841 Broadway
New York, NY 10003

Distributed by Publishers Group West

www.groveatlantic.com

08 09 10 11 12 13    10 9 8 7 6 5 4 3 2 1

To Sally Eckhoff
Fabulous transcender of the mundane
With love

*Whom will you cry to, heart? More and more lonely,*
*your path struggles on through incomprehensible*
*mankind. All the more futile perhaps*
*for keeping its own direction,*
*keeping on toward the future,*
*toward what has been lost.*

—Rilke


*I am a pilgrim and a stranger*
*Traveling through this wearisome land*
*I've got a home in that yonder city*
*And it's not (good Lord it's not) not made by hand*

—American gospel song

Sometime in the not-distant future. . . .

# ONE

Loren and I walked the railroad tracks along the river coming back from fishing the big pool under the old iron bridge, and I couldn't remember a lovelier evening before or after our world changed. Down by the rushing stream, banks of wild yellow irises shimmered in the twilight, and up in the vaulted corridor that the tracks cut through the trees, the mild June air was filled with twinkling green fireflies. We'd both been drinking some of Jane Ann's wine.

"It reminds me of Christmas at the mall," he said.

"I don't miss the mall," I said. "I miss a lot of things, but not that."

"Do you think I'm pathetic?"

"You're obsessed with the old days."

"Most of my life happened in the old days. Yours too, Robert."

It made me sad, but I didn't say so because the evening was so beautiful and that was something to be grateful for. Now and then, the fireflies pulsed in unison, mysteriously, as if they all agreed on something we humans didn't know about.

"I wish I had a jar. I'd catch some," Loren said. The fact that he was our minister and fifty-two years old had not diminished his boyish enthusiasm, which was one reason we were such close friends. He pulled out the bottle again, and polished off the dregs. Jane Ann, Loren's wife, made good wine, considering what we had to work with around here. She flavored this batch with sweet woodruff to round off the foxy roughness. When the bottle was empty Loren pretended to try to catch fireflies with it, but he was obviously just clowning around. Finally, he stuck the bottle in the back flap of his fishing vest to take home and reuse. We resumed walking the tracks.

2 JAMES HOWARD KUNSTLER

"I've been thinking lately," he said.

"It's not healthy to obsess about the past."

"No, I've got an idea."

"Oh? Let's hear it."

"We should start a laundry."

"A laundry?"

"Yeah, a community laundry. A place where people bring their clothes and bedsheets and all, and they get washed there."

"What about Mrs. Myles?" I said. Lucy Myles was my neighbor. She took in quite a bit of other people's washing.

"She could work for us," Loren said.

"Us?"

"Well, that's why I'm telling you about this. We'd be partners."

"I don't know the first thing about running a laundry."

"No, your job is to help me start it up. Fix the building. Figure out the water system. Get the tubs going. Keep things running. You know how to do all that stuff."

"Where do you think you would do this?"

"We can use the old Wayland-Union Mill building. The title's open," he said, meaning that the owners were known to be dead with no heirs and assigns, a common condition in these times. "It would be useful for everybody. And we could make a little honest profit too."

"What do you do with the dirty water?"

"Into the river," he said.

"It's got soap in it."

"It's just gray water. It'll go downstream to the Hudson."

"That's not right."

"It's below where we fish. And mostly from town. It's just soapy water."

"That's a hell of an attitude."

"Don't get all *environmental* with me," he said.

"I wouldn't dump soapy water in the river."

"It wouldn't affect anything."

"I wouldn't be so sure."

"You're being an asshole."

"Nice talk, Reverend."

"I've been thinking about this for a long time."

"Maybe you should think about it longer."

"Condescending prick."

"Vulgarian."

"Nabob of negativism."

I let him have the last word. It was always better that way with Loren. He could keep it up forever. We walked a ways more, enjoying the silence and the fireflies.

"Nabob of negativism?" I said. "Where'd you get that one?"

"Spiro T. Agnew."

"Who was he?"

"Vice president under Nixon."

"Oh? I don't remember Nixon too well."

"Agnew used to call news reporters 'nattering nabobs of negativism.'"

"He wouldn't be able to say that nowadays, would he?"

"No, he'd have to call them nabobs of nothingness," Loren said and laughed at his own joke. I guess I didn't think it was that funny, since we didn't have news reporters anymore and you barely knew what was going on five miles away. "Hey, look," he said. "Give this laundry idea a chance. It would be good for the community. Try not to be negative."

"I'm not negative."

"Contrary then."

"I'm not contrary."

"You should hear yourself."

Eventually the train tracks crossed over Lovell Road, and we got off them there while the road took us across the river on a steel and concrete bridge that was falling to pieces now. It had been years since the state of New York repaired any of these things. There were big holes in the deck you could see clear through. Another couple of spring floods and it might be swept away altogether. On the far bank stood an old hydroelectric station, or the brick shell

of one. An inscription in the masonry lintel over the door said it
was built in 1919. The big power company, Niagara Mohawk,
closed down all these little generating plants in the 1960s because
they were supposedly inefficient. Nothing was left but the walls
and part of the roof. The turbines and metal parts had long since
been sold for scrap and every other useful thing was scavenged out.
We couldn't replace them anymore. It was too bad because it might
have lit up our whole town. Anyway, the little dam there had been
breeched, and rebuilding that would have been more than our community could manage. I don't know if anybody would even have
known how to do it. It was chilling to reflect on how well the world
used to work and how much we'd lost.

We stopped halfway across the bridge in the lovely pink light
that remained of the long June day and peered down to the water.
Scores of big trout finned in the current beside the crumbling bridge
abutment. A nice hatch of cream-colored mayflies fluttered off the
water and mingled with the fireflies. The swift little mud swallows
that nested under the bridge did an aerial ballet through it, gorging
themselves. Plenty of mayflies would still get away for their one ec-
static night of reproducing in the treetops. They would return to the
river to die the next morning. It was called the "spinner fall." They'd
been doing it for millions of years before we showed up.

"Want to go down and try some?" I said.

"My creel is full," Loren said.

"We could put back what we catch."

"I've fished enough tonight, Robert."

"Okay, let's go home."

It was about a three-mile walk home to Union Grove. In the
old days, you'd drive it, of course, but now you walked. I didn't
mind. I enjoyed the peacefulness and easy pace of the walk. In a
car, I remembered, you generally noticed only what was in your
head or on the radio, while the landscape itself seemed dead, or
at least irrelevant. Walking, it was impossible to not pay attention. On a mild luminous evening like this, the landscape came
alive. The crickets had started up. In the distance a last glimmer

of sun caught the top of Pumpkin Hill where men were still out mowing the first hay crop on the Deaver farm. You could hear their horses from down where we were, and someone was singing while he worked. Washington County is a terrain of gentle hills and close valleys that grows more rugged as you get east over toward the Vermont border, where the Green Mountains begin in earnest. In the early twenty-first century, farming had all but died out here. We got our food from the supermarket, and not everybody cared where the supermarket got it as long as it was there on the shelves. A few elderly dairymen hung on. Many let their fields and pastures go to scrub. Some sold out to what used to be called developers, and they'd put in five or ten poorly built houses. Now, in the new times, there were far fewer people, and many of the houses outside town were being taken down for their materials. Farming was back. That was the only way we got food. Ben Deaver employed at least twenty men from town on his farm. You could smell the horses down where we were on the bridge. Sometimes the whole world smelled of horse. It was my fond wish to own one some day.

Across the bridge, Lovell Road came to a T at old Route 29, which used to be the main route between the Hudson Valley and Arlington, Vermont. It was a standard state two-laner. We headed west toward town on it. When the sun finally went down, the sky above the hills remained pale blue, the cloud bottoms all salmon and orange. We walked right down the middle of the highway, over the faint ghost of the double yellow line. After years of neglect the pavement was broken with great fissures and potholes the size of a bathtub. In some stretches, it had gone back to dirt. Loren and I were both lost in our own thoughts when we heard horses at a distance coming up behind us. We turned together.

It was an open cart with two wooden-spoked, iron-rimmed wheels, not the old automobile tires that you used to see on a common utility wagon. You could still find rubber tires here and there, but you couldn't get patch kits or the kinds of adhesives that would stand up to a repair job anymore, so we had no choice but to go back to wooden wheels with iron rims. This sort of vehicle was sometimes referred to as a Foley rig. I couldn't tell you who Foley was, but that's what it was called. There were stories, as about so many things in these new times, where the actual facts were sparse or elusive, but they named the rig after him. There were two figures aboard, a man driving and a woman beside him.

The rig came trotting out of the twilight, bouncing on the rough road, until it reached us and the driver slowed his team to a walk. They were fine, tall, stout matched blacks with some feathering on their lower legs, a mix of some kind. Since the world changed, there had not been much time to breed horses, so around here anything distinct from the American quarter horse or a common draft animal tended to stand out. These looked like they had some Percheron or other cold blood in them and their size, at least sixteen hands, was another sign. The driver brought them to a halt beside Loren and me.

He was a stranger, a clean-shaven, middle-aged man, with a nose too small for his face. It made him look oddly boyish. Among men in Union Grove, beards were the norm so any clean-shaven man was apt to look young. He took off his broad-brimmed straw hat so as to show off, or so it seemed, his full head of black hair with a few strands of gray at the temples. His skin had a pinkish cast, as though he spent a lot of time indoors.

"Brother Jobe," he said, reaching down from his seat to press our flesh like a politician. We would learn later that he spelled it this way, with an *e* on the end.

"Loren Holder's the name."

"How'd you do?" Brother Jobe said.

"Fine," Loren said. "Beautiful evening."

"No, I meant how did you make out fishing?"

"Oh, pretty good," Loren said.

"I hear the river's better'n it ever was before," Brother Jobe said.

"It's quite good," Loren said. "Less angling pressure nowadays."

"I haven't had the time to try it myself. Busy tending to my flock."

I couldn't help glancing at the young woman beside him. She had been sitting very still, like a startled doe, as if stillness might enable her to remain unscrutinized. Both she and Brother Jobe were dressed in the severe clothing of the pious. He had on a black sack suit, a cotton shirt with collar points, and a floppy black bow tie. She wore a straw hat secured under her chin with a black ribbon. She'd gathered her thick red hair into a single braid. Her skin was so pale as to appear luminous in the low light. The longer I looked the more I noticed that she had a good figure within her plain muslin blouse. Though it was buttoned to her throat, you could see the shadows of her flesh within. Her delicate face suggested she was not much more than sixteen. Few young women were left in our town. The Mexican flu had been especially vicious among the young, though death by other means had not spared any age group.

"Say, aren't you the chief over at First Congregational?" Brother Jobe asked Loren.

"I'm the minister there, yes." Loren said. "How'd you know?"

"I've got an outfit of my own," Brother Jobe said, as if that answered the question.

"Oh?" Loren said. "Whereabouts?"

"Why, right here in Union Grove."

Loren cut a puzzled glance my way.

"Bought the old high school day before yesterday," this Brother Jobe said.

With the recurrent sickness and the problems with electricity and everything else, the sprawling, low-slung high school complex at the north edge of town had fallen into disuse. Once, it had collected pupils spread out over half the county in a fleet of shiny yellow buses. The small number of children in our community went to the church school now.

"That's a surprise," Loren said.

"We've been on a hard and prayerful search," Brother Jobe said. "This place looked about perfect."

"How many of you are there?"

"Seventy-three adults."

"Where'd you come from."

"We were last in Pennsylvania."

"Why did you leave?" I said.

Brother Jobe regarded me closely for a moment, as though my question were impertinent.

"We weren't comfortable there," he said. "Who are you?"

"Name's Robert Earle."

"Robert Earle what?"

"Just Earle. That's the family name."

"Oh? Down where we're from that'd be a man's given name."

"Like Billy Bob."

"Exactly."

"I take it you hail from Dixie," Loren said.

"Indeed I do," Brother Jobe said, running a sleeve across his damp brow. It must have been uncomfortable for him in a suit on a warm summer night like it was.

"A troubled place these days, isn't it?" Loren said.

"There's plenty of mischief to go around this poor country of ours. What's left of it."

"We don't get much news of the outside anymore," Loren said. "The electric's hardly on these days."

"We've noticed," Brother Jobe said. "But you've got something here maybe even more valuable."

"Yeah?" Loren said. "What's that?"

"Peace and tranquillity."

"The last real news we had was when the bomb went off in Los Angeles."

"California got dealt a bad hand, all right," Brother Jobe said, "but things are rough from sea to shining sea. It's no fun in Phoenix or Albuquerque either, so I've heard. From Texas clear to Florida, there's folks shooting each other and trouble between the races and all like that. Seems like the law is on the run everywhere. We were on our way up out of Virginia when the other bomb hit Washington, D.C. Pennsylvania wasn't no picnic after that, I can tell you. We tried it for more than two years, but it wasn't any go for us there. We pulled out the end of April."

"I'd like to hear what you've observed on your travels sometime," Loren said.

"Hardship. Not a whole lot of brotherhood."

"This is a friendly place," I said. "But it would have been nice if the powers that be had consulted us about selling the school. We weren't informed."

"It's all signed and legal, I assure you."

"It seems to have happened under cover of night," I said.

"Are you up to the Lord's business too?" Brother Jobe asked me pointedly.

"In a manner of speaking,"

"How's that?"

"I'm a carpenter," I said.

Brother Jobe pointed at me and laughed, the way comedians used to do long ago on TV. The girl beside him cracked a trace of a smile too, but looked away self-consciously when she saw me notice. Eventually Brother Jobe's strenuous hilarity ebbed.

"Let's have a look in those creels, boys. I've got to see those whoppers you bragged on."

Loren opened up his creel and held it up to show.

"*Hooo-weee,*" Brother Jobe said. "I'll take 'em."

"Excuse me?" Loren said.

"Five hundred bucks, American."

"They're not for sale."

"Aw heck, okay, seven hundred fifty."

"No, I—"

"You boys drive a hard bargain," Brother Jobe said and whipped out a fat roll of bills. "Here's a thousand. Lay them babies right down there under the dash by my boots."

Loren shot a look at me that attempted to convey a humorous appreciation for all this but really signaled his discomfort. He liked to make other people happy but not usually at his own expense.

He had lined his creel with ferns to keep his four nice trout cushioned and moist, and he now laid them all down, including the ferns, like a kind of grocer's display, at the driver's feet up under the Foley's curved mudguard.

"Let's see yours now," Brother Jobe said to me.

"I didn't get any."

He guffawed. "Like fun you didn't. Let's have a look."

"There's nothing to show."

"I thought you said it was good fishing down there tonight."

"It was good for him, not so good for me."

He held up the bankroll again. "Sure you won't talk to the old persuader?"

"A dollar isn't what it used to be."

"That's the God's truth. But heck, I've got a flock to feed."

"Sorry."

Brother Jobe made a kind of show of looking deflated for a moment, then pulled himself upright and puffed out his cheeks.

"All right then. I hope you have better luck next time. We'll be starting a regular service soon in that old school auditorium. Maybe you'll come by sometime."

"I'm in his outfit," I said, cocking my head at Loren.

"We put on a hell of a show. Hymns and preaching. I got a 1930 Schwimmer pump organ. It's like the old-timey times."

Smiling broadly, Brother Jobe raised his whip and sort of dusted both horses over the hindquarters. They snorted and began to walk. They were well trained. We watched them set off and a little way down he got them trotting. He never did introduce us to his companion.

# Two

We walked the next mile in silence. The brilliant salmon-colored sky turned to a yellow-gray clotted pudding as darkness came on. I wondered what the weather would be like. You never knew in advance anymore. A warm breeze had come up, and I surmised it would be hotter tomorrow.

"What are you going to spend all that money on?" I said finally.

"It's not like I wanted to sell them," Loren said.

"Then why did you?"

"You saw how he was. Might as well have been a holdup."

"Well it looks like you've suddenly got some competition in town."

"The church isn't a business."

"I don't know about that. Sometimes it seems like the only business left."

"That's why you should take my idea seriously," Loren said.

"Okay, I'll think about it."

"I want you to go look through the building with me."

"All right."

"It'd benefit everybody."

We hiked past the raggedy commercial strip that used to mark the eastern built-up fringe of town, but the town had shrunk back into itself. The strip mall stores were vacant. Spiky mulleins and sumacs erupted through the broken pavement of the parking lot. The plate glass was gone and the aluminum sashes, and everything else worth scavenging was stripped out. A fragment of the plastic Kmart sign remained bolted to the façade—the piece that said—*art*. The irony did not move me. I wasn't sorry that it was out of business, but I was sorry that the remnants were still there.

"Did you notice the girl?" Loren said.

"Of course I did."

"Kind of young, didn't you think?"

"Maybe she was his daughter."

"Didn't look a bit like him," Loren said. "How can they come in here and buy the school and we don't even know about it?"

"It wouldn't be the first time Dale made a deal on his own." Dale Murray was our mayor. The apparatus of our government had fallen way off, along with the population. It was Dale and a drunken constable for the most part, and a magistrate who said he wouldn't do the job if elected—before he was elected. Sometimes things just happened and then you heard about it. Mostly nothing happened. "The school was just sitting there, rotting," I said.

"It must be worth something," Loren said. "I don't like giving up on the idea that we might need it again in the future."

"It's your nostalgia working overtime."

"Well, it bothers me. And more to the point, I'm not sure I like that fellow," Loren said. "Why did they have to pick this town?"

"People are on the move again. We should expect it. Maybe some of them will break off from his bunch and come our way."

"I doubt it. Those sectarians are tight as ticks."

"We'll see. It's still a free country, isn't it?"

"I don't know what kind of country it is anymore," Loren said, "and neither do you."

We hiked past the burned-out hulk of the old wholesale beverage center.

"Do you want any of these trout to take home?" I finally said, offering my creel to Loren.

"You don't have to."

"I'm just going to put them in the smoker. Go ahead. Take two."

"Okay. Thank you."

"Tell Jane Ann I appreciated the wine."

By now, we'd entered the town proper. The streetlamps were off, as usual. Many of the houses we passed were dark. I would venture that the population here was down by three-quarters. The safety net for the elderly had dissolved, with so much else, and since a disproportionate number of houses in town had been owned by older folks who had died off, many were now vacant. It was nice to see the Copeland kids running around playing in the yard beside their big old place, with candles burning inside, welcoming and homey. Jerry Copeland was our doctor. He was a GP but he had to do it all, becoming an excellent surgeon by necessity. The hospital in Glens Falls had closed after the flu killed more than half the staff. Jerry had trouble getting medicines and supplies, but he was also resourceful. His wife, Jeanette, was an able assistant and a dazzling soprano. Their boys were polite and well behaved. Being so few in numbers, children no longer enjoyed solidarity in rebellion, and our society was too fragile to indulge much symbolic misbehavior. The flu had carried off Jerry's youngest, a girl named Fawn. There was nothing even he could do.

We eventually came to Loren's parish house next to the big white wooden church on Salem Street. The church was in excellent condition because those of us who remained did not have diversions like television or recreational shopping anymore, and the church had become our get-together place in a way churches had ceased to be for generations. So we took care of it. We worked on it and we kept it painted, though of course paint wasn't what it used to be either. We made it ourselves out of slaked lime, milk, and chalk.

I gave Loren two nice trout of my five and we said goodnight.

My house was a block and a half past where Linden Street met Salem Street. On nights like this the surface normality of small-town America overwhelmed you with sadness. Here and there a candle glowed in a window, but people worked hard and were likely to turn in when the sun went down, so it was difficult to tell occupied houses from vacant ones. My own house was haunted by the ghosts of my family: wife Sandy, gone from an outbreak of encephalitis, daughter Genna, taken by the flu, and son Daniel, who left home and did not return. The sight of the place plunged me into memory and feeling no matter how many times I came upon it.

Just as things were starting to fall apart, Sandy had painted the house a gray-violet with sage green trim. She was a stickler for quality materials, and the paint had stood up well in the years since. The house was built in 1904 in the arts-and-crafts style, which was a romantic reaction to the juggernaut of industry, and perhaps because of that it worked well under these new conditions of austerity. The front porch was deep and graceful, though I had lately been using it as a woodshop in the warm part of the year. Inside it was generous for a bungalow, with four bedrooms in all, and it had many fine touches, including oak wainscoting, a cozy inglenook beside the fieldstone fireplace, built-in bookshelves everywhere, and graceful windows with arched sashes that still slid beautifully and closed snugly after more than a hundred years.

I lost Sandy and eleven-year-old Genna in two successive years. Daniel was thirteen when his sister passed away and nineteen when he set out from here, which was two years ago, and I wished I knew whether he was alive and well, and where he had gone and been to, but there were no more phones or mail as we once knew them. I tried to avoid nostalgia because it could destroy you. I was alone now.

# THREE

I don't think the electricity had been on for half an hour all that month. When it did come on it was always at some time you least expected it, before you could do something useful with it, like run a board through a planer. It cut out as mysteriously as it came on, so you didn't dare start any job of work involving machines. When the electricity was on, you didn't get much over the radio. We apparently had a president now named Harvey Albright, but I would be damned if I knew how he got elected because they didn't hold it here. This was well after the short, unhappy reign of General Fellowes, who removed President Sharpe from office on account of the fiasco in the Holy Land and might have been instrumental in his death. Fellowes himself was taken down by the more constitutionally minded generals, and Vice President Beebe was installed to finish Ted Sharpe's term, with the army looking over his shoulder. The various shifting factions worked hard at managing the news even as the TV, newspapers, and Internet were failing in one way or another from irregular electric service.

The bomb in Washington put an end to that revolving cast of political characters. We heard rumors that a federal government had been reorganized in Nashville and then Chicago under Speaker of the House Rhodes, who was out of town when Washington was bombed. By that time we weren't getting any oil from the Middle East or Venezuela, and even the mail stopped. The last election evidently happened around the time of the flu, when every community was shuttered up in desperate quarantine, at least here in the upper Hudson River Valley. It seemed to me that the federal government was little more than a figment of the collective memory. Everything was local now. We liked to think the worst disorders were behind us, that we came out on the other side of something. But the truth was we didn't know what the truth was anymore.

I had put some raspberry canes in the side yard three years ago, and they had filled in nicely. I noticed drupes were forming on the canes but were still green and hard. In a week or so I would have all the raspberries I could eat. I could also trade them for bacon. I was lighting a stub of candle on the kitchen counter when I heard a sigh and wheeled around to see Jane Ann's face emerge out of the warm light as the wick took flame.

"It's only me," she said.

"You scared me."

"Sorry."

"It's not your night."

"I know."

"Loren's back too, of course."

"He can find his way around the house okay without me."

"He'll worry."

"I brought you a brown bread," she said. Jane Ann was resourceful in the kitchen. We had trouble getting wheat lately because trade had fallen off, and we couldn't grow it locally because of a persistent wheat rust in the soil that returned no matter how you rested a field. Mostly we had to rely on corn and buckwheat, with some barley, rye, and oats. Buckwheat, of course, is not even remotely related to real wheat. It has no gluten in it. Ground into flour, it was good only for pancakes. Otherwise, we ate the whole groats boiled, like rice, or baked like a pilaf with other things mixed in. Jane Ann's brown bread was corn and rye, sweetened with honey and steamed rather than baked. It was her New England heritage.

"Thank you."

"You're welcome."

For some time now, Jane Ann had been visiting me one night a week in a connubial way. Usually she came Thursday nights. It was an arrangement. She was my best friend's wife. My wife was dead. No suitable single women were around. Loren was apparently no longer able to have sexual relations with Jane Ann for reasons that I did not delve into but were probably not that mysterious. After all, things happened to people and between people and it was not necessarily anyone's fault. We were able to manage things among the three of us this way. Perhaps we flattered ourselves to think it could go on like that indefinitely. But Jane Ann had no intention of leaving Loren, and I didn't want her to. It wouldn't have helped her or me or any of us if she did. She had been in a state of despair since her girl was taken by the flu and her son, Evan, went off to see the country with my Daniel, who was a year older than him. We used to call people like her "depressed," but we dropped those clinical locutions because despair was a spiritual condition that was as real to us as the practical difficulties we struggled with in everyday life. Jane Ann could not stop mourning. She was not the person she used to be, but she resembled her.

She reached up and undid my belt buckle in the candlelight. At forty-seven, Jane Ann was still a beautiful woman, with deep breasts, a slim waist, and a small behind. Her qualities of physical beauty were undiminished by the constant sorrow she carried like a burdensome cargo. These days, most anyone who had survived was in good physical condition because life was so relentlessly physical, unless they drank too much. She generally kept her silvery gold hair in a fat braid. Sometimes she let it out for me because I asked her to, as a favor, but only if I asked. She told me she was beyond capable of conceiving a child, but I secretly believed that our relations were, on her part, an enactment of the wish to do so. I loved Jane Ann but I was conscious that I was making love with a ghost. She was so unlike my Sandy that I could not have pretended she was Sandy, and Jane Ann was not altogether present herself either.

This night we made love quickly as though doing each other a routine kindness. I felt sorry for both of us, and for Loren too, old as we all were and rather hopeless in our strange circumstances. Afterward, Jane Ann sat on the edge of the bed lacing her doeskin slippers. Her shoulders seemed to slump in the candlelight.

"I heard somebody bought the high school," she said. "A preacher with a congregation, they say."

"We met him on the road coming back from fishing."

"Oh?"

"He was driving a rig with two fine horses."

"What was he like?"

"Pushy. Seemed full of himself. Loren will tell you about him. Why did you come here tonight? It isn't Thursday until tomorrow."

"Oh? I lose track."

"Feeling sad?"

"Yes. A bit more than usual, I guess."

"Loren's an upright man," I said.

"It's true. But I'm still sad."

"He's got two nice trout waiting for you."

She finished lacing her slippers and turned around to face me. "How do you keep from going crazy, Robert?"

I had to think about it. "I'm not sure. Disposition maybe."

"Sometimes I wish you were as sad as me."

"Why would you suppose I'm not?"

She shrugged her shoulders.

"We're not the first society who fell into hardship," I said.

"I can't find much consolation in that."

"Maybe I am crazy. I live with hope."

"What for?"

"That we'll recover some. Maybe not back to before, but some. I live in hope that my Daniel will walk into this house again some fine morning, and your boy with him."

Jane Ann sighed.

"It's not all bad now," I said.

"We've lost our world."

"Only the part that the machines lived in."

Jane Ann patted my thigh, but said no more and got up to leave.

"Thanks very much for the bread," I called after her.

She was careful not to let the screen door slap on her way out.

# Four

In a recurrent dream, I was sitting in a comfortable padded chair gliding swiftly over the landscape in a way that felt supernatural yet oddly familiar. I did not feel any wind in my face, despite the speed, which was much faster than anything I was accustomed to. I was deeply at ease in my wonderful traveling chair and thrilled by the motion. Familiar sights whizzed by: the Larmon farm on the Battenville Road, Holyrood's cider mill, the old railroad over-pass outside the village of Shushan, pastures and cornfields, hills, hollows, and houses I had known for years. In the dream, I came to realize that I was moving inside some kind of protective enve-lope, not just sitting in a wonderful chair. Then, a dashboard resolved before me with its round glowing gauges, and then the steering wheel. Of course, I remembered, with the bottom fall-ing out of my stomach, I am driving a car! It had been so many years since I had done that! It was a dream-memory of something that now seemed hardly different from the magic carpets of my childhood storybooks. But then the speed picked up alarmingly and I was no longer at ease. I careened around curves in the road just missing gigantic trees. I couldn't remember what to do with my feet. I had lost control . . .

I woke up gasping to a great commotion of preaching on the radio. Even after I caught my breath, I could not overcome the sink-ing sensation in my gut. I recalled Jane Ann visiting me the night before and wondered what we thought we were doing together. The purity of my despair astonished me. The uproar on the radio finally wrenched me out of it. Roosters crowed off in the distance behind the din. I never turned off the old FM receiver in the living room anymore so as to be aware when the electricity kicked back on. It hadn't been on in weeks. I wasn't even sure who or what was putting juice through the wires when it did come on.

Sunlight was already filtering through the curtains, so I supposed it was around six. We lived more by the sun than by the clock, but I did own a clock. It was an eight-day windup console clock which I kept on the mantel in the living room, and it was the only timepiece in the house that worked anymore. It was made by my friend Andrew Pendergast, the town librarian, a man of broad talents: portrait painter, sometime theater director, leader of our church music circle, and a wonderful piano player. He repaired instruments and made strings out of sheep intestine for those of us who played instruments that required them—in my case, fiddle.

Living by the clock was an old habit that died hard. Not much that we did required punctuality, but people still wanted to know what time it was. Andrew had old almanacs that told the sunrise and sunset for a given date so he always had the correct time. If you asked him, Andrew would stop by your house and check your clock against his pocket watch, which was accurate. It was not so hard to keep track of the date, probably because holidays were important to us in ways that might be inconceivable to people whose sole conception of Christmas had been based on frantic excursions to gigantic chain stores. We lived by the seasons now. Our survival depended on it. And we marked the seasons by frequent holiday celebrations, fetes, levees, balls, and solemn days of remembrance.

The racket was coming over what used to be our public radio station, WAMC out of Albany, but the familiar reassuring voices of normality were long gone. Some febrile evangelist was railing from the Book of Revelation:

*"I know thy works and where thou dwellest, even where Satan's seat is; and thou holdest fast my name, and hast not denied my faith, even in those days wherein Antipas was my faithful martyr, who was slain among you, where Satan dwelleth . . ."*

I switched on the television on the outside chance that something might come through. Nothing had been on for years. The local network affiliates withered away after the national network of cable channels went out, until there was nothing. But when the electricity did come on, I automatically turned on the TV and roamed around the stations to see if anything had changed. It hadn't.

I searched the FM band but there was nothing besides other pious pleaders, and they didn't come in too well. The AM band offered about the same thing, only with worse reception, nothing remotely describable as news, and no music because commercial entertainment as we knew it was no more, and its handmaiden, advertising, had gone with it. No shortwave bands were on my old receiver, so I returned the signal to the ranter on 90.3 FM just to hear another voice while I addressed myself to the project of breakfast. Even if the world had gone crazy, I preferred to know what was on its addled mind. Among us survivors were many who were confused and despondent.

*"I have a few things against thee, because thou hast there them that hold the doctrine of Balaam, who taught Balac to cast a stumblingblock before the children of Israel, to eat things sacrificed unto idols, and to commit fornication."*

What used to be the rear patio of my house was rigged up to be a summer kitchen. You didn't want to run a wood-burning stove indoors when it was ninety degrees, and it was that hot much of the time, May through October. I had a sheet-metal wood-burning cookstove out there under a roof with open side walls, a sturdy eight-foot pine table I'd made, and a cupboard with pierced tin panels to keep my salt and cornmeal and honey safe from little animals while it let air in. A smoker sat a way back from there, an old refrigerator on blocks, over by the fence. It was hard to imagine that we used to cultivate lawns. My yard was now a raised bed garden. It was geometrical, a cruciform pattern, the beds transected on the diagonal as well, with brick paths carefully laid. With our many material privations, it was not possible to live without beauty anymore. I spent a lot of time in my garden, and the feel of being in it was as important to me as the vegetables I grew. At the center, I built a birdbath out of stacked granite blocks with a concave piece of slate on top that caught the rain. The birds seemed satisfied with it and it was pleasant to look at. I would have preferred a statue of the goddess Diana in the manner of Augustus Saint-Gaudens, but I hadn't managed to scrounge one up. The smoker, much as I needed it, was an insult to the garden. It galled me to see the damned thing: a scarred old Kelvinator that mocked our failed industrial dreams. I intended to replace it someday with a proper brick smokehouse.

I prepared to smoke the trout I had left from the evening's fishing because they'd be worth something in trade and for breakfast I had plenty of eggs and the brown bread Jane Ann brought me. We didn't have a lot of things, but we had plenty of eggs. Half the people in town kept chickens, and rabbits too, which was the reason I didn't. Much of the year we had plenty of milk and butter as well, though milk was more difficult to keep in high summer because we lacked refrigeration. Butter in a covered crock would keep on a sideboard for a week or more, even in hot weather. Many farmers made cheeses and traded for them, and Bill Schroeder, who ran the creamery, made several kinds.

So I had two fires to get going that day: cookstove and smoker. I split up ash kindling splints and whittled down some of them to shavings and started a fire under the smoker with one match. You didn't like to waste matches. I put apple wood chunks on the burning ash kindling and let it work. By then I had the cookstove kindled up and brought fire to it from the smoker, and soon they were both going.

I generally ate a big breakfast. The amount of walking I did required it. In the old days, as a corporate executive, I kept going on little more than continuous cups of black coffee until dinnertime. I had one of those steel thermal mugs you carried everywhere with you as a kind of signifier of how busy, and therefore how important, you were. The people in my office joked that my thermal mug was surgically attached to my arm. In those days, in a life that now seemed as if it had taken place on another planet, we lived in Brookline, Massachusetts, and I worked for a software company called Ellipses on Route 128. Our division made network security programs:

antivirus, antispam, antihacker, firewalls. I was head of marketing and spent the bulk of my time organizing promotional events at national trade shows in places like Atlanta and Las Vegas. We'd pay big-time rock and roll bands to get the customers in for the CEO's sales pitch. We'd buy out whole vintages of California wineries to impress our clients. We'd hire celebrity chefs to feed them. My job paid well and we enjoyed the status of a nice house, German cars, and private schools for the children. I multitasked so hard I had panic attacks. I suppose all the coffee I drank didn't help. Then, within a short span of time, our world changed completely.

We came here, to Union Grove, Sandy's hometown, after the bomb went off in Los Angeles. That act of jihad was extraordinarily successful. It tanked the whole U.S. economy. The authorities finally had to start inspecting every shipping container that entered every harbor in the nation. Freighters anchored for weeks off Seattle, Norfolk, Baltimore, the Jersey terminals, Boston, and every other port of entry. Many of them eventually turned around and went home with their cargoes undelivered. The earth stopped being flat and became very round again. Even nations that were still talking to us after the war in the Holy Land, stopped being able to trade with us. Ellipses went down by stages, one division at a time. Ours was the last to go.

I was thirty-six then. We sold the house in Brookline at a substantial loss just to get out. We dumped the big BMW and kept the sedan. You could still get gasoline, though it was expensive and scarcities were worsening. We wanted to be as far away from the action as we could get without leaving the northeastern region of the country. Sandy's father, Bill Trammel, was alive then, a retired vice president of the nearby Glens Falls National Bank. He was glad to have us all in the house in Union Grove because Sandy's mother had died of cancer the year before, and it was a bad time to be old and lonely. Pneumonia took Bill two years after we arrived. Common antibiotics were in short supply. In a way, I was glad he went before Sandy and Genna and everything else that happened, because it would have broken his heart. He was absolutely a man of the twentieth century. His last coherent words, in the delirium of illness, were *"Don't worry, I'll bring the car around . . ."*

By the time he passed away, it was obvious there would be no return to "normality." The economy wouldn't be coming back. Globalism was over. The politicians and generals were failing to pull things together at the center. We would not be returning to Boston. The computer industry, in which so many hopes had been vested, was fading into history. I was fortunate to have carpentry skills to fall back on and to have a decent collection of hand tools.

The evangelist on the radio cut out, and I realized that the electricity had gone off. I felt relieved, even though I had only myself to blame for leaving the radio on. Listening to these maniacs had gotten to be a compulsion for me. I was desperate to learn anything about the world outside Washington County, because I worried constantly about my Daniel and where he might be, and whether it was dangerous there.

We didn't have coffee anymore, or any caffeinated substitutes for it. I made a pot of rose-hip tea, which was our chief source of vitamin C, and fried up three slices of Jane Ann's brown bread with plenty of butter in a cast-iron skillet that I had owned my entire adult life—I actually remembered buying it in a Target store in Hadley, Massachusetts, the year after I graduated from Amherst College. When the bread slices were crispy and fragrant, I took them out and dropped in three small pullet eggs. I missed black pepper terribly. We hadn't seen any for years. Cinnamon too. Anything from the Far East was no longer available. But over the years I had developed some skill in brewing my own hot pepper sauce. It was worth something in trade. I put plenty on my eggs.

Once the radio went off you could hear roosters battling for supremacy of the village. Some people were annoyed by them, but I found them pleasantly reassuring. Their crowing and the vapors of the hot sauce helped clear enough room in my head to think about what I had to do. Planning my day was a way of not giving in to despair. It really is not possible to pay attention fully to two things at once—for instance, carpentry and suicide.

I had to continue the work I had started on a cupola above Larry and Sharon Prager's garage, which they were turning back into a stable. Larry Prager was our dentist. With the electricity off most of the time, he did not have the high speed drill anymore. He got ahold of a 1920s pulley drill in Glens Falls, and Andrew Pendergast helped him rig it up to a foot treadle which Sharon could operate like a pump organ while she assisted her husband. He had become adept at working with gold in the absence of complex polymers and advanced cements. His patients usually brought in their own gold, most often jewelry, which he converted into castings or foils. For anesthesia he was limited to tinctures of opium and marijuana. Nobody looked forward to a session with Larry, but we were lucky to have a dentist.

The job on his cupola required trips to the sawmill and the general supply, often called simply "the general." So, I tidied up the breakfast things, hung the trout in the smoker, tossed more apple wood on the smoldering embers, and washed myself in the outdoor shower I'd rigged up next to the summer kitchen. We were fortunate to still have running water in the village. The town established its water system in the early twentieth century. The reservoir lay a hundred feet higher in elevation above the village, so the system was gravity fed and still worked. It wasn't treated anymore but it was good potable water—though the pressure was noticeably lower lately. I had a little sheet-metal tank with a firebox rigged above the shower, all held up on a steel pipe frame. It was such a warm morning that I didn't bother firing it, and the cool water brisked me up. Finally, I put on my work clothes: cutoff denim shorts and what used to be a Brooks Brothers pink pinstripe dress shirt, now minus the sleeves.

We didn't use bicycles much anymore—rubber tires being unavailable, not to mention the poor condition of the pavements. For many ordinary chores, therefore, I was what we all jokingly referred to as a foot cowboy. I had a small wooden tote wagon that I'd built for my toolbox, which I'd left on the job over at Prager's. I dreamed all the time about getting a horse, almost as much as when I was a six-year-old boy. They couldn't breed them fast enough, and they were still very costly. You could rent one from Tom Allison here in town: saddle horse or horse with a rig, if you needed to transport something bulky or go visiting with your family. Anyway, I set off that day on foot with my old backpack to carry the nails and things I needed from the general. The sawmill would send my wood down by wagon after I went by and ordered and paid for it.

Out in the dooryard, I heard the distant clip-clop of hooves on pavement, and then I saw a wagon glide up Salem Street toward where the high school had been. That was the extent of the traffic. The tranquillity was pleasing, despite what it signified about what had happened to our society. You could tell it was going to be a hot day. A gauzy haze already hung over the sun-struck little town. The birds sounded discouraged.

Mrs. Myles, my neighbor, was outside firing up the immense copper tub that she used to do the laundry she took in. Her given name was Lucy, and she had been an English teacher in the high school, which was no more. She had lost her husband, Dexter, as I'd lost Sandy, from the encephalitis. He had been the Washington County family court judge. Since she was at least seventy years old, and was used to being addressed a certain way by children, everybody called her Mrs. Myles rather than Lucy. I'd helped her out by constructing her laundry system, a drywall fieldstone hearth under the tub, and the pipe system, and two long pine tables for sorting and stacking things, and the pavilion that sheltered it all from rain and snow. We'd run the gray-water drain pipe out of the copper tub and into the ground across the yard to her substantial patch of currents and gooseberries. She was an excellent gardener. Forty years ago she had been a Cub Scout den mother and member of the town zoning board. Back then, she went to the supermarket every week, like everybody else. She was never once cold or hungry until she was an old woman. She no longer knew where her children were or even if they were still alive.

"Want some eggs, Robert," she called from across the fence.

"No thanks. Hey, the electric was on for a while just now."

"Was it?" she said. "I don't even notice anymore."

"I'm going to the general. You want me to pick up anything for you?"

"I could use some mason jar lids."

"I'll ask."

"You going up with the truck?" She meant my tote wagon.

"No. Not today."

"All right."

"Why?"

"I could use a couple more buckets. Tin, plastic, whatever they've got."

"I'll get you some real soon."

"Peas are coming in like gangbusters."

"That's good."

"You get me a nice trout, we'll be in hog heaven."

"I've got two smoking up right now."

"I like 'em fresh, fried in butter."

"Okay. Will do. You have a nice day now, Mrs. Myles."

"You stay out of trouble, Robert." She said that to me every time I said goodbye to her. I suppose that was what she used to tell her kids back in school.

# FIVE

In a world that had become a salvage operation, the general supply evolved into Union Grove's leading industry. When every last useful thing in town had been stripped from the Kmart and the United Auto, the CVS drugstore, and other trading establishments of the bygone national chain-store economy, daily life became a perpetual flea market centered on the old town dump, which had been capped over in the 1990s. The general was run at first as a public cooperative, under the illusion that the ongoing catastrophes would ebb and normality would return. But the flu and the bombing of Washington put an end to that illusion, and the general eventually came under the management of Wayne Karp and his gang of former motorheads.

In the old days, Wayne Karp worked as a trucker for the Holland and Vesey paper mill in Glens Falls. Sometimes he hauled loads of pulpwood down from Saranac. Sometimes he took giant rolls of machine-finished magazine paper from the H & V plant to the big web-offset printing operation in Schenectady where regional editions of *Newsweek* were run off. In his leisure time, Karp was addicted to sporting entertainments that required gasoline engines: motorcycling, motorboating, snowmobiling, off-roading, jet-skiing, and watching NASCAR racing on television. He couldn't relax unless an engine was roaring somewhere near his head. He lived four miles outside Union Grove in a former trailer park near the general supply along with about a hundred like-minded former motorheads, greasers, bikers, quasi-criminals and their families who had drifted in over the years.

In normal times, Wayne Karp would have passed through life as just another lumpen American Dreamer, a hardworking consumer of shoddy products, chemically tweaked foods, and rude popular entertainments, a taxpayer subject to the ordinary restrictions of the social contract. But in the new era, he blossomed into a local kingpin.

He was married for some years to a barmaid from a now defunct tavern called Waterhole No. 3, which occupied the even longer defunct Boston and Maine train station. The barmaid earlier had a son out of wedlock with a guard from Comstock State Prison up at the northern end of Washington County. The guard ended up incarcerated in his own joint for selling heroin to the inmates. Wayne Karp raised the child. This stepson ended up in Comstock himself at age nineteen for stabbing to death another teenage boy one summer night at the quarry outside town where kids gathered to drink and hook up with girls. His was one of the last cases tried in the county criminal courts. A month later, flu swept through Comstock prison and killed seventy percent of the inmates, including the stepson and his natural father. Wayne's wife died under mysterious circumstances a year later. By then the justice system had ground to a halt like so many things that had once seemed woven into the fabric of regular life. The rumor was that Wayne strangled her in their trailer. He had more or less bragged about it openly. The phrase *with his bare hands* always seemed to crop up whenever you heard someone whispering about it.

As well as taking over the general supply, Wayne Karp had for a while organized the drug trade in Washington County, meaning marijuana—because manufactured pharmaceuticals, and anything linked to them, like methedrine made out of cooked cough syrup residue, had ceased to exist. At the onset of the hard times quite a few people had begun growing pot, to have something to trade, to simply survive. It was a form of currency, like eggs. After a while, if Wayne Karp learned that you were growing, he would demand an exclusive "contract" on your crop on terms very favorable to himself. Those who resisted or cheated had unpleasant things happen to them. But after a few short years, Wayne lost control of the dope trade. So many people were growing so much weed that the stuff became valueless as a means of exchange, no matter how the traffic was organized. Wayne himself was even growing it in quantity, queering his own market. Then, it started showing up wild all over the place, in the hedgerows and roadsides. I had sowed plenty of seeds myself up along the old railroad tracks by the river. It was a hardy and potent low-growing, shaggy Afghani strain of cannabis that was now naturalized in our corner of the world like the orange daylily. It put out buds the size of plums.

Since then, several farmers around the county had taken up cultivating opium poppies, a venture promoted by Dr. Copeland, who made his own laudanum, tincture of opium, for use in surgery and other medical emergencies, since it was no longer possible to get advanced pharmaceutical painkillers. He also made a kind of sedative tea from boiling the seedpods. Lately he'd been working on a procedure for refining morphine. People wanted him to be well supplied. He made sure, in turn, that our dentist, Larry Prager, had plenty. Nobody had dared burgle Jerry Copeland's lab for laudanum out of fear that someday they might be lying on a stretcher with a compound fracture of the femur in need of a potent analgesic.

We regarded opium as a godsend. It did not develop into an illicit trade, though. There was no legal prohibition, no police running around trying to suppress drugs, driving up the price artificially, and no marketing system. There were no distant markets to send it to because shipping anything was slow at best and often unreliable, and travel was something you just didn't do anymore. Anybody could grow their own poppies or buy raw opium paste from one of the growers. Farmers made more money growing raspberries or asparagus. They grew poppies as a public service. A few people took to smoking opium, but those with an extremely apathetic attitude toward survival tended not to last long in the new disposition of things.

So, Wayne Karp turned the focus of his energies to running the general supply. He had a large crew out there systematically digging up the old landfill and sorting out valuables, especially glass, plastic containers, pipes, hinges, screws and nails, anything that could be reused. He sent other crews around the countryside to disassemble abandoned houses for their materials. Back in the glory days of the suburban expansion, many split-level houses had been built on roadside out-parcels far away from the towns, the stores, and the jobs. The people who built them expected to be able to drive cars everywhere to work and meet their daily needs forever. Now, with the population so far down, and many empty houses in town itself, and the oil gone, and no ability to drive heroic distances, these buildings had no value except for salvage.

# SIX

To get to the general supply, you had to go past the old high school at the edge of town on North Road. I was interested to see suddenly quite a bustle about the place. Several wagons stood before the main entrance, and men were off-loading things: furniture, trunks, crates, a big iron wood-fired cookstove with shiny chrome appointments. Another gang worked up on the roof. You could smell tar boiling from where I stood. Yet another crew was out in what used to be the parking lot, breaking up the asphalt with picks to feed the tar-boiling operation. In this weather, it must have been brutal work. A column of white smoke curled up in the breezeless air.

The old high school football field was in the process of being turned into a large garden. It had been returning to scrub in recent years anyway. The newcomers had done an impressive job of clearing the sumacs and other weedy trash. They had already plowed up the field and harrowed and raked it smooth. A dozen women were out there now in long skirts and straw hats, stooped over and inching their way up new rows planting seeds. It was a little late to be starting most vegetables. I hoped they knew what they were doing.

I paused on the road there watching at a distance for a while, fascinated by the scale of enterprise and wondering how it was organized. In my old corporate days, I was considered a good organizer. That's what my job was mainly about, getting things done on time, pulling things together. I had a fascination with how people managed other people in the corporate world. In our world now, the freehold farmer was the new chief executive. The authority in town was a lot less clear-cut, to put it mildly, with the population so diminished and no money to do anything and schooling reduced to the little church-affiliated academy that Jane Ann was in charge of. We musicians in the First Congregational submitted to the direction of Andrew Pendergast who ran the choir, the music circle, and the spin-off chamber ensemble. And of course the Reverend Loren Holder was in charge of the church itself, and most of the activities organized within it. It was not always so easy to understand or accept the authority of the God that our church was organized to honor, given all the hardships he had brought down upon us.

The people working over at the high school ignored me as I stood watching them from the road. There wasn't any sign of Brother Jobe, but I supposed that all this activity was directed by him. I certainly wondered how these newcomers were going to fit into the life of our town. It was obvious that the balance of things was going to change with them around. I reflected on the possibility that it might be for the better, since at least they would set an example of cooperative labor, something we had gotten sloppy about, especially where the upkeep of the village was concerned. There would also be new blood in town, people with new skills, maybe some good musicians among them, perhaps even an eligible woman—but this led me into a rueful consideration of my relations with Jane Ann, which was something I could hardly bear to think about. I supposed that this outfit was a covenanted sect and you'd probably have to sign on with them to meet a woman, and no doubt they had a lot of special rules of behavior, and for all I knew maybe they followed celibacy like the old Shakers had. I did not see any children anywhere.

The old high school complex itself was a 1970s-vintage modernist monstrosity, a U-shaped set of low-slung rectilinear boxes like ten thousand other schools around the nation from the period. Seeing the building usually made me deeply sad and even a little angry, the way that refrigerator in my garden did. Its vision of yesterday's tomorrow seemed pitiful. Children like my Daniel and Genna had sat in those very box buildings under buzzing fluorescent lights listening to their science teachers prattle about the wonders of space travel and gene splicing and how we were all going to live to be a hundred and twenty five years old in "smart" computer-controlled houses where all we had to do was speak to bump up the heat or turn on the giant home theater screens in a life of perpetual leisure and comfort. It made me sick to think about it. Not because there's something necessarily wrong with leisure or comfort, but because that's where our aspirations ended. And in the face of what had actually happened to us, it seemed obscenely stupid. Thinking about all that got me so agitated, I took off up the road. Motion is a great tranquilizer.

# Seven

Halfway out to the general supply I ran into Shawn Watling, a big, shambling young man who so typified our times. He'd been born in a hospital and raised on computers, and then all of a sudden the world fell out from under him. I met him coming onto North Road where Black Creek Road joins up with it. There is a bridge there over the creek, which is a tributary of the Battenkill. Shawn worked as one of several hands on the Schmidt farm up the hill, which was in fruit, oats, buckwheat, and hay, with some beef cattle, and goats for milk and meat. Agriculture had changed completely without oil. We'd gone from a few people using machines to grow monoculture crops and process them for everybody else, to a society in which at least half the people used tools skillfully with human and animal muscle to feed the other half. With the population down so much, labor was at a premium. Shawn was probably paid decently, but his opportunities were limited.

His father, Denny Watling, had run a real estate office in town. His mother, Margie, was the leading sales agent. Shawn's parents played in a country music band all tricked out in matching cowboy outfits at local bars and the county fair every August. They were regular small-town folk who read spy novels, got new cars every three years, and once took a vacation to see Paris. They were gone now, along with Shawn's little brother, Cody, who had been my boy's age, taken by the flu. Shawn inherited his father's instruments (violin, mandolin, guitar) and was part of our music circle in church. He was a hell of a musician. He was in the last graduating class that Union Grove high school ever produced and he spent one semester at Colgate University before it, and most colleges everywhere as far as I knew, had to close on a temporary basis that now seemed permanent. Shawn went to work for Bill Schmidt because that was what there was to do for a young person like him. He was strong in a way that you hardly ever saw in the old days, strong from real work, not from lifting barbells or aerobics classes. At age twenty-three, he married another young survivor, Britney Blieveldt, and they had a girl named Sarah. Shawn was not a kid anymore. He and his family lived in town in his parents' old house, which was one of the nicest ones on Salem Street, our nicest street. Having a nice house didn't make him wealthy or boost his status, though. There were plenty of empty houses in town and no one to sell them to. The real estate industry no longer existed.

When I met up with him on the way to the general supply, Shawn was leading a big furry black dog pulling a two-wheeled cart. The dog was part Newfoundland with some mastiff in him, Shawn said. It belonged to Mr. Schmidt. Few dogs were around anymore. Some had been eaten during the hunger that followed the flu in the spring of that year. People didn't talk about it, it was so demoralizing. And now, with no manufactured pet food, you had to have a productive household to be able to feed one, which Mr. Schmidt certainly did.

"We need you on Tuesday night for Christmas practice," I told him because he'd skip it if you didn't pester him about it. Rehearsal for the Christmas carol service went on year-round and was more like an excuse for the circle to play regularly. At this time of year we usually played everything but Christmas music just because we liked to play. Sometimes we played string band dance music, sometimes old rock and roll, sometimes Handel. With the electricity off, you didn't hear recorded music anymore. You had to make it yourself.

"You come by the house and collect me, I'll go, Robert," he said.

"I wish I didn't have to drag you there."

"I get awful tired, especially this time of year."

"We're supposed to play a levee at the Shushan grange July Fourth, you know."

"We'll just play the same old crap. "Possum Up a Gum Stump," and all. We don't need to practice that."

"We do if we want to sound crisp."

"I don't care how it sounds."

"That's not a very positive attitude."

He laughed bitterly. "We'll be haying up at Schmidt's all next week. He'll probably have us out there until pitch dark, anyway."

I know deep down Shawn loved to play. We just continued on for a while, enjoying the quiet road and the creak of the little cart's axle. But the big black dog was panting from the heat, and a big gobbet of foamy spit hung from his jaw. Shawn limped slightly.

"Did you hurt yourself?" I said.

"I fell off Mr. Schmidt's barn roof."

"What were you doing up there?"

"Fixing it. What do you think?"

We walked a ways again in silence. I hadn't known him to be so irritable before.

"It's been mighty hot lately," I said.

"It's not just the heat. Jesus, Robert, look how we live? I'm practically a serf. You know what a serf is?"

"Of course I do. I went to college," I said, and regretted it right away.

"Lucky you," he said.

"Music always cheers me up," I said.

"I'm glad it works for you."

"Music salves the soul."

"Nothing can salve my soul."

"You know, Shawn, even back in normal times people got down and depressed. In fact, you could argue that people are generally better off now mentally than we were back then. We follow the natural cycles. We eat real food instead of processed crap full of chemicals. We're not jacked up on coffee and television and sexy advertising all the time. No more anxiety about credit card bills—"

"I don't want to debate."

"I bet it's true, though."

"Find somebody else if you want to have a debate."

"It's just conversation."

"Whatever you call it, quit trying to persuade me that everything's great, okay?" he said and stopped in his tracks. I stopped too. His face was red and tendons stood out on his neck. He was a large young man, and he looked a little scary.

"You frustrate the hell out of me, son," I said.

"Do I? I work like a dog. Harder than this dog. From sunup to sundown, like a medieval peasant. I do it with hardly any sense of a future, and the last thing I need is a lecture from the generation that screwed up the world. Come on, Merlin," he said to the dog.

He marched off stiffly. I watched him leading the dog for a few moments and then hurried to catch up with them.

"I apologize," I said.

He shrugged.

"I didn't mean to lecture you."

He shrugged again.

"Hey, can we still be friends?"

"Sure," he said.

I didn't want to give him more reason to stay away from the music circle. We needed him. Further up the road, we had to stop again. Shawn unhitched the dog from the cart so it could climb down into the ditch off the shoulder and drink from the rill that ran alongside there.

"Do you ever hear anything of your own boy?" Shawn said.

"No."

"Daniel's his name, right?"

"That's right."

"My little brother Cody and him were friends, I think."

"Yes they were. I remember Cody."

"They were both good kids. Cody would be twenty-one now."

"Daniel would too."

"Yeah, I'm sorry—"

"He's not dead. As far as I know. Just gone. He had to see what was out there."

"I hope he found something good out there, Robert."

The big dog, Merlin, suddenly busted up through the cattails and orange daylilies, like a monster from the depths, dripping and slobbering. It startled me. He obligingly allowed Shawn to hitch him back to his cart.

"Smart dog," I said.

"You don't know the half of it," Shawn said, and we walked the rest of the way to the general.

# EIGHT

The general supply consisted of a pole barn housing the "store," the yard behind the store where salvage was sorted, and five large sheds where the sorted salvage was kept out of the weather. Most of the stuff in these sheds was lumber, plywood, sheet metal, and other materials collected from derelict buildings that had entered ownership limbo. Back behind the sheds was the ten-acre filled hollow that used to be the town dump. Now, instead of putting things into it, things were taken out of it. A dozen men with shovels and pry bars worked a section close to the sheds, while a team of heavily muscled bay Belgians stood by stoically hitched to a wagon in the heat, swishing at flies with their tails.

You came up to the general supply by way of a wooden gate rigged on a counterbalance with a guard shack beside it, where you were checked to make sure that anything leaving the premises was paid for. The fellow on duty there today was Bunny Willman, who had years ago worked as a janitor at the middle school when my son was there. Bunny was the opposite of what his name suggests. He was a six-foot-three hulking menace, muscled like a hyena. His bacon-colored hair was worked up into sinister pigtails tied with scrap cloth bows. Like many of Wayne Karp's crew, he wore a droopy mustache and goatee. He also sported the tattooed wings over his eyebrows that Wayne Karp's cohorts had adopted as their tribal insignia. The shack had windows front and back and a door. On the side facing the gate, someone had nailed up a coyote pelt. It stank ferociously in the heat.

Shawn and I came up together. Bunny Willman didn't lift the gate to let us in, which seemed odd to me. He reposed comfortably outside the shack, tilted back against the wall in a beat-up

chrome and vinyl dinette chair, chewing on a twig. Though he was
not exerting himself, beads of sweat stood out on his forehead.

"That dog ain't coming in here," he said.

"He always comes in," Shawn said.

"Not today with me here he don't."

"I've got to load the cart."

"You can drag it in yourself and hitch him back up when you
come out."

"What's the problem with the dog?" I said.

"Are you with him?" Bunny said.

"Yeah," I said, even though it wasn't strictly so.

"I don't like the way that dog looks," Bunny said. "Like he has
the rabies. It's all over the county. Raccoons and coyotes is full of
it. It's this damn heat. So get him the hell away from me."

"I'll watch the dog while you're inside," I said to Shawn.

"No, you go, Robert. It'll be better if I stay out here with him."

"Okay, I'll get both of our stuff," I said.

"Lookit, here," Bunny said and paused to spit to the side.
"However you two work this out, just get that damn dog away
from my shack."

"He doesn't have rabies," Shawn said, letting a little too much
disdain creep into his voice.

"How do you know?"

"I'm with him all day long."

"He's foaming at the mouth."

"It's the breed. They slobber a lot."

"You just take him over to there right now," Bunny said with
mounting impatience and pointed at a maple tree down by the road.
Like all our maples, it had a lot of dead branches. We didn't know
whether it was the heat or a disease, but they weren't getting on well
and sugaring was way off. We went down to the tree with the dog.

"What did you need, then?" I asked Shawn.

"Fifty pounds of roofing nails," he said. He took a roll of bills
out of his pocket and peeled off a thousand dollars in fifties and
twenties. "Take the cart in, why don't you."

Shawn unhitched the dog and held onto it by its leather harness. A hot breeze rattled the dry leaves above us. He took a seat on the ground against the dying tree and the big dog lay down peacefully beside him. I pulled the cart by its harness up to Bunny's guard shack. He raised up the gate, and I entered the general.

Wayne Karp himself was back behind the long counter in the store. I was surprised to see him there. He didn't often work the customer end of his establishment. That was usually left to an underling. He was sitting in a battered easy chair in a tranquil pool of dimness, sorting through a splint basket of steel springs. In a peculiar way, he was about the only person who qualified as a celebrity anymore in our locality, more potent in his remoteness from things than in his actual presence, larger than life when he wasn't around. In reality, he was physically unassuming, wiry, with close-cropped salt-and-pepper hair, droopy mustache, and a goatee. You wouldn't pick him out of a crowd as a natural leader. His left eyelid was a little droopy from an old motorcycle accident, it was said, but he had a set of wings tattooed over his eyebrows that sort of evened out the look of them. I suppose it was designed for that purpose, and it set a fashion trend for those under his sway. He didn't get up when I entered, or more than glance my way.

Wayne had access to things you hardly ever saw anymore. His crew came up with all kinds of stuff scavenging, and being their boss he often got the pick of their gleanings. This day he had on a pair of blue jeans that looked well broken in but not raggedy, while his camouflage T-shirt might have come off the shelf at the Wal-Mart the day before yesterday, if Wal-Mart had still existed. The short sleeves were rolled up so as to display his lumpy biceps. He wore a pair of red clip-on suspenders too, apparently to emphasize the bulge of his pectorals, not to hold his pants up. He was well nourished and fit and renowned as a fighter for defeating men much larger than himself. On the rare occasions when I saw Wayne, the phrase *with his bare hands* always echoed in my mind. I waited for him to indicate that he was aware of me standing there, but he seemed oblivious, so I spoke up.

"When you've got a moment," I said.

He held a spring up to the window as if sizing it up in the light.

"Time passes slowly these days, don't it?" he eventually said.

"The pace is different," I said.

"Move slower, you live longer, I always say."

"I'm not in any tearing rush, but I've got things to do."

He finally looked over my way.

"You're the fiddler, ain't you?" he said, and chucked the spring in a wooden box, which was actually an old drawer.

"That's right."

"I seen you fiddle last fall one time up in Belchertown, didn't I? Some levee up there."

"That would have been their harvest ball."

"Those plowboys can party."

"Yes they can."

"It's a harsh life, though. I wouldn't want it."

"Well, you've got a situation for yourself, after all."

"That's true," he said. "We all got ourselves a situation, don't we?"

"It's not what I expected of life earlier on."

"Me neither, but you play the hand that's dealt to you. Say, you remember Charlie Daniels?"

"Yup."

"He was a hell of a fiddler."

"I wouldn't know."

"You said you remembered him."

"I remember the name. I never listened to his records, though."

"Never listened to Charlie Daniels? And you call yourself a fiddler?" Wayne finally got up and took a winding way to the counter, as though he were trying to elongate the trip as much as possible so I might observe how he moved. He did have a sinuous way of carrying himself. It was obviously intended to be intimidating. "Too bad," he said. "Those recordings are hard to find nowadays."

"Well, the electricity's hardly on anyway."

"Yeah, you're right about that. Remember Guns n' Roses?"

"Never listened to them either."

"What the hell did you listen to?" He finally looked straight at me.

"Mostly old-time. String band stuff. What they used to call folk music."

"You just plain folks?"

"Pretty much," I said.

"What'd you do back in the real world?"

"Computers."

"Oh? Well that shit's down for the count, ain't it?"

"Looks like it."

"Funny how the old times came back with a vengeance."

"You've got a point there."

"Well, I just miss rock and roll like crazy, I do," Wayne said. "Things have got a little too old-time for me in every way. I suppose you came in here for a reason today, Fiddler. What do you need?"

"To start with: fifty pounds of roofing nails and ten of ten-penny common, galvanized if possible. You got any mason jar lids?"

"By the dozen."

"I'll take two dozen."

"We can do that. Let's say thirteen hunnert altogether. What did you have against Guns n' Roses, if you don't mind me asking?"

"They made my ears hurt," I said. While I was counting out the bills three gunshots rang out sharply from outside. My heart flew into my throat.

# NINE

We rushed out of the store and down to the gate area, Shawn lay crumpled facedown with his right arm twisted unnaturally behind his head and bright arterial blood spilling out of him, actually raising tiny spumes of dust as it ran downhill, like fingers clawing the ground. The dog lay a few feet away with his head facing uphill. One of his eyes was shot out and he was motionless, with blood puddling around the margins of his deep fur.

"Oh, what the hell now, Bunny!" Wayne said as we arrived on the scene. He repeated himself several times with increasing anger until he was shouting at the much larger man, who seemed to draw inward trying to make himself look smaller.

I was so overcome with fright that I started hyperventilating. I kneeled down just uphill of Shawn's head. The truth was I could barely remain upright and had to kneel to keep from passing out. I tried to straighten Shawn's arm out, as if that would help. I soon understood that both Shawn and the dog were dead.

"You shit-for-brains!" Wayne said and smacked Bunny in the head. "What the hell happened here?" A revolver still dangled from Bunny's right hand.

"He fell asleep," Bunny said, "and his dog come up on me."

"Asleep! Who goes to sleep in the middle of the road!" Wayne shouted and smacked Bunny again.

"No, down by that tree," Bunny said.

By now, the other men working back in the dump had ventured down to the front of the general and gathered around us in a semicircle.

"If he was sleeping down there, how in hell did you happen to shoot him up here?" Wayne said.

"I shot the damn dog and then he woke up and he come up on me."

"What'd you shoot the got-damn dog for?"

"He got the rabies. Lookit how he's frothing at the damn mouth!"

"He just needed some water is all," I said.

"What the got-damn hell you know what the dog needed or didn't need, got-dammit," Wayne said and then turned wrathfully back to Bunny. "Gimme that got-damn gun!" He wrenched it right out of Bunny's huge fingers and then brandished it at him. "You're lucky I don't put a bullet in your got-damn brainpan, you stupid sonofabitch. And I'll tell you something else: this is the last time you'll ever draw shack duty."

The other men mumbled among themselves.

"Shut up," Wayne said to them. "That your cart up by the office?" he said to me.

"It was his," I said.

"Go get that cart," Wayne said to one of the other men.

He hopped to and trundled the cart down in short order.

"Load him in there," Wayne said.

Several of the men picked up Shawn's body and put him in the cart faceup, but with his arms dangling. One of them got blood all over his hands and tried to rub it off on Shawn's shirt. You could see part of Shawn's jaw was shot off.

"Fix him right, damn you," Wayne said, and the men got Shawn's arms tucked inside.

"Why are you putting him in that?" I asked.

"Because you're going to take him back."

"What about that team and wagon up there?"

"It's staying put."

Wayne and the rest of the men stared blankly at me. Flies began landing on Shawn's wounds. My clothes were soaking wet. I was trembling as though it were a winter day, while sweat dripped off the end of my nose.

"I guess you plan to pretend this didn't happen here?" I said.

"I'm truly sorry. It's mostly a downgrade to town from here," Wayne said. "You'll get there by and by."

"You expect me to say anything other than what really happened?"

"I don't expect nothing. You say what you will. It'll be word against word."

"It was a accident," Bunny said.

"Did I ax you?" Wayne shouted. "Here," he said, suddenly turning to me with an air of disgusted resignation and held out the big pistol, as if for me to take it. "You do us all a favor and shoot this stupid sonofabitch."

"Look . . ."

"He was your friend, wasn't he? You got any doubt who done it?"

"For Pete's sake, Wayne . . ." Bunny said.

"I'll just . . . leave," I said.

"We'll all swear it was self-defense," Wayne said. "Won't we boys?"

A few of them mumbled something, but they didn't seem all that enthusiastic.

"Go on, take it," Wayne said. "Take the got-damn pistola, amigo."

"Forget it."

"You pass up this chance for justice, it might not come again."

"I'm not an executioner."

"Well, you take this iron anyways." Wayne grabbed my hand and literally pressed the pistol into it.

I tossed it back down in the dirt.

"I don't think you understand," Wayne said. He picked it up and jammed it into the waist of my pants. "This piece ain't staying round here. Let's not argue. Wally, go up to the store and get me a length of stout rope." Wally jogged briskly away. "We're going to fix this cart so you can tow on it."

"People back in town are going to want to know what happened here," I said.

"I know they are. You go with it, Fiddler. Tell your story, whatever you think you understand about this unfortunate accident. Give them the weapon if you feel like it. Whatever you need to do. We'll do what we need to do." He came closer and pushed me a few yards away so the others were out of earshot. "Lookit, we both know who done this. It was a reckless act of stupidity, and I will tell you so straight up this one time only. But it's done and nothing I can do will bring this young man back to life. This will all come out in the wash, I promise you. But don't expect too much from the law. The truth is, we're our own law in these times, like it or not. Apart from all that, I'm personally sorry this has happened, and I wish you luck in dealing with it. Who was he anyway? I know I seen him."

"He was a hand on Mr. Schmidt's farm. Shawn Watling."

"Watling? I once bought a double lot from that Watling agency."

"That was his parents. They're dead."

"Well God bless us the living, anyway."

Wally returned with a length of rope and was rigging it to the harness so I could pull it more easily. Then there was nothing to do but leave with Shawn's body. It was a substantial load. As I pulled the cart away from the general, all I could think about was whether they would eat the dog.

# TEN

The day had turned deathly hot with no breeze. On the first steep downgrade, I had to turn the cart around to keep it from running away on me, only to confront Shawn's face with the flies darting at the terrible wound. When we got to a flatter stretch, I stopped the cart and put my shirt over his head so I wouldn't have to look at him. The rest of the way I endlessly replayed what might have occurred between Shawn and Bunny Willman, trying to imagine the part that I hadn't seen. It occurred to me that I had put Shawn in a bad mood earlier, which perhaps had made him say or do something reckless . . .

I brooded over what I would do with the gun. There were still plenty of guns around, but manufactured ammunition was nearly impossible to get, and Wayne was the sole supplier anywhere near our town. Three rounds remained in the cylinder. I looked. I decided to hide it along the road, somewhere I could find it in the future if I had to. I wasn't going to bring it into town with me because, for all I knew, people might draw the wrong conclusion. There could be some kind of legal proceeding, I thought, an inquest, a grand jury, some effort to pretend that we were still civilized because a human life still mattered. There hadn't been an incident like this in our town—the killing of one person by another under any circumstances —as long as I could remember. Even back in his heyday running the dope trade, Wayne hadn't killed anybody, though his boys had roughed people up and lighted some fires. Perhaps Wayne could influence the outcome of a proceeding, maybe even shift the blame to me. Stephen Bullock, the wealthiest farmer in our area, and a friend of mine, was the magistrate, but nobody knew what to expect of him because he'd declined the honor of serving.

I parked the cart, with Shawn in it, among the daylilies along the road at the Black Creek Bridge where we'd met up earlier that day, and climbed down under the bridge and tucked the gun up along one of the old steel girders underneath where the swallows made their nests. It was dim under there even with the sun blazing like an ingot in the sky. I doubted anybody would find it.

The Schmidt farm lay more than a mile up the junction there, uphill the whole way, and I didn't want to leave Shawn in the cart, drawing flies in the lilies while I went up for help, so I decided to get him the rest of the way to town myself. I couldn't imagine just bringing the body directly to his house and presenting it to his wife and child. Freer's funeral home was long shuttered because both Freer brothers were carried off by encephalitis and nobody took up their business, so I couldn't bring Shawn there. Besides, there was no refrigeration in their morgue with the electricity off. In recent years, most of our funerals took place in the church. There hadn't been a police department for years and Heath Rucker, the constable, didn't have an office and was a useless drunk on top of that. I decided to take Shawn's body directly to Dr. Copeland's house, since he might be called upon to act as a medical examiner in any legal proceeding.

As I passed by the old high school, nobody was left out in the garden in the midday heat, nor was the roofing crew still at work. I assumed they were inside at lunch, or prayer, or just preserving their energy for the cooler hours of the day. The streets of town were deserted too, though I heard the sound of hammer blows from Doug Sweetland's wheel shop and saw Linda Allison hanging wash in her yard. The smell of something sweet emanated from Russo's bakery. It nauseated me in the heat. Finally, I hauled the cart up behind what had once been the driveway to Dr. Copeland's office, formerly a carriage house and garage. I left Shawn beside the yew hedge there and went in to find the doctor.

He had no patients in his waiting room. I called out and his voice said come into the back. He had a lab behind his examining room. He was in there pouring off a jug of grain alcohol into an

odd lot of smaller bottles and jars. He had become an adept herb-
alist through the years. He had to make his own antiseptic, like
everything else. The room was heavy with fumes.

"Heat getting you, Robert?" he said without looking at me.

"There's been a terrible accident, Jerry."

He looked up, peering over the rim of his eyeglasses while he
managed to finish filling an old soda pop bottle without spilling a
drop.

"What sort of accident?"

"Shawn Watling got shot up at the general supply."

"That doesn't sound like an accident."

"I've got him in a cart outside."

Jerry, lean and lithe at thirty-nine, slipped past me and I followed. He knelt beside the cart. He had the shirt off Shawn's face
and was studying him, feeling for a pulse on his neck, though anyone could see that he was beyond saving. Pretty soon, Jerry began
cursing, saying "goddammit, goddammit" over and over in a harsh
whisper. Sweat dripped off the end of his nose onto Shawn's chest.

"You didn't say he was dead."

"I'm sorry."

"Goddammit . . . How did this happen?"

I told him everything I had seen up at the general, but I seemed
to be blabbering. The simple truth was, I didn't know.

"God*dammit*!"

Out of nowhere, the doctor's older son, Jasper, ten, appeared.
I heard him gasp as he saw Shawn's body.

"Go to the rectory and get Reverend Holder," Jerry said. "And
don't talk to another soul on your way over or back about what you
saw here, understand?"

Jasper nodded but remained fixed in his footsteps like a statue.

"Go on!" Jerry said and the boy finally obeyed him. "Robert,
help me move the body into the springhouse."

The springhouse was spacious inside and carefully built. I
know because I had helped build it a few years earlier. This was how
people kept perishable things cool in the days before mechanical

refrigeration, and this was how we did it now—if you happened to be lucky enough to have a spring on your property. The fieldstone structure was bermed into the hill behind Jerry's house. The Copelands had about a half acre of fruit trees above it. At the time we built it, there had been many deaths in town, and I understood that he had designed it to receive human bodies awaiting burial as well as for everyday things.

It must have been thirty degrees cooler inside. Meager light seeped through a small triple-pane transom window above the door. I remember fitting it into the fieldstones there, scribing the wooden sashes. Now, the light filtered through an additional layer of cobwebs. A long wooden slab table stood inside with trugs and wooden bowels of the year's first peas and radishes, along with shelves of preserved fruit, straw-filled bins where they kept onions and squashes, and hams hanging from the ceiling with their protective coats of mold. Even under the circumstances, you couldn't fail to notice that the Copeland's food supply was impressive. As the town's only doctor, he received a bounty in barter for his services.

"Let's get him onto the table," Jerry said. Shawn weighed well over two hundred pounds. The two of us struggled to lift him out of the dog cart. Jerry bent to examine the ugly wound that had left half the jaw hanging by a few tendons. The shot had also severed the carotid artery, he said. Then, still cursing under his breath, he pulled a bottle out from behind a five-gallon stoneware crock, took a pull on it, and passed it to me. It was a very fine pear brandy, and very powerful. We didn't have to make any lame excuses about why we needed it. Between the brandy and the cool air, the situation began to clarify. Loren found us in the springhouse easily enough. Jerry told his boy to stay outside.

"Oh hell," Loren said when his eyes adjusted and he saw Shawn laid out on the table. He let out a sound like a gulp or a sob. Jerry passed him the bottle too. Loren had baptized Shawn's child.

"God help that son of a bitch if he ever comes to me for help," Jerry said, and I assumed he meant Wayne.

I repeated to Loren what happened at the general supply, and he said we three should all go together to Shawn's house and tell his wife, and Loren said he would see that everybody in town was notified so we could have a funeral tomorrow. I realized that I would be up all night making the coffin.

# ELEVEN

Britney Watling was picking black currants with her seven-year-old girl, Sarah, pale like her mother and barefoot, at the back of the garden as we approached. Both of them seemed to flinch at the sight of us. Loren didn't even have to say anything. He went over to where she stood and guided her gently by the elbow to the shade beside the barn and sat her down on a marble slab bench that had probably been there for a hundred years. Jerry hoisted the child up and carried her down there hitched up on his waist, as he would a child of his own.

Once we were all there in the shade of the barn, where the family cow took refuge from the heat, and where the hostas that Shawn's mother planted long ago bloomed purple, Loren explained to Britney that her husband was not just hurt but dead. The little girl, Sarah, seemed to search for a cue from her mother, whose mouth fell open without producing any sound. The child repeated, "Daddy, Daddy, Daddy," and began keening. It was left to me to try to briefly tell Britney what had happened, making it clear I hadn't actually witnessed the incident. She did not ask me any questions about it. For the longest time, nothing was said. Finally Loren began to quietly explain what would happen next, how the funeral would be arranged and the sequence of events that would entail. Britney took it in stoically. She was a young person who herself had endured large losses, including parents incinerated in Los Angeles, a brother and many friends gone, and one child stillborn. She gave the impression of great solidity even though she was petite and pale. She asked if she could see her husband's body. Jerry warned her that the wound was awful.

"I don't care," she said raising her voice so it broke. "I'm going to see him. You take me to him."

The five of us walked the three blocks back to Jerry's house. He carried the little girl hitched on his hip. She cried on his shoulder all the way there. He stayed outside with her while Loren and I went into the springhouse with Britney. I could hear Jerry's wife, Jeanette, out there now. "Jasper told me," she said to her husband. "Oh Jesus Lord almighty."

"Is my daddy in there?" I heard Sarah say.

Inside, in the dimness, Britney stood mutely over Shawn's body for a long time.

"All right, I believe he is dead," she eventually said with stoical resignation and let out a long soblike sigh. "Oh Shawn. What are we going to do now? What are we going to do?" Then, she suddenly flew into a rage and cried, "What'd you have to go and get shot for!" and actually swatted his inert shoulder. Finally, she collapsed in a heap on the damp dirt floor, clutching the leg of the table as though she were a child herself holding onto a father's leg. She stayed there weeping for the longest time.

"Robert will build the coffin," Loren said finally.

"I want an open coffin at the funeral," Britney growled back between her sobs.

"You don't have to decide that now."

"I want everybody to see what they did to my husband."

"We'll keep him here until tomorrow morning," Loren said, apparently eager not to quarrel. "Ten o'clock we'll start at the church."

"I'll fetch his good clothes before that," she said.

# TWELVE

By evening, a stream of callers had come by the Watling house, and many lingered to lend a sense of solidarity. Loren had informed a few key individuals, and the news of Shawn's death spread quickly through town and out into the countryside. Jeanette Copeland and Jane Ann Holder volunteered to stay the night with Britney and her daughter. Neighbors brought dishes over to give both sustenance to the callers and some focus to the gathering. Ellen Weibel brought a ham and Jane Ann several bottles of her wine, and Eric Laudermilk brought jugs of new ale, and my neighbor Lucy Myles brought her sausage, and several women brought "pudding," a savory staple of our tables made from leftover bread scraps, which we no longer throw away, mixed with anything else you have around, say bacon, squash, kale, chestnuts—like Thanksgiving stuffing. There was samp, which used to be called "polenta" in the upscale restaurants of yesteryear, cornmeal grits doctored up with cheese, mushrooms, or what have you. Maggie Furnival brought a buckwheat pilaf, Nancy Deaver a barley pilaf. There was, of course, corn bread, our staple. Donna Russo brought two coffee cakes made, she said, with the last of their wheat flour. And insofar as it was June, we had plenty of fresh greens, spinach cooked with bacon and green onions, radishes, rocket and lettuce salad, peas with mint. Elsie DeLong brought new beets. Katie Zucker brought honey cakes made of ground butternut meal. Annie Larmon brought fresh cream from their farm and whipped it up for the cakes. Felix Holyrood, who ran the leading cider mill in Washington County, brought a keg of his powerful "scrumpy," which was stronger than beer. For all that, the evening was hardly festive, but a very somber, measured gathering, with fussing over the dishes a way to signify that life would continue, as well as to give people something to do with their hands.

It was a warm, sticky evening. Mosquitoes rose out of the long shadows in ravening clouds, and people who sought fresh air outdoors were eventually driven back inside to escape them, while big furry moths banged away at the screens. The neighbors had considerately brought extra candles, and the first floor seemed almost as bright as if the power were still on, but the candles also added to the heat inside.

What had originally been the keeping room when the house was a tavern after the Revolutionary War—and then became first a law office, then a nursery, then a parlor, then Shawn's grandfather's optometry shop in the 1950s, and finally a television room in the late twentieth century—had been converted into a broom-making shop by Britney. Here in the large south-facing room with good light she made brooms out of rush and willow and birch, and baskets out of split ash, and wooden spoons out of whatever hardwood scraps were left over. The household had been reorganized in a way that Shawn's parents would have never understood. What had been the Watlings' real estate office from the 1970s until 2003 was now a suite of pantries, food storage, and canning rooms off a kitchen centered on an enormous wood-fired cookstove for processing the output of the garden. No one years ago would have anticipated how much production moved back into the home when the machine age ended. The family's personal quarters were upstairs, including a sitting room. It was a large old house and they kept it in good condition.

Surprisingly little curiosity was expressed about the incident that had left Shawn dead, once I had related what I knew two or three times and it got around to all present. It was eerie, a portentous signifier of our true social condition beyond the conventions of a funeral. Nobody wanted to disturb Wayne Karp and his bunch any more than they would poke a nest of rattlesnakes with a stick. We all knew the apparatus of justice had dissolved. Heath Rucker, our good-for-nothing constable, didn't come around that evening.

For all anyone knew he was drunk or off fishing. Our mayor, Dale Murray, turned up among the later arrivals. He sought me out and cornered me and made a little show of saying, "We're going to get to the bottom of this."

"How," I said. "By what kind of procedure."

"We'll convene a grand jury," he said, "and you'll testify."

"I didn't see a damn thing. And anyway have you noticed the county courts are suspended?"

"I don't think Mr. Bullock will remain unmoved in the face of a cold-blooded murder."

"We'll see about that," I said. Dale Murray had once prosecuted a lawsuit against my father-in-law and ended up getting stung in a countersuit. Though he had turned up late at this impromptu wake, he was not altogether steady on his feet. "By the way," I said, "I'd like to get to the bottom of how you happened to sell the high school to this Christian bunch that just landed."

"They made an offer. I accepted."

"On whose authority?"

"You look here. Nobody else in this burg takes an interest in civic affairs, yourself included. The building's been empty for years and the roof is falling in. These people, whoever the hell they are, they're going to keep the place from falling apart completely."

Before I could ask him where the money was, Laura Holyrood, wife of Felix, who apparently had also been drinking some, came between us with a plate all loaded with a supper for Dale, and in her amorously restless way started flirting Dale up, making sure he noticed her substantial bosom. So that was as far as we got on the school matter. I excused myself and went and found Loren and some of our music circle. We had to discuss what hymns and pieces we might play at the funeral.

Through the windows, the sun sank below a distant hilltop. There was a commotion across the room. Brother Jobe appeared in the open door with a delegation of his followers.

# THIRTEEN

There were five of them besides Brother Jobe, all men, wearing the somber black suits of their sect and carrying hats in their hands. They were all clean-shaven, not like most of us Union Grove men. It struck me as an odd reversal of the way things used to be long ago: the secular clean-shaven and the pious bearded. Only Brother Jobe wore a necktie, a black ribbon cravat, as though it were an emblem of rank. He was sweating impressively. The others were all younger, in their twenties and thirties, uniformly large and powerful men, a different breed almost, like draft horses are to quarter horse stock. You could see how Brother Jobe would feel confident in their company, and you wondered whether he had selected them for their heft and strength.

The whole clutch of them paused at the door while the low buzz of conversation throughout the room dropped away. I think Brother Jobe was aware that he had given himself a theatrical entrance, and he was prepared for it with a little speech.

"Evening to you all," he said, and introduced himself and the others by their given names, Brother Joseph, Brother Elam, Brother Eli, and so on. "I suppose you know by now that we are setting up over at your old high school. We are called the New Faith Brotherhood Church of Jesus and we have come out of Virginia by way of Pennsylvania because of what has happened in our nation's capital. We are happy and grateful to have found this situation and look forward to uniting, so to say, with your community. We come here tonight in recognition of the sadness that has touched upon you today, to pay our respects and begin introducing ourselves, because we do not want you to fear us or think us to be alien beings. We are upright Americans, like yourselves, banded together in faith, praise Jesus, to meet the unfortunate circumstances of these our times. We expect to find new friends here and work fruitfully alongside you, and I hope you will feel the same amongst us. Well, that's all I got to say. Except," he added with a fresh attack, "I wish to reassure you of our friendly intentions by saying we have brought a barrel of good Pennsylvania whiskey on the cart outside and we invite you to partake of it. Now that *is* all I got to say."

Several of our men headed outdoors at once with their cups and glasses. I wondered as how the New Faithers were not against drink per se. Brother Jobe spotted Loren and myself in a corner along with Andrew Pendergast, Bruce Wheedon, and Dan Mullinex who built the grain mill on Bright Creek. Brother Jobe came over like a politician working a room.

"I hear this poor devil was shot dead in cold blood," he said, "and the one that did it is still at large."

Nobody replied to him for an awkward moment. We took refuge in our supper plates.

"That isn't right," he went on. "Can't have folks shooting folks."

"The machinery of justice isn't working too well around here these days," Loren finally said.

"That is exactly what I gather," Brother Jobe said, "and that's why I suggest someone get the ball rolling on it. I understand you do have an elected magistrate."

"Yes, we do. His name is Stephen Bullock."

"Is he here in this house? I'd like to talk to him."

"No."

"Why not?"

"I don't know why he's not here," Loren said, "except he lives several miles out of town and perhaps he hasn't heard the news."

"Why wouldn't this matter come before him?"

"He didn't run for the office, and he said if he got elected he wouldn't serve."

"That's some civic spirit for you," Brother Jobe said. "What does this Bullock fellow do as a livelihood?"

"He's a gentleman," Dan Mullinex said.

"Ain't we all?" Brother Jobe said.

"He owns lands down by the Hudson River," Loren said. "A large establishment. Two thousand acres at least."

"You might even call it a plantation," Bruce Wheedon said, cracking a slight sardonic smile as he speared a piece of ham on his plate.

"Oh?" Brother Jobe said. "Like Ole Massa? We know *that* type."

Our group fell silent again. Whatever one thought about Brother Jobe, we clearly all felt embarrassed about the slovenly state of our local affairs.

"I'd like to go see him," Brother Jobe said. "Would one of you fellows take me to his spread and introduce us?"

Loren and I exchanged a glance.

"You know him best, Robert," Dan said.

"Don't he come to your church?" Brother Jobe said to Loren.

"No."

"Which outfit does he attend?"

"None, as far as I know."

"Hmph. A man who don't have religion, won't serve his community when called. What kind of fellow is that?"

We all swapped more glances around on that one, because we knew Stephen Bullock. He went his own way and always had. He ran a bountiful farm. He had altogether perhaps fifty people living and working for him there, and it was rumored that many of them had entered into a relationship with him of extreme dependency, people who, out of one misfortune or another, or perhaps just a desire to be led or to live a structured existence, sold their allegiance to him for security and a full stomach. He took care of them. It was an old old story, but one that hadn't been seen in America for a long time.

"His farm has come to be a sort of world of its own," Dan said.

"All right. Whatever it is, I'd like to go visit with him. Can we do that sometime after this poor fellow's funeral?" Brother Jobe asked me directly.

"All right," I said.

"I'll send for you, and we'll take the wagon," he said. "People getting shot for no reason. That don't stand with us. Come on out now, boys, and let me buy you a ding-danged dram of life's righteous comfort, praise Jesus."

# Fourteen

I was up until four o'clock in the morning making Shawn's coffin—a sorrowful task as I struggled with the idea that I might have provoked him to anger in the hour leading to his death. It was a plain hexagonal pine box, doweled at the joints, with his initials carved on the lid in a small beaded border. The long day's heat persisted well into the night and the little sleep I found at last was febrile with inchoate dreaming.

Several of us reconvened at Doctor Copeland's place at nine o'clock in the morning. It was already warm. Jane Ann brought Shawn's good clothes over. We dressed the corpse and placed it in the coffin and brought Shawn's remains up to the church on a plain truck wagon from Allison's livery, which the women had draped in some black bunting. Loren and several others fetched Britney and the little girl up from the Watling house to the church and the funeral got underway. Britney still appeared angry on top of being distraught. Jane Ann seemed to struggle with her briefly in the front pew. It was because Shawn's coffin was closed, after all, I surmised. Loren and the other elders had decided that his wound was too terrible and would scare the children. They'd asked me to nail it shut and I did.

We townspeople had settled into the pews when all seventy-three adult members of the New Faith Church entered behind Brother Jobe. They filled in the remaining seats, and took places standing in the sides and rear when all the seats were occupied. I couldn't remember when the church had ever been so full. It was strangely thrilling. Curiously, all the New Faith men stood on one side, and the women on the other. Of course, neither Wayne Karp nor any members of his bunch appeared. We in the choir took our places and began the funeral service with the hymn, "Awake, My Soul, and with the Sun," also called the Doxology.

At the conclusion of the verses, Andrew Pendergast continued playing the hymn softly in the background on piano while Loren came into the pulpit in vestments that he rarely wore except at funerals, and gazed out over the congregation as if to the more distant scene beyond the doors, which were open to keep the air circulating.

"The death of a young man in the early summer of life, seemingly senseless, sudden, and violent, can test our faith. We've been tried over and over in recent years by violence and loss, by the crumbling of society's touchstones, by illness, darkness, hardship, and even the wrath of the earth's weather, out of our gleeful avarice. We elders remember our former lives and we have a lot to answer for. We regret what our lost riches have cost us, even while we miss them. Shawn's brief life bridged these two worlds. By the time he came of age, the days of miracles were over. He assumed a role in our little society, and he went manfully into a life of hard work making the ground yield our bread and caring for his family. He was a generous member of our music circle and will be sorely missed there. There is no telling where another destiny might have led Shawn if this tragedy had not intervened. We'll never know now, because his life was snatched away in a moment of reckless confusion."

A wave of low murmur flowed through the congregants. More than one person coughed.

"We don't know where this land and its people are tending. But we hope for an end to our losses, and we pray to be worthy of this beauty-filled, God-made world that we are still grateful to live in, for all our startling difficulties. Would that the Almighty might stop plucking our young away and reap us instead, the long-lived, who disgraced his world and led it down into weeds and ashes. But his design is not revealed to us and his will only known through our acts. Dear God, death reminds us of our true nature. While in your world we are in you. We are your servants. We thank you for your lessons and your mercy. We ask for your blessings upon the spirit of our friend and kinsman, Shawn Watling, as he enters into the light of your grace."

Loren paused a long moment, then said, "We will continue at the cemetery. All are invited to follow along."

Much bustling and bumping in the pews concealed the sound of Shawn's child crying for her father as everybody moved for the doors. We pallbearers carried the coffin back out to the wagon. The people of Union Grove made a long procession behind the wagon to what had been the edge of town until the 1950s. By a strange irony, several of the houses built afterward, which had encroached on the cemetery for years and dishonored it with their graceless vinyl split-level facades, had been among the first disassembled by Wayne Karp and his crew for salvage, so the cemetery had regained some its original character as the place where the town met the rural landscape. And of course no cars were disturbing the peace of the late morning. Loren had gotten a crew together earlier in the morning to dig out the grave and set the straps for lowering the coffin. When we'd gotten the coffin off the wagon, Tom Allison drove the rig off and left the horses tied to the iron fence in the shade.

We in the choir took up our places behind Loren at the head of the grave. The New Faith people ended up in a crowd on one side and the Union Grove people on the other. Loren began the burial with a Psalm, number 100:

*Make a joyful noise unto the Lord, all ye lands.*
*Serve the Lord with Gladness:*
*come before his presence with singing.*
*Know ye that the Lord he is God:*
*it is he that hath made us, and not we ourselves;*
*we are his people, and the sheep of his pasture.*
*Enter into his gates with thanksgiving,*
*and into his courts with praise:*

*be thankful unto him, and bless his name.*
*For the Lord is good; his mercy is everlasting;*
*and his truth endureth to all generations.*

When Loren had concluded, Brother Jobe took a step forward from his people, cleared his throat in a demonstrative way, and began reciting another Psalm, number 1:

*Blessed is the man that walketh not in the counsel of the ungodly,*
*nor standeth in the way of sinners,*
*nor sitteth in the seat of the scornful.*
*But his delight is in the law of the Lord;*
*and in his law doth he meditate day and night.*
*And he shall be like a tree planted by the rivers of water,*
*that bringeth forth his fruit in his season;*
*his leaf also shall not wither;*
*and whatsoever he doeth shall prosper.*
*The ungodly are not so:*
*but are like the chaff which the wind driveth away.*
*Therefore the ungodly shall not stand in the judgment,*
*nor sinners in the congregation of the righteous.*
*For the Lord knoweth the way of the righteous:*
*but the way of the ungodly shall perish.*

There was more than a little coughing and chuffing among our townspeople as he concluded.

"Thank you, Brother Jobe," Loren said, "for that interesting choice."

"The hundredth there that you spoke. That's on the cheerful side, given the circumstances. Wouldn't you think?"

"I thought it might reflect the gratitude of we the living."

"The Lord is busy judging, and by death do we know it."

"I suppose so. Now, if you'll permit us."

Brother Jobe appeared to think better of saying more and stepped back among his people.

"Lord our God," Loren said, "you are the source of life. In you we live and move. Keep us in life and death, in your love, and, by you grace, lead us to your kingdom through your Son, Jesus Christ, our Lord."

"Amen," the crowd said.

"Almighty God, look on this your servant, lying in great weakness, and comfort him with the promise of life everlasting, given in the resurrection of your Son, Jesus Christ, our Lord."

"Amen."

Loren turned and nodded to those of us in the choir behind him. We began the hymn named "Africa" by William Billings. It was not about the continent of Africa per se, or any of the doings within it, but it was a very beautiful hymn of the American Revolutionary period. It was a favorite of ours and one that Shawn himself had sung with us many times. His strong baritone was conspicuously absent.

*Now shall my inward joy arise,*
*And burst into a song;*
*Almighty love inspires my heart,*
*And pleasure tunes my tongue.*

There were five more verses. When we had concluded, out of nowhere, and much to our surprise, the New Faith people raised their voices in song, all seventy-three of them. The song they commenced was an ominous tune I had heard once or twice, called "The Great Day." It went like this:

*I've a long time heard that there will be a judgment,*
*That there will be a judgment in that day,*
*Oh there will be a judgment in that day.*
*Oh, sinner, where will you stand in that day?*

*I've a long time heard that the sun will be darkened,*
*That the sun will be darkened in that day,*

*Oh the sun will be darkened in that day.*
*Oh, sinner, where will you stand in that day?*

*I've a long time heard that the moon will be bleeding,*
*That the moon will be bleeding in that day,*
*Oh the moon will be bleeding in that day.*
*Oh, sinner, where will you stand in that day?*

The New Faith people sang the hymn in the shape note manner, all modal harmonies full of terror and dread and nasal harshness. It was an impressive display. Our people seemed cowed by it.

When they had concluded, we immediately sang "Shiloh" another hymn by Billings. As we laid down our last note, they answered with "Mortality" by Isaac Watts:

*Death like an overflowing stream*
*Sweeps us away; our life's a dream,*
*An empty tale, a morning flower,*
*Cut down and withered in an hour.*

Loren glanced behind at us in the choir and gave a little shake of the head which we took to mean we should not answer with any more music. In this fraught interval of silence, Brother Jobe spoke out.

"Reverend, I've always thought the minor key better suited this sort of occasion," he said. "I can't help but remark on your employment of the major keys."

"We sing to honor the beauty of God's creation and the joy of the living who remain in it."

"Funeral is a time of sadness."

"I don't think we need to be instructed on how to feel."

"Didn't mean any disrespect, Reverend. But D-major always puts me in mind of dancing, not burying the dead."

Not a few of the other New Faith people seemed to titter at that, though they tried to hide their faces. Some of our people turned and began to walk away from the gravesite. Others gaped across the yawning grave in wonder at the newcomers. Britney glanced pleadingly at Loren.

"If you'll excuse me, Brother Jobe," Loren said, "we are burying our dead, and we're doing it in our way."

"Sorry. Go ahead."

"Thank you."

"I'll just shut up now."

"If you don't, Brother Jobe," Loren said, "I am liable to come over there and bust you in the mouth."

Brother Jobe recoiled slightly, then lowered his head and did not utter another word. His people likewise looked down.

"Almighty Lord," Loren said, "we commit the body of Shawn Watling to the peace of the grave. From dust you came, to dust you shall return. Our Father, who art in heaven, hallowed be thy name. Thy kingdom come, thy will be done on earth as in heaven. Give us this day our daily bread. Forgive us our trespasses, as we forgive those who trespass against us. Lead us not into temptation, but deliver us from evil. For thine is the kingdom, and the power, and the glory, for ever and ever. Amen."

"Amen."

At that, we laid Shawn into the comfort of his everlasting resting place and left the burying ground in silence.

# FIFTEEN

In the days that followed Shawn Watling's funeral, everyone made an effort to attend the needs of his widow and their daughter. There were no official safety nets in our little society, no more social services, no life insurance, nothing but the goodwill of neighbors. I went over twice: once with Todd Zucker, to get in stovewood for her, using his horse cart to bring maple cut from his dying sugar bush; the second time on my own, bringing five pounds of cornmeal from Einhorn's store. It was eight o'clock in the evening when I came by, after working a full day on the cupola.

I could see Britney through a front window sitting in the broom shop, but she didn't come to the door after I'd knocked twice, pretty loudly the second time, so I let myself inside and went to the shop.

"Excuse me for barging in," I said.

She turned to me as if shaking off a reverie and leveled a gaze my way, as fierce as a kestrel. It was unnerving.

"Just checking to see if you're okay?" I said.

"I'm okay," she said, and she turned her gaze back down to her handiwork.

"How's your little girl getting on?"

"She's over to the Allisons," Britney said with a sigh. The Allisons had an eight-year-old girl and a boy, six. Tom Allison operated the only livery in Union Grove in a time when most of us did not yet own our own horses or rigs. The family had a nice household untouched by personal tragedy, apart from Tom's never again working as the vice president for administration of the Washington County Community College, which had closed its doors, and his wife Linda's losing her graphic design business.

"The world seems to be burning up out there," I said.

"It might as well," Britney said.

I glanced down at my sandals, made by our cobbler, Charles Pettie, out of old automobile tire treads and leather straps.

"How are you doing for food?" I said.

"All right."

"I brought you some meal."

"Thank you."

"Anything else you short of?"

"People have been very kind," she said and put on a wan smile, as if speaking from inside a globe of loneliness. I knew what that place was like. Maybe I was projecting my feelings too much, but it was troubling to think what would happen now, with no one to care for her. Less than a week after her husband's funeral, it seemed indecent to imagine who she might eventually pair up with, but that was the direction my mind went in and I couldn't help it. There were few single men in our town. The absurd Heath Rucker. George Murdlow, the candlemaker, who never washed. Perry Talisker, who lived in a shack by the river and made bad corn whiskey and decorated the outside walls of his shack with the stinking pelts of beaver, otter, and raccoon. Buddy Haseltine, who was "slow" and helped out at Einhorn's store in exchange for a cot in the storeroom. Wayne Karp's tribe. Myself. We were the single men in town. What a sorry bunch we were, I thought. Yet I was shocked to imagine for a moment having a young woman such as Britney in my care, and then to take that a step further into the dark territory of conjugal relations. It was a fugitive thought but I was ashamed of myself. Her father, who did not survive the Mexican flu, had been younger than me when he passed on.

"Are you getting any meat?" I said.

"We could stand some."

"Ben Deaver mentioned he would slaughter a kid for me. You like goat?"

"I'll eat it," she said.

"I'll bring some by when I get it? You like smoked trout?"

Watching her sit in a beam of evening light, I couldn't fail to notice how well formed she was. A troubled look came over her. She stood up and brushed bits of broom straw off her apron.

"They came around here," she said.

"Excuse me? Who came around?"

"That New Faith preacher and some of their women."

"A lot of damn nerve, after how he behaved at the funeral."

"What I thought too."

"What did they want?

"Trying to get me and Sarah to move over to the school."

"They're a weird bunch. Why would you consider that?" I said.

She shook her head. Then her features crumbled. She tripped forward into my arms, weeping. Her hair was full of the spice of fresh grass and childbearing. It made me a little dizzy in the heat. I held her until she was cried out. "You don't have to put in with them," I said. "You have this fine place here."

"Maybe," she said and drew away, pulling herself together. "But this making brooms and baskets won't do all on our own. People have all they need of those things."

"We're your people and we won't let you go hungry," I said.

"This being alone is something else," she said and squeezed her eyes shut as if to keep more tears from coming out. But they did, of course.

# Sixteen

I made the trip out to Bullock's with Brother Jobe the following morning. They'd sent a young man over the night before to notify me to be ready. It was more like being issued instructions through a subaltern than being invited along on a social call, but I didn't hassle the messenger about it. I went over to the old high school at nine o'clock in the morning, as instructed. The New Faithers were turning the old school bus garage into a barn with thirty stalls and had fenced off the adjacent baseball field into four paddocks. They had twenty-odd horses, several mules, and a big tan jackass, not counting that team of handsome blacks hitched to the Foley cart, and they seemed all set up for breeding operations now. A muscular chestnut stallion grazed in a separate paddock on the hillside beside the old school cafeteria.

"I see you like horses?" Brother Jobe said.

"I do."

"There's a lot to like there," he said and bid me to climb aboard the rig. We took off at a trot.

It felt grand to sit high up behind that team and exhilarating to move so swiftly down the street, like the dream I had about the magic chair. He drove confidently. There was nothing I had yet seen that he was not confident about. The few people out on Main Street stopped to watch as we flew by. The temperature was rising, though, and he slowed the horses to a walk as soon as we got outside of town where there was no more need to show off, and the pavements got bad again. We passed the ruins of the Toyota dealership with its defunct lighting standards lording over a phantom inventory of sumac bushes where the Land Cruisers and Priuses used to sit parked in enticing ranks.

"I have work for you, old son," he said.

"You're not of any age to be my daddy," I said.

"Figure of speech," he said. "Relax."

"You're a cheeky son of a gun."

"'Course I am. I'm a leader of men," he said and cackled and gave me a little poke in the ribs. "Word is you are a fine woodworker."

"Is that so?"

"You any good, then?"

"I'm plenty busy so I must be good enough."

"Like I was saying."

"You have plenty of hands among your followers," I said. "Surely some of them are carpenters."

"They're coming along. I'd like for them to work with you, though. Learn a thing or two. There's a particular special job over our way that needs doing."

"What would that be?"

"You come by, I'll show you."

"Are you trying to recruit me?"

"Wouldn't dream of it."

"Just so we understand each other."

"Oh, I think we do. No strings attached."

"I hear you've been coming around the young widow's house."

"We've dropped by, like everybody else, trying to help out."

"You're leaning on her to come over your way?"

"What's wrong with that? You all bring her pies and meal and joints of meat. We offer that and more. We offer warm hearts and busy hands and shelter from the storm—and let me tell you, old son, in case you ain't noticed, we got plenty of bad weather out there."

We rolled on for a while without speaking, and I couldn't resist the sheer enjoyment of the journey. The landscape had changed so much over the years. A lot of what had been forsaken, leftover terrain in the old days, was coming back into cultivation, mostly corn, some barley, oats, hay, and lots of fruit trees. Everywhere that had been a parking lot, the pavement was breaking up and growing over with scrub, sumac, and poplar mostly. The roadside commercial buildings going out of town to the west were in various stages of slow disassembly: the discount beverage warehouse, the strip mall where the movie rental, dollar store, and a Chinese take-out joint used to be. All the metal was stripped off. One particular building fascinated me whenever I came out this way: a bungalow that obviously once had been a regular house before it was engulfed by commercial sprawl, probably in the 1970s. The bungalow had finally evolved into a gift shop selling all kinds of poorly made and perfectly useless handicrafts to motor tourists bored by the interminable hours behind the wheel and desperate for any excuse to stop for a while. The word *Gifts* was still there in fading four-foot-high letters on the asphalt shingle roof.

"We don't strong-arm nobody," Brother Jobe said after a long interval of silence, bringing me out of myself. "If folks come over to us, it's because of what they see we got to offer."

"Our people are sore about the way you carried on at the funeral," I said.

"Really? You all appear to be sunk in laxness and lassitude here."

"It may seem that way to you, but they don't like being pushed around any more than anybody else."

"They're demoralized, from what I can tell. Folks crave some structure in their lives. You want to see justice done? Don't you? Ain't that why you agreed to come along?"

I didn't reply.

"You can't live in fear of murderous thugs. And I tell you, we won't tolerate them now. We have seen too much on our journey and come too far, and by God we are going to make a decent home here. Death has been our outrider all the way. We have learned how he drives men's spirits, and the kind of respect he demands, and it ain't in the key of D-major, my friend. Death ain't no may-pole dance. We seen what he did down around Washington."

"How close did you get?" I said.

"We cut past the edge of the suburbs, coming out of Leesburg and across the highway bridge there into Montgomery County, Maryland. You couldn't go any nearer. It'd be like committing suicide. We ran into people fleeing west, upwind of the city. Many of them were burned and had the radiation sickness. You'd come across bodies along the road. We couldn't stop to bury them all. We did not linger."

"You say you were in Pennsylvania a few years?"

"That's so. The flu sickness was terrible there. It rained all winter, two in a row, and the summers were fierce. I think you might grow palmettos there now, the way this screwy weather is going. The white against black and so forth was spilling over from Philly too, and we had trouble with it."

"What did your group live in there."

"We had the use of a large spread, gratis, so to speak, but between the weather, the sickness, and the violence it was no go. I've got a good feeling about this little corner of the country, though. I don't think the sorrows of the cities will make it up this far north, and I take it you still got something like winter up here."

"It still snows and the ponds freeze."

"Snow," he said, breathing deeply. "I look forward to it like a little boy waiting on Christmas."

# SEVENTEEN

Stephen Bullock strode out of the dark interior of his carriage barn as we came into his driveway at a trot. Brother Jobe told the team to *get up* on the approach to the big house to give himself a perky entrance.

"That's Bullock right there," I said, and Brother Jobe brought the horses to a snorting halt.

Bullock was about sixty, hale and brawny, six foot three in boots, with silver hair that hung to his shoulders and was only starting to thin in the front. He was clean-shaven like the New Faithers. His blade of a nose and penetrating blue eyes added to his look of Roman authority. His white linen shirt looked freshly laundered and he wore close-tailored tan riding trousers tucked into black boots. Striding toward us, he wiped off his hands with a rag and handed it, without a glance, to a chunky man in coarser apparel who had followed him out of the barn, as though he had every expectation that the man would be there to take it at the moment he wished to dispose of it. That would be Roger Lippy, who was long ago a salesman at the Chrysler dealer in town and now was Bullock's chief factotum.

When he saw it was me up on the high seat, his forbidding expression gave way to a friendly smile. We'd always gotten along. He had a harvest ball every year that people came to from far and wide around the county, and he hired me and the usual suspects from the music circle to play. He played a fair flute himself, went to Yale undergraduate and Duke Law, and admired things Japanese, having spent time after college teaching English in Osaka. I had built him a little traditional teahouse beside his pond behind the main house, which he was well pleased by. He prepared a set of plans from

memory of what he had seen in the Far East years ago. I just followed them. The lumber came from his own land, milled on
the premises, mostly cherry. It was nice wood to work with. Self-
sufficiency was not new to him, but the necessity of changed times
made him take it to higher levels.

I introduced him to Brother Jobe, who gave a compressed version of how he and his followers had landed in Union Grove, but
did not exactly disclose the purpose of our visit.

"Will you stay for lunch?" Bullock said. Without waiting for
an answer, he told Roger Lippy to have Mrs. Bullock set two extra
places. I could tell from the way Brother Jobe was craning his neck
around that he was anxious to get a look at the operation, and
Bullock, who was not modest, readily offered to give him a tour.
He called the name "Kenneth" into the barn, and another man came
out with grease on his hands to take Brother Jobe's team over to
where a great old stone watering trough stood in the shade. I did
not recognize this Kenneth, but new people were added to Bullock's
rolls on a regular basis as life everywhere else grew more difficult,
and people gave up on it.

For the two-hour duration of the tour, Brother Jobe goggled
and gaped unself-consciously while entering notes in a little handmade book of folded foolscap that he carried. There were, first, the
impressive workshops in the vicinity of the house, several of them
new fieldstone buildings: the creamery, the smokehouse, the brewery, the harness shop, the glass shop, the smithy, the laundry.
Brother Jobe took a particular interest in the brewery, where Bullock not only made beer, but distilled an annual supply of rye whiskey and applejack, some for trade and some for his own use, and
some pure grain for running small engines on the place. Bullock's
farm was the only place I knew where you might still hear engines
running. Not even Wayne Karp managed that. Back in the days
when I had been building the teahouse, when it was still unclear
which way the country would go, Bullock sometimes ran an English sports car around with the engine tricked up for alcohol. Then
he broke a front axle over in Hebron going through a pothole the

size of a bomb crater, and had to tow the car home behind a hired team of oxen. It took three days to go the twenty miles. The roads were much worse now.

Bullock poured us each a generous sample of his whiskey from a cask in the rear, where many barrels were racked, into jade green pony glasses made there on the premises too. Brother Jobe tossed his dram straight back, said it was "fit for all occasions and all weathers," and Bullock refilled his glass. I had not been there for a while, but it seemed that everything was coming up at Bullock's establishment whereas everything in our town was running down. You could understand the allure of the place.

We proceeded to the horse-breeding barn. Bullock was raising big Hanovers for the cart and saddle, and Percherons for freight loads. Brother Jobe said he favored a mule in the field, that it was the coming thing with all the hotter weather. Bullock said he hadn't seen a jackass in Washington County that was worth breeding a mare to. Brother Jobe said he had just such a one and would lend it over.

"Have you tried oxen?" Bullock said. "They're peachy in the woodlot and behind the plow."

"I don't know the first thing about an ox," Brother Jobe said. "We're all about mules where we come from."

"I'll tell you something about an ox," Bullock said. "You can eat him when he's past his prime for work."

"That makes sense, I suppose," Brother Jobe said. "I confess, I never tried to eat a mule either in or out of its prime."

Bullock refilled our glasses. He said he admired Brother Jobe's team of blacks, but the latter said that the sire had been left back in Virginia.

"We're miserably short of new blood," Bullock said.

"Your welcome to try our stallion. He's a liver-chestnut, fifteen-and-a-half-hands Morgan. Maybe sometime we can swap out."

They were in excellent spirits by the time we strolled through the orchard to the beginning of Bullock's extensive fields. The corn seemed to go on forever, but we crossed a hedgerow over a stile and came to what Bullock really wanted to show.

"Why, iddin that sweet sorghum?" Brother Jobe said. It was not a crop that I recognized.

"You are correct, sir," Bullock said. "With the maple borers killing our sugar trees, and mites on our bees, we're a bit hard up for sweetening lately."

"Is that a fact?"

"Well, it's this heat, you know."

"We always had sorghum syrup on Momma's table."

"It'll be a new thing here, but our people will like it, won't they Robert?"

"I suppose they will, Stephen," I said, not really knowing.

"It beats heck out of blackstrap molasses, I'll tell you," Brother Jobe said. "Milder."

"It's got a flavor all its own," Bullock said.

"My point," Brother Jobe said.

The two of them seemed to be getting on like boon companions. It made me a little sick to see it, or maybe it was just the heat and the whiskey.

We made our way around the extensive property, down grassy lanes between fields of one crop and another. The corn was knee-high and lush. The buckwheat was in flower. From his years in Japan, Bullock was fond of soba noodles made from the grain. He was particularly proud of his experiments with spelt, an antique precursor of our common wheats and apparently immune to the rust disease that lurked in our soils. It did not have the gluten content of modern wheat, he said, but it was better than rye. He hoped to expand production to a hundred acres next year, he said. The hillsides above his grain fields were dotted with brown and white cattle, some dairy and some steers for beef. Coyotes had been killing his calves lately. He'd had to post sharp-shooters. There were ten acres alone in potatoes and as much in kitchen vegetables. He had mostly women and a few children chopping weeds among the crop rows out there, and men on

construction and heavy labor jobs around the plantation. We saw
a crew coming in from the woodlots with a load of red pine logs
behind a team of massive oxen.

"There you are," Bullock said. "Red and white Holsteins. Trac-
table, steady, strong. And not nearly as dumb as they say."

"Maybe we'll try some," Brother Jobe said. "Holsteins," he said
to himself, scribbling in his little book.

Soon we got over to the new sorghum cane crushing mill and
refinery that Bullock was building on a high bank beside the
Battenkill River. It stood about a quarter mile above the place where
that stream runs into the Hudson, on a site that had been the Kiernan
and Page cardboard box mill early in the last century, of which little
remained but foundation stones and some giant pieces of iron machinery so rusted that their exact purpose was no longer identifiable.
The men working around the new cane mill greeted Bullock enthu-
siastically. I recognized at least two of them from the old days: Jack
Hellinger, who used to be the Rite Aid pharmacist in town, and
Michael Delsen, who had a little insurance agency with his dad on
Main Street. It was hard to tell whether the workmen's enthusiasm
on seeing their boss was that of free, happy men or of people who
had to put on a face to authority. Bullock's relations with the people
who lived on the plantation was the subject of much speculation
among us who lived back in town. Being a world of its own, there
was no way we outsiders knew what his people had to say about
how things worked there, except that it pretty obviously wasn't a
democracy.

Bullock's new mill certainly was impressive. They were lever-
ing a great shallow iron evaporation pan into position over a rect-
angular stone hearth where the cane juice would be boiled into
syrup. The building was all fieldstone, mortared up nicely. Bullock had a lime kiln up on the plateau above the river valley where
he burned limestone to make the adhesive component of cement:
quicklime. Brother Jobe scribbled away. Altogether, the mill was
a big new thing that looked like it was well thought out, well made,
and would work. Nothing in town compared so well. We had built

virtually nothing new there in years. It got me thinking about Loren's idea to start a laundry, and that maybe I should show a little more enterprise and help him get something going.

We followed the road along the extensive hay fields and oat fields where they raised animal feeds and came, at last, to the collection of little cottages that Bullock had erected over the years for his people. It really amounted to a village, but of a kind that had not been seen in America for a long time. The cottages were deployed along a picturesque little main street with a few narrow lanes off it. There were about thirty buildings in all. This main street lacked shops or places of business because the only business there was Bullock's business. There was a commissary building, where his people could get their household needs. I didn't know if they used money in it or whether Bullock's people even got paid. Two new cottages were under construction, meaning I supposed that more people were joining up. This too seemed to pique Brother Jobe's interest.

"What do you call the place?" he said.

"Metropolis," Bullock said.

"Ain't that were Superman lived?" Brother Jobe said.

Bullock grinned and winked at me, and Brother Jobe grinned too, back at Bullock. It was grins all around.

"We just call it the New Village," Bullock said.

"I like that," Brother Jobe said. "It's plain and to the point."

"Maybe when I'm dead they'll name it after me. Bullocktown."

"They ought to."

"Doesn't really roll off the tongue, though, does it?"

"There's worse. Near us back in Virginia was a little burg name of Chugwater. And another one called Stinktown. Well, that was more like a nickname for Stickleyville."

One larger structure stood out at the center of things, and that was the meeting hall, offset from a little grassy square at the end of the main street. Bullock's people all generally took a midday meal together there and schooled the few children they had managed to produce. It was a plain but dignified clapboard building, with large light-gathering windows, and a cupola on top for additional light. All the buildings were whitewashed.

"Is this your church?" Brother Jobe said.

"Sometimes," Bullock said.

"Where do you stand on religion, if I might ask?" Brother Jobe said.

"I'm not against it."

"But you don't minister to them."

"Beyond my competence."

"Maybe you're unnecessarily modest."

"Well, I'm not Superman. After all."

The streets and lanes of the little village communicated only with the wagon roads between Bullock's fields and works. We rarely saw his people over in Union Grove, unless they were on a specific errand for him. Otherwise, he had a landing on the Hudson River. The things he needed came up from Albany and beyond. The cottages where his people lived there in the plantation village were of a common vernacular type, also very modest, though some were decorated more than others, with brackets and moldings, according to the tastes of who lived in them. I suppose they were allowed to do as they pleased with them. Some had summer kitchens out back. All had brick chimneys. Nobody was working on the new houses now. I supposed they did that in their off-hours.

While we stood out in the grassy square, a stout woman in an apron stepped out of the meetinghouse and pounded a tubular iron gong that hung from a stock beside the door. She regarded the three of us with a kind of wary respect, as if our presence portended something. Then she bustled back inside, wiping her hands on her apron. An appealing familiar aroma of baking corn bread emanated from the place. Soon Bullock's people began streaming in from the fields and forests. All nodded their heads at Bullock in deference.

"They seem well fed," Brother Jobe said.

"They're not fed," Bullock said.

"Excuse me?"

"Well, I'm not running a zoo here. They feed themselves."

# Eighteen

Bullock's own house was built in 1802, when the area was first coming up after the American Revolution, a handsome old clapboard thing that now looked like it had grown out of the ground along with the two-hundred-year-old oak trees around it. It had belonged to Bullock's great-great-great-great-grandfather who acquired it from a Colonel Templeton who was wounded heroically at the battle of Saratoga and later ran a flax mill in town, which burned down in 1811 and ruined him. The Bullocks acquired the house, afterward ran a big farm there, and also sent barges of molding sand down the Hudson River to the cast-iron works in Troy. The exceptionally fine sand was a gift of the retreating glaciers that had carved out the Hudson Valley eons before and laid a big ragged deposit along the bank where the Battenkill met the Hudson on his property. In the twentieth century, when mechanization came on, the Bullocks planted thousands of fruit trees, mostly apples but some pears and plums too.

This is what I understood about Stephen Bullock: In the 1980s, his father, Richard, was producing cider commercially on contract for the Star supermarket chain. Stephen was in his second year of law school at Duke University, after his sojourn in Japan, when his father was killed in a highway accident. Stephen was the only son and he went back to run the place. It wasn't what he had planned to do, but Richard had been a controlling and difficult father, and without having to rebel against him anymore, Stephen found that he liked the farm life and did a good job of running the place, and he decided he hadn't really cared for the law after all. His mother passed away two years later and he didn't have to answer to anyone anymore.

As the modern world came apart, and the local economy with it, Bullock took the opportunity to acquire at least eight other properties adjacent to the original family farm. They were not all in agriculture. One was an auction yard for secondhand farm equipment and trucks. Another was a marina for pleasure boats on the river, which now served as Bullock's landing (and was called Bullock's Landing by everybody else, if not Bullock himself). Several others were derelict dairy operations with ruined barns, pastures gone to poplar, and houses that let the rain in. Some of the owners had died off. Others sold out only to end up working for him. It was clear to me from the conversations we had in the days when I was building his teahouse—and they were many, often over a glass—that Stephen Bullock had a comprehensive vision of what was going on in our society and what would be necessary to survive in comfort, and I don't think he ever deviated from that vision for a moment.

Bullock met his wife Sophie one night at the Asia Society in New York City. He used to go down (he told me this) to meet girls, and he met Sophie there. She was a young assistant curator at the Metropolitan Museum, fresh out of graduate school at Brown University, and she quite liked the idea of visiting her new boyfriend on this prosperous apple farm upstate where, I suppose, he charmed her with autumn rambles in the orchards and evenings before the fireplace in his lovely 1802 house. She married him, of course, and for many years in the old days they carried on the family orchard business until things fell apart. They had two daughters. The daughters had grown up, and each moved to exactly the wrong cities at the wrong time: Los Angeles and Washington, D.C., and now they were gone, or at least presumed to be gone because they had not been heard from since so many perished in those cities, and that was before the mails and telephones went down.

Sophie Bullock greeted us at the side door. I had not seen her in a while. Coming along into her fifties, she was still commandingly beautiful. Her wheat straw hair had more of a silvery glint in it now. Her face was a little more lined. She was dressed in a simple white cotton gown puffed at the shoulders with roses embroidered at the bodice, a costume of leisure. She gave the instant impression of a person effortlessly enjoying her position in the world, and I sensed that Brother Jobe was awed by her.

"How nice to meet you," she said. She seemed to regard Brother Jobe with the amusement that a kindhearted but essentially superior being would show to an obvious primitive, with a dash of bewilderment as to why such a curious creature had turned up at her house this day.

Bullock led us into his dining room. The walls were filled with pictures, including a portrait of a Bullock ancestor, a landscape of the upper Hudson River Valley, two colorful abstract blobish compositions done by Bullock's mother in the 1960s, and some large old engraved maps of the area. But what really caught Brother Jobe's eye was the ceiling fan, which was revolving.

"How's that work?" he said, pointing.

"Electric," Bullock said.

"You got electric?"

"We run a small hydro outfit."

"I'll be dog."

Next Bullock opened a cabinet under the sideboard and turned on recorded music. Mozart. A piano concerto. Brother Jobe was now speechless.

Mrs. Bullock asked us to sit down and pretty soon an older servant woman brought in our plates through a swinging door from the adjacent kitchen. On each plate sat a grilled hamburger on a round bun with fat golden slivers of fried potatoes along with a mound of cabbage slaw. The servant woman returned with a pitcher of sumac punch and a little serving bowl of ketchup, made on the premises, Mrs. Bullock said.

"My goodness," Brother Jobe said pointing at his bun. "This wheat?"

"It is," Bullock said.

"Where'd it come from?"

"Originally? I don't know. Ohio maybe. I send things to Albany and get stuff back in trade. We got a store of wheat in April, but we've seen a sharp falling off."

"You run boats down there?"

"I lost a crew ten days ago."

"What do you mean lost?"

"They didn't return."

"Oh my . . ."

We addressed our hamburgers. Mrs. Bullock cut hers in quarters daintily.

"Why, this is better than what we used to get at the Sonic drive-in," Brother Jobe said, "and it didn't get much better than that. My compliments."

"A hamburger amuses me," Bullock said.

"Just like old-timey times."

"Pickle?" Mrs. Bullock said, proffering a dish.

We ate silently for an awkward interval.

"What do you aim to do about that boat crew?" Brother Jobe said.

"Right now I'm waiting to see if they'll return," Bullock said.

"What if they don't?"

"I'll most likely have to organize another bunch to go down and search for them. But I'll need some outside men. I can't spare many more from here."

"Maybe I can spare some of my men," Brother Jobe said.

"How many have you got?"

"I have thirty-eight men in all."

Bullock seemed impressed, but didn't take him up on it right then and there. Instead, he just said, "From now on I'll have to arm my crews."

"Did you pass through Albany on your way here, Brother Jobe?" Mrs. Bullock said. "I understand you've come a long way."

"No, ma'am. We avoided the cities."

"Probably a wise thing," she said.

"You say your trade has fell off?" Brother Jobe said.

"Things have gotten more disorderly down there," Bullock said. "We were already paying excise taxes, as they called them, that amounted to extortion. I expect it will get worse, not better. But we are doing everything we can here to become as self-sufficient as possible."

"Yes, well, that unfortunate bit of news about your boat crew sort of brings me to the purpose of my visit," Brother Jobe said. "There's been a killing over in town and no law brought into the picture, and you being the only law in the jurisdiction I want to persuade you to come in on this here business and establish a little authority."

"I declined the honor of the election," Bullock said.

"I heard. You can't do that," Brother Jobe said.

"Of course I can."

"Where's your community spirit."

"It's here on the farm."

"Surely you have a little left over for your neighbors?"

"I'm not going to start a feud with Wayne Karp."

"So you must already know about this business," Brother Jobe said.

Bullock pushed his plate forward with the half-eaten sandwich on it.

"Yes, I heard about it," Bullock said.

"How's that, you being so disconnected from things over here?"

"I send a man to Einhorn's store at least once a week, and I have to get things from Mr. Karp like everybody else."

"Then you know that Robert here was the chief witness to the crime?"

Bullock sighed. "I heard the bare bones of the story." He shifted his gaze to me. "You were up there with this young man who was shot."

"I was in the store with Wayne," I said. "I didn't see what happened."

"Something about a mad dog, I was told," Bullock said.

"There wasn't anything wrong with the dog. It was hot. It was a big dog, some kind of Newfoundland. You know how they drool. But I don't know what the dog did, if it did anything, or what Shawn Watling might have done to get shot."

"My feeling, Mr. Bullock, sir," Brother Jobe said, "is that what you do might never lead to any prosecution in this matter, but it would be a moral support to the town for you to at least authorize an investigation, reestablish some rule of law. I tell you, sir, I have been around this country some in recent years, and once the law goes altogether, the center don't hold."

"Why don't you set up to govern things over there yourself, Brother Jobe? You seem to have a substantial organization in place. I assume you have some reliable people with you."

"We only just come. It wouldn't look right. The people in town might not stand for it."

"You think? Did the people mount any effort to look into this crime, if it was a crime?"

"Exactly what I'm saying—"

"Why would they object if you took over matters that they're too busy, or lazy, or too disorganized to take on?"

"If I set up as judge or sheriff or whatever you want to call it, why, I'd have to rule over you then too, wouldn't I?" Brother Jobe said.

Bullock smiled. "I don't know that we would require your attention over here," he said.

"I'm just laying it out, to be frank. Are you comfortable knowing you send a trade boat down to the state capital and the goldurn thing don't come back? And there ain't no one to look into the matter?"

"I'll find out what happened. Don't you worry about that," Bullock said and turned to me again. "Robert, you're a capable fellow. There are things that need to be done in town. I hear from Einhorn that the town water system is about shot."

"Is that so?" Brother Jobe said.

"There's something wrong with the outflow up at the collect pond," I said. "And the main coming down from it leaks in more than a few places."

"Now that you mention it, we've noticed the pressure is low as heck over our way," Brother Jobe said. "We're at the high school."

"I've heard," Bullock said.

"Goldurn roof was falling in."

"You fixed it, I suppose."

"You're well told, we did, sir."

"Why, then I suppose the water will be next," Bullock said.

"We'll get to it," I said.

"What I've been trying to tell you," Brother Jobe said. "You see, all these individuals in the town trying to live like it's still old times, each on its own, each family alone against the world. You can't have that in these new times or things will fall apart. See what a splendid show Mr. Bullock is running here," he said, evidently for my benefit. "Everyone has a part to play and does its job and the whole adds up to more than the sum of the parts. Am I right? That's exactly like how we do in New Faith, only we bow to a higher authority. You never got Jesus, I take it, sir."

"Never did," Bullock said.

"Well that's a goldurn shame. Ever tempted to try?"

"Not really."

"How about your folks on the farm here?"

"My people are free to believe what they want to believe."

"Maybe some of them would like to take a look over our way, then, and come to the Lord."

"I don't have any to spare, Brother Jobe. I just lost four hands on the river. Robert," Bullock turned once again to me, his patience visibly ebbing. "Why don't you talk to the Reverend Holder and the other men over there and see if you can get them going on repairing that water system. Brother Jobe here is right. You people over in town need to show a little initiative."

"Loren and I aim to start a laundry operation," I said, surprising myself by sounding so deliberate.

Brother Jobe perked up. "First I heard of it."

"Where will you do this," Bullock said.

"In the old Wayland-Union Mill," I said.

"Well then you'd better fix the water supply."

"Of course."

"I can cast you some lengths of concrete pipe here," Bullock said "and get them over to you, if that'd help. You've got at least six feet of head on the Battenkill in two locations up there. You could be running hydroelectric for the whole town. There's enough metal parts lying around this county to build a steam locomotive, if you looked hard enough. We built a five-kilowatt generator out of the automotive scrap on Bacon Hill."

I couldn't help but feel that Bullock was looking to purchase Brother Jobe's goodwill as a tactical measure.

"I like the sound of that," Brother Jobe said, rubbing his hands. "I'll tell you what: we'll examine those water pipes right away. We have the manpower to repair them and we'll do it. And we'll see to the electric this summer, if your offer to lend a little guidance still stands. And my offer still stands to help out in case your boat crew don't report back. I've got some fellows that have been trained in this sort of thing."

"What? Military types?"

"Holy Land vets."

"Really? Well, great," Bullock said, pushing away from the table. "It was sure nice of you to visit. We don't get many breaks from the routine here."

"You notify me if you want our boys to help turn up those boys of your'n. They're stout fellows, upright and fearless."

"Very kind of you."

"And maybe you'll consider starting up those wheels of justice."

"I'll consider those things."

"It's been an honor to meet you too, sir," Brother Jobe said. "But say, if you're not going to eat the rest of that fine hamburger, why I'd like to take it with me, if you don't mind. It's been years since I've seen such a thing and, you know, waste not want not, especially in these times."

"Of course," Bullock said with a strange broad smile that didn't seem altogether natural, while he handed the plate to Brother Jobe. "By the way, this hamburger came from one of our oxen."

"You don't say?"

"His name was Dick."

"What happened to him?"

"Freak accident. A scaffold fell on him down at the new cane mill and crushed his spine. We had to put him down."

"My condolences. Well, he sure come to a tasty end, though."

"Come back some time for hot dogs," Bullock said. "We make those here too."

The sky had darkened and it looked like a storm was gathering when we stepped outside. On the way back to town in the cart, not much was said. I suppose we were both lost in our own thoughts. But as we passed the old Toyota lot just west of town, Brother Jobe surprised me by muttering, as if to himself, "That fellow is a dangerous man."

# NINETEEN

Lightning played crazy patterns on the walls all night, though the storms stayed off in the distance and no rain fell. I kept waiting for it to come closer, work its fury, and be over. Even more, I longed for a cool front to drive off the relentless heat. At times I imagined that maybe it wasn't thunder and lightning at all but a terrific battle beyond the horizon between whatever was left of the great war machines—though I hadn't seen an airplane in the skies for years, civilian or military. In any case, the distant storms kept me awake, so I got out of bed and sat in a soft chair by the window to watch the sky until I was satisfied that it was indeed lightning and not Armageddon. I must have fallen to dozing there because I woke up with a jerk. I quickly recognized that the scream which woke me up was real, not in a dream, and noticed an orange glow reflecting off the side of Lucy Myles's house next door. I strapped on my sandals and hurried outside.

Lucy was out in her yard in her nightclothes.

"Someone's house is burning down," she said.

An orange aura flickered over the nearby rooftops. A hot wind blew leaves and dust down the street, as if every loose particle in town was being prompted into motion by unseen forces. I rushed around the block toward the fire, joined by half-clad neighbors, till we all converged in front of the Watling house on Salem Street. Flames licked through the tall windows of the broom shop and up into a dormer. The fire visibly gathered strength in the few seconds that I stood there gaping at it. Bonnie Sweetland, the Watlings' next-door neighbor, was screaming. Loren and Jane Ann, Jason LaBountie, Sam Hutto, Andrew Pendergast, Tom Allison, Terry Einhorn and his older boy, Teddy, the Copelands and their kids, Larry Russo the baker, who generally started work before dawn, and many others all soon arrived on the scene, some half-dressed, many carrying buckets. Even Heath Rucker and Dale Murray, the constable and our mayor, showed up. Bruce Wheedon, a foreman on Deaver's farm, who was the nominal chief of our pathetic fire department, appeared with a huge box wrench, but was not able to open the valve on the nearby hydrant. Who knows how many years it had been since the valve head had been turned, and I was not aware that anybody went around testing them. The nut was rusted frozen.

Loren tried banging the wrench handle with a big rock. He only succeeded in snapping off the handle from the box end. Bruce cursed and there was some yelling back and forth, and Doug Sweetland dragged his garden hose over, which got everybody to stop yelling until they realized that we couldn't fill the buckets fast enough with it, and then Charles Pettie, the town cobbler and bass fiddle player in our music circle, showed up with a yard-long Stillson wrench that must have weighed thirty pounds. Two men pushed and one pulled the long handle until the valve nut turned with a shriek and water started flowing out of the hydrant. Everybody cheered and rapidly formed a bucket brigade. But it was soon obvious that our flung buckets made no impression on the fire.

All this happened quickly, no more than a few minutes. Meanwhile, other women joined Bonnie Sweetland in screaming and pointing up into the end dormer where two figures, Britney and Sarah, were dimly visible huddled together inside. Tom Allison brought over an aluminum extension ladder and threw it against the eaves below the dormer. At the same moment, the needles of a big white pine tree close by the most involved end of the house reached kindling temperature and exploded into flame. Bruce Wheedon yelled at the bucket men to forget the Watling house and start wetting down the Sweetland's place next door so it wouldn't catch, and they all rushed to reform the bucket line there. Up on the ladder, Tom smashed the window in the dormer, but Britney remained frozen inside clutching the girl. I tossed my bucket aside, rushed around the back of the house, and slipped in the kitchen door.

My hand sizzled when I turned the doorknob, and there was a smell like grilled meat. The back stairway ran right off the mud-room, and I raced up into the smoke. They were in the little girl's room, the wallpaper dirty pink through the smoke. Everything happened fast. In the confusion it seemed that Britney was trying to prevent me from helping her. I scooped up Sarah under my left arm like a meal sack and grabbed Britney's hand so she would fol-low me out. But she resisted. I hollered, "This way! Come on!" By now, flames were probing into the hallway, and I doubted we could make a run out the back stairs. Tom shouted something from the window, where he stood atop the ladder, his words smothered in the rising roar. To hand Sarah to him, I had to let go of Britney. She slipped out the door back into the fiery hallway. I realized she didn't want to escape. But the maw of flame deterred her long enough for me to reach out and seize her. She flailed ineffectively. I yanked her back into the pink bedroom and shoved her toward the dormer until I managed to push her out the window. Tom grappled her down with help from the boys below. By then flames had invaded the little room itself. The heat was ferocious. I launched myself through the dormer headfirst.

The next thing I remember was lying in the weeds hacking my lungs out with faces bobbing above me, and then I rolled over and vomited in the grass. Warm blood ran down the side of my head into my eyes. Someone pressed a rag against my scalp and then they were carrying me somewhere. Gray daylight gathered in the tree-tops as raindrops the size of marbles spiraled down from an infi-nite height and stung my face.

# TWENTY

Jerry Copeland had a small infirmary in the second story above his office and lab where people too sick to be home sometimes stayed so he could keep an eye on them. That's where I woke up. I was in a fog. My lungs felt heavy. A big bandage like a mitten was swaddled on my left hand. I had a similar bandage around my head. I began to recall what had happened the night before in odd documentary detail, without emotion. I lay there for quite a while in a strange care-free exhausted state of mind, hearing the muffled sounds of Jerry padding around down below, doing whatever he was doing, seeing patients or cooking up medicines. After a while, he came in with a tray of food for me.

"How are you feeling?"

"Pretty stoned."

"That's the laudanum."

"It's wicked strong."

"I had to put a few stitches in your head."

"What happened to my hand?" I said, holding up the mitten-like bandage.

"I'd say you burned it on a doorknob."

"Where?"

"The Watling house."

"No, where on my hand?"

"The palm mostly."

"I need those pads on the tips to play my fiddle, you know."

"I think they're okay. Try to sit up."

As I did, I noticed an impressive pain in my shoulder, but felt detached from it, like it was somebody else's pain and I was only a casual observer of it. I must have made a face, though.

"You came down pretty hard on that side," Jerry said. "Nothing's broken, in my judgment. There would be more swelling. No reason why you can't go home."

"Okay," I said, trying to imagine how I might hold the fiddle with a bum shoulder. I had fiddling on what was left of my brain.

"Eat some," he said. "It'll help clear your head."

The tray had legs on it so a person could eat comfortably in bed without having to balance it on their lap. On it was a plate of scrambled eggs, two squares of corn bread, a little dish of creamed spinach, and a mug of rose-hip tea. I must have been staring at the tray.

"This is beautiful. Your wife makes a lovely breakfast."

"You're a hero now, Robert."

"Huh?"

"Saving those two."

"Oh."

"Eat something."

I picked up a fork. "I don't think she wanted to be rescued."

Jerry sat down at the end of the bed.

"What makes you say that?"

"She tried to run back into the fire. I had to catch her and shove her out the window."

"Maybe she was confused."

"I don't know. Maybe."

I lifted a forkful of scrambled eggs, golden and buttery. Jeanette had panfried the corn bread in butter too.

"It's a good thing we all work as hard as we do around here," I said. "All the butter and cream we eat."

"Do you suppose she set that fire herself?" Jerry said.

"Huh?"

"You think Britney Watling torched her own house?"

"It hadn't occurred to me."

"Well, now I wonder," Jerry said. "At first I figured lightning. But now I'm not so sure."

"I don't know either. The storms kept me up a long time but they were far off. I fell asleep sometime before the fire broke out."

"Lightning can strike far from the center of a storm cell," Jerry said.

"Maybe. I hope she didn't try to harm herself and her kid. I stopped in on her two days ago with some cornmeal. She seemed mighty glum."

"She'll have to put in with someone," Jerry said. "Sooner rather than later. Maybe with your neighbor Lucy Myles. Lucy could help with the child."

"Who are they staying with now?"

"Allisons. I think."

I finished the eggs and turned to the creamed spinach and finally the corn bread. Sandy used to think it was funny that I ate things in sequence off a plate. Never some of this and some of that. One item at a time. Who knows, maybe it was what made me a good organizer in the old days on the job. My head was clearing.

"Last night, before all this happened, I was thinking."

"About Britney and the girl?"

"No. About the town. We really have to get our act together around here."

"Yeah? How are we going to do that."

"I'm calling a meeting of the trustees tonight," I said after a while. Any of us on the town board could call a meeting. We just hadn't done it in at least a year. "Can you help get the word out? Ask Loren to send for the farmers, and make sure Dale Murray is there."

"All right," Jerry said. "Any particular purpose?"

"For one thing, the water pressure used to be much higher than it is now. We really have to fix it."

"I doubt it would have mattered last night."

"We'll never know, will we?"

"I suppose."

"You see how we give in? It's some kind of reflex negativity."

"We're conditioned by adversity."

"We don't have to surrender to conditioning. Brother Jobe says
we're demoralized. I think it's true."

"Since when are you tight with him?"

"I took him over to see Bullock. He's a cheeky bastard. He put
it right to Stephen about taking up his duties as magistrate."

"Stephen's a proud man. I don't imagine he rolled over for him."

"He got Stephen to agree to help fix our water system. He can
cast some concrete pipe for us, he says."

"Maybe we should all take turns falling out a window," Jerry
said. "It seems to have pepped you up."

"I'm just sick of sleepwalking through life. Can you take this
tray up off me?"

"Of course."

I got up and out of the bed. Everything felt wobbly, but I stayed
on my feet. Sun streamed through the windows. It felt like a new
day.

"Also, ask Loren to get Brother Jobe to the board meeting
tonight. That new bunch has to be in on this."

"All right," Jerry said.

"Tell them eight o'clock at the old town hall, upstairs."

# Twenty-one

The top floor of our three-story town hall, an 1879 Romanesque red sandstone heap, was the old council chamber that had also served for generations as the community theater and civic ballroom. It had a proscenium stage at one end. The seats were not fixed, so they could be arranged for official meetings, shows, dances, banquets, what have you. In the 1950s, they held boxing matches up there. The high coffered ceiling was partitioned into twelve octagons that had been painted long ago to depict the signs of the zodiac. They were so faded and flaked you could barely make out which sign was which.

Back of the stage, a painted flat from the last community theatrical production remained in place: the musical *Guys and Dolls*. It showed a Times Square scene of the mid-twentieth century. It was startling to be reminded that people had lived in a world of skyscraper apartments, night clubs, neon lights, and taxicabs. I remembered the excitement the week the show ran. We so looked forward to coming here and putting it on each night, no matter how hard we'd worked during the day or how frightened we were about what was happening around the country. Sandy played Sarah Brown, the Salvation Army girl, sweetheart of gambler Sky Masterson (Larry Prager). Loren was Nathan Detroit. Linda Allison was Adelaide. I played violin in the orchestra, of course. My Daniel was in the chorus of Nathan's gambler chums, with a painted-on mustache. We lit the stage with footlights fashioned out of candles and tin cans dug up from the general supply, and it all looked perfectly enchanting. You didn't need a thousand watts to put a show on. The people came from all around the county night after night to see it. Many came more than once. The chil-

dren seemed baffled about the world that the play depicted. Since
the flu hit, we hadn't put on any more plays.

This evening the old wooden folding chairs were arranged in
a few concentric circles with twelve at the center reserved for us
trustees. I had slept most of the afternoon and felt nearly normal
again, mentally. My shoulder hurt, but I had full rotation. The sun
still lit the big arched windows when the trustees straggled in at
eight. In late June, twilight would last until nine thirty. It was warm
up there in the top floor of the old building and the big room
smelled faintly of bats.

Before the meeting got underway, the trustees and some observers stood around in knots. They all stopped gabbing when I
came in. Many acknowledged me with a nod, I supposed because
of what happened at the fire. But then I realized it was because I
was the one who'd called the meeting, and they were looking to
me to explain why. The trustees were Ben Deaver, Ned Larmon,
and Todd Zucker, all farmers; Cody DeLong, who still pretended
to be a banker at the Battenkill Trust but barely survived off the
big garden in the back of his house; Jason LaBountie, the veteri-
narian; shopkeeper Terry Einhorn; Rod Sauer, the mason; Victor
Gasparry, the tinsmith; Loren, Andy Pendergast, and Dale Murray,
the mayor. All the trustees were men, no women and no plain laborers. As the world changed, we reverted to social divisions that
we'd thought were obsolete. The egalitarian pretenses of the high-
octane decades had dissolved and nobody even debated it anymore, including the women of our town. A plain majority of the
townspeople were laborers now, whatever in life they had been
before. Nobody called them peasants, but in effect that's what
they'd become. That's just the way things were. Shawn Watling,
rest his soul, had called it clearly.

Jane Ann was among the few women there. She and Loren
had an understanding that she always stood by him in public,
whatever went on in private life. She explained to me more than
once when we were together, as if she needed to explain it to
herself. The idea was to reassure those whose families had been

blown apart by catastrophe that the minister and the minister's wife remained a continuing presence for them, like a father and mother in the greater household of the town, and that therefore some kind of benign order still prevailed in our little corner of the universe. Jane Ann cast a haunted gaze at me when I came in, and I realized that we'd failed to get together that week.

Loren bustled over to me with Andy Pendergast. I'd taken that awkward head bandage off at home and they admired the stitches that Jerry had left in my scalp.

"Where'd you learn how to leap out of a burning house like that?" Andy said. "You looked like one of those old Hollywood stunt men."

"Self-preservation is a great motivator," I said.

"We're all proud of what you did," Loren said.

"It could have been anyone," I said.

"I don't know about that," he said.

"Well, you're our hero," Andy said, "so, hey, when are we all going to get together?" I knew what he meant by that. It was his code for prompting our music circle to meet. It had become his job to get the rest of us to make it to practice, especially this time of year when there was so much else to do.

"I'm not sure if I can play," I said, showing my bandaged hand.

"Well, you better heal up. It's important to keep things going, especially the way things are now."

I supposed that he meant Shawn Watling getting killed.

"It does keep the morale up around here," Loren said.

"It's more than that," Andy said. "It's light in the darkness. And I wonder if I'm alone thinking there's ever more darkness around us."

"You're not alone," I said.

"Uh-oh," Loren said.

Just then Dale Murray sauntered over, as though he still had the liveliest law practice in Washington County. He was actually wearing a necktie—the only one in the room. It was red silk foulard patterned with golden crests of some long lost fraternity or civic organization, and had a dark stain on it. His shirt collar was all nubbly too. His face had that flushed look, so I assumed he'd been drinking.

"Evening, gentlemen," Dale said. You could smell the liquor now, poorly made corn whiskey with a lot of fusel oil in it. "What's this all about, Robert?"

"It's about running the town's affairs."

"Anything about them in particular?"

"I have a whole list of particulars."

"Any you'd care to share before things get underway?"

"No."

He flinched theatrically, the way a drunk will, as though to register an insult when he can't quite put the words together. The fact that he was a genuine clown made it seem less comic.

"Should I take that as unfriendliness?" he said.

"Since when were you and me friends, Dale?"

"I'm everybody's friend."

"And I expect you'll stay that way," Loren said.

Brother Jobe suddenly emerged at the top of the stairs with two cohorts, Brother Elam and Brother Seth, who might have been defensive backs in the National Football League. Next to those two, with his hat on, Brother Jobe looked like a cookie jar. All eyes in the room went to them.

"There's your next mayor, if you ask me," Dale said.

"You're a little off on that," I said.

"See if you can stop him."

"Evenin' all," Brother Jobe said, doffing his hat with a flourish.

Some of the others mumbled "good evening" back.

Brother Jobe came directly over to us.

"What's up, old son?" he said.

"You're going to commence your civic duties tonight," I said.

"That a fact?" he said with something like genuine glee and he turned to Dale. "Howdy-do there, Mayor?"

"I was just telling Robert here, I expect you'll be mayor yourself here before too long," Dale said.

"Oh Lordy," Brother Jobe said. "I don't know that I can fill your shoes."

"A fellow like you could do this job barefoot," Dale said.

"Maybe so," Brother Jobe said. "I hear you've been doing a fair amount of it in your sleep."

Brother Jobe cracked up at his own joke. That got Loren and Andy cackling. Dale Murray seemed to grasp that the jokes would continue at his expense, so he cut his losses and called the meeting to order.

# Twenty-two

Naturally enough, the first order of business was a call for an account of how the New Faith Brotherhood happened to buy the high school, and how it was paid for exactly, and that was when Dale Murray disclosed that Brother Jobe had signed a contract to buy the school on a ten-year option term at five thousand dollars per year on an eventual purchase price of five million dollars.

"What become of the first five thousand?" Victor Gasparry asked.

"We've, uh, received that in the form of a note," Dale said.

"In other words, they didn't pay nothing."

"Since when does anybody pay cash for real estate around here?"

"And what the hell is that five million going to be worth in ten years?" Ned Larmon said. "Why five thousand bucks'll barely buy a wagon wheel now."

"Fiat currency: that's what did us in," Rod Sauer said.

"I don't believe there's going to be any U.S. dollar in ten years, way things are going," Jason LaBountie said. "I do almost all barter these days, myself. Unless someone has hard silver."

"Then how come we don't get some kind of barter agreement out of these people over at the school?" Cody DeLong said. "Payment of some kind in lieu of cash."

"Funny, coming from a would-be banker," Dale said. "I thought you liked money, Cody."

"Money's important, all right." Cody said. "You don't have civilization without it. But these aren't normal times."

"Make-believe money," Ned Larmon said. "Phooey."

"There's more than one way to do a deal," Terry Einhorn said.

"The contract is signed," Dale said.

"Maybe this council can vote to nullify it," Jason LaBountie said.

"You can't nullify a duly signed contract like that," Dale said.

"Why the hell not?"

"Because I'm an attorney, and I'm telling you the law doesn't allow it," Dale said.

"Maybe that law don't apply no more," Victor said.

"I'd like to know what the hell value that school has standing around empty, nobody using it, with the roof leaking?" Dale said.

"As I understand it," Andy Pendergast said, "the disposal of any significant town asset requires a vote of the trustees. That's what we did when we sold the snowplow garage to Bill Schroeder for his creamery operation."

"Look at it this way," Dale said. "These newcomers are an asset to the town, and the school wasn't anything but a liability. So it's a win-win for the community."

"I hate that goddamn phrase, win-win," Ben Deaver said. Long ago, before he farmed, he had been a United Air Lines executive. He didn't say much at meetings, but when he did, it was usually pungent.

"That building was nothing but a damn safety hazard," Dale said.

"How in the hell was it a safety hazard?" Todd Zucker said.

"Children were playing in there. Messing around."

"Hell, it used to be a school. Wasn't a safety hazard then."

"Messing around a place without supervision is something else. They could hurt themselves," Dale said. "Lock themself in the walk-in refrigerator."

"Now you're talking like a lawyer," Victor said.

"I am one," Dale said.

"Too bad there's no law anymore."

"Of course there is."

"It's all pretend," Ned Larmon said. "Where are the courts, then?"

"They'll reconvene by and by," Dale said. "When things settle down."

"Things are about as settled as they're going to get," Todd Zucker said, and several of the men laughed ruefully because they knew exactly what he meant.

"I didn't see any courts convene in the case of that Watling boy," Cody said.

"We'll get to that separately," I said. "Let's go back to this school deal. Maybe we can work something out. Maybe it's a good thing no cash was involved. There was nothing to get mislaid—"

"Are you insinuating—"

"Oh, shut up now, Dale," Loren said.

"You all talk about how there's no law, and you don't even observe the order of the council chamber."

We went around in that vein for quite a while. But finally we gave up gibing each other and I proposed a solution: the New Faithers would work in lieu of payment, and that work would consist of civic improvement projects, starting with repair to the town water system so the next time a house caught fire we might have a chance to put it out. I further proposed that Brother Jobe be appointed to the vacant post of public works director at a salary of one dollar a year. The trustees voted him into the job unanimously with Dale Murray abstaining.

Brother Jobe said he would accept the post and the financial arrangement and he would begin making an assessment of the water system and the town reservoir right away.

Dale Murray, as mayor and chair of the board of trustees then moved to adjourn the meeting.

"We're not done," I said. "I told you I had a list of particulars."

"All right, all right," Dale said. "Don't get all touchy."

We turned to the matter of Shawn Watling and the fact that nobody was doing anything about it. Stephen Bullock, the elected magistrate, hadn't commenced an inquest. Heath Rucker hadn't started even the most elementary investigation—I knew that for a fact because I was the only person at the scene besides Wayne

Karp's bunch, including Bunny Willman, and Heath had not even
spoken to me about it. So I made a motion to begin by replacing
the constable, Heath Rucker. The other trustees glanced around
at each other, and that's when it occurred to me that nobody else
wanted the job, I suppose because nobody wanted to go up against
Wayne, when it came down to it.

"I move formally to remove Rucker," I said. "Second?"

Andy Pendergast seconded.

"Mr. Rucker's not here to defend himself," Dale Murray said.

"He isn't charged with anything," I said. "We're just firing
him."

"And anyway, why isn't he here?" Terry Einhorn said. "He's
required to be present at town board meetings, if I remember the
charter right."

"Probably off drunk somewhere," Cody DeLong said.

"So, who's going to replace him then?" Dale said. "Any nominations?"

"Is that a move to call for nominations?" Ned Larmon said.

"Yes it is."

"Then say it," Dale said.

"Okay, I make a motion for nominations to the post of town
constable," Cody said.

There was no rush to nominate anyone. You could hear birds
twittering their evening songs outside the open windows.

"You can nominate yourselves," I said. "If anyone wants to
volunteer."

More birds singing. A horsefly buzzed across the circle of
chairs. Someone coughed.

"I'll nominate you, Robert," Todd Zucker said finally.

"I decline because of where I stand in the Watling case."

"All right," Jason LaBountie said, "then I nominate you for
mayor."

That brought everybody up short, and a silence followed wide
enough to drive a team of oxen through.

"That post is occupied," Dale said eventually.

"We can vote you out, just like that good-for-nothing constable," Jason said.

"There's a different motion on the table."

"Well, I move we suspend that motion and move on with my motion," Jason said. "Anyone second?"

"I second," Victor Gasparry said.

"I don't know that you're in order on that," Dale said.

"I don't give a damn," Jason said. "Discussion?"

"Let's vote him the hell out," Rod Sauer said.

"Look at what's become of our town under him," Cody DeLong said.

"Point of order," Dale said. "You are not following proper procedure here. Didn't any of you bring the *Robert's Rules*?"

"If proper procedure means so much to you, why didn't you bring the damn *Robert's Rules*?" Jason said.

"We've never had these disputes at town board," Dale said.

"Maybe we should have," Ned Larmon said.

"I call a vote on the motion to get rid of Mayor Dale Murray," Todd Zucker said, "and replace him with Robert Earle."

"Wait a minute," I said. "How come nobody asked me if I want the job?"

"Sometimes duty just calls, son," Brother Jobe said from the outer circle of the few nonvoting observers. He was grinning.

"You're out of order, sir," Dale Murray said.

"Those in favor of the motion to give Dale the boot and put Robert in, raise your hands," Jason said.

"You can't call the vote," Dale said. "That's the chair's job."

All the trustees except Dale raised their hands.

"The motion is carried," Jason said. "You're out, Dale. Robert's the mayor now."

"And the chair of this board," Rod Sauer said.

"Congratulations, son," Brother Jobe said, and everybody in the room except Dale Murray clapped their hands briefly. Terry Einhorn actually got up, walked across the circle, and made to shake my hand—the one that wasn't bandaged up. I was flustered by this

recognition from my peers, of course. But I also realized that somebody had to be responsible for things in town after years of apathy
and paralysis, and that I was ready to try. I figured if I managed to
accomplish the least thing it would be an improvement over the
current situation.

"I guess you can always vote me out if you're dissatisfied," I
said.

"You're damn straight we can," Ben Deaver said.

"All right, then, let's get back to the business of this meeting,"
I said. Meanwhile, Dale Murray made a big show of shoving his
chair into the center of the circle and stalking out of the hall.

"Go easy on the corn liquor," Ned Larmon said, as Dale clomped
across the big room to the exit.

And that was how the gavel passed to me, except there wasn't
any gavel. By God, I thought, I could make one, though.

We went on with the meeting. Loren was nominated for the
post of constable and the board elected him. I was surprised that
he agreed to serve, considering all the rest of his duties around the
community. We couldn't agree what to do about the Shawn
Watling case. Victor Gasparry wanted to convene a special court
and haul Bunny Willman in—Andy Pendergast called it "a kan-
garoo court"—but anyway that meant going up to the trailer park,
Karptown, and placing Willman under arrest, and that posed additional problems.

Andy brought up for discussion the related matter that Wayne
Karp's bunch had no legal right operating the former town landfill as their own private resource mine, and that we should investi-
gate some means for getting it away from his control altogether
and running the place as a public utility.

"Good luck with that one," Victor said.

"My people could run it," Brother Jobe said.

"How do we know you wouldn't turn it into a racket for your
own selves?" Jason LaBountie said.

"Because we walk upright in the sight of God," Brother Jobe
said.

"I've heard that before," Ben Deaver said.

"It can't be said enough," Brother Jobe said.

"All right, let's just back off that for now," I said. "Loren, I'm going to instruct you as constable to send a letter to Stephen Bullock formally recommending an inquest. I'm sure Heath Rucker never put it in the form of a legal document."

"All right."

"One of my boys can ride it over to Mr. Bullock's, post haste," Brother Jobe said. "Maybe there's something we can do for him in return."

"We'll need a town attorney with Dale gone," Loren said.

"I'll talk to Sam Hutto," I said. Sam had dropped law for running a turpentine distillery on the back side of Pumpkin Hill, but I thought he could be induced to help out.

Finally, I moved that we form a committee to meet and make an inventory of the town's needs—everything from meal sacks to medicine—and start an organized effort to obtain these things. By then, the true darkness of night was creeping over town and stealing into the third floor of the old town hall, and since nobody had brought any candles, I moved to adjourn the meeting.

# Twenty-three

Jane Ann stole into my house, as she always did, without knocking, an hour or so after I'd returned from the meeting. I was sharpening my ripsaw with a file out back in the summer kitchen. In a world without electric powered saws, you had to take care with hand tools. She found me out there, slipped into the rocking chair I had pegged together out of some maple limbs, ash splints, and willow canes, filled a corncob pipe with some marijuana bud that she carried in a little leather pouch on the belt of her long skirt, and lit a splinter of stove wood off my candle to fire up the bowl.

"Want some?" she said, passing the pipe.

"All right."

The weed was just past green and very resinous. I knew I was getting stoned when I lost track of which saw tooth I was working on.

"Are you just going to keep toiling away on that?" she said.

"Not anymore, I guess."

"You've taken on quite a lot the past couple of days. All these heroics. And now you're the big pooh-bah around here."

"I'm hardly a pooh-bah. This sad little town just needs someone with organizational skills."

"I always pegged you as more of a background kind of person."

"Are you angry at me?"

She didn't answer. She relit the splinter and the bowl.

"I don't know what Loren thinks he can do as constable around here," she said.

"People look up to him."

"He's not the warrior type."

"There's no war on around here."

"Could be, though. Between Karp and this new bunch and everybody else."

"I think we can get some law going."

"I hope you're right," she said. "Here." She took a lace napkin out of the big pocket in her skirt and unwrapped a generous square of the walnut cake she was famous for. It was almost all ground nut meats and butter. "For you," she said.

"Why, thanks." I was suddenly rather hungry. I put the file and saw aside. "Tell me about your day. What did you do?"

"What didn't I do? Milked goats. Weeded. Forked compost. Put up rhubarb jam. Walked halfway to Battenville to call on Esther Callie. Her mom finally died."

"Oh? What of?"

"She was ninety-seven years old, you know."

"I knew she was very old."

"I think she'd just finally had enough. She was a nurse in the Second World War. The things she remembered were incredible."

"The things I remember seem incredible," I said. "Air-conditioning. Cold beer. Baseball on television." I started to get lost in the maze of my own stoned mind remembering all the things we didn't have anymore.

"She'd seen so much. I asked her how she could maintain any faith in the human race." Jane Ann lit the pipe once again.

"Well, what was her view on that?"

"She said on balance she preferred the way things are now."

"Wow," I said.

Jane Ann stood and undid the ties along the front of her white blouse revealing her dark-nippled breasts. They shifted liquidly in the flickering candlelight as she swayed to unheard music. "Let's comfort each other a while," she said and went inside. That was her code. I knew to follow in a little while with the candle. She was naked when I came to her. We enjoyed our efficient carnal ceremony as we had so many times, and it concluded, as usual, with Jane Ann in tears.

"You know what bothers me most," she said.

"What."

"That in the sight of God we don't matter."

"Maybe it's enough that we act as though we do."

"We can't even act as if we matter to each other."

"You mean you and me? Or everybody in general?"

"You and me."

"Well, we can't advertise it," I said.

"No, I'd prefer to pretend it doesn't matter."

"Maybe God's pretending we don't matter too. He's got plenty to be pissed off about us."

In a few minutes she was gone again, leaving me in the dark and the heat with my mind on fire.

# Twenty-four

Sometime later that night a cool front blew through upstate New York and swept away weeks of spirit-sapping heat. You never knew the weather in advance anymore. You might be said to have a good weather eye but nobody knew anything for sure and some were just better guessers than others. In this case it was as though all of Washington County were suddenly *air-conditioned,* as we used to call refrigerated air, and it allowed me to sleep well for the first time in days. The change in the weather seemed to energize Union Grove. I had two callers before eight o'clock the next morning.

The first was Brother Joseph, one of the New Faithers. He came to the door, calling me "Mr. Mayor," just as I was frying up slabs of leftover hominy for breakfast and preparing to return to work on the cupola at Larry Prager's place.

"Hope I'm not interrupting your breakfast, sir," he said.

"It doesn't require all my attention, and you can call me Robert."

"All right, sir."

"Does this butter smell a little off to you?" I held the crock up for him to sniff.

"I'd eat it," Brother Joseph said with a smile after reflecting earnestly a moment. He looked oddly boyish for his considerable height, which must have been about six foot four. But all the New Faith men had that young look because they were clean-shaven.

I slathered honey on the fried hominy and laid into it as he stood there.

"Want some?" I said.

"Oh, I had a big breakfast just a while ago. Eggs, ham, corn bread."

"From the sounds of things, I'd guess you have fifty roosters over there at the school."

"We've got more than a few. Anyway, I bring you news. Hope you're not rushing out of here to start running things."

The way he put it, I had to chuckle. He had a winning manner.

My new position in the world had not exactly altered my habits overnight, or my estimation of myself. There was a mayor's office in the old town hall, but there was no electricity, no staff, no secretary, no telephone, nor even the common office supplies we took for granted in the old days, including paper and writing implements. We had no use whatever for the *new* town hall, which had been built out on the highway strip in 1983. Anyway, Wayne Karp's crew had removed the windows and aluminum sashes there. Dale Murray had used his own private law office on Main Street, but only as a drinking establishment, since he didn't do any official business, nor did he have any law business, as far as I could tell.

"You can tell Brother Jobe that he and I should meet at the soonest convenient time and begin organizing the repair of the town water system."

"Something else has come up, sir. Mr. Bullock from over the grand plantation has entreated us to form a party to search for his missing boatmen."

"Entreated you?"

"Yessir."

"That's a mouthful."

"Yessir. And he would like you to be along on it."

"Why's that?"

"Because you will know the men we are searching for by sight, he says. And because he trusts you, I gather."

"Well, he doesn't really know your bunch."

"My point, sir."

"Have you got their names?"

He reached into his vest and pulled out a piece of good vellum paper. It was penned in a decorative hand, official looking, though it didn't pretend to have any legal standing as a warrant or a sum-

mons or a commission, as far as I could tell. Among the instructions were the names of the missing crew. Thomas Soukey once
ran the video rental in town and played softball with a bunch of us
in a weekly game before the flu hit and he lost his family and went
over to Bullock. Jacob Silberman used to print promotional T-shirts
and coffee mugs for companies. Skip Tarbay had been a landscaper,
mowing lawns and bedding annuals. And Aaron Moyer taught art
history over at Bennington College. All lines of work which were
no more.

"How many will be in this search party?" I said.

"Five, including yourself."

"How long."

"As we have planned it, maybe two days down, two days search
around the locks and port of Albany and such, and then two days
back."

"That's most of a week, Joseph."

"Yes it is, sir."

"I just assumed new duties here in town."

"We're aware of that."

"Can't you find somebody else?"

"Nosir. The other townsmen that don't have family, they're
mostly ne'er-do-wells, drinkers and such. Anyway, Mr. Bullock
stipulated for you to go."

"Is he lending us a boat?"

"No, we're going on horseback. That way a couple of us can
bring his boat back, if we find it."

"If we don't find the crew themselves?"

"I suppose that would be the size of it, sir."

"Do you have to call me sir?"

"It's New Faith manners, sir. Anyway, we hope to find the men
too."

"Of course."

"Do you have a personal weapon, sir?"

"A weapon?"

"A firearm."

"No. Well, sort of."

"What is it?"

"I don't know. A revolver."

"What caliber?"

"I can't really say."

"You don't know?"

"I've never actually used it. It's a large pistol."

"We have .38 wadcutters that'll go into a .357. Some nine millimeter. Do you have it at hand, sir?"

"No."

"Well, can you get it?"

"It would take me an hour or so."

"I'd suggest you fetch it, sir," he said. "We're looking to depart by midday. We'll come by for you at one o'clock, say, with a mount. We'd encourage you to bring along some of your own meal, bacon, what have you. We'll have some company provisions too. The rest we'll scrounge along the way. Okay, sir?"

"Okay. Are you in charge of this expedition?"

"I suppose I will be, sir."

"Then I'll have to call you sir."

"No you don't. You can call me Joseph, like everybody else does. It's only the five of us."

"Were you in the military, Joseph?"

"Yessir. I saw action at Damascus and Qiryat Shimona before the pullout," he said.

"Did you shoot at people."

"Yessir, and killed a fair number of the ones I shot at, I suppose."

# TWENTY-FIVE

Brother Joseph had not been gone ten minutes when another knock sounded on the front door. I was a little annoyed, what with being obliged on short notice to go on a possibly dangerous journey far from home that I was unprepared for, and because, at the moment, I was pouring cornmeal from a sack into one of the few decent plastic storage tubs I had left with a lid that closed tight, and I spilled some on the brick floor of the summer kitchen.

"Just a minute," I said. The bandage on my left hand was driving me crazy. I took it off hurriedly. The blister on the meaty edge of my palm was the size of a half-dollar. I threw open the door.

It was Britney Watling. She had some visible scrapes and scratches on her face from the misadventure the night before last.

"Can I come in?" she said.

"Sure," I said, remembering the sizzling sound of my palm frying on her doorknob. "Would you mind following me out back, though. I'm getting some things together out there."

I wondered whether she had come to apologize for nearly getting both of us killed in her burning house. She followed me.

"That's a very pretty garden," she said. She looked on edge, as if she had been sleeping poorly. "What's that thing in the center?"

"It's a birdbath."

"Oh? Looks like a pile of rocks."

"It's that too, I suppose. Are you feeling all right?"

"What do you mean? Am I okay in the head?"

"No, that's not what I meant—"

"Because folks are acting like I'm a crazy person."

"Well I don't know whether you are or not," I said, "and I wouldn't try to judge."

She glared at me a moment and then seemed to soften up. "Can I sit down?" she said.

"By all means."

"Folks seem to think I started that fire."

"Well did you?"

"No! A candle set it off. I couldn't sleep in the heat. I was reading a book. I must have drowsed off and knocked the candle over. The bedclothes caught and then a curtain, and then it got up into the window sashes, I guess."

"Can you tell me why you went back into the fire when I tried to pull you out?"

"I don't know," she said, sweeping the floor with her eyes, as if she might turn up an answer there. "I lost heart, I suppose. First Shawn. Then my home. I didn't really want to die. I have a child to look after. It was moment of . . . selfish confusion."

"I'm sorry so many bad things have happened to you."

Looking down at her sitting there only emphasized her small size. Shawn must have been at least twice her weight. I seemed to remember them dancing together once at a levee in Battenville. Like a bear with a doe, each full of youth and life in its own way, but an odd pair.

"I know you've seen your share of heartache too," she said.

"Life remains a precious blessing for us the living."

"I hope I come around to feel that way."

"I hope you do too."

I hadn't been away from home for a week in as long as I could remember, and it was hard to determine how much food I ought to bring for myself. I had a hunk of Terry Zucker's smoked hard sausage, which I wrapped carefully in a piece of waxed canvas and tied with an old piece of string. I saved absolutely everything.

"Are you going somewhere?" Britney said.

"Yes."

"Is it a secret?"

"I have to go to Albany. I'll be gone most of a week."

"Albany? What's down there?"

I told her about Bullock's missing boatmen.

"Tom Soukey used to babysit me when I was a little girl," she said. "He was in high school. I beat him at checkers. I hope you can find them."

"I don't know what we'll find down there," I said. "I haven't been out of the county in years. Anyway, they're coming by to get me soon and I have to go see about something before that."

"Okay, then," she said resolutely. "I came here for a reason. I have a proposal."

"What's that?"

"I thought you might need somebody to keep house."

It took me a moment to absorb that.

"I can't pay someone to keep house," I said.

"That's not what I had in mind."

Now she was making me nervous. I put some corn bread, hard cheese, three onions, and a head of garlic into an oilcloth and tied it with more string into a compact package. Anything you cook will taste okay with onions and garlic. I figured we could get eggs along the way. Everybody had chickens nowadays.

"What did you have in mind?" I said.

"Like I said. Keep house for you."

I just stared at my bundle.

"To be on the premises," she said.

It took me a moment to get it.

"You want to live here?" I said.

"We don't have any place to live."

"You just lost your husband."

"Thank you for reminding me."

"I mean, how would it look?"

"You can say yes or no."

"I hear you're with the Allisons?"

"We can't stay there. It's not a comfortable situation."

"There are quite a few vacant houses in town."

"This isn't a good time for a single woman with a child to live alone."

"Mrs. Myles lives alone right next door. Maybe you could live with her."

"She was my fifth grade teacher. I don't want to live with her."

"Well, why do you want to live with me?"

"I would feel safe here."

I went over to search the shelves above the counter for my purple Lexan water bottle. I hadn't seen it in a while and they sure weren't making them anymore.

"It looks to me like you could use somebody to keep house around here," she said.

"I'm not used to living with other people," I said.

"You had a family once. Look at this place," she said. "It's like some old trapper dude lives here."

"Thanks."

The Lexan bottle was not where I thought I put it. Did I leave it over at Pragers'? It was making me upset.

"It wouldn't look right," I said. "You moving in here."

"You have been alone for some years now, isn't that right, Robert?"

"Yes."

"Do you want to be alone to the end of your days?"

"I'm old enough to be your father, and I was present where your husband was murdered. People might get some strange ideas."

"I'm well aware," she said. "But I need a helping hand, and these are not normal times. I'm old enough to remember the difference. I once had my own television. My mom drove a pickup truck. We used to go to the Target in Glens Falls and buy stuff when she got paid. Those days are gone, and so is any idea of what's normal or decent. I don't want to put in with that New Faith crowd and pray three times a day and have some pack of busybodies raise my child. And I won't put in with Bullock and be a damn serf. We can help each other, you and me. Just let me and Sarah stay here while you're gone. We'll weed your garden for you."

I gave up looking for my water bottle.

"All right," I said. "You can stay while I'm gone."

"What about when you're back?"

"I mean you can move in after I leave today, and we can see how it works out when I return."

"I still have a big garden of my own behind where the house used to be, plus the cow, so you don't have to worry about feeding us."

"All right."

She gave me an intense studying look. I worried now whether she would throw her arms around me and sob, and make me feel uncomfortable. But she just took my right hand in hers and shook, like a sales representative sealing a deal.

"You were kind to me when I was very low," she said. "I'm grateful, and you won't regret this."

"There's four bedrooms upstairs," I said "It'll be obvious which one's mine. You and Sarah can have any two of the others. Please don't go rearranging things too much, especially the kitchen setup. I've got everything where I know how to find it."

"I will be very respectful of your stuff and your ways."

She said she didn't have much to bring over, that pretty much all she owned had been lost in the fire. I showed her around, how the outdoor shower worked and where I kept my store of meal and honey and things. Finally, I saw her to the door. She said they'd come back later in the day after I'd gone.

"Have a safe journey," she said. "I hope you find Tom and the others."

"Thank you. I'm a little nervous about it, to tell you the truth."

"Think about coming home to a clean and orderly house."

I watched her walk a ways back up Linden Street. She was a good walker, with a strong, purposeful stride.

Soon, I left to fetch that pistol I'd hidden under the bridge over Black Creek on North Road, and all the way up and back my mind reeled with terrible thoughts of what it would be like to not be alone anymore, and what Jane Ann would think when she found out.

# TWENTY-SIX

Riding along in a band with four other mounted men in fine summer weather was so exhilarating that I cast aside my worries and apprehensions for the rest of the afternoon as we made our way south on the old county highway along the Hudson River. The other three besides Joseph were Brothers Elam, Seth, and Minor. Elam and Seth were large, broad-shouldered earnest men, like Joseph, but Brother Minor was skinny and smaller than me. He had a sharp, weasely face and a joking demeanor, and when he laughed at his own jokes, which was often, his eyes creased and seemed to close up tight, while his laughter was nearly silent, more like air huffing through a pipe. He joked incessantly.

"You hear about the farmer was milking and a fly went in one of the cow's ear 'n out th' udder?" was a typical Minorism, as the other men called his constant banter.

Joseph and Elam carried rifles, and Seth wore a sword, a saber, some kind of museum piece he had come across in their journeys. All had pistols. Brother Minor carried a sawed-off shotgun scabbarded off his saddle and two daggers in his belt, one long one he called a "pigsticker" and another he called "the last resort."

I'd found that pistol where I had stashed it, all right, under the Black Creek Bridge, the one that killed Shawn Watling. It proved to be an old Ruger .41 Magnum, an odd "bastard caliber," Brother Joseph said, and they didn't have any ammunition for it. There were three rounds left in the cylinder. I brought it along thinking I could not possibly run into three situations in a few days that would require me to fire at another man. I carried the pistol tucked in my belt, and I must confess it was reassuring to feel its heft there as I rode along all afternoon and we ventured into what was, for me, unknown country—at least country I had not been to in years, since we stopped going places in cars. My mount was an eight-year-old bay gelding named Cadmus, a full sixteen hands high with white stockings and a blaze from lips to forehead. He was responsive and forgiving, considering my paltry experience, though we barely moved faster than a walk that day.

The first settlement we rode through was the town of Starkville, seven miles altogether from Union Grove and on the other side of the river. The old highway bridge there was in terrible condition. In places the cement roadway had rotted out and you could see daylight down to the water through twisted, rusty filaments of iron rebar and flaking girders. We dismounted and led the horses across with the utmost care. In a few years the thing would be completely shot and there would be no connection across the Hudson River for twenty miles in either direction, unless somebody started a ferry.

Then there was the town. It was hard to believe that as recently as 1971 Starkville had an industrial economy—a wallpaper factory and a cardboard box mill, using wood out of the Adirondacks up river. They employed hundreds at decent wages a family could live on. Back in the 1950s, the town had its own movie theater and even a newspaper. Now, the little business section of Main Street was deserted in midafternoon on a weekday. The windows were broken in all but one shop front. The one remaining had a *Sorry Closed* sign in it. We stopped and peered through the dusty glass. The shelves and counters inside were bare, and Elam remarked that it was probably closed for good. The commercial buildings themselves along Main were in sorry condition. In some cases blue sky peeked through the ceilings in the upper stories, and scraggly shrubs had taken root in the decayed gunk along the parapets, so you knew the roofs were ruined.

I had heard Starkville was particularly hard hit by the Mexican flu. We didn't know anyone from there, and I wasn't aware of anyone from our town who carried on trade down there these days. Now

I had to wonder if anything was left. Beyond the modest business district, Main Street reverted to old state Route 4. Some of the houses along there were occupied by gaunt, slovenly adults and a few half-naked children dressed in tatters hanging around the front porches doing nothing. Even the few pigs running in the street seemed mostly skin and bone. No dogs came out to greet us. They had probably succumbed to the roasting spit or the stewpot as life grew harder over the years. The yards were filled with weeds and shrubs. Only here and there had anyone made an attempt to grow potatoes or corn. The inhabitants regarded us suspiciously as we walked our horses by, probably frightened by the well-fed New Faith men in their imposing broad-brimmed hats and the weapons they carried. Brother Minor ventured to banter with these people in his joking way as we walked by, but they did not respond to his gags and most skulked indoors when he spoke at them.

"Sometimes I think I'm a chicken," he said to one ill-looking old man with his face sunk into his beard, sitting on his porch on a broken-down sofa. "Felt this way ever since I was an egg." The old fellow just stared hollowly. I was glad to leave the place behind.

South of Starkville, we passed some individual farms that looked like going concerns, not exactly prosperous, but at least as though the owners had not given up. The corn was in and their gardens were laid. But you had to wonder what held them together as a community. Whenever we approached, if there was anybody outside, we'd see them head into their houses at a distance. Possibly they took us for marauders or scavengers, and for all I know they went inside in order to train rifles on us. Along in that stretch we came upon one particular young man, perhaps sixteen, leading a swayback horse pulling a hay wagon. He did not seem afraid of us.

"Are you militia or pickers?" he said.

"Neither," Brother Joseph said and explained as how we were on a search to Albany.

"They's all thieves down there," the boy said. "Got any sugar? You can have a flake of hay each if you spare a little sugar."

"We don't have no sugar," Brother Minor said.

"I've got some honey," I said.

"I don't have no vessel to carry no honey. I'll give you all a flake for a spoonful."

"All right," I said.

We stopped and made a little trade. The hay was good, sweet timothy grass.

Brother Minor sang to himself as he fed his flake to his mount.

*"A swarm of bees in May is worth a load of hay.*
*A swarm of bees in June is worth a silver spoon.*
*But a swarm of bees in July isn't worth a fly."*

The pavements on Route 4 were badly broken, and we walked in line along the shoulder, where the asphalt had worn away altogether and the dirt was beaten soft by hooves. Black-eyed Susans, blue bugloss, chicory, and Queen Anne's lace bloomed there. Here and there, carcasses of the odd truck and automobile that had not been collected years before in the great drive for metal sat rusting in the flowers. Now and then the road came very close to the river, and we could see through the trees along the bank. We did not see a single sail or an oar craft on the water wherever we were afforded a look.

By the early evening we had gone about twenty miles since leaving home. My hips and rear end hurt from rocking in the saddle. In vivid evening light we came upon a house sited on a barren sweep of scrubby fields on a hill overlooking the river. Thinking it deserted, like many other dwellings along the way, we dismounted to see if we might stay there for the night and make ourselves a meal. Joseph knocked firmly on the door. To our surprise, a woman answered. It was hard to tell her age because she was extremely thin, but I guessed about sixty. I imagined she had been pretty when young. She seemed friendly, unlike the others we'd encountered that day, and welcomed us all inside warmly, and even volunteered right away to cook us supper. Her name was Gladys Raynor, she said, and she was waiting for her husband to return from a journey he had made out to Utica to see about some relatives there. The house was orderly but smelled funny, like rodents had got into the walls and maybe died there. In fact, one would surmise that the Raynors had once been well off. The furniture was good quality, and the paintings on the wall were above the grade of art fair kitsch.

Joseph offered some of our provisions to help her with that supper she had offered to make us, some bacon, meal, butter, onions, but she declined, said she was all set, if we didn't mind lamb stew with new potatoes, fresh peas, and corn bread. As far as we were concerned, that was sumptuous fare. She said we could turn our horses out in her pasture, which was still well fenced and that we could pitch a camp on any level spot we pleased outside on her property. When we got all that going, we collected out on her spacious back porch, which was furnished with nice wicker and offered a broad view across the Hudson Valley. The sun was lowering in the opposite direction, behind the house, and the few thin clouds hanging in the eastern sky blazed in rosy-golden reflected light. Mrs. Raynor banged around in her kitchen and eventually she came out with a pitcher and some glasses on a tray.

"How are you fellows doing?"

We all said fine, thank you, and offered some vague pleasantries.

"I thought you might want to try some of my strawberry wine."

We all said thank you. She put the tray down on a round wicker table.

"This used to be a sod farm," she said. "We had all the sod business between Albany and Glens Falls."

"Is that so?" Brother Minor said. He managed to refrain from making a joke. Perhaps he sensed, as I did, that something was off.

"Well, there's not much call for sod these days, as you might imagine," Mrs. Raynor said with an attempt at a plucky smile. The effort only made her face seem more skull-like. "I'll go back in and see to supper."

Brother Seth, no shrinking violet, had a go at the pitcher as soon as she went back inside. The twilight had reached the purple stage where things were no longer very distinct. He filled the five glasses. One by one we all had our sips and soon enough we were all cutting looks about at each other.

"This here's plain water," Brother Minor said in a low voice, "or I'm a durn mud turtle."

"Well, it's nice clean water, at least," Elam said, "and sometimes I think you are a mud turtle."

"Maybe she made a mistake," Seth said.

"Any of you all see a garden about this place?" Minor said.

"None that I noticed," Seth said.

"Ssshhhhh," Joseph said.

We didn't speculate about it further. We just sat along the porch there in a row watching the last glimmers of daylight dissolve in the shadows of the far hills, enjoying our water. Time went by. We watched a quarter moon swing above the treetops while glimmers of its reflection on the river played through. An owl hooted off in the distance. We slapped at mosquitoes. Our stomachs growled. I didn't notice any cooking aromas emanating through the screen door.

Finally, Mrs. Raynor called for us to come inside. She had no candles going in there, not even further back in the kitchen. The moon cast a pallid glow through the windows. She directed us into the old formal dining room. It contained a large oval table and padded chairs. I had a candle stub in my pocket and lit it. Elam found a tall crystal candlestick on the sideboard to put it in, while Joseph went out to get more candles from his pannier. The table was set for six with cloth napkins and nice cutlery.

"Sure smells good, don't it," Brother Minor said. Banter was his way of allaying nervousness.

We all sat down. Joseph returned with more candles and soon the big table, at least, was lighted.

"Can we help you with anything in there, ma'am?" Seth said.

"No, you fellows just get comfortable."

She soon appeared with a heaping dinner plate in each hand, put them down in front of me and Minor, went back for two more for Joseph and Elam, and then two additional for Seth and herself. We all swapped glances around at each other in the candlelight.

"Potatoes and peas coming right up," Mrs. Raynor said and she came back in with two serving bowls. I took the one full of potatoes. It was not the least bit warm. I took one and put it on my plate. It was a rock. I passed the bowl left to Seth and he took his and so on. When the peas came around I took a helping. It was grass. The lamb stew on our plates was watered up dirt: mud. Mrs. Raynor told us to dig in. I pantomimed eating and the rest did as I did, except Brother Minor, who could barely conceal his mirth. Of course, I did not regard this as a mirthful situation, and I doubt the others did either.

"Excuse me, ma'am," Brother Minor said. "I don't have much appetite tonight." He got up from the table gingerly and left the room.

The rest of us went through the motions long enough to be polite. Brother Joseph volunteered our services to help with the dishes, but Mrs. Raynor wouldn't hear of it and the four of us remaining retired to our camp. Minor had a fire started down there and a big fry pan of bacon working. I opened up my oilskin larder and got some corn bread and the hunk of sausage I brought along. The others got out their provisions. Joseph produced a jug of that Pennsylvania whiskey the New Faithers seemed well supplied with, and it felt good going down with river water. They also had a sack of little oatmeal "sticky cakes," as they called them, that their women made with dried currents, honey, and plenty of butter, and gladly gave me as many as I wanted. Joseph laid aside a rasher of bacon, a square of bread, and a hunk of sausage and a sticky cake on a plate, and when he was done eating, he ventured back up to the house. Mrs. Raynor came to the door and in the moonlight we watched him go in. In a while we heard shouting. Mrs. Raynor was letting Brother Joseph have it. We couldn't make out what she was saying, but she was loud for such a frail person. Then the door

opened and she shoved him out on the front portico, and that was
that. She began to wail and continued up there in her darkened
house the whole way Joseph was coming back to us.

"She sounded right grateful," Brother Minor said when Joseph
returned to the firelight.

"I guess I insulted her."

"Well, clearly she is off her rocker," Seth said.

"What'll we do about her?" I said.

"I'd say her man run off," Elam said. "She's liable to starve here."

"We should stop on the way back and take her with us," Joseph
said, and without much discussion it was pretty much agreed that
we should do that. Then it was a final dram, and we tucked ourselves into our bedrolls in nice cool sleeping weather, for a change,
and all fell out rather quickly from our day's exertions.

# TWENTY-SEVEN

Brother Minor might have been an irritating little fellow, but he was diligent, regular, and capable. He was awake before anybody else, had the fire going again, had watered our horses, and was boiling up a pot of cornmeal samp for our breakfast when the rest of us stirred from our bedrolls. The weather had a fractious look. The sky to the east was red and an ominous breeze was already making the weeds dip and sway. I sensed it would get hot again. We did not linger at the sod farm. On our way out, we paused in front of the house. I accompanied Joseph to the door to say thank you and farewell, so as not to leave on unfriendly terms. The others stayed on their horses.

Mrs. Raynor did not answer our knocks. Joseph said we'd better go inside. In daylight, the house was drearier than it had appeared by candles and moonlight. A coat of dust lay over most surfaces. As we entered from out in the summer meadow, the bad smell inside made its impression again. We called out to the lady of the house but she did not answer. With the electricity off, and no appliances humming, the place was stone silent. Joseph and I started poking around by unspoken mutual consent. Nothing was out of order on the first floor, except the muddy dishes remained unwashed on the kitchen counter from the night before along with the bowls of rocks and grass. Of course, Mrs. Raynor's electric well pump was not functioning, along with everything else, and to get water she would have had to fetch buckets from the livestock pond on her property, or else walk all the way down to the river, a good quarter mile.

"Well, let's have a look upstairs," Joseph said.

In the second bedroom we looked in, we found the source of the odor that pervaded the house. The body of a man was laid out on a bed. In actual fact it was mostly the clothed skeleton of a man, since even the insects seemed to be mostly done with the flesh of him. We could only guess how long he'd been laid out there. A month or more. We recoiled from the sight and the stench and very quickly went through the three other bedrooms and back through the ground floor again, including the back porch, looking for the old woman.

"She's gone," I said.

Brother Joseph gave a kind of dubious grunt. I followed him down to the basement. It was much cooler down there. In the meager light that came through window wells that hadn't been cleared of dead leaves for years, and among the odds and ends of a family life that circumstance had now obliterated—the old stroller, a broken bicycle, plastic incunabula, unsold yard sale junk, and trunks full of memories—we found Mrs. Raynor hanging from a pipe by a lamp cord. The ceiling was so low that she hadn't used a chair or a box to step off. She had merely bent her knees to allow her neck to receive the remaining weight of her body. Whatever the agonies or difficulties involved, she had succeeded in ending her life.

We cut her down and took much of the morning digging a single proper grave for the both of them in the back of the house, where we had lingered in the beautiful twilight the night before, looking east toward the river. We put the missus down first and then the remains of what we presumed to be her husband, wound in the bedspread we found him on. Then we covered them both up, another hour of work with one shovel among us.

"We don't know who these people were," Brother Joseph spoke over their mound when we were done with our work. "Who their relations or children are or where they might be. But these two will be together in eternity now. It is an awful thing when anyone falls into despair and takes their own life. If it was up to us, Lord, we would have rescued this poor soul in a few days time. But your ways are mysterious and you didn't allow it. So may Mrs. Raynor—I'm sorry, but I have already forgotten her given name—"

"Gladys," Seth said.

"—may her troubled spirit come into your love and dwell in your house forever. *Like as the waves make towards the pebbled shore, / So do our minutes hasten to their end.* Amen."

"Amen," all around.

We mounted our horses.

"You know what I think?" Brother Minor said.

"What?" Seth said and Elam echoed him.

"I think she was waiting for some folks to come along who could give them a proper burial and we were elected," Minor said. "Ain't these times something?"

The heat was definitely back with us and we were tired from digging and hadn't made any progress yet that day. Among the few things from the premises we helped ourselves to, we found two fishing rods, with good open-faced spinning reels and monofilament line, along with a box of lures, plugs, spinners, hooks, swivels, and bobbers. An hour or so later, we had made some headway down the river road again, and we stopped to water the horses at a place where a cool rill formed a sandy delta on the shore as it entered the Hudson. There were big flat rocks to sit on, and a grove of locust trees for shade. I took the opportunity to bathe away two days of grime. Joseph and Seth bushwhacked upstream a ways with the fishing rods. Elam was off looking for raspberries while Minor made a fire on the rocks.

The blister on my burned left hand had broken open from helping to dig the Raynors' grave. I was concerned that it might get infected. You couldn't be too careful about infected wounds when there were no more antibiotic medicines. I asked Minor for some whiskey I could apply as disinfectant. He asked to see it. I held my hand out to him. He studied it a while, told me to wait right there, and bustled off into the woods. He returned in a minute with several stems of some kind of leafy weed.

"What's that?"

"Solomon's seal," he said. "This here might seem uncouth, but it's necessary."

He picked off one leaf after another from the stems and put them in his mouth until he was masticating a great chaw of them. Meanwhile, he took a bandana out of his pocket. By and by, he extracted the wad of chewed leaves from his mouth and laid them on the bandana.

"Give me your hand."

I did. He arranged it so the chaw was over my blister and then rather tenderly tied the bandana around my hand.

"You keep it like so the rest of the day and overnight," he said. "That burn blister'll be healed up in the morning."

He stated this with complete assurance. I didn't want to act contrary about it or seem ungrateful so I agreed.

Our fishermen came back in surprisingly short order with more than enough good-sized fish for our lunch: several largemouth bass and a northern pike the size of a Yule log. We were hungry after all that digging.

There had been a lot less angling in the Hudson River in recent years as epidemics drove down our numbers and motorboats stopped running, and there was no more factory-made tackle. Less pollution of all kinds ran into the river, no more factory fertilizers and pest control poisons, no more detergents. So the fish had returned in numbers not seen in anyone's memory. Land-based game, on the other hand, was noticeably sparser now, as nobody observed hunting seasons anymore. The deer, especially, were down, even though commercial grade ammunition had also gotten scarce. People jacked deer all year round, by any means possible, including pitfalls, deadfalls, and traps. Rabbits were down because nobody cut lawns anymore and the grassy margins they thrived in were returning to woods. Coyotes were up in tandem with sheep and goats. Ben Deaver swore he saw a mountain lion on the roof of his chicken shed one morning the previous September, and further north of us, in Hebron, where the human population was back to the pioneer level of the mid-1700s, a "catamount" reputedly killed a four-year-old boy inside a house.

Minor butchered the fish expertly with his short knife. His grandfather ran a catfish farm in South Carolina when he was little, he said. He could cut fillets all day long and into the dark.

"How do you stop a fish from smelling?" he asked and before anyone could come up with a quip, he said. "Cut off its nose."

He dipped the bass fillets in cornmeal and fried them in last night's bacon grease, which he had saved in a can.

"What has big sharp little teeth, a tail, scales, and a trunk?" he asked and immediately answered. "Pikey fish going on vacation. Y'all are slow. Maybe retarded."

The pike he just gutted and roasted whole on crisscrossed green sticks. The New Faith boys all brought jars of their own pickled peppers and onion relish. It did make everything taste interesting when salt and pepper were scarce.

Elam had discovered a thicket of raspberries growing up along the roadside and we filled our hats with them as Minor cooked off the fish. We packed up directly after this lunch and resumed walking our horses toward the city, as well fed as if we had been home.

# TWENTY-EIGHT

The afternoon weather resolved into an uncomfortable drizzle, driven by hot winds out of the south. I had an old ripstop nylon poncho from my collegiate camping days, but it had lost its waterproofing. We began to enter what had been the suburbs emanating out of the capital city, Albany, and its neighbor, Troy, and a handful of other industrial towns in and around the confluence of the Mohawk and Hudson rivers. We planned to cross the Mohawk at Waterford on the railroad bridge there.

Waterford began its existence as the gateway to the Erie Canal system, the first stretch of which was built to bypass several waterfalls on the Mohawk River. But the locks there no longer functioned because they were rebuilt and enlarged in the early twentieth century to open and close on electric power. Now there was no way to operate them. They were too big for human or animal power.

We began to encounter more people now, inhabiting the ruined suburbs, the lawns replaced by potato patches, the split-levels and raised ranches turned into hovels now that the electric amenities and the plumbing were out of order, including the wells and toilets. Ill-clad, scrawny children played in mud puddles in the broken streets and stopped to blink at us as we passed on our horses. When Brother Minor offered up one of his jokes, they just gaped. By and by, we crossed an old commercial highway strip with its complement of dead gigantic discount stores, strip malls, and defunct burger barns. The buildings were all in various stages of disassembly as materials of value were stripped from them—copper pipes and wires, aluminum sashes, windowpanes, steel girders, and cement blocks. The parking lots seemed especially desolate with nothing in them but mulleins and sumacs poking through the cracked pavements.

At Waterford, the bridge connected two bluffs about a hundred feet above the surface of the Mohawk River. It was one of those engineering marvels from the early twentieth century that could never be replaced now, any more than the Coliseum in Rome could be rebuilt by the most talented subjects of Frederick Barbarossa. Near the northern approach to the bridge, we came upon a man beating his donkey with a long-handled whip. The donkey was hitched to a cart full of bricks and made a terrible racket with each blow. The man, a hulking, well-fed brute, wore a pair of homespun pants tucked into crude ankle boots and a chewed up straw hat that was little more than crown. His belt was a rope. Shirtless in the drizzle, his wet muscles bulged as he laid into the donkey, which was as starved-looking as the man was stout. The donkey already had several bleeding stripes on his back.

"That ain't right," Brother Minor said as we came upon the scene. Minor rode up to the man. The rest of us hung back.

"Afternoon," Minor said.

"What do you want?" the man said, drawing back his whip hand as if not to miss a stroke.

"You ever hear this one?" Minor said to him. "There's this here zebra lived her whole life at the zoo, and the kindly old zookeeper decided to put her out to pasture on a farm in her last years."

"What the hell—" the man said.

"Just listen up, you'll like this."

"You get the hell out of my sight," the man said to Minor and turned to lay on his stroke. The donkey cried out as the lash fell.

"So, this here zebra was so excited," Minor said, without skipping a beat, "when she got onto that farm and was amongst all these strange new animals. And she come up on this big fat brown and white critter. 'Hey thar, I'm a zebra, what're you?' 'I'm a cow,' it says. 'That so? What do you do?' the zebra asks. 'I make milk,' the cow says—"

"I'm warning you," the man with the whip said.

WORLD MADE BY HAND 139

"So what do you know?" Minor said. "Next this fluffy white ball of feathers steps by. 'What're you?' the zebra asks. 'Why, I am a chicken and I lay eggs,' it says. So next, what do you know, the zebra sees an animal that looks exactly like her only without no stripes, and the zebra asks, 'What're you—?'"

"Didn't you hear me," the stout man with the whip said.

"I heard you," Minor said.

"You're still here."

"Don't you want me to finish the joke?"

With that the man tried to lay into Minor with his whip. But before he could the more nimble Minor slipped down from his horse with his sawed-off shotgun drawn and leveled it at him. Seth came and got Minor's horse under control.

"I'm anxious to tell you the rest of this story," Minor said as he stalked the big man with the shotgun leveled.

"You regulators or something?" the man said.

"Yeah, that's right," Minor said. "At the moment we're regulating the animal cruelty situation. There's a fair bit of it these days. Where was I now . . . Oh yeah, so this here zebra is on the farm and met the cow and the chicken, and now she meets this animal that looks just like her only without no stripes, and the zebra says, 'What are you?' And the jackass says, 'Take off them striped pajamas, little honey, and I'll show you.'"

Minor nearly fell over with laughter at his own joke, as usual. The man turned away with a snort and drew back his whip once more to strike the donkey. Minor rushed up behind him, swung the heavy barrel of his weapon, and struck the man in his right kidney. The big man crumpled onto all fours emitting a bellow as loud as the cries of his donkey had been. A kick from Minor to his ribs fetched him over on his back. Then Minor perched on his chest with the point of his pigsticker poised under the man's chin and the shotgun barrel pressed to his cheek.

"Want to hear another one?" Minor said.

# Twenty-nine

And that's how we acquired a donkey—which Brother Minor named Jenny because it was a jennet, a female—and also the cart, which we unburdened of its cargo of bricks and helped ourselves to, thinking it might be useful if we found anything worth trading for in whatever remained of the capital city of New York state. We left the previous owner of the donkey and cart in the mud by the bridge to reflect on his conduct. I felt no qualms about confiscating his property. Jenny seemed happy to come with us once her load was lightened.

The drizzle had turned into a driving rain with thunder and lightning added by the time we got near the heart of the city, such as it had become. We were hungry, weary, and uncomfortable in our wet clothes. Perhaps a half an hour of daylight remained, and it was meager light given the dreary weather. I remembered Albany years earlier as just another down-on-its-luck small American city that had sacrificed its vitality to a whirring ring of homogenous suburbs. A flickering residue of life had persisted in the row house district near the capitol building. But that phase of its history was over, and the whole place had fallen apart from the edge to the center. Meanwhile, a strange new settlement had grown up like fungus on a log along the riverfront underneath Interstate 787 and the tangle of ramps that soared off the once mighty Clinton Avenue interchange. This new settlement was no shining city or science-fiction fantasy of gleaming towers. Rather, it was a patchwork of spare parts, salvage, and refuse, both material and human.

Along the riverbank itself, which for decades had been a little-used "park" functionally cut off from the city by the freeway, now stood ranks of rickety wharves, some with boats docked along them, rowing crafts of different kinds, homely prams, skiffs, even canoes, and a number of the shallow-draft, gaff-rigged catboats that were the workhorses of the Hudson River trade. There were quite a few larger pilot cutters, sleek, fast boats with a lot of deck, that came from as far away as Baltimore, and skipjacks that were favored by the fishermen downriver in the broad Tappan Zee. A battered sloop sat in a drydock with its mast down and hull scraped. These wharfs led onshore to boathouses, warehouses, and stores associated with them. None of the new buildings were up to the quality of the ones that had been demolished earlier to make way for the freeway.

Albany once again looked like a frontier town. A few of the new buildings along the waterfront were brick, almost surely salvage, and fewer were a full three stories. The majority of wooden ones were generally clad in unpainted rough-sawn board-and-batten or clapboard. They fronted a new unpaved street called Commercial Row. Not all of the buildings had been completed, and it looked as though work had ceased months ago due to some calamity and had not resumed. Some wooden scaffolds remained in place but no sign of tools or materials. The buildings were designed to contain trading establishments on the ground floors, but at least half were vacant, and nothing was open for business when we rode in at eight thirty on a stormy evening. Overall, the place gave off the odor of a society that was struggling desperately to keep business going, and largely failing.

As it happened, we found one fellow working on accounts by candlelight in an establishment called Ricketts Finished Goods. We stopped before his lighted window and he looked up at us arrayed out there on our horses. Joseph and I went in to talk with him. The others remained outside under the shelter of the elevated freeway. The ground floor storeroom contained a scant few rows of barrels, crates, and empty pallets, but not much else was visible in the gloom beyond this fellow's guttering candle and the occasional lightning flash. He said his name was Jim Ricketts. In the old days, he said, he was a purchasing agent for the state's department of health. His current business was wholesale textiles, yarns, findings, fasteners, and paper products, ". . . and frankly anything I can get my hands on these days," he said, "which isn't much." He said he was sick of being there, and sick of corn bread morning, noon, and night, and nearly sick of this world. He had been writing letters to his suppliers in Baltimore and Philadelphia, whose communications had fallen off, and he doubted that the packet boat mails were getting through anymore.

"New York City is finished," he said. "They can't keep order there, and you can't have business without order. It'll take a hundred years to sort things out and get it all going again."

"What do you hear of the U.S. government?" I said. "We don't have electricity an hour a month anymore and there's nothing on the air but the preachers anyway."

"Well, I hear that this Harvey Albright pretends to be running things out of Minneapolis now. It was Chicago, but that may have gone by the boards. Congress hasn't met since twelve twenty-one," Ricketts said, using a common shorthand for the destruction of Washington a few days before Christmas some years back. "We're still fighting skirmishes with Mexico. The Everglades are drowning. Trade is becoming next to impossible, from everything I can tell, and business here is drying up. It all seems like a bad dream. The future sure isn't what it used to be, is it?"

"We believe in the future, sir. Only it's not like the world we've left behind," Joseph said.

"How's that?"

"We're building our own New Jerusalem up the river. It's a world made by hand, now, one stone at a time, one board at a time, one hope at a time, one soul at a time. Tell me something: do you know Jesus Christ."

"No, I never met the fellow."

"Would you like to?"

"Is he outside there on one of those mounts?"

"He's in your heart."

"Well, that's news to me," Ricketts said. "All these years I thought it was single occupancy. And who the hell are you, sir?"

"We're the New Faith brotherhood, sir, and if this enterprise isn't working out for you any longer, come north and join us. We're always looking for new blood."

"You're not the only ones out for blood," Ricketts said. "Anyway, I'm not your man. Count me out. The more I hear of religion —and any of it's more than I want to hear—the less I like it. In God we trust! I curse the idea. All these different gods is what started this mess in the first place. Allah, Jesus H. Christ, and What Have You Almighty! Haven't we seen enough vengeance and punishment? To hell with them all—and I suppose they each have their own hell to go to anyhow."

"We're more into the practical side of things," Joseph said.

"Sure, whatever that is. Maybe one of these gods will have mercy on me and send a hundred yards of four-hundred-count cotton moleskin and another hundred each of calico, gingham, muslin, buckram, and voile. Now what can I do for you gentlemen at this late hour on a such a dismal night?"

I explained that we were looking for a particular boat, the bateau *Elizabeth,* a twenty-five-foot-long rowing packet with a single gaff-rigged sail, and her crew of four, and how she belonged to the planter Stephen Bullock of Union Grove, forty miles north. Ricketts said he had traded with Bullock now and then, though he hadn't seen the boat or its crew recently or heard anything about them. But, he added, the new scarcity of goods had induced a lot of desperate behavior up and down the river, and he was not confident that things could move around safely nowadays, which only made him despair again for his business. I didn't want to bother him further, except to ask for someplace we might put up for the night, and he said Slavin's Hotel at the south end of Commercial Row.

# Thirty

Slavin's was a ramshackle structure cobbled up against a trestle of the old elevated freeway running to Clinton and Pearl Street. A lightning flash lit it up in its stark fullness. Ironically, it was a stone's throw from the old Albany train station, still standing and visible in the downpour, a beaux arts period Greco-Roman temple that had been rescued by preservationists in the 1980s and turned into a bank, and was now an empty, looted hulk in need of rescuing again. *Hotel* was perhaps a grandiose term for Slavin's three-story log and clapboard jerry-built eyesore that was more accurately a flophouse for river rats, as boatmen were called, with a tavern on the ground floor that served pretty good food, Ricketts had said, when the cook was not drunk.

The tavern room in Slavin's was a lively scene in contrast to the desolation of the streets and wharves outside. Whatever its other shortcomings, the management was liberal with the candles. The rain had driven the denizens of the waterfront inside that night, rough boatmen, wranglers, dockmen, plus half a dozen bar girls who were "friendly and available," we were told. Some card games were in progress. Smoke wreathed the ceiling beams, both cannabis and some real tobacco. A wan youth about fifteen played tunes on a small accordion while a younger female child—his sister? —performed a loose-limbed clog dance beside him. Both seemed to be drunk. The aroma of things cooked in butter wafted from the pass-through window to the kitchen behind the bar. It put a keen edge on my hunger. With rain dripping off the eaves and thunder crashing outside, even this squalid scene was a relief.

The barkeeper, a keg-shaped man about forty with close-cut black hair and a Vandyke beard, a damp bar towel over his shoul-

der and a stained apron on, introduced himself with a kind of distracted patter: "I'm Henry Slavin and this is my place and you can
apply to me a drink, a meal, a bed, a chippie, or any combination,
what'll it be, boys?"

We asked first for someplace to stable our animals and he said
they maintained a boarding barn on the other side of the trestle. It
was "self-serve." They couldn't afford to keep a man out there and
couldn't vouch for security and suggested that some member of our
party might put up in there with the animals. The diligent Brother
Minor volunteered if we would bring him something to eat and a
bottle of anything potable. So we helped Minor get the tack off
and settle the animals. The stalls lacked fresh bedding and Minor
took it upon himself to rake them out, since the management
didn't. Elam tossed down a bale of stalky hay from the lofts above.

We couldn't turn up any oats or other grain. But to our surprise
there was a faucet on an iron pipe with running water, and when we
returned to the tavern, Slavin explained that the "boss" of the city,
or what remained of the city, Mr. Dan Curry, had installed a waterworks the previous year near the old Rensselaer Bridge ramp, with a
great undershot wheel that used the river current itself to lift water
to Commercial Row and a few streets beyond. Curry was regarded
as a hero because of it. It had required the digging of a half-acre
reservoir pond on what had historically been Cornelius Place. They
hoped someday to resume water service "up the hill" to the former
heart of the city, Center Square, now largely uninhabited, and the
area around the capitol, but that day was still somewhat over the
horizon. Curry also ran a fire department, policed the docks, operated the justice court, deported "pickers" (vagabonds) downriver, and
collected substantial taxes in connection with these ventures. For
practical purposes, he was mayor, but disdained the title, Slavin said.
Brother Elam volunteered that Slavin was talking to the new mayor
of Union Grove, up in Washington County. Joseph told Elam to
shut up. Slavin cocked a knowing grin at me and said, "I hope you're
thriving, sir, like our Mr. Curry is."

"It's not a paid position," I said.

146 JAMES HOWARD KUNSTLER

"Neither is Mr. Curry's," Slavin said with a wink. "But he manages pretty smartly all the same. Now, how do you boys propose to pay for your rooms and meals? Paper dollars or real money?"

"Silver coin good enough?" Joseph said.

"We take that here. Two bits each, bed and a meal. One dollar for the horses. Drinks are extra, of course."

Joseph took out a leather drawstring purse and dropped a handful of old quarters and half-dollars on the wooden bar, where they rang musically. Slavin looked impressed. Whatever the other failures of the U.S. government were, it had managed to print an excess of dollars which, combined with the collapse of trade and communication, had severely eroded the currency's value. People always liked silver better, if it was offered. Gold, on the other hand, was rarely seen. People tended to hoard it.

In a little while, Slavin's kitchen produced a chowder that he said was made from a locally caught sturgeon "the size of a Nile crocodile," stewed with plenty of butter and cream, green onions, and firm new potatoes. The portions were substantial, befitting a place that served hardworking men. We sent Seth out with a crock of the stuff to Minor in the stable, along with several slabs of buttered corn bread, a big hunk of what they called Duanesberg cheddar, and a quart bottle of pale ale Slavin swore he brewed himself.

We asked Slavin if he'd heard anything of the *Elizabeth* and its crew. He snorted saying boats were coming and going all the time and he had no idea, but I might inquire in the morning at Dan Curry's office at the waterworks; his people seemed to track every last corncob that passed in and out of the port.

Finally, we were advised to "double up," two to a bed because the other rooms were let out to the girls quarter-hourly, and by the way, Slavin said, were we interested in some of that action, for an additional two bits each? We declined. Joseph and I paired up, and Seth and Elam together, and soon we went to the rooms above.

# THIRTY-ONE

Joseph and I lay side by side on a rank mattress in the close dank room. I had been ruminating sleeplessly about the young widow and child whom I had perhaps rashly agreed to let move into my house, worrying what people would think, worrying about her getting into my things, worrying about being so far from home, just worrying, anxious in the storm-lashed darkness.

"You awake?" I said. Joseph's breathing had not seemed the regular pattern of a man asleep. The rain had not even succeeded in cooling off the jungly night air.

"Yessir, I am," Joseph said.

"Do you remember air-conditioning?"

"Yessir, I do." He gave a mordant little laugh. "If it's not raining out tomorrow night, I say it's back to camping for us in the fresh air."

"I'm with you on that. Should we pay a call on this Boss Curry tomorrow?"

"Not right off," Joseph said. "I smell something."

"What?"

"Just a feeling. I say we comb the docks and the boathouses first."

"What feeling?" I said.

"Some kind of trap," he said. "We saw situations like this in the Holy Land, when things were not what they seemed to be."

"Do you think this Curry has done something to Bullock's crew?"

"I think they may be in his custody."

"Hostages?"

"Yessir."

As I paused to reflect on this, a vicious thunderbolt, like a gunshot, crackled across the rooftop and reverberated against the concrete slabs of the old ruined highway above.

"Like a ransom situation?"

"Yessir."

"But nobody sent any message to Bullock demanding money for his crew," I said.

"How do we know that?"

His question caught me up short.

"Leastwise, Bullock didn't mention any," I said.

"Why risk sending a messenger all the way up there," Joseph said, "when sooner or later Mr. Bullock would surely send someone down here to inquire, which he has now done, namely us."

"Then I suppose we can't be too careful."

"Exactly so."

"I see," I said, trying to take measure of what I didn't see. "I hardly recognize this city. It's frightening how much has changed here in just a few years."

"Everything's gone to the devil all over our poor country. Believe me. We've seen a lot."

"Why did you leave Pennsylvania, Joseph?"

For an awkward interval, we lay silently there in the moist darkness. I wondered if he had heard me.

"Well, sir," he said finally, "race trouble, to be honest."

"What do you mean?"

"A lot of people cut loose when Washington got hit, you know. They left there with nothing but the clothes on their backs and some firearms. You had civil disorders in Philadelphia and Baltimore, refugees fleeing, what you folks call pickers, bandit gangs. Pennsylvania became a desperate place. After a while, it was like cowboys and Indians."

"What happened?"

"There was no getting along."

"Did you fight?"

"Yessir. Over two years we lost twelve of our number."

"Why did you stay as long as you did?"

"It was mighty good land. Some of the best I ever seen. But, obviously, we decided to move on."

"I've got a boy out there somewhere," I said.

"Where?"

"I don't know, exactly. He set out two years ago with Reverend Holder's boy. We haven't heard from them since."

"I hope he turns up, sir," Joseph said. "I had a boy myself."

"Had?"

"He was one of the twelve that was killed."

"Oh . . . gosh . . . I'm sorry."

"He was sixteen. Name of Aaron. He was a brave boy. Yours?"

"Daniel. Nineteen when he left. We haven't seen that kind of strife up in Washington County, New York."

"I know. That's how come we like it."

"I didn't know it was so bad out there."

"There's grievances and vendettas all around at every level. Poor against whatever rich are left. Black against white. English-speaking against the Spanish. More than one bunch on the Jews. You name it, there's a fight on. Groups in flight everywhere, ourselves among them. I haven't seen any black folks or Spanish in Union Grove so far. You got any, sir?"

"Some black families lived in that hollow down by the Wayland-Union Mill, the old factory village. The mill closed up before I moved to town. There was a fellow named Archie Basiltree who worked in the Aubuchon hardware store when we first came. The store is gone and so is Archie. Another black man worked on the county road crew."

Thunder had been pealing and lightning flashing all along, some strokes so close that they shook the building.

"I haven't been anywhere in years," I said. "I don't really know what's going on out there."

"Let me tell you something, sir," Joseph said. "There has been considerable churning of the population and warring among different sorts of people all over. Why do you think we left Virginia in the first place? I think the separate regions will go their own way."

"It would be a sad and sorry thing if it came to that."

"Well, it has come to that, sir."

In a little while, Joseph's breathing fell into a regular rhythm, and I assumed he'd gone to sleep. I lay awake longer, listening to the rain drip from the eaves and thinking of the big map that hung from the top of the chalkboard in my primary school in Wilton, Connecticut, so many years ago, back in the days of cars, television, and air-conditioning. The states on this map were muted tones of pink, green, and yellow. Over it hung the flag that we pledged our allegiance to every single morning. "One nation, under God, indivisible . . ."

# THIRTY-TWO

In the morning, the sky had been swept clean again and, of course, the heat was rising. I had kept the bandana on my hand overnight and, when I took it off before breakfast, was astonished to see that a florid pink spot on my palm was all that remained of the blister. A new layer of skin had seemingly grown over the spot.

Minor joined us from the stable for a breakfast of fresh eggs, smoked fish, and corn bread downstairs, again paid for in silver coin. The animals were rested, watered, and ready, he said. He had straw in his hair from bedding down in the stable, but he didn't complain about his duties.

I showed Minor my hand and asked him how it was possible that such an injury could actually heal overnight.

"Solomon's seal has powers," he said. "But you add a little Jesus juice to the mix and that puts her in overdrive, so to say."

It wasn't an explanation that squared with my understanding of how reality worked. But I couldn't argue with the results either.

"I'm grateful to you," I said.

We decided over our meal to devote the early hours of the day to shopping for wholesale goods and necessities along Commercial Row. New Faith needed everything from salt in quantity to candlewicks. I wanted to find machine-made paper and good steel pen nibs for the town so we could resume recording things again in a coherent way, medical supplies for Jerry Copeland, and whatever else I could scrounge up. We didn't have a whole lot of cargo space in the donkey cart. After that, we'd break into two groups and search the wharves for the *Elizabeth*. If we found her, perhaps we could bring more goods back to Union Grove. But that remained to be seen.

When we turned out onto the street, the first thing we saw was the figure of a large man seated in the dirt, slumped against a rain barrel across the way with a hog rooting in his lap. The figure was inert. As we came closer, we could see a vivid red and gray mess of stuff that looked like sausage links in his lap, where the pig was rooting. Seth sent the animal off squealing with a blow across the hams with the flat of his sword.

"He's dead," Elam said. "Why, I'll be dog."

"What?" Joseph said.

"This is that same drover we took that jenny off of. Lookit."

Elam took a kerchief rag out of his pocket and used it to hold the dead man's head up at the chin for us all to see. The face was distorted in death, and the whites of his still-open eyes were shot through with blood as if he had suffered a severe blow to his head. But it apparently was indeed the same man we'd quarreled with at the Waterford bridge.

"I believe you're right," Seth said. "That'd be the one."

"Did you kill him, Minor?" Joseph said.

"I didn't do nothing," Minor said. "Sumbitch probably fell out drunk and cracked his durn head."

I stooped down. The stench he gave off was impressive up close. Around the ragged edge of his dirty shirt, above the gross wound to his abdomen, you could see a pattern of small round holes, like shotgun pellets would make. I did not point it out, but I don't think the others failed to notice either. I remembered that gunshotlike blast of thunder the night before and imagined this nameless wretch reeling out the stable door and collapsing where he now sat, to die in the rain, with a pig in his guts.

"I judge that this poor soul is beyond our assistance," Minor said, "and if I linger here, I'm liable to lose my breakfast."

"I suppose we can leave him for the constable," Joseph said.

"If they got any law here," Elam said.

"Anyway, it ain't our business," Minor said.

And so we went about our business, but not before Joseph in-voked Matthew 5:13: *"Ye are the salt of the earth,"* he said, *"but if the salt have lost his savor, wherewith shall it be salted? It is thenceforth good for nothing, but to be cast out, and to be trodden under foot of men."*

# THIRTY-THREE

Traders from elsewhere along the Hudson Valley were already out on Commercial Row, and men with drays and carts were busy moving goods off the wharves in a clatter of wheels and dust. Some smaller vendors had joined them along the street, selling fish, vegetables, and odd items of salvage from wagons and tarps spread on the ground. Here and there, snatches of songs of the loaders could be heard. Not everybody's business was off, but it seemed a very dull trade in necessities. No groups collected on the street to socialize, as one might expect in a livelier marketplace. Hardly any women were among the traders, and the men were furtive in their movements. They scuttled in and out of the trading houses like wary rodents or bugs and left with whatever goods they'd purchased without lingering.

We found some of the things we needed among Minnery's General Stocks, Hyde's Salvage and Made Goods, and VanVoast's Import and General Trade Articles, the three largest competing establishments on the row, and Aulk's Provisions, the food wholesaler. I found aspirin, reusable hypodermic syringes, IV catheters, and adhesive tape for Doc Copeland. I could not find antiseptic or antibiotic medicines of any kind. Nor did they have any lidocaine or topical anesthetic for our dentist. I purchased a five-ream box of plain white twenty-pound bond paper (Xerox brand from the old days) and a gross of Phinney no. 4 steel pen points. They didn't have any manufactured ink in stock, but you could make that easily enough yourself from lampblack or walnut shells. The New Faithers were delighted to come across a fifty-pound sack of peanuts, which they had not seen any of in some time, they said, as well as the other articles on their list, and some of Mr. Ricketts's remaining inventory in linen fabrics at a very high price, which they apparently could afford—Joseph's fund of silver seemed bottomless. VanVoast's actually had on hand a small inventory of manufactured instrument strings, and I bought several sets of guitar, violin, and cello strings. It had been years since we'd had any new ones, making do with the gut strings Andrew produced.

We loaded all these things onto the cart, covered it with our waxed ground cloth, and set out on a systematic search of the wharves and their attached boathouses.

We divided into two groups, Joseph and myself to go one way, Elam and Seth the other, leaving Minor again in charge of the animals in a scrub pasture that used to be the football field of a public school on DeWitt Street. The school building itself was a scavenged ruin. One of the goalpost uprights remained in place. It was already hot out in the field. Plenty of rainwater stood in puddles for the animals. Minor found a spot of shade under a sumac tree and seemed content there while the horses grazed peacefully. I gathered that Joseph didn't trust Minor's hot head in the kind of search we were about to undertake, mixing with the locals and all. Joseph and I said we would work the wharves from the north end down. Elam and Seth would start near the waterworks and work up. We said we'd meet up in between somewhere.

So we set off, making like we were looking for a boat to buy. In fact, there were a lot of boats for sale along the wharves, given the depressed conditions lately, and we had to pretend to inquire about them, so it took the whole morning to work down the row, but we didn't come across the *Elizabeth*. Along the way, we caught quite a bit of news chatting with the owners, traders, and dockmen and boatmen. For instance, we learned that a recent hurricane had crossed the east end of Long Island and swept up along the New England coast, drowning many of the towns east of Providence before swerving out to sea at Cape Cod. Boston was spared, but Boston might have benefited from a bath, one sloop owner said with a gallows laugh. The violent thunderstorms we'd seen in the Hudson Valley were a backwash of all that rough weather, he said.

We heard that a gang of pickers had nearly burned down the town of Kinderhook while plundering the place. Several were captured and hanged. A bad gypsy moth infestation was moving north and had reached as far as Rhinebeck. At night, they said, you could hear the caterpillars munching on leaves, their numbers were so great. In some places down there, the trees were so denuded it looked like November. One boatyard owner said that the Chinese had landed on the moon, but his partner scoffed at the notion and said that the other man also believed there was still plenty of oil in the world, and a conspiracy between the Arabs and the Asian Co-prosperity Alliance had deprived America of its share because "they hated our freedom." Who really knew anymore? On the bright side of things, the shad run in the Hudson had been the best ever seen by people still living, though a lot fewer people were living than a decade ago.

At half past noon, having found nothing up along the north end of the waterfront, we met up with Seth and Elam, who said excitedly that they were sure they'd found the *Elizabeth* in the fourth place they looked, a boatyard associated with VanVoast's Import. It was inside a big red boathouse which stood out in the distance against the china blue sky.

"How do you know it's the right boat?" Joseph said.

"Oh, it's her all right," Seth said.

"The name *Elizabeth* is spelled out on the transom with a rose painted to each side of the name," Elam said. This was what Mr. Bullock had specified in his written instructions. No sign of the crew. There was a manager on the premises and a few idle dockmen, waiting for a cargo. Elam and Seth had looked over the boat and left the place with a cursory thank you. We decided to go back immediately all together and ask some hard questions.

The manager of the VanVoast terminal, a well-fed man named Bracklaw, he said, sporting a set of bright green suspenders to hold up a pair of slovenly linen trousers, showed a high degree of alertness as the four of us entered the dim, cavernous boathouse, with swallows careening through the sturdy trusswork overhead. In fact, he seemed downright nervous seeing how Seth and Elam had suddenly multiplied to four of us. A couple of cat-boats occupied one side of the main slip, and there were side slips too, where the *Elizabeth* sat among an assortment of small craft. Bracklaw's dockmen were not on the premises, perhaps off on lunch.

Joseph suggested we all go into the office and talk. Bracklaw resisted the idea but Joseph more or less shoved him in and we all followed. Elam closed the curtain on the window that faced Commercial Row. Seth kept his eyes on the opposite window, looking into the interior of the boathouse. Bracklaw was allowed to occupy his own ancient swivel chair behind a very disorderly desk piled with old cargo manifests and assorted junk. The chair squeaked every time he moved.

"Can you imagine what we're after?" Joseph said.

"I ain't clairvoyant," Bracklaw said.

"Do you suppose we came to rob you?" Elam said.

"That would be very unwise."

"We're looking for the crew of that light bateau yonder that you have took in," Joseph said. "The *Elizabeth*."

Bracklaw didn't answer. He glared at us as if we had a nerve for asking.

"Four men came down here on her," Joseph said, "Out of Union Grove, with families and all. Any notion about 'em?"

Bracklaw just crossed his arms.

"How'd you come across that boat out there?" Joseph said.

"Mr. Curry's people brought it in," Bracklaw said.

"That'd be Mr. Curry of the waterworks and such?"

"The very one."

"I understand it was carrying ten kegs of cider, among other things."

"That so?"

"I don't suppose you'd have a bill of landing for that here on your desk."

"I don't recall any such a cargo recently."

"Not of slight value, I'd think," Joseph said. "Given how times are."

"Whatever."

"You're not inclined to say?"

"I'm not inclined to being put upon in my own place of business," Bracklaw said.

"Well, we're hardly putting upon you. We could I suppose. Actually, it hadn't occurred to me until you suggested it—"

"You'd be wasting your time. And in the end you'd have to answer to Mr. Curry anyway, and he would be displeased."

"I wouldn't want to displease Mr. Curry."

"No, you wouldn't."

"Then do you suppose we might go see Mr. Curry about the crew of that boat?"

"That's exactly what I would do if I were you."

# Thirty-four

Joseph and I proceeded down to the waterworks, leaving the others behind with Bracklaw to keep down any news of our doings. It was a five-minute walk. The great waterwheel itself was a marvel of construction. It groaned on its axle as it turned in the sluiceway. Beside the big brick cube that housed the pump machinery, stood a gallows, a place of execution, a symbol of order and terror meant to reinforce the basis of Dan Curry's administrative authority. Just up the bank from that loomed a building designed to be formal and dignified, but in a crude approximation of Greco-Roman construction: Dan Curry's headquarters. It sat on a high sturdy brick foundation, above the hundred-year flood level, which required an imposing flight of stairs to reach the portico, where four squared-off columns of rough-sawn boards held up a pediment. The columns had neither bases or capitals. The windows were salvage, and not identical in either size or the number of lights within each sash. The whole thing was unpainted, as though it had only recently been finished, and you could even smell the sawn wood at some distance. It made up for its roughness by its impressive mass, and altogether the place radiated an aspiration to be dignified within the limited means of our hard times. It possessed a kind of swaggering charm, of something new, alive, and breathing in a time when most things were shrinking or expiring. This was reinforced by the numbers of people, mostly men, hanging around the portico, which was a good fifty feet wide by twenty feet deep—a spacious outdoor room in its own right, well supplied with chairs. They were gathered in groups and knots, some dressed in clean summer linens like businessmen, and others the kind of roughnecks who might have worked the wharves and flocked to Slavin's taproom at night. I assumed they were all, in some way or another, dependent on Curry's favor. They hardly glanced at us as we stepped up and made for the entrance.

Inside, at an old steel school desk, a guard or clerk sat vetting visitors. He had two boys, about twelve, seated at either side of the desk like bookends. They were runners, evidently, used to dispatch messages to the different offices throughout the building. To the left side of his desk was a double row of splint chairs where those who had checked in to do business with Curry waited their turns.

We were told to write out our business on a slip of paper, supplied to us with a lead pencil, and take a seat—and be sure to return the pencil, the guard said. Our note said: *Seek information about the crew of the trading boat Elizabeth out of Union Grove missing several weeks,* and gave their names. We were called within ten minutes. One of the messenger boys led us up another flight of stairs in the center of the hall to the floor above.

Curry sat at his ornate wooden desk eating lunch off a tray. For a moment I thought we had been taken to the wrong office, because the man behind the desk was so young. He couldn't have been over thirty years old. But even seated, he gave the impression of being physically imposing, like his building. He had a full head of curly dark hair, a trimmed beard to match, and wore a clean white cotton shirt with puffy sleeves under a fawn-colored linen vest—with a napkin tucked in at his throat. He gestured at us to sit down, while taking a mouthful of rare-cooked meat there on his plate, along with a savory pudding and fresh peas. A tall glass of milk and a smaller plate of corn bread sat on the tray too. It made me hungry. To Curry's right, a well-dressed woman with silvery hair worked writing letters at a desk along the wall of the large room. She was old enough to be his mother. To his left at a desk dog-legged off Curry's was a slight, hollow-chested man working at ledgers. Apparently both were secretaries. Behind Curry, a big arched window, a wonderful piece of old salvage composed of many panes pieced artfully together, framed a picturesque view looking down the river: blue sky, white clouds, and a few buff sails on darker blue water.

"I was wondering when someone would send for these boys," Curry said in a booming voice when he finished chewing.

"Where are they?" I said.

"Why, cooling their heels in my custody," he said.

"For what reason?"

"For the reason that they couldn't come up with bail among them."

"For what?"

"Charges, of course."

"What charges?"

"How should I know. Birkenhaus here would know. What charges," Curry said to the drudge at his left.

"Willful avoidance of excise tax. Lack of insurance documents. Battery upon a chippie. Oh, and resisting arrest."

"What's this excise tax?" Joseph said.

"You come into this port, you have to get the proper stamps and clearances," Curry said. "You can't just move cargoes as you please. We don't stand for smuggling."

"Since when are you taxing cargoes?" I asked.

"When did we come up with that?" Curry asked Birkenhaus.

"March," Birkenhaus said.

"Why'd we do it?" Curry said.

"We needed the money," Birkenhaus said. "The waterworks and all."

"Oh?" Curry said, spearing more meat. "There you have it."

"Perhaps they didn't know about it," Joseph said.

"Know about what?"

"This new tax of yours."

"Ignorance of the law is no defense," Curry said. "Well, if you've come here to get them, let's talk turkey, shall we? Actually, I'd like a little turkey. All they give me around here is beefsteak. Every damned day. A fellow gets sick of it."

"Maybe they think you're still a growing boy," Joseph said.

"That's a smart remark," Curry said, giving his napkin a tuck while he cranked his head. "What are we looking at in terms of bail, penalties, and all?"

"Hundred thousand each," Birkenhaus said. "U.S. paper dollars, that is."

"That's a lot," I said. "Even by today's standards."

"And another hundred thou for storing the boat," Birkenhaus said.

"I hardly remember when paper money was worth more than a curse," Curry said. "You fellows would, though. I hear you could buy a shoat for twenty bucks in the old days."

"That's so," Joseph said. "How do we know these men are alive?"

"You want to see them? They're down below, in stir."

"I'd like to talk about these charges with them," Joseph said. "Hear their side of the story."

"Be my guest. But in the end you'll have to pay. We both know that. Jojo," he said to the messenger boy who now occupied a chair near the door. "Bring these fellows down to Mr. Adcock. And take this corn bread. I'm getting fat as pig." He turned his attention back to us. "You weren't far off about how they feed me around here. Price of success, I guess. Nothing I courted, you understand. This is just a time when nobody seems to know how to do anything, to get things done. A fellow makes a few things happen, and the world falls at his feet. You come back before four o'clock today if you want to spring these boys. We don't conduct business after that hour. I'd like to discharge these fellows as much as you'd like to bring them home. It costs me to feed them, you know, and new ones come in all the time. It adds up. Whenever you're ready to settle, you come back. They'll show you right up, I'm sure. Oh, and if you don't come get them in twenty-four hours, I'll have to hang them. They're cluttering up my jail."

# THIRTY-FIVE

"What did you make of that?" I said to Joseph as we followed the boy downstairs.

"I make that he's a fantastic rogue for such a young buck, and probably not bluffing," Joseph said.

"He's holding them for ransom, all right. Just plain extortion."

"Yes he is. And if we don't pay it, I believe he'll kill them."

"How can we pay him?"

"Oh, we can pay him," Joseph said. "We're prepared."

"Are you going to offer him silver? I imagine he'd lower that figure for hard currency."

"We have several ways of paying him."

The basement of the building contained what can be described only as a dungeon, a dim, dank, raw masonry chamber fitted with wrought-iron cagework. Light came through in a shaft from a single slit of a window up near the ceiling, barred both inside and out. The basement stank fiercely of human excretions, mold, and filth. Within the cage, about twelve men sat inertly on benches or lay on triple-decker wooden shelves along the wall, apparently bunks on which they had to rotate in shifts, because there weren't enough for all the men to sleep at any one time. The boy delivered us to Adcock, the jailer, a tall, skeletal, pallid figure who looked like he had stepped out of a medieval engraving of the apocalypse. Adcock bent down to listen to whispered instructions from the boy.

"You men of Union Grove," Adcock called into the cage, "your saviors have come." The crewmen of the *Elizabeth* leaped from their places in the dimness to the wall of their cage.

"Robert!" It was Tom Soukey, the one I knew best, whom I used to play softball with on summer evenings in the old days. "Oh thank God, thank *God*!" he said, almost blubbering.

"Is it true?" Skip Tarbay said. "You getting us out of this hellhole?"

"Yes," I said. "Bullock sent us down to find you."

"Thank God . . ."

They didn't look healthy. They were scrawny and filthy.

"It's all trumped up crap!" Jacob Silberman said.

"I know, I know. But we're here to get you out, don't worry."

"I can't believe it," Tom said. His sobs racked him and he shuddered, despite the heat—and it was very close down in that hole.

"Pull yourself together, Tom, for Chrissake," Jake said. "We're not out yet."

"Aaron's not doing so well," Skip said, and canted his head at the bunks.

"Is he hurt?"

"Sick."

"What with."

"I've no idea. Shitting blood."

"Who's he?" Jake said, pointing to Brother Joseph. I explained who he and his people were, and how it happened the five of us were sent down to get them.

"We will get you out of here," Joseph said. "Today. I promise."

"They want money," Jake said. "It's all about grift—this nonsense about excise taxes and tariffs and all that. There never was such a thing before in the years we've been trading down here."

"I know," I said.

"Are they going to let us free now?" Skip said.

"We came down here to verify that you're actually alive," Joseph said. "We have some arrangements to make now for your release. We'll come back later for you."

"Please! Don't go," Tom said. "They keep saying they're going to hang us."

"Don't worry," I said. "You'll be out of this shithole and homeward bound before the day is over."

"How you talk," Adcock the jailer said, overhearing. He clucked at us. "Don't let Mr. Curry hear you talking like that. He don't like to be insulted. He'll hang 'em just for spite, he gets wind."

"We'll be back," I said again.

"Okay," Jake and Skip said.

Just then, two other men, strangers, rushed up to the wall of the cage like bugs to a lighted screen. They were young, no older than twenty.

"Wait, please! Can you get a message to our father, Mr. Dennis Marsden of Greenport."

"I don't know how I could," I said.

"I beg you, mister," one said. Both were in tears.

"Greenport's pretty far south of here," I said. "We're headed north today. I'm sorry."

Adcock showed us to the stairs and shut the door behind us.

The stairs took us back to the ground floor. I asked the clerk at the front desk what time it was. He pointed to a big case clock over the door. One thirty.

"This is just plain gang rule is all it is," I said to Joseph as we came back out into the sunshine. "It's like a bunch of pickers have taken over the city, or what's left of it."

"Of course it is," he said. "This Curry's no better than a petty warlord. I know the type."

"Look, I have an idea," I said. "Maybe it's a waste of time, but I want to make a side trip to the state capitol building to find out if there's any government left in this state, any authority besides this Curry."

"Everything I've seen tells me he's running the show here," Joseph said.

"Give me an hour," I said. "It's just up the hill."

"All right," Joseph said. "An hour. Meet up right back here. After that, we'll do things my way."

"Are you actually prepared to pay this guy?"

"Don't you worry," Joseph said. "I'm ready right now to pay him in full."

# THIRTY-SIX

I took off in the direction of State Street, Albany's old main drag, with my pulse quickening, worrying whether Joseph meant something other than payment of these fines and charges and how I might figure in the transaction.

It felt strange to be in a place that had been a functioning city last time I saw it, now transformed into a vast ruin. I walked past James Street, once the haunt of lobbyists and lawyers, to North Pearl Street, where a few shabby vendors sold salvage from carts, a sort of permanent flea market for the riffraff who lived in the ruins. The office buildings and old hotels on State Street, dating from the 1920s heyday of the business district, were desolate after years of neglect. Bricks had spawled out of the facades, and littered the weedy sidewalks. One actually fell from an upper story as I walked up the empty street and missed splitting my head open by a few yards. I wondered if somebody had lobbed it at me from above but didn't see anyone skulking up there. The plate glass shop fronts were blown out, of course, and everything of value inside had been stripped.

The once meticulously groomed grounds of the state capitol building, an impressive limestone heap in the Second Empire style, were now choked with box elders, sumacs, and other woody shrubs. Knapweed, vetch, and blue chicory sprouted from the cracks between the broad front steps where a few ill-nourished layabouts sat listlessly surveying the scene. Inside the grand old building, every surface had been stripped down to the bare masonry. Carpets, draperies, chestnut wainscoting, metal fixtures, all gone, probably long gone. The stink of urine and excrement told the rest of the story. I would have turned and left had I not heard a familiar tapping sound seeming to come from distantly above somewhere up the southeast stairs.

I ventured warily to the second floor. The tapping grew louder, echo-ing off the limestone blocks in the stairwell. I recognized it now as the sound of a typewriter, something I had not heard for a very long time, something that I had only really heard in old movies.

Off the stairwell and down the hall, I came to a set of rather grand arched oak double doors. They stood ajar. Gold-on-black lettering on the window said OFFICE OF LIEUTENANT GOVERNOR EUGENE FURMAN. I knocked on the glass. The tapping within stopped. A voice said, "Come in." I shoved the door open. It creaked on its hinges. Inside at a large and ornate desk, bathed in glorious afternoon light from a ten-foot-high window, sat a man in a clean dark suit complete with a blue oxford button-down dress shirt and necktie, behind a pink portable manual typewriter. He was neatly barbered and even shaved and looked like he had come to life out of a photograph.

"What are you doing here?" I said.

"Carrying on," he said, cheerfully, without any guileful over-tones. "I'd ask the same of you."

"I came to see if there was anyone here."

"I'm here," he said. "Please come in. Have a seat."

His office was tidy to a fault, an oriental rug on the floor, book-shelves groaning with volumes, a sofa and chair set arranged be-fore a carved limestone fireplace on the far side of the big room, the U.S. and New York state flags deployed on standards in a cor-ner, his desk full of documents and papers, all neatly arranged around the surface. The pervasive stink of decay intruded on the scene, but everything else gave the weird impression of decorum and normality. I sat down in one of a pair of tufted leather arm-chairs at a side of his desk.

"What's your name and where from?" he said. His manner was smooth, practiced.

"Robert Earle. Union Grove, Washington County. Are you really," I glanced back at the door, "the lieutenant governor, Eugene Furman?"

"Yes," he said and nodded with a boyish smile. "I am."

"What on earth is going on around here?"

"Well, obviously, things have changed," he said. I wondered whether he was a crazy person. Perhaps he sensed my thought, because he quickly added, "I'm not trying to be cute."

"Of course not. But why are you still here?"

"I was elected. Swore an oath to serve. Here I remain."

"But there's nothing left."

"Well, I don't know about that. We're in rough shape. I mean, look at what a pigsty this building has become. But the state of New York is still out there. Washington County's still there, right? A physical fact. Populated with citizens."

"The ones still left. Yes."

"Your neighbors are still there, doing things, living their lives."

"Getting by, barely."

"Okay. And St. Lawrence County's still there too, where I'm from. Potsdam. Though I haven't been there in some time."

"If you're here, where's the governor?"

"I honestly don't know. He was in Washington when, you know."

"What was his name?"

"Eric Champion."

"I don't remember voting for any Eric Champion."

"Out of Rochester. The Energy Diet campaign?"

"I don't think we heard about it."

"Yeah, the election was carried out under, uh, less than ideal conditions."

"I don't even remember the two of you running. But, wait a minute, you mean to tell me there's still a functioning government?"

"There's a few of us left in this building. Stan Obermeyer in budget, third floor. Hector Oliveres over in emergency services, a few others—"

"What emergency services?"

"Well, there's not much, but there could be, if we had resources."

"If the governor is dead, then you must be governor now."

"He hasn't been declared dead. Officially. He's missing."

"But that was years ago, the bomb in Washington."

"Okay, he's been missing for a while now. But I wouldn't presume to just declare myself governor. Look, I'm not that kind of pushy person, or else it would have been me heading the ticket and not Champ, right."

"But someone must have declared you acting governor."

"To be perfectly frank, there's nobody around with the authority. But let's say I'm acting as if I were the acting governor even though I haven't been legally declared any such thing."

"Where in the hell did everybody go?"

"Everybody?"

"In the state government. You had tens of thousands of workers, agency heads, department chiefs, appointees, staff, civil service, judges, police."

Furman just blinked at me.

"I mean, as a practical matter, there is no government," I said.

"Oh. I see what you're driving at. Well, again, frankly, that's a fair appraisal of things. I guess you could say we're keeping the chairs warm, under the theory that this . . . this whatever it is . . . this rough patch we're going through . . . that it eventually comes to an end."

"What do you think the chances of that are?"

Furman leaned closer to me, over the top of his typewriter. "Again, to be really candid, it doesn't look so good. You asked about the government. The people who worked here? Well, there's an answer to your question. Most of them stopped coming to work when they stopped getting paid. Another bunch of them died— you get that Mexican flu up your way?"

"Yes. Sure."

"Well, you know what that was like." Furman made a kind of whistling sound sucking air between his teeth. "The ones who survived just walked away, walked home, wherever that was, or walked somewhere else. There's a term for those few of us who stuck around here running this ship. I forget what it is just now—"

"A skeleton crew."

"That's right! Sailing a kind of *Flying Dutchman* of government. Doesn't mean we're a bunch of ghouls, you understand. We do what we can. Which leads me naturally to ask if there's anything in particular I can do for you? Or did you just stop in to chat?"

At this point I told Furman as concisely as possible how I had come to Albany with four other men to find the crew of the *Elizabeth*, and how Dan Curry was running a hostage and ransom racket down at the waterfront, which these men fell prey to, and finally I asked whether there was any state authority or legitimate law enforcement that might intervene.

Furman swiveled toward the window and gazed out across State Street at the empty Empire State Plaza, Governor Nelson Rockefeller's long-ago fantasy of a futuristic administrative utopia. Now it looked like an abandoned UFO landing strip.

"There's not a damn thing I can do about Dan Curry," Furman said. "I know exactly what he's up to. His operation has nothing to do with us. It's not authorized. It's beyond our control. But politics hates a vacuum, if you know what I mean." He swiveled back around to face me. "On the bright side, Mr. Curry says he's going to run water back up the hill here pretty soon. That'd be nice wouldn't it?"

"He wants us to pay half a million dollars to release these four men."

"Can you pay it?"

"I think so."

"Half a million isn't what it used to be. You better pay it, if you can. He's a ruthless son of a gun."

"I guess you've answered my question," I said.

"Sorry I can't be of more help. I wish you the best of luck. If they get the mails going again, drop me a line and tell me how it all worked out."

"Sure," I said. "Only you tell me something before I go: what if I was a picker or some psycho coming up here looking to steal something?"

"Is that what you *are*?"

"No. I'm just asking out of curiosity. How do you protect yourself up here in this nasty building?"

I barely saw Furman move a muscle but he seemed to instantly produce a very large automatic pistol, which he held level with my chest.

"I think I understand," I said.

"You're not a psycho, right?" he said.

"No."

"That's good. You had me going there for a moment. This is the U.S. Army model Colt .45, first issued in 1911. Used through most of the last century. My father carried this piece in Vietnam, sixty-six through sixty-nine. It'd blow your liver clean out of your ribcage."

"I wish you wouldn't point it at me, though."

"That's exactly the feeling it's meant to impart."

The odd thing was, I had a pistol every bit as lethal tucked in the rear of my belt, next to my skin, underneath my shirttails. I'd been carrying it so many days that I had almost forgotten it was there. This was the kind of world we now lived in.

"Good luck with Mr. Curry," the lieutenant governor said as I left his office.

# THIRTY-SEVEN

I hurried down the hill through the ruins of State Street to the grassy riverbank in front of Dan Curry's headquarters as quickly as I could, reentering another world, another reality. In the time I had been away—under an hour, actually—Curry's minions had managed to hang two men from the gallows down beside the pump house. Apparently, the hanging had just concluded. Some spectators up front were turning to walk away, while a separate contingent remained up on the broad portico gazing over the balustrade down at the scene in muted conversation. The legs of one victim still twitched, and I recognized that they were the two young Marsden brothers who had importuned me only a little while ago to contact their father in Greenport. I wondered whether this was an object lesson for our benefit. I was still goggling at the swinging bodies when I felt a hand on my shoulder and reflexively spun on my heels. It was Joseph.

"Look what this monster has done now," he said.

I was speechless.

"Well, let's go and get Mr. Bullock's boys before he stretches their necks too," Joseph said.

"Where are the others?" I said.

Joseph cocked his head. Seth and Elam waited at a remove beside a warehouse under the freeway overpass, perhaps a hundred yards away, mounted, with two more of the horses.

"Where's Minor?"

"I sent him up ahead with our goods. We'll catch up with him later. What did you discover up yonder at the statehouse?"

"There's nothing left up there that can stand up to this."

"I didn't think so," Joseph said. "Well, then, let's go pay Mr. Curry, then, and be gone, and leave them to their wickedness."

My knees knocked from the sight of those boys hanging as we climbed the stairs and entered the building. We stopped at the first floor desk as we had before. Joseph told the guard that we had come to pay the fines owed for the release of our four men in custody. He scribbled a message and sent a boy up, as before. A minute later we were ushered back into Curry's office. Curry was in the act of being barbered in his seat behind the desk with a smock tied over him. An old factotum had just finished shaving the whiskers on Curry's neck with a straight razor and took up a pair of scissors to groom the beard and mustache.

"Ah, gentlemen, I'm told you've come to the right decision."

"Yes, we have," Joseph said.

"Excellent," Curry said. "Birkenhaus, draw up discharge papers on these birds."

"Yes, sir," the secretary said.

"People complain about these taxes and duties," Curry said, "but how else would we pay for the many improvements we've started, not to mention the ones planned? They don't give out grants for this kind of thing anymore, you know. We're on our own here—that's enough, dammit. Get away from me!" he said to the barber and shoved him aside. The old fellow gathered up the tools of his trade off the desk, rolled them into the smock, and slunk out of the room like a whipped dog.

"Where was I?"

"Civic improvements," Birkenhaus said.

"Right. It all comes down to good government. And local government is all that's left, so we have to take every advantage where revenues are concerned. The people expect it. You see what I mean?"

"What about the cargo that was taken off the boat?" I said.

"What cargo?"

"Ten kegs of ninety-proof cider among other things."

"I don't know a thing about it," Curry said, putting on a face of indignant surprise.

"Don't you have some record?" I said.

"Why should we have a record?"

"How could you calculate an excise tax if you don't know what the cargo was?"

Curry seemed to flush for a moment, as though embarrassed to be caught in an obvious lie.

"My tax people calculate that," he retorted, a moment later. "And I'll thank you to show a little respect for this office. Remember, I still have these persons of interest in my custody, and I enjoy hanging riffraff."

Curry shot out his cuffs. He was wearing cufflinks in the shape of little acorns. He seemed to make a show of recomposing himself.

"Please, sit down," he said. "All I know is what my people tell me. I can't concern myself with every detail of what goes on around here. I'd go insane. A good leader knows how to delegate. These operations run on trust, on my ability to depend on people to discharge their duties. Now, if everyone were as honest and diligent as the people who work for me, we might become a great nation again—and perhaps we will be. And so you see another reason for weeding out the criminal element, the parasites, the tax evaders. Anyway, you can remit payment directly to me. You have the cash, right?"

"What about gold instead of U.S. paper dollars?" Joseph said.

Curry's eyes widened perceptibly.

"What do you propose?" Curry said, obviously relishing the idea.

"Would an ounce satisfy these charges?"

"In lieu of half a million U.S. scrip?"

"That's right."

"You've *got* gold?"

"I do," Joseph said.

"You just carry it right on your person?"

"In some situations only gold will answer."

"My motto exactly—but one measly ounce for four men?"

"That's what I said."

"Seems . . . less than altogether required."

"We're talking about some tax owed on freight, aren't we?"

"Why, yes, of course," Curry said. "But each man is charged with evasion so the fine is additional and would be multiplied by four. Plus all the other misdemeanors. And there's the slip fee for that boat of theirs—"

"Maybe you could find a way to calculate the total so it all worked out to what I am offering you," Joseph said.

"Well, the thing is: is that all the gold you have?"

"You're a piece of work, sir," Joseph said.

"I know." Curry said. "Nervy bastard, aren't I?"

"I'll say."

"But you! You drive a hard bargain."

"An ounce of gold is a tidy sum these days."

"You're right there," Curry said. "But does it equal the pleasure I would get from hanging these four river rats? That's what dogs me."

"How much pleasure did you derive from hanging those two young fellows yonder just a while ago?"

"At least half as much," Curry said and broke into a braying laugh. Birkenhaus, meanwhile, sprinkled some blotting sand on a document, waved it around to dry, and dangled it before Curry, who snatched it out of the air. "Ah, look, your paperwork's ready. Now, you sir. Show me the goods."

Joseph got the leather purse out of a pocket inside his coat. He untied the cinch and drew out a gold coin, placing it in the center of Curry's desk. Curry hesitated a moment, then reached for it, emitting some little grunts of satisfaction.

"Is there anything prettier in this world than the shiny yellow metal that never tarnishes?" he said, admiring it in the sunlight from the big window behind him. "What've we got here?

Hmm. Mexican gold peso. *Oro puro*. I like that." He bit into it, then held it very close to examine it. "What do you think, Mr. B?" he said, passing it over to his secretary, who used a penknife to check for lead.

"Appears to be the real thing, Mr. C," Birkenhaus said.

"By the way," Curry said to Joseph, "how'd you come by this?"

"Earnest toil," Joseph said. "May I ask you something, Mr. Curry?

"Sure, what?"

"Do you know the Lord?"

"What? You mean, like, Jesus Christ?"

"Yes."

Curry stood, puffed out his cheeks, looked to the left and then to the right of himself and said, "Frankly, I don't have time for that crap."

Just then, gunshots rang out down below. There were shouts and imprecations. Screams. More gunshots.

"What the hell?" Curry said.

"Don't worry. You're headed there directly," Joseph said.

"Excuse—"

Before Curry could finish, Joseph had drawn a small pistol from his pocket and emptied the chamber in Curry's forehead. A little red spot appeared there, just under Curry's dark forelock, and his athletic body crumpled behind the desk like a puppet whose strings had been cut. Joseph then turned the pistol on Birkenhaus, who tried to dodge the line of fire only to be hit in the neck. Joseph must have gotten an artery because Birkenhaus spun around screaming as bright blood shot out between his fingers with such force that it literally splattered high up on the wall. The older woman who worked on the opposite side of the room watched all this agog.

"You shot my son!" she said, as Birkenhaus crashed to the floor.

"Which one was yours?"

She pointed where Curry lay.

"Him! You raised up a fiend!" Joseph said. "I ought to shoot you too, if I weren't a Christian."

"Oh, please, no," she said, sobbing. "Don't kill me!"

"*Abominable wickedness the Lord hates,*" Joseph screamed at her, with the tendons standing out in his neck and blue veins bulging in his forehead, while he waved his pistol at the terrified woman. "*Then the just shall rejoice to see his vengeance and bathe their feet in the blood of the wicked . . .*"

More gunshots resounded outside.

"For Christ's sake," I said, "let's go!"

I had to drag him away. The woman collapsed in sheer fright. Joseph pulled himself together quickly. He remembered to retrieve his gold coin from Birkenhaus's desk before we hurried out of the room.

"I thought our boys'd never make their move," he said as we faced the stairs. "Good thing I actually had that dang peso."

# Thirty-eight

People seemed to be running in all directions outside. More gun-shots rang out. But at the center of the human maelstrom, near the foot of the exterior grand stairway, Elam waited mounted on his horse, calm as a drover, holding the reins of three other horses as well as a rifle hitched up under his arm. Several bodies lay strewn in the weedy grass. Then Seth emerged from the mob with a smok-ing pistol, leading Mr. Bullock's boatmen out into daylight for the first time in weeks. Tom and Skip struggled to assist Aaron Moyer, who was unsteady on his feet from sickness. A path cleared for them as Seth brandished his pistol and men scattered. Joseph launched himself onto his big gray, Temperance, while Tom and Skip helped get the weakened Aaron up behind him. Seth helped Tom aboard behind him. Skip mounted behind Elam. I followed on my bay gelding, Cadmus, giving Jake the stirrup to climb up behind me. Finally, all of us were double mounted.

More cracks of gunfire sounded. Gray puffs of smoke appeared up on the portico where they were shooting at us from behind the balustrade. Elam and Joseph answered these shots with several of their own. We wheeled our horses back around toward the elevated freeway. Seth raised his sword to hack at a man who attempted to grab his mount's bridle, and I thought I saw the man's hand sepa-rate from his sleeve in a gout of blood. I heard another shot much closer by and felt a bullet pass so near to my head it made a ripping noise in the air. Just ahead of me, perhaps twenty feet, a white cloud of gun smoke hung over a fat man with a red beard wearing dirty cream-colored pants held up with suspenders. I registered these details as I watched him level a pistol at me again and squeeze off another round. It was as if I was watching myself watching him, my amazement at being fired on was so great, and it all seemed to happen in slow motion. He was a poor shot and he missed the second time too. My wondrous detachment persisted as I reached behind, drew the big .41 out from my belt there, leveled it at the fat white target below the red smudge of beard and pulled the trigger. The report nearly knocked the gun out of my hand. My bullet took the red-bearded man off his feet and drove him backward like a rag doll against the dusty ground. His shirt and pants quickly turned red. I could hear him groan like a steer. Joseph yelled to follow him up the riverbank. We rounded the corner at Slavin's Hotel under the freeway and galloped up Commercial Row where the traders gaped at us silently from their doorways while the last shots, cries, and screams from Curry's headquarters faded into the distance.

We rode at a gallop for at least a mile, and then trotted for a long way until we crossed the Waterford bridge, where we had encountered the man beating his donkey on the way down. We dismounted there to rest the animals, which were foaming from exertion. Bullock's men fell into swoons of gratitude, saying that Adcock the jailer had promised that morning it would be their last day on earth. Tom Soukey, the captain of the *Elizabeth*, made noises about going back to Albany under cover of darkness to get the boat, but Joseph quashed that idea. In a little while we resumed riding north, to meet up with Brother Minor, who was waiting for us at the Raynor farm in Stillwater.

Except for Aaron Moyer, who was very ill, the other boatmen were happy to walk freely along the pleasant country roads north of Waterford. I walked for much of the way too, giving them turns on Cadmus. They didn't talk much, but they seemed keenly attuned to the sights and sounds along the way, as men would who had been locked up for weeks. We covered roughly fifteen miles, with ample rest stops, in five hours, making it over the last hill to the Raynor farm with the sun half lapped over the western horizon. Minor's horse and the donkey stood hobbled peacefully in the shrubby field where we had passed such a strange night recently.

Smoke from a campfire ribboned straight up in the soft breezeless air.

Minor was extremely glad to see us when we rode up. He could barely contain his high spirits.

"Listen up," he said. "A momma mole, a daddy mole, and a baby mole lived in a hole in the ground up by yonder house. One day, the daddy mole poked his head out of the hole and said, 'Mmmmmm, I smell bacon a'frying!' The momma mole stuck her head outside and said, 'Mmmmm, I smell pancakes!' The baby mole tried to poke its head out of the hole but couldn't get past the momma and the daddy. 'Dang,' he said, 'all I can smell is mole-asses.'"

Minor appreciated the joke more than anyone, of course.

Bullock's men obviously didn't know what to make of Minor. But he had caught several large pike and had roasted them up and fixed a pot of buckwheat groats, onions and fresh nettles to go with them, and boiled two dozen eggs that he'd traded for along the way, and that was all Bullock's men concerned themselves with. They ate like wild animals, and when the fish and eggs and groats were gone they asked for more, so Minor turned out pan after pan of corn cakes, which they ate with butter and honey. Aaron was able to choke down a few of them too, and the others said it was the first they had seen him eat in days. By then, the sun had set, while the air remained mild. Joseph brought out the whiskey bottle and passed it among us. Elam sang a song about East Virginia in a reedy, mournful voice, and Joseph sang a brighter one about fair and tender maidens, with Minor playing harmonica softly behind him. I wished I'd had my fiddle there. Shortly, Bullock's boatmen were snoring in the fragrant grass.

Joseph and the brothers discussed the attributes and shortcomings of various New Faith women, and which ones would be nice to "get with," and I didn't know whether this was their argot for getting married, or whether more casual arrangements prevailed among them. They teased Minor remorselessly about his interest in a girl named Zilpah, and Minor retreated into playing his harmonica. They said that anyone who had been in the vicinity of Washington, D.C., as they had, seemed to have trouble bearing children. It concerned them that their community had so few. I told them that the same was true apparently of people who had recovered from the flu or one of the other illnesses that had visited us. They said a good deal of their prayer every day was devoted to asking God for children. I asked if it bothered them that their prayers weren't answered, and they said it must be God's will. Seth said God had decided the earth was overpopulated, and I asked how come he let it get that way in the first place. Seth said that God loved his children so much that he couldn't bring himself to cut back until all this climate wickedness started and then he had to do something to save the planet from overheating and killing every last living thing on it. I argued that the human race should have known it was in for trouble, at least we in the United States should have, given how insane our way of life had become. Minor quit blowing into his harmonica long enough to say that John D. Rockefeller and the Bush family had made a deal with the Devil going back all the way to the 1900s.

By this time, my head was swimming with whiskey and the others sounded like they were far gone themselves. We let the fire run down. It was a warm night. Smoke from the smoldering embers helped keep the mosquitoes away. I lay back against my saddle to gaze at the stars twinkling against the incomprehensible depth of space and eternity, reflecting that I had shot a man, probably to death, that afternoon and had been an accessory in the killing of Dan Curry and his secretary, Birkenhaus. And the others had killed at least several more. Could we even pretend the law still existed? Or was it something you made up now, as the occasion required?

# THIRTY-NINE

The rest of our journey home would have been unremarkable, even pleasant except for a disturbing encounter on Route 4, the River Road, some five miles south of Starkville in midafternoon the next day when we came upon an old man driving an automobile. Yes, an automobile.

I had not seen a car in motion for years. This one was a Ford, the big *Explorer* model, the color of dull brass, with daisies of rust around the wheel wells and a broken rear window. It was creeping down the road slower than our horses might go at a moderate walk. The pavement on Route 4 was badly broken with potholes, and the driver was obviously steering around them with the utmost care. He came to a stop as we approached. His engine knocked, sputtered, and backfired.

"What you running that thing on, old-timer?" Minor said.

"Who wants to know?" the old man said. He might have been eighty years old given the wizened face beneath a stained and tattered baseball cap. "You pickers or regulators?"

"Naw, just regular folks," Minor said and flashed a big grin around at all of us. He'd been walking, leading Jenny and the cart. Aaron Moyer was up on Minor's horse, sitting straight in the saddle on his own now, feeling better after a day in the fresh air and sunshine. The rest of us soon formed a circle around the car. "Where you going in that thing, anyway?" Minor said.

"None of your damn business."

"Excuse me for breathing," Minor said.

"I got a firearm," the old man said.

"Well you should," Skip Tarbay said. "But keep the safety on. We're men of Union Grove."

"Far afield, ain't you?"

"Far enough, and coming home from Albany now, thank God."

"Is the mall still there?"

"I wouldn't know, sir. That wasn't the part we were at. Hope you're not aiming to go down there in your car."

"Nope. I just like to keep her running," the old man said. "You know, use it or lose it."

"Sounds like she's losing it," Minor said. "What's she running on?"

"Grain spirits."

"A waste of the taste, if you ask me," Minor said.

"I can't taste nothing anyway," the old man said. "And who asked you?"

"Must be uncomfortable driving that thing on this busted up road," Skip said.

"It's a damn sorry excuse for a state highway. The state won't fix it. How do you like that? The taxes we paid all those years and look what we got to show for it."

"Don't hold your breath waiting for improvements, old-timer," Minor said.

"We got a right to decent roads. This ain't the American way."

"The American way has kind of lost its way," Minor said. "Maybe you should get a horse."

The old man snorted scornfully and spat out the window onto the fissured asphalt. "This is supposed to be the modern age."

"The modern age went to hell some time ago."

"Is that so? Well I don't like it."

"It's a fact we all got to live with."

"You should have been around in the 1960s, boy. *Hooo-weee.* Gas was twenty-five cents and the roads were smooth as a baby's behind. You could buy good bread and ground round anywhere, and the TV came on when you felt like it. Now nothing's on when you want it."

"It ain't even on when you don't want it," Minor said, to everyone's amusement. "Do the home folks know you're out and about?"

"They don't give a damn whether I live or die."

"You must be lonesome, then, old man."

"It ain't none of your damn business what I am."

"Have you found the Lord?"

"No, I ain't."

"You could find some comfort there."

"I'll pass, thank you."

"Why don't you try letting him into your heart?"

"I don't care to. I got this far without it."

"This far ain't nothing," Minor said, raising his voice shrilly. "What about the trackless eternity you're going to spend down in hell, old man, where the modern age is still going strong, waiting patiently for you to show up and sign back on? And you'll get there pretty durn soon, I imagine, from the looks of you."

"Are you crazy or something?"

"Hell no."

"Well, you talk like a goddamn crazy man."

"And I ain't drunk, neither. But if I was, I'd be sober tomorrow. And you'd still be a godless old sumbitch."

"Sonny, I'd put a bullet in your ass if I wasn't saving it for something worthwhile."

"And what'd that be?"

"You got more goddamn questions—get out of my goddamn way."

The old man put the engine back in gear and continued on, hardly giving Seth a chance to step his mount aside. He wove the car around a stretch of divots, ruts, and potholes and we watched him go, the very sight of an automobile going down the road a marvel, like seeing history come back to life. He had gone perhaps a hundred yards when we heard a little *pop*. I thought, oh no, he's gone and blown a tire, given how old they must have been, and how rough the road, but the car did not stop. It veered to the side of the road and then clean off the shoulder and into a shrubby field where it plowed over a series of poplar saplings before coming to rest with a crunch against the trunk of a mature black ash tree. Even

so, the engine kept running and the horn blared. We hurried down
to it.

The old man lay slumped against the wheel. Tom and I helped
get him out. He had a gash above an eyebrow. We laid him down
in the weeds—black-eyed Susans and Queen Anne's lace—and
realized he was no longer breathing. Then we discovered it wasn't
the crash that had killed him. Rather, his tattered flannel shirt was
dark and sopping with blood. We ripped it open. Underneath he
had a clean purple hole in his chest with a slightly raised dough-
nut of blue flesh around it, just over his heart. Minor rooted around
the interior of the car and emerged holding the pistol. He examined the cylinder and said, "One spent shell, all right. Sumbitch
done himself in. How do you like that?"

Joseph slid down off his horse as though he was suddenly all
in a hurry and stalked over to Minor.

"Give me that damn thing," he said and wrenched the gun out
of Minor's hand, and proceeded to cuff him across the head, driving the smaller man to the ground. "You think death is just another of your jokes," Joseph said. "I'm sick of it."

"I didn't have nothing to do with this—"

"You got to talk trash with everybody that crosses your path?"

"You think he kilt himself 'cause I made a little chitchat?"

"Calling him a godless sumbitch! I got half a mind to strop
you skinless."

"Just you try it!" Minor reached for the dagger he called *the
last resort*. Joseph kicked it out of his hand and, using a move that
he might have learned in the military, had Minor flipped over with
his face pinned in the weeds, a knee on his neck, and both of his
arms nearly dislocated, held painfully behind him.

"Ow, ow! Damn you, you're hurtin' me!" Minor said.

"I aim to hurt you," Joseph said. "If you ever raise up a weapon
against one of your brothers again, you'll get hurt so bad you'll never
recover. Understand?"

"Yes."

"Say you're sorry."

"I can't breathe!"

"I don't care about your comfort just now."

"Okay, okay, I'm sorry."

"I can't hear you."

"I'm sorry, I'm sorry, I'm sorry . . ." Minor said. Joseph released his arms and his boot from Minor's neck, but Minor remained face-down. His body shook and he seemed to be blubbering. The Union Grove men turned away, in embarrassment I suppose. Elam and Seth eventually helped Minor back up on his feet. Jenny stood at the edge of the road in front of her cart blinking at us.

# FORTY

We made inquires up the road and eventually found the old man's people living a mile away in a miserable split-level house that sat alone on a hill, with two windows over a gaping garage door that gave it the look of a woeful human face. All around it lay a poorly kept garden composed of little more than squash vines, the garden of people who had lost the will to cultivate anything, as well as the knowledge to do so. Stumps around the house indicated that the shade trees had been cut down over the years, probably to heat the place. Now, with the temperature above ninety, the sun beat down remorselessly on the asphalt shingle roof. It was one of millions of such cheap houses erected in the last century in rural places on one-acre road frontage out-parcels cut from old farms when nobody cared whether they lived near a town or a job because they could always hop in the car and drive somewhere. If the place had a drilled well with a submersible electric pump, then it probably didn't have running water these days. It was exactly the kind of place that Wayne Karp's crew was disassembling for materials all around Washington County as the owners died or went crazy.

A living scarecrow answered the door looking enough like the dead man to have been his son. And so he proved to be. He barely registered any emotion when we told him what happened. The old man's body was slung facedown over Joseph's horse but the man said he recognized the clothes.

"We're sorry about it," Joseph said.

An equally scrawny woman stood behind the man in a pool of darkness, with her hand over her mouth. The inside of the house stank fiercely. You could smell it wafting out the door.

"Would you care to help us bury him?" the man said, adding, "We can't pay."

"Sure, we'll help you," Joseph said.

So we, the able-bodied, spent an hour digging another grave out beyond the squash vines, and Joseph conducted another funeral. Minor didn't speak a word, but he did more than his share of the digging. I noticed that Joseph did not give the couple the old man's gun, though he did hand over the car keys. Nor did he bother to proselytize them. We were anxious to return to the road, being within striking distance of home. Once we passed through Starkville proper, the landscape grew recognizable, and I felt tears of gratitude well up inside as the familiar contours of Willard Mountain and the little range of hills known as the Gavottes came into view.

At our journey's end another long day had spent itself. When our party entered the front drive of the Bullock farm, we'd marched twenty miles since breakfast, pausing to dig a six-foot hole in the ground. The sun was down, but plenty of purple afterglow remained and to the east a coppery quarter moon was rising in the warm haze. The antique foursquare manse never looked lovelier, with trumpet vine blossoming over the pergola outside the kitchen, roses in the arbors, two potted fig trees beside the door, swallows dipping around the eaves, and purposeful human activity evident everywhere your eye came to rest. Lights glowed warmly inside the big house and a Debussy recording played. It was the epitome of what you would want to return home to after a harrowing journey to a dark place.

I could see Stephen and Sophie Bullock at their dinner table through the French windows as we rode up. We must have made quite a commotion in the stillness of that hour. They put down their forks and bustled out of the house. The courtyard between the big house and the barns and workshops soon filled with Bullock's servants, and someone rang a bell that tolled out over the fields. The four boatmen seemed overcome with emotion. Tom was weeping again. Skip fell to his knees by the big oak tree. Even Jake uncharacteristically shook and blubbered. Bullock helped Aaron down from the horse and held him up in his arms until Aaron was steady on his feet. Roger Lippy hooked leads on and led Temperance and Cadmus to the soapstone water trough. Sophie helped Skip up off the ground, and he subsided in her arms, sobbing. Shouts rang out in the distance in the still evening air. Soon most of the inhabitants of Bullock's village swept down the lanes between the fields and the barns, answering what was generally construed to be an alarm bell, to find their friends, husbands, fathers returned from the dead. Sophie called for cider and soon pitchers of the potent brew went around.

Bullock steered Joseph and myself away from the celebrating throng to his office inside the house. It was a spacious, airy room, with walls of built-in bookshelves, a long trestle table laid with engineering drawings for his various projects, and a beautifully carved cherry wood desk that had been his grandfather's. I had tossed back a tumbler of cider and the warmth was flooding through my veins. Bullock now poured shots of his best whiskey from a cut glass decanter. He allowed as we were surely anxious to continue on home to Union Grove but wanted to know briefly how things had transpired in Albany. I told him about Dan Curry and how he was running an extortion and ransom racket there, and how we had found the boat and then the crew in his custody, and how he demanded payment outright for their release, calling it excise taxes and fines. Bullock said he could see it getting to this over the preceding year.

"What a bold sonofabitch he's become!" he said. "You didn't pay, did you."

"No, sir," Joseph said.

"Good. But then how could you? I didn't send you down there with that kind of money."

"You didn't?" I said.

"Of course not. Excise tax, my ass!" Bullock said, smacking the tabletop for emphasis. "This idiot could disrupt all the trade in the Hudson Valley. All right, then: how did you spring my men?"

"By other means," Joseph said.

"Such as . . ."

"Such as was required in lieu of payment," Joseph said.

Bullock was clearly frustrated. "Did it require force?" he said.

"You could say that."

"To what extent?"

"To the extent that some people got hurt, sir."

"Who. This Curry?"

"Yes, I'd say Curry was among them," Joseph said.

Bullock took this in. "What do you mean by hurt, exactly?" he said.

"Do you really want to know?" Joseph said.

"Go on, tell me," Bullock said.

"I had to shoot him in the head, sir."

"You killed him?"

"I believe so. It's not the kind of injury that people get over."

"Was it necessary to kill him?"

"Yes, sir," Joseph said. "But it wasn't necessary to tell you."

Bullock flinched, then retrieved the whiskey decanter, and poured another round of shots.

"Were you there when this happened, Robert?" Bullock said.

"Yes."

"Was this necessary?"

"He was going to hang your men," I said.

"You sure he wasn't bluffing?"

"He said he would in so many words. And he hanged two boys earlier that day. When I say boys, I mean boys. Two teenagers from Greenport. He told us he enjoyed it."

"Believe me," Joseph said. "Stopping this fiend was the Lord's work."

Bullock brooded a while. "I suppose they'll hold me responsible," he said.

"I'm the one who shot him, sir," Joseph said. "Anyway, he wasn't the only one."

"How many more?"

"I don't know," Joseph said. "A good many."

"Like what? A baker's dozen?"

"Something like that," he said.

Bullock poured himself yet another shot. His hands trembled visibly. "Oh, Jesus . . ." he muttered to himself.

"Curry was all the law there was down there," I said. "It began and ended with him. There won't be anybody coming up here after you. I'm pretty sure of that." I described my side trip to the capitol, the lieutenant governor rattling around the ruined building like a BB in a packing crate, the total absence of state authority.

Bullock reflected as I spoke, sipping more liquor.

"Hmm. I suppose the boat is a loss," he said.

"You could send another party down for it, sir," Joseph said. "But if it was me, I'd forget about it for now and build another boat until things settle out down there."

"I take the point," Bullock said. He seemed a little walleyed suddenly, as if the liquor was finally getting to him, and he ran his fingers down through his long white hair as if he were combing something out of it. "By the way, Robert, your man Jobe has kind of opened up a rat's nest over in town with that water project."

"Oh? Did he get started on that?"

"We can't make pipe fast enough. It's taking my men away from haying."

# FORTY-ONE

Most of the town was already asleep when we rode through in the moonlight. The few businesses on our little Main Street were closed. Here and there a candle glowed in a window on Salem Street and then down Linden. My own house was among the lighted ones. I swung off Cadmus for the last time and collected my gear from the panniers, a little sorry to be on my own again and wary of the uncertainties that awaited me. Elam retrieved my few parcels from the donkey cart. I thanked them all for their valiant efforts in our adventures, especially Brother Minor, for his caretaking of the animals, for the many meals he had cooked, and his attention to my injury. As I said goodnight to them, the front door swung open and there stood Britney. I had thought of her in only the most abstract terms since setting off, and now it was a shock to see her in the flesh. It was too difficult to imagine the changes she might represent in my living arrangements, not to mention my spirit. The others looked at her as though she were a perfectly roasted chicken.

"Welcome home," she said.

Joseph tipped his hat, then led the others and their mounts down the street toward their new home, the old high school. I stood in the dooryard watching them, afraid to enter my own house, as the horses clip-clopped into the moonlight.

"Are you hungry?" Britney said.

"I suppose I am," I said.

"You come in now."

She helped me take my stuff inside. Sarah, her seven-year-old daughter, sat by a lighted candle in a rocking chair in the living room, braiding reeds into fat coils. Several new baskets sat on the floor beside her chair.

"Welcome home, Mr. Robert," she said.

"Thank you, Sarah. Just plain Robert is okay, though."

"Mama told me to say that."

"Oh? Those are very nice baskets."

"Mama and me trade for them, you know."

"I expect you'll do real well with those."

I followed Britney out back, to the open summer kitchen. The house had obviously benefited from her being there. It smelled fresher, like strewn herbs. Yet nothing was really out of place.

"Thank you for cleaning up."

"You were kind to take us in," she said.

"I've been nervous about this. About how we would inhabit this house together."

"What are your thoughts?" she said.

"I've been trying not to have any."

"We'll stay out of your way."

"I don't know as I'd like that, exactly."

"What would you like?"

"I don't know. A normal household."

"This isn't a normal situation, and these aren't normal times."

"Don't I know it."

"And I'm a young woman."

"Yes, you are. And I'm what I am. Let's maybe start by not having to apologize for ourselves."

"All right," she said.

"Mostly I'm exhausted from riding and walking more than twenty miles today."

"I have a spinach pudding made earlier tonight with some of Carl Weibel's goat cheese. There's no meat on hand. I didn't know you'd be back tonight."

"Pudding's fine."

"We have fresh lettuce and the first little sweet onions—"

"I would love some kind of fresh greens—"

"And I can make you some eggs too."

"Please."

"How do you like them?"

"Scrambled. But not runny. Five or six if they're pullet eggs."

I rooted around a cupboard and found half a bottle of Jane Ann's wine.

"Here, sit down," Britney said, pulling out a chair for me. She lit a candle in a tin can holder on the table.

I watched her load some splints in the cookstove and blow on them until they caught from the embers left over from their supper earlier. It was hard not to admire the delicacy and economy of her movements.

She proceeded to fill me in on what had happened in my absence. Greg Meers, a farmer from nearby Battenville, had died in Larry Prager's dentistry chair. He was forty-seven and seemed to be in good health. He had received a substantial dose of laudanum for a root canal and his heart just stopped. He left a wife and two boys, nine and twelve.

"I knew him slightly," I said. "He dropped out of Wayne Karp's bunch some years ago to farm on his own. Sold snowmobiles back in the old days. Not a bad fellow."

"Dr. Prager is very upset."

"I expect he would be."

The main news, she said, was that the New Faith gang had commenced fixing the town water system.

"Bullock told me they were at it," I said.

"But some problem's developed and the water's been cut off altogether for three days now," she said. "People are coming around here looking for you, grousing, and demanding that something be done."

"I'll see about it first thing tomorrow."

"Those that stop by look shocked to find me here."

"What do you tell them?"

"I tell them I'm keeping house for you."

"Good. It's the truth. It's exactly what you're doing."

I very much enjoyed seeing somebody else bustling around in

my kitchen. In a little while, she served me a big square of the spinach and cheese pudding and a mound of scrambled eggs.

"May I sit with you?" she asked.

"Sure. Would you like some of this wine? It seems to me you could use some."

"Thank you, I will."

She got another glass out of the cupboard while I ate. Her cooking was first-rate.

"I want you to know a few things," she said.

"All right."

"My husband, Shawn, was a troubled person. Our life together was not what other people might think."

"I'm sorry."

"Don't be. It was what it was. For some time before he died, more than a year, we didn't sleep in the same room. It was his choice as much as mine, in case you're wondering. I think he had something going with the dairy girl up at Mr. Schmidt's. A girl named Hannah Palfrey. Came down from Granville a couple of years ago. Lives out at the farm now. I don't know much else about her. She was at the funeral, of course."

"Was she?"

"Oh, yes. A big cushion of a girl, especially up in here." Britney pushed up her compact breasts. "Shawn liked that. What could I do? It was a little late to go get implants."

Luckily, my mouth was full and I couldn't comment.

"Do you think Doctor Copeland could fix me up that way?" she said.

"There's nothing wrong with you."

Suddenly the electric lights went on and someone was screaming about Jesus on the radio. The power could not have been running for more than five full seconds, and then it cut out again.

"Mama! Mama!" Sarah came dashing into the kitchen and practically leaped into her mother's lap.

"It's all right, darling. It's over."

"Who's that man shouting?"

"Just a crazy preacher."

"Why?"

"Shouting makes them feel important."

"If I shout, will I be important?"

"You're already important. You don't have to shout. Maybe Mr. Robert will fix it so it won't come on again like that."

I went and hit the power button on the old stereo. In doing it, I was conscious of putting something behind me: the expectation that things would ever be normal again. There was a kind of relief in it. I also turned off the electric lights so they wouldn't come on and scare anybody again. Britney was standing now, holding Sarah on her hip, the way one would hold a toddler, except Sarah was way beyond that stage.

"We're going to bed now," Britney said. "There are some buckets of clean water by the sink, in case you want to wash up."

"Thank you." I was quite desperate to bathe. "Where did you get it?"

"The river."

"That's a long way to carry water."

"I'm strong," she said. "I hope you sleep well, Robert. Goodnight."

I watched as she went inside with the sleepy child, picked up the candle from the table beside the rocking chair, and climbed the stairs. Years ago, I'd watched Sandy go up those same stairs with a child on her hip.

Of all the things that no longer worked, we'd never lost our water before, because the town system relied on nothing more complicated than gravity. We'd never *not* had water, even during the worst times. The system had been put in place long ago and it was a given condition of life, like the oxygen content of the air. We never thought of it until the pressure went down that summer.

I had that outdoor shower rigged up off the summer kitchen with a steel tank over a wood-burning firebox, all built from salvage. I had soldered a supply pipe going into the tank, and a shower nozzle coming off the bottom. It had a piece of old screen over the top to keep bugs out. I brought a chair over, poured half a bucket of water in the tank, and made a little fire in the box with some splints. Over the years, I'd developed a pretty good sense of how long it took to heat up. In the meantime, I went and fetched my fiddle from inside. I hadn't played in weeks. I was eager to put on the machine-made strings that I picked up in Albany. I switched them out with the old gut strings, one at a time, so as not to unseat the bridge. My bow was in fine condition because two things we had plenty of were horsehair and rosin. The wound steel wire strings were wonderfully even, with a clear, bright sound. I played a slow, sad favorite tune called "The Greenwood Tree" in the key of D. In a little while, the water in the shower tank was heated. I got wet enough to soap up, shut it off, and used the rest to rinse. It left me a changed man.

# FORTY-TWO

A commotion of voices downstairs woke me up. The sun was well above the rooftops outside my bedroom window, so I must have slept unusually late. I threw on my summer work clothes and hurried down to find Victor Gasparry and two other local men there, Roger Hoad and Frank Arena, bullyragging Britney with complaints about the water situation.

"Where the hell you been?" Victor said when I appeared on the stairs. "They got this deal all screwed up—"

"We ain't had water for days now," Frank said.

"You've got to do something!" Roger said.

"All right, all right—"

"What the hell you mean taking on leadership here and then leaving your people high and dry for the better part of a week?" Victor said.

"Well, I'm sorry, but I had some other obligations."

"If we wanted nothing done, we could have stuck with old Dale."

"I'm going up there personally this morning and see what this is all about," I said, "and don't you ever come in here again raising a ruckus like this—there's a young child around!"

"And whose child, I'd like to know," Roger muttered.

I never did like him much, and now I liked him even less. He lived alone in the shell of the former Dunkin' Donuts and made matches by a secret process, they said, that involved boiling down large quantities of his own urine. I suppose the basic resource was easy enough for him to come by, since he drank so much. His matches were sold by the dozen at Einhorn's store. I kept mine in an old mint tin. He must have made enough off it to stay alive

because everybody needed matches and they were the only kind
you could get lately. They made a smell like fireworks and probably a quarter of them were duds. At this moment, I would have
liked to pick Roger up by the seat of his coarse-woven pants and
toss him into the street, but it occurred to me that the essence of
politics was to not act on your impulses.

"She's a child of someone who has passed away," I said. "And
in these times we had better look out for each other, or there is no
point to what remains of this life."

They left us in peace, but it would be a long day ahead.

The Union Grove water system began in a six-acre reservoir
created where Alder Brook was first dammed up in 1879. The
original crude wooden aqueduct system was replaced in 1921 with
buried iron pipes that carried the water by gravity to the town a
total of a mile and three-tenths. The earthen dam was replaced at
that time by one made of concrete. A treatment station was added
below in the 1950s where Hill Street dead-ends. It had not been
attended to since the station superintendent, Claude Wormsley,
died in the flu several years ago. We couldn't have got the chemicals to run in it now anyway.

The service road up to the dam was overgrown after years of
neglect, and a crew had evidently worked hard to clear it the past
week. The pungent smell of freshly cut trees and raw disturbed
earth made for an exciting aroma of enterprise. The scale of the
operation was impressive when you consider it was all done without machines or power tools. We hadn't mounted a collective effort like this in town for years. Some New Faith men were working
at a sawbuck there, cutting the felled trees into eight-foot lengths
to send back down below for stove wood.

I found Brother Jobe and a large gang of men further up in
the vicinity of the dam. The work crew included twenty New Faith
brothers, among them my recent companions Joseph, Elam, and
Seth, and five of our own town men: Tom Allison, Doug Sweetland, Rod Sauer, the mason, Jim VanMeter who used to run an ex-
cavation service, and Brad Kimmel, a talented fellow whose fix-it

shop was vital in a society that was forced to recycle virtually every-thing. It was the first time I'd seen Brother Jobe without his frock coat and some kind of necktie. He was dressed in muddy linens with his sleeves rolled up, and was right in there working with the rest of the men. I stood back and watched them lay a six-foot length of ten-inch-diameter concrete pipe in a trench, about a hundred yards from the dam. They had rigged up a portable crane out of timbers and a chain winch, with a box at the leverage end for field-stone counterweights, and this allowed them to jockey the heavy pipe into place. When the new concrete section was positioned to their satisfaction, they yanked up a length of rotted iron pipe from the trench.

At the conclusion of this operation, Brother Jobe called a break. News had obviously gotten around about our successful return from Albany with Bullock's boat crew, and the town men gathered round to greet me and ask me about what was now being called the Big Breakout. It frightened me to think back on it, about the horror and confusion of the moment, and the man with the red whiskers who pointed his gun at me, and what I did. But I was grateful that their spirits were high. Both the Union Grove men and the New Faith men seemed energized by the new experience of working shoulder to shoulder at a task that would make life in our town better for a change.

They had set up a camp kitchen under an open-walled tent nearby, and several New Faith women were in there along with townspeople Marsha Kimmel and Joanne Pettie turning out a mid-morning snack for the crew: big buckwheat-and-potato-flour flatcakes rolled up with butter and jam, and rose-hip tea to wash it down. Brother Jobe steered me over to the face of the dam while the others got their food. It was about fifteen feet high. A trench ran up to it and I could see a new copper fitting that had been run up into the original supply pipe at the base of the dam below the frost line.

"I hear you had quite an adventure in Albany," Brother Jobe said.

"We accomplished what we set out to."

"Yes, it come out pretty well," Brother Jobe said and cleared his throat. "I know that some people got hurt down there. From what Joseph told me, they asked for it. This is exactly the kind of lawless monkeyshines we saw everywhere coming up from Virginia. Gangsterism. Hostages and ransoms and whatnot. But I'm sorry you had to discharge a firearm at somebody."

"He was aiming to kill me."

"Quite a feeling, ain't it? Getting shot at."

"I would have been happy to pass on it."

"Yeah, well, this is the kind of country we live in now, old son. Your own people who speak English and wear the same kind of clothes as you do aiming to blow your brains out for sheer greed and sinfulness. That's why we have to build something lawful here, if we can. You see what I mean now?"

"I see where we've been pretty lucky here for the most part in recent years."

"You're goldurn straight," he said and spit into the trench. Then his face lit up all smiling. "Speaking of which, your dam's straight now too. Ain't that something? We'll be done with her before the end of the day if our Mr. Bullock manages to get one more length of new pipe up here."

"That's very good news indeed."

"You wouldn't believe what we dragged out of the intake," he said and jerked his chin up the face of the dam. "A dead coyote. Turtle shell the size of a dadblamed wheelbarrow, among other trash. Don't you all know that you got to pay attention to a system like this?"

"Things just slipped. Especially under Dale."

"You all been drinking dead coyote juice for months. You're lucky it didn't start no outbreak. You better appoint a water commissioner or some such of a responsible party first thing, and get some volunteers to come up here reg'lar and clean the trash out—"

Just then, we saw a wagon lumbering up the hill, creaking loudly under its load. It was a flatbed behind a team of ghostlike gray Percherons.

"Looks like we're in business now," Brother Jobe said.

The final length of cast concrete pipe lay tied down and padded up in the flatbed. We went down there. It was driven by Bullock's man Jack Hellinger. Jack leaped down from the driver's bench and came straight over to me while others held onto the harnesses and worked the crane around to unload the new pipe.

"Mr. Bullock sends his greetings and regards," Jack said, "and says that he wants to put on a grand levee tonight in honor of you and these brotherhood fellows who went and got back Tom and the boys in Albany. And if it isn't asking too much, he says, would you mind getting up your bunch to furnish the music? What do you say, Robert?"

"Why, tell him I'm honored as to the first part, and I'll be glad to arrange the second."

"That will please Mr. Bullock, I'm sure. Festivities to begin in the early evening. He says he'll send every wagon, carriage, and cart over to town to help fetch those that need it."

"We've got wagons too," Brother Jobe said. "Don't forget."

"We're going to roast a whole steer and more than a few hogs," Jack said. "The women are baking up a storm. And the liquor will flow."

"Hot diggity," Brother Jobe said. "You need any pointers in the barbeque department, we'll be glad to lend a hand."

# FORTY-THREE

The last length of cast concrete water conduit was laid down around two that afternoon. It was obvious we'd eventually have to replace more of the main trunk below, but for now the system was restored. We got the trench filled in and the worksite all squared away by late afternoon. Our boys put the word out around town about the levee at Bullock's as they filtered home. Tom Allison sent his boy off on horseback to alert the farmers outside of town, and many of the successful ones like Deaver, Weibel, and Zucker, who employed townspeople, let their hands off work early. Brother Jobe sent a wagon around with two "sisters," Helen and Emily, offering to take anyone's little children to an evening of babysitting over at the old high school with the New Faith youngsters. Even the weather seemed to cooperate as a cooling northerly breeze cleared out the persistent haze and dropped the humidity.

I went around myself to alert the music circle members about the engagement at Bullock's request that night—Eric Laudermilk, our guitar player, Dan Mullinex, flute and clarinet, Leslie Einhorn, cello, Charles Pettie, our bass player, Bruce Wheedon, second violin, and Andy Pendergast, who was delighted to hear we were called to play. I distributed the rest of those new wound steel strings I'd picked up in Albany. As far as I recalled, Bullock had a piano on the premises somewhere, but Andy wanted to bring his harmonium out just in case. On my way home, going down Van Buren Street, I ran into Loren pulling a handcart heaped with manure from Allison's stable, I suppose for composting in the rectory garden. Loren's face was bright red with exertion, and half moons of sweat darkened the underarms of his frayed blue shirt from pulling the load uphill. We both paused by the cemetery fence in the shade of a horse chestnut.

"Remember Gatorade?" Loren said.

"You know me. I don't think of the old days as much as you."

"Well that stuff could really pick a guy up. I miss it. I really do."

"Try some honey and sumac punch. That'll work."

"For what it's worth, I never gave a shit about the chemicals or the fake coloring they put in it."

"Give me an ice cold beer," I said. "Straight out of a refrigerator. With dewdrops running down the side of the bottle."

"Dream on," Loren said.

Screen doors slapped and voices carried all over town as households prepared for levee, singing as they pulled clothes off the line, neighbors visiting among neighbors to borrow finery, harnessing their horses—the few who had one. Children caught the spirit and squealed as they were packed off for babysitting.

"We got the water back on again," I said.

"Hooray for that," Loren said. "I had to jump in the river last night or Jane Ann wouldn't let me in the bedroom." Loren looked momentarily uncomfortable, as though a passing cloud had brought on a chill. He wiped his brow with the back of his hand. "You're quite the hero. First the fire, then you shove Dale off the plank, then the Big Breakout, and now the water system finally gets fixed."

"Do you think I'm out for brownie points?"

"Gosh no."

"We can't not have running water," I said. "That would be the last straw for civilized life around here."

"It's been a harsh week without it. I can tell you that."

"Anyway, it was the New Faith and Bullock that solved the water problem, not me."

"Remember that laundry idea of mine?" Loren said.

"Yeah?"

"This Brother Jobe seems interested in getting it going. We had a sit-down about it, him and me."

"Did you?"

"He likes the idea."

"They must have a lot of wash every week."

"They've got manpower too. I believe he's serious."

"Kudos to you then."

"Not out for any kudos. But I could still use your help."

"Okay. Sure. I'll help," I said.

"Can you get someone to make sure the titles are clear on the Wayland-Union Mill property?"

"I'll ask Sam Hutto."

"And then maybe you and I can walk through the place and talk about what it would take constructionwise, where things might go."

"Sure, I'll do that."

"Brother Jobe's got a decent metalsmith over there."

"I saw that they put a new copper fitting on the water line outflow."

"I expect they could fabricate some big pot kettles."

"I expect that's so."

"Things are happening again in this town, aren't they?"

"Apparently."

"It's a good thing, isn't it?" Loren said.

"I think so."

"It's like we've been living in . . . in Jell-O. Trapped. Immobilized. Watching everything around us slowly fall apart through this thick, gummy, transparent prison of Jell-O, and unable to do anything about it."

"To me, it was like time had stopped."

"So, what do you make of him?" Loren said.

"Jobe? He's not so bad beneath all the bluster, if you can get beneath it," I said. "Well, I really don't know what they're up to over there. I mean, underneath the trappings of brotherhood and fellowship, who knows what they do amongst themselves."

"Like what? Orgies?" Loren said.

"That wasn't what I was thinking."

"Human sacrifice?"

"I don't know. After all, it's what we used to call a cult."

206 JAMES HOWARD KUNSTLER

"Then we better not drink the Kool-Aid. Have you been drinking the Kool-Aid, Robert?"

"No."

"Because right now there's our people, you know, us, the town, and our church, and there's this New Faith bunch that has all of a sudden become a rather large presence in our world here. I'm hoping we can coexist, Robert, because they obviously have something to offer as long as we don't drink that old Kool-Aid."

"I'm not going over to them, if that's what you mean," I said. "Don't worry."

"Because it could be a kind of narrow line we're walking."

"We'll walk it."

"Not to mention we've got Mr. Bullock setting up like a Scottish laird with his own peasants and everything, and Wayne Karp and his maniacs up North Road on top of everything else. And sometimes lately I worry about us getting squished in the middle of it all."

"I know. I think about it too."

"I've heard there was gunplay down in Albany."

"I think I killed a man there, Loren."

He flinched slightly.

"Wow. Tell me about it."

So I did. All of it. The Raynor farm. Brother Minor probably killing that donkey drover. What Joseph told me that night in Slavin's hotel about their difficulties in Pennsylvania. Dan Curry. The guy with the red beard firing at me.

"I don't know if I feel bad about taking somebody's life or just afraid that I'll be held responsible for it," I said.

"By whom? God?"

"I keep on thinking about the legal system coming after me. And then I realize that there isn't any. There's nothing left. No real police, courts. No state government. Nothing. But I'm pretty sure I killed the man."

"Your conscience is weighing on you," Loren said.

"Yes. And now I've got Shawn Watling's widow in my house."

"I've heard. That kind of complicates things, doesn't it?"

"I'm sure people will get the wrong idea," I said. "They already have."

"How'd she come to settle under your roof?"

"Well, her house burned down, you know."

"I know. There are empty houses in town."

"Do you think I should throw her out?"

"Not at all. Are you banging her?"

It was my turn to flinch.

"No," I said.

"Because that could make you feel bad, given that her husband's only been in the ground a few weeks, and you happened to be present when he got killed."

"Do you think I did it, Loren?"

"No. But I understand why things are weighing on your mind."

"It's pretty straightforward," I said.

"I'm sure it is."

"These really aren't normal times."

"Quite so."

"Plus, there's the child."

"God bless the child."

"Are you being facetious, Loren?"

"I shouldn't be even if I am. Forgive me."

"All right. Are you going out to Bullock's tonight?"

"I wouldn't miss it for the world," Loren said. "I might even tie one on out there."

# FORTY-FOUR

The levee at Stephen Bullock's farm was the greatest social event around Washington County in decades, even going back into the old days, when television and all the other bygone diversions held people hostage in their homes after the sun went down, and you could hardly pry people out of their living rooms—as we used to call the place where the TVs lived. In the new times, Bullock's levee beat the Harvest Ball at Hebron, the Spring Frolic in Battenville, the Labor Day Picnic at Holyrood's orchard, and even the Christmas levee we put on every year at the First Congregational. Bullock's levee brought us out of ourselves, out of a dark wilderness of the spirit where we had sojourned for so long in anxiety and isolation.

As the afternoon merged into evening, everybody who could muster a wheeled vehicle and a horse or team began marshalling them in the vicinity of our church for the trip over. Bullock sent several wagons to town as promised, while the New Faith had its own too. Altogether they made a train of horse-drawn vehicles that stretched a quarter-mile long heading west into the sun, which still hung ten degrees above the treetops. Britney decided to stay behind, a relief to me, since it would have made an awkward public statement for us to appear as a couple at a festive event like this, apart from how things actually were between us. I didn't try to talk her out of it.

I rode over in Terry Einhorn's wagon with Leslie and her cello, Eric Laudermilk, and the Russos. Eric and I broke out our instruments en route, playing "Sail Away Ladies" and "Grey Eagle," and some other lively numbers as we rode past the vacant car showrooms and strip mall ruins at the edge of town. Leslie kept her cello under wraps since the rig had no springs to speak of. Eric was him-

self a cidermaker of some distinction, and we traded slugs from
the bottle he brought along, so we were already in a mellow frame
of mind when Terry followed the rest of the wagons into one of
Bullock's new-mown hay fields where we hitched them to picket
lines for the evening.

Bullock had strung colored Christmas bulbs all around the big
circular drive between the barns, the workshops, and his house. It
reminded me of the patio of a popular bar in Key West where I
had gotten drunk a long time ago. Many of the Union Grove people
were not aware that Bullock had his own hydroelectric setup, and
as they were informed, their reactions ran from amazement to veiled
jealousy. Sam Hutto just goggled at the lights like a kid at a carnival. I heard Debra Gooding say to Maggie Furnival, "I don't see
why he can't send some of that juice over our way—I'd pay the
sonofabitch!"

A beverage bar was set up on a long table under the arbor off
the kitchen, with pitchers of Bullock's own cider, sparkling and jack,
and beer, and jugs of whiskey, and a vast punchbowl with some sweet,
potent brew flavored with lemon verbena and raspberries. Across the
way from the bar stood more long tables groaning with puddings,
new potato salad, sugar snaps, radishes, pickles, sauerkraut, creamed
new onions, corn bread, cakes (real cakes made with wheat flour),
pies (ditto the flour), berry crumbles, cookies and confections, butternut fondants, even a tray of fudge made from chocolate—an in-
gredient that few of us had seen for some years. Among all these
things the Bullocks had placed enormous bouquets of purple loose-
strife, now coming into bloom wherever the ground was damp, and
black-eyed Susans. Removed from the center of things, where the
smoke would not be bothersome, they had set up a barbeque operation. Over one fire, a pig roasted on an iron spit turned by a teenage
boy who nipped at a cup of something as he worked the crank. Over
another fire, a Bullock servant wrangled rows of beefsteaks on a steel
mesh grill. Next to him, yet another Bullock man turned sausages
with tongs. Meanwhile, the procession of wagons kept rolling into
the adjacent hay field, and a steady stream of townspeople and New

Faith people entered the courtyard until the outdoor room grew crowded. The aroma of grilling meat seemed to affect the people like a powerful drug, as much as their first stimulating drinks of the evening. For the first time since they came to town, the New Faith people of both sexes mixed openly and easily with the regular Union Grovers and Bullock's folks. The din of conversation was as intoxicating as the beverages.

Here and there around the big circular drive, barrels stood on end, each presenting a deployed basket of—what?—triangular corn tortilla chips of the kind that used to be manufactured by the great snack corporations of yore and were the ubiquitous national party food until that part of our history ended. Evidently Bullock's cooks had made them from scratch for the occasion, along with a pickled hot pepper condiment—salsa!—to scoop up. The sweet herbaceous aroma of marijuana also began wafting around the courtyard. I saw Bullock himself take a hit on a pipe passed by Todd Zucker. A few of the New Faith men indulged too.

I had a toke or two myself, on top of the cider coming over and a tumbler of Bullock's own since I got there, and I was reaching a plateau of expansive amiability, shall we say, when Andy Pendergast took me by the elbow into the carriage barn.

"Isn't this great?" he said, excited as a little kid.

"It's something, all right."

The vehicles were removed from the barn for the evening and the place was all cleaned and beautifully lighted with those strings of little white minibulbs that fancy restaurants used to always put in their potted fig trees. Along the far side of the enormous room, going lengthwise, a plank stage was set up. The lumber was fresh cut. You could smell it. Somehow Bullock had come up with a sound system—four microphones on boom stands and two speakers at the sides coming out of a one-hundred-watt amp with a mixer. We tested the damn things and they actually worked. There was no piano, however, so Andy and I went to get his harmonium out of the wagon he'd come in.

On the way back, we heard that they were serving hot dogs in real wheat flour buns, and I went over to check it out as soon as we had Andy's keyboard set up. You could have your dog with sauerkraut or sweet pickle relish and a coarse, grainy mustard. It was just like Bullock to serve such a thing for the sheer theatricality of it, to demonstrate how the old luxuries were all available at his plantation, in case anyone was thinking of coming over to live there and work for him. The way the crowd carried on, you'd think these were the greatest culinary delicacies ever contrived by mankind. The truth was Bullock's hot dogs were far superior to any commercial hot dog I'd ever had back in the old days. Everything was handmade, including the sauerkraut and the mustard. The dogs themselves tasted more like bratwursts, and the buns were just out of the oven. The fact that so many of us were either drunk or stoned or both made them seem even more amazing, I suppose. Anyway, I ate two: one with kraut and mustard and one with sweet relish, and when I was done I went and got a chunk of beefsteak the size of my hand.

By now, a dense purple twilight had gathered and the courtyard took on an enchanted glow. The stars came out, fireflies began twinkling among the colored lights, and the moon was rising above the woods behind the field full of wagons. None of the New Faith women—thirty-five of them altogether—were older than middle age and most of them in their twenties, with a few apparently older teens, including the shy, pretty girl I saw that night we first came across Brother Jobe in the wagon, coming back from fishing. The New Faith women dressed differently than our people. They wore a kind of uniform: a long, herb-dyed linen skirt and a sun-bleached white muslin blouse buttoned primly at the throat. The only real difference between them was in the sleeves. Some long, some short, and some no sleeves. But their figures were on display despite the superficial modesty. They apparently did not wear anything in the way of underwear. Perhaps they dressed for the summer heat, but their muslin blouses were surprisingly sheer, and here and there, if one of them was standing in the light a certain way, you could see her figure outlined through the fabric. Our women were generally older, and despite the décolletage on display, and the variety of fabrics and styles they wore, they came off more modestly than the New Faithers.

I was standing by the bar, holding a piece of beefsteak between my thumb and forefinger, trying not to look like a slob, with a glass of Bullock's excellent sparkling hard cider in the other hand, when one of the New Faith ladies came up to me.

"Hello there," she said. "My name's Annabelle."

"You're a handsome creature, Annabelle," I said. It was the weed and the cider talking. I was feeling frisky for the first time in years.

"Are you somebody's husband?"

"No, ma'am," I said. I felt a passing twinge of guilt for failing to say I used to be.

"Do you know the Lord?"

"Bullock and I go back through the years."

"No, the Lord of heaven and earth," she said.

"Oh, him. Jesus."

"Yeah, him."

"Probably not in the way you mean."

"Can I have a bite?"

I held out the chunk of beefsteak so she could have some, and she nibbled off a piece, gripping my hand to steady it in the process, and giving an excellent demonstration of how her lips worked.

"Would you like to know the Lord?" she said. The buzz of chatter was so loud we practically had to shout into each other's ears. I could smell the scent of her skin and fresh laundry.

"I'll pass for now," I said.

"Knowing Jesus is like an orgasm, I find."

"That's more than I could bear," I said. "It'd give me the vapors."

"Are you mocking me?"

"No. Where are you from, Annabelle?"

"Raleigh-Durham area, originally."

"And what were your people originally?"

"Greek," she said and covered her bashful smile with four long fingers. "My daddy had seven pizza shops."

"Were they Eastern Orthodox?"

"No, they were just regular pizza, but you could get lots of toppings."

"No, I meant your parents."

Annabelle giggled and kind of slapped my shoulder and then sort of pressed herself into me so I could feel the yielding curves of her torso.

"They were pagans," she said. "Our religion was pizza. You're cute."

Just then I heard an electronic crackle from inside the barn. Bullock was onstage. He started making a speech. His amplified voice was garbled from where we stood, far over by the barbeque. There was applause. A lot of the crowd had begun to migrate inside the barn. More speech, more applause. Then Brother Jobe took over the mike, and whatever he was saying provoked several outbursts of laughter as well as applause. He knew how to work a crowd.

"Would you like to stroll up into yonder field with me?" Annabelle said.

I was amazed at her forwardness. And, I must confess, more than a little aroused at that point.

"Did Brother Jobe put you up to this, by any chance?"

"Huh?"

Something about her smile told me she was playing dumb.

"I think there's more going on here than meets the eye."

"I swear I don't know what you're talking about," Annabelle said, still beaming radiantly.

"You're very charming, Annabelle," I said, "but your bunch has got to stop trying to recruit me. Especially on such a lovely night as this when we should all relax and have a good time."

Just then, Loren found me and took my elbow and dragged me away into the barn, where I had to get up on stage with Joseph and the three other brothers who I went down to Albany with, and Tom and Skip and the boys from the *Elizabeth*, and there was more clapping and hugging and good fellowship and salutations. I still had the rest of the beefsteak in my fingers. Finally Bullock said the music and dancing would commence presently, and the rest of the Union Grove music circle came up and traded places on stage with the heroes of the occasion, and I got my fiddle out of its case, and the others started tuning up to Andy's harmonium, and I could see Annabelle way over to the side with Brother Jobe, no doubt reporting the outcome of her mission. The cheeky rascal saw me looking at him, raised his cider glass in my direction, and gave me a big wink.

# FORTY-FIVE

We warmed up with some nice loose-limbed old-time tunes starting with "The Maysville Road," "Big Scioty," "Saint Anne's Reel,"
"Lost Indian," "Granny Will Your Dog Bite," "Speed the Plow,"
"Hell among the Yearlings," and "Blackberry Blossom." We played
the tunes in clumps, medley-style, and either we were in especially
fine form, or we were pretty lit, or both, because we all swapped
glances around the stage, Andy and Dan and Eric and Charles and
Bruce and Leslie and me, and all of us had big goofy smiles plas-
tered on our faces like we hadn't felt so good in a long time, and
how could we be so dumb as to have neglected the music circle all
these weeks. And the crowd below got into the spirit right away,
with no bashful waiting around for somebody else to step out on
the dance floor first. They all went right to it. By the time we got
some traction on "Big Scioty," what do you know but Brother
Minor emerged from the crowd, jumped up on stage, and began
calling figures. You could tell that he knew what he was doing. Between calls, he plugged a Jew's harp in his mouth and twanged
along with our tunes—another of his strange talents.

When we completed the opening medleys, Loren came over to
the stage with a big pitcher of cider for us. Jane Ann, I couldn't fail
to notice, lingered off to the side of the dance floor with her arms
wrapped around herself, as if holding on for dear life. She was wearing a beautiful old peacock blue sequined satin gown that seemed to
hark way back to the mid-twentieth century, something that Bar-
bara Stanwyck would have worn to the Academy Awards in 1953.
It frightened me to think how gone the past was, and to see Jane
Ann looking so beautiful and so desolate. But then Eric sent a pipe
around the circle, and we hit the cider again and started in on the

main part of the program, which was the contra dance part, the pieces we really excelled at, the English eighteenth-century dance tunes out of John Playford's English Dancing Master anthologies. These tunes included "Juice of the Barley," "Newcastle," "Lord Burghley's Maggot" (meaning a "whim," not a worm), "Liliburlero," "The Chestnut," "The Rakes of Rochester," "Gathering Peascods," and a few of the beautiful Irish O'Carolan tunes that Shawn Watling had liked so much: "Sheebeg and Sheemore," "Planxty Irwin," and "Fanny Power." The Union Grove people knew what to do, but everybody else was confused by the antique steps, which were more complex than square dance figures, and the New Faith people stood off to the sides watching. Eventually, a few at a time, they ventured to join in the lines and quadrilles on the dance floor, and our people showed them every consideration in teaching them how it all went.

Our set ran over an hour. At the break, I climbed down from the stage and was immediately engulfed by Elsie DeLong, Cody's wife, a rather large woman of about sixty, with breasts like Hubbard squashes, and evidently quite drunk. She planted her lips on mine and said, "I'll take him," to her surrounding girlfriends, who howled and cackled. I slipped out of her clutches and made off through the crowd. Near the door, Brother Jobe took me aside by the arm.

"The jenny's yours," he said.

"Huh?"

"That little donk you all rescued down in Albany. You can have her and the cart she come with. I daresay you could use her."

"Why, thank you. But I have nowhere to keep her."

"You can keep her over our way for now. Come and get her when you need her."

"Okay. Gosh. I appreciate that."

"I'd like to breed her to our jack, though, if you don't mind."

"By all means."

"It can only help to have a few more donks. Especially a younger jack. Oh, say, suppose you could manage a turn at the old 'Virginia Reel' when you boys come back on? It'd mean a lot to my people."

"Sure," I said.

"Didn't you like that other little gift I sent your way?"

"I don't want to seem ungrateful, but . . ."

"You're a hard case, old son."

"Just an old heathen."

He reached up and tousled my hair like he was my camp coun-selor and then peeled off to flirt with some of the Union Grove ladies.

I made my way out of the barn. It was mercifully cooler in the fresh air, and the night smelled sweetly of hay. My head swam, as much from playing hard for an hour as from all the cider and pot. I found a quiet spot in the vicinity of the bar where I had run into Annabelle earlier. Stephen Bullock stepped up to me there.

"Robert," he said. He proffered a pitcher but I declined for the moment.

"Swell party, Stephen," I said and burped. "Pardon."

"The pleasure is ours, I assure you. Tell me something: are you shacked up with the young widow of the unfortunate fellow who got shot some weeks back?"

"I wouldn't call it that."

"Doesn't look so good."

"People have got the wrong idea," I said.

"I'm going to have to convene a grand jury on that killing."

"I thought sooner or later you would."

"And you'll be called to give testimony."

"I expected that too."

"Just so you know."

Musicians were tuning up over the PA system inside the barn. It seemed like it had been an awful short break. Something sounded off.

"Who's that playing inside?" I said.

"That'd be our boys," Bullock said. "I told them they could play the breaks. They're not as good as your bunch, but it'll be good practice for them to play in front of strangers."

We stood there listening for a while. It was a weird mix: more than one guitar, banjo, bass, a trombone, and a saxophone in there somewhere. When the tuning was done, they went into a raggedy Dixieland version of "Bye Bye Blackbird," the kind of thing you might have heard on a Carnival Cruise in the old days.

"Hey, let me ask you something, Stephen: just what do you suppose I'm doing with that young widow?"

"I really don't know," he said. "Is she here with you tonight?"

"No, she's back in town, because she knows everybody would be giving her the hairy eyeball."

"That was prudent, at least."

"Goddammit, Stephen."

"I'm not being facetious."

"Do you think she should go out and get a job selling real estate or something? Maybe rent an apartment and mail-order a sofa from Crate and Barrel?"

"Well, obviously . . ."

"Her house burned down and she has a little girl."

"She can come over here and live," he said. "We could use a young female. And a child too. Our people are not reproducing that well."

"You're as bad as Brother Jobe."

"Well, we've got similar problems, both of us having to look out for large organizations with complicated social considerations in extraordinary times. You think this all just runs itself?"

"I'm well aware of your responsibilities, Stephen."

"Hell, you're welcome to come over here, Robert, and bring the young widow and child with you. I'd build you all a house if you did."

"Thanks, but I like living in town."

"The invitation stands if you change your mind."

He patted me on the shoulder and headed back to the party. The band had moved on to "Mack the Knife." It made me wonder what Bertolt Brecht might think of how we were living now. It made me painfully aware of how *over* the twentieth century was. Even more oddly, it prompted me to remember the night long ago when, by happenstance, I sat through part of a Wayne Newton show in Las Vegas. Where did Wayne Newton go when the USA went to shit? I was more stoned than I had realized. And so when I saw Jane Ann come toward me in her sparkling blue gown in the moonlight I was dazzled by the sight of her.

She took me by the hand, and we walked up a grassy lane into the orchard behind Bullock's house. She didn't have to say anything. I was suddenly on fire for her. We sat down in the cool grass up in the orchard, and she hiked her gown over her head in a single swift motion so that she was just pale skin, silvery hair, and fragrance lying before me in the grass. I was less agile getting free of my own clothing, and my hunger for her was, as always, sharpened by the ache of my moral failure. Then we were upon each other, and everything beyond the field of our senses fell into darkness for a while as we enacted the old urgencies.

Afterward we lay side by side under a plum tree looking at the stars through boughs laden with early fruit, waiting for our hearts to stop pounding. Bullock's band was playing an old standard I recognized, but I couldn't remember the title to save my life.

"What's that tune?" I said.

"Beyond the Sea," Jane Ann said. "Has she come to your bed yet?"

"No," I said.

"She will."

"Maybe she's got more moral fiber than I do."

"Women are not moral animals," she said.

"What a thing to say."

"Look at me: the minister's wife."

"I see someone sweet and beautiful and kind."

I heard voices and saw shapes moving darkly up the grassy lane. Jane Ann and I automatically shielded our faces. A man and a woman tumbled past us perhaps ten yards away. Apparently they didn't see us. The woman tripped on something and giggled. I thought it sounded like Annabelle. The man said, "Sssshhhh," drunkenly. Whoever it was, he had a beard, so he was not one of the New Faith men. He helped her up. They both laughed and continued on. You had to marvel at the determination of that bunch.

"You must think I'm pathetic," Jane Ann said when they were out of earshot.

"You don't have to run yourself down."

"What *do* you think of me?"

"You're a human being in an odd situation in a strange time."

"How diplomatic."

"It's how it is."

"Maybe we're just wicked, Robert."

"I wouldn't encourage you to think so."

"It's getting to Loren."

"Do you two ever talk about this?"

"Are you crazy?" she said.

"I'm not there when you two are alone. I don't know what you talk about."

"Do you ever talk to Loren about how you're fucking his wife when the two of you are off on one of your fishing adventures?"

"Of course not. Do you want me to?"

"Don't be ridiculous."

"Maybe we should just stop this, then."

"If you do, I'll kill myself."

"That's a heckuva thing to say."

Jane Ann started to cry quietly. "Why her and not me?"

"I can't bust up you and Loren."

"Why not?"

"Do you want to leave him? Is that what you're saying?"

"I don't know," she said and cried some more.

We didn't speak for a while. Jane Ann continued crying quietly, squeezing my hand. Meanwhile the music had stopped, and then I heard instruments tuning up again, including a fiddle, Bruce Wheedon of our bunch, since the others hadn't had a fiddle, and I realized I had to get back down there.

"We're on again," I said. "I have to go back in and play."

"Okay," she said. "You go. I'll come down in a little while, after a decent interval."

"You know if you killed yourself I would be very sad and guilty for the rest of my life."

"I know," she said. And I then left her up there under the plum tree.

# FORTY-SIX

I grabbed another pitcher of cider from the bar on my way inside, relieved to be back in the crowd with the electric lights and the laughter. We played some more square dance tunes, including a grand version of Brother Jobe's requested "Virginia Reel." Eric's pipe went around again, and someone passed a whiskey jug and after a while we found our way into the old rock and roll songs, starting out with "The Midnight Hour" and moving through "Bring It on Home to Me," "Under the Boardwalk," "Twist and Shout," "I Can't Get No Satisfaction," and "Be My Baby." It felt pretty odd with only acoustic instruments—and my fiddle parts on the last two numbers were flat-out ridiculous—but Andy and Eric were both good singers (and had been in electric bands when they were kids), and Linda Allison, Bonnie Sweetland, and Jeanette Copeland climbed onstage to sing backup, vamping it up with all the little hand claps and steps in unison, and the saxophone player from Bullock's band joined in too, and it was sure fun, whatever it sounded like. Out on the dance floor, everybody was dancing in the old style, orgiastically, with hips swinging and arms flailing—even Brother Jobe and the New Faithers—and things got a little blurry for me after that.

I don't remember much about loading out, except when we stopped playing—or rather, got too wasted to keep playing—Bullock's servants went around the barn with trays full of grilled hamburgers on real buns, stacks of them, which everybody greeted with astonished delight. I gobbled down two and stuck one in my pocket. Then I was in the box of Jerry Copeland's wagon, lying in fresh hay looking up at the stars with several other people from town, jouncing our way down the rough roads back home. We were all too tired and drunk to talk anymore. I fell asleep more than once, and remained mostly asleep through the journey until the rig stopped in front of my house on Linden Street and Jeanette shook me awake. You could hear horses clomping elsewhere around town as other wagons wended through other streets, and here and there a cry of "goodnight," and screen doors slapping. Laughter.

I was careful to close my screen door gently so as not to wake anybody, but discovered that Britney was up anyway. She was sitting in a big stuffed chair in the living room with a candle burning on the table beside her. She wasn't reading or anything, just sitting huddled and small under an old blanket in a tattered cotton nightdress.

"How was the levee?" she said.

"I wouldn't know where to start," I said. I had sobered up some on the ride home, so I didn't say anything foolish like *You should have been there*. "Bullock served hamburgers before everybody left for home. Real ones on real buns."

"That's nice," Britney said.

"I brought one back for you."

It was not easy to extract the thing from my pocket. When I did, it was all compacted into the bun, a soggy mess with a deal of pocket lint around the edge. I tried to clean it off as I held it out for her.

"That's all right."

"There was nothing to wrap it up in."

"Don't worry about it."

"No tin foil or plastic wrap. Not even a paper napkin."

"I understand," she said.

I put the squashed, linty hamburger on the table beside her. The clock on the mantelpiece said ten after three.

"What are you doing up so late?" I said.

She seemed to shudder in the dim light but didn't reply.

"Are you okay?" I said.

She drew her knees up under the blanket to make herself look even smaller than she actually was. I went over and stooped down beside her chair.

"What's wrong."

"Those men from the general were here," she said. Her voice quavered.

"Who was?"

"Wayne Karp and two others."

"They came in here? Inside this house?"

"Yes."

"You let them in?"

"They let themselves in."

"What'd they want?"

"I think they were looking to steal things. I surprised them. Just being here."

"What happened?"

Britney sighed and made a choked sound like a sob that couldn't quite come out.

"Tell me," I said.

"They demanded 'refreshments.' That very word."

"What'd you do?"

"I told them there was some milk and leftover corn bread. They went out to the kitchen on their own and rooted around and found some of your apple jack."

"Did they take anything else?"

"I don't think so."

"Is that all?"

"No."

"What else?"

"They touched me."

"Touched you?"

"In my personal places."

"What do you mean by 'touching'?"

"I mean touching."

"Nothing more?"

Britney looked into her lap and shook her head. "They talked about coming back another time for more 'refreshments.' They like that word."

All kinds of blustery phrases echoed through my head. *If they set foot in here again, I'll kill 'em*, and things like that which I had probably heard on TV years ago. I didn't say any of them. I was sober enough to know that they sounded stupid.

"Where was Sarah?" I said.

"She was upstairs. Asleep, I think."

"Look, forgive me for asking, but I want to make sure I understand—they didn't force you to have sex?"

"No, they didn't rape me."

"Look at me. Listen. Two things: I'll make sure you're not left in this position again. And these guys will pay some kind of price for what they did."

She nodded.

"I don't think this is the only house they went into," she said.

She didn't especially want to move out of that chair, but I persuaded Britney to come upstairs, and I literally tucked her into her bed. Her room was Daniel's—my son's—old room. His collection of birds' nests was arrayed along a narrow shelf that I had built for that purpose high up along one wall. There was a large map of the world salvaged from the final days of the high school. On it, the great pink amoeba of Russia was still called the Soviet Union and Germany was divided in two. Britney had no belongings of her own to speak of, everything she owned having been consumed in the fire that destroyed her house. Some of the other women in town had given her a few items of clothing, a comb, a pin cushion, and sewing implements.

"We can find a place to store Daniel's things if you like," I said, "so you could make it more like your own room."

She nodded. The sadness she carried was a palpable force, like gravity doubled. I wondered, if someone tried to lift her up now, would she weigh two hundred pounds?

As I sat there on the bed, her hand searched along the thin summer covers until it found mine. I held it a moment, then joined my other hand, and she hers, and we held each other's hands for a while.

"The world has become such a wicked place," she said quietly, just a statement of fact.

"There's goodness here too."

"Where is it?"

"In all the abiding virtues. Love, bravery, patience, honesty, justice, generosity, kindness. Beauty too. Mostly love."

"I'm afraid sometimes that we drove those things out of existence."

"No, we carry them in our hearts. They're always with us."

"I don't know what's in my heart anymore. It's too dark to see."

"Light follows darkness."

"Thank you for saying so," she said, and let go of my hands. She rolled over on her side and I left her there.

I looked in on Sarah before I went to bed. She was in what had been Genna's room, full of the little wooden dolls and puppets I had made over the years, with doll and puppet clothing made by Sandy. Sarah was fast asleep, small, innocent, and perfect.

# FORTY-SEVEN

Larry Prager was out in the extensive garden behind his house (and dentistry practice), on Locust Street, on the northeast side of town, not far from the defunct Wayland-Union Mill. I liked to come over to his place because he was one of the few people in town who still had a dog. Bogie was some kind of a retriever-terrier mix, about fifty pounds with a terrier beard. He was a playful, happy dog, and he met me as I came around back of the house.

Larry's garden was among the most beautiful and productive in town, a half acre of well-established raised beds with bluestone paths between them and a twelve-foot-high south-facing brick wall with pear and plum trees espaliered against it, and a full complement of berry bushes in disciplined ranks on the other three sides. He cultivated intensively, getting several crops of different things out of some beds in a season. When I came along that morning, he was tying up tomato vines to their stakes. He watched me come through the garden gate—which I had reconstructed for him the year before—with Bogie jumping up at my side. The dog let me rub his belly as I stooped down to talk to Larry.

"They love this heat," Larry said of his tomatoes.

"It looks like they're really taking off. Hey, I'm sorry I haven't been able to get back to the job here," I said.

Their garage had originally started out as a carriage barn when the place was first built in the 1870s. It was upgraded to a garage sometime in the 1920s, and the original cupola was removed. I was converting it back to a barn now. It required a new cupola because the hayloft needed to be well ventilated. Larry and Sharon had plans to acquire a horse of their own. Larry bartered with most of his patients. I was one of his patients, of course. Sometimes he paid me in dental work and sometimes in cash money. Under the circumstances, they lived well.

"I've heard about your recent exploits, Robert," he said, "so there's no pressure at this end. And it's nice to have the water back on again too, thank you very much."

"You can thank New Faith. And Bullock for making the pipe. I just came by to check in, let you know you were not forgotten."

I stood there watching him tie off some more vines. Something seemed wrong because usually Larry was a much more voluble person, always ready to palaver.

"We missed you over at the levee last night," I said.

"I couldn't go. A man died in my chair last week."

He was referring to Greg Meers.

"Yes, I heard. Terrible."

"It wouldn't have been decent."

I was unprepared for what happened next. Larry, a self-possessed, dignified man of forty-nine with a professorial air and a graceful bearing, just fell apart. He began weeping, quietly at first and then with greater and greater vehemence. After a while, he put his fists up against his ears, like a little boy protecting himself against a flurry of physical blows, and keened in the utmost despondency. Finally he put his head down against ground, like a Muslim at prayers, and sobbed into the dirt. I crouched down beside him to try to give him some comfort, but I honestly didn't know what to say. I just patted him on the shoulders. Bogie, the dog, tried to nuzzle him. Larry kept at it for a couple of minutes, and then with equally surprising suddenness pulled himself together. I stayed there with him. He eventually kneeled upright again, sniffled some, dried his cheeks with each sleeve, and finally gave a big fraught sigh as if letting go of all that emotion.

"It got to me, Robert," he said.

"I guess it did."

"He appeared healthy. He just slipped away."

"Nobody's blaming you."

Larry let out another tortured sigh. "I don't know if I can practice anymore."

I listened to the birds and insects for a moment, noticing that the peas in one of the raised beds had about gone by. He had peppers coming along nicely in another bed.

"We don't have another dentist in town, Larry."

He was scribing in the dirt with a pair of Japanese garden shears that he had probably gotten from some fancy mail-order catalog in the old days. In his other hand he held a bunch of cloth ties, torn from some old rags, which he was using to secure his tomatoes to their stakes.

"He needed a root canal so I had to put him under pretty deep," Larry said. "I finished the damn tooth before I even realized he wasn't breathing anymore. Man, when I got out of dental school, we had no idea what we were in for. All that fabulous high-tech stuff we took for granted, gone! Now I've got to put patients under crude general anesthesia and drill with a damned foot treadle. It's madness. You know, what really bothers me is the thought that I'm going to lose some little kid the same way. There's no precision with these crude opiates."

"It's better than nothing, isn't it?"

"The effective dose is sometimes close to the lethal dose," he said.

"Even back in the old days, in the big hospitals, the docs lost patients," I said. "What they gained in technological magic, they lost in bureaucracy and inattention and sloppiness."

"Dentists didn't lose patients," he said. "This is not thoracic surgery."

"Well, whatever else is happening, you've still got your knowledge and skill. And the people here in town aren't dying of simple abscesses."

Larry resumed tying up his tomato vines.

"This Greg Meers had a couple of kids," he said. "God knows what happens to them now. There's no social safety net. There's nothing."

"He used to run with Wayne Karp's bunch," I said. "The wife too. Maybe they'll end up back there, in Karptown."

Larry glanced up at me.

"They came around here last night," he said. "Wayne Karp. And two of his cronies."

"Tell me about it."

"Sharon and I were back here in the garden, sitting outside around sundown. Bogie ran barking around the front of the house. I went in from the back and found Wayne on the entrance portico with his, uh, associates, when I opened the front door."

"Did they seem surprised to find you at home?"

"Actually, I assumed at first that they came over because of what happened to Greg Meers. I was afraid they were going to, I don't know, rough me up, or maybe something worse."

"Did they do anything?"

"No. But they did seem kind of surprised that I answered the door, now that you mention it. I wasn't too comfortable finding them there, of course."

"Did they say what they wanted?"

"They said the town hired them to act as security for the night while everybody went off to Bullock's and they were just making rounds."

"Security? That's a laugh. I sure didn't hire them. And I'm certain Loren didn't either."

"Do you think they were up to no good."

"Of course they were," I said.

# FORTY-EIGHT

The more I thought about it, the more pissed off it made me. Now I'd have to go all over town alerting everybody to check and see if any of their belongings had been stolen, and make up some kind of inventory of missing articles, and in any case, sooner or later, I would have to go up to Karptown and have a discussion with Wayne about the whole deal, and about him barging into my house and manhandling Britney, and probably have him arrested—meaning Loren would have to be involved, and that suddenly didn't seem like a very good idea, since Loren was not exactly a tough guy—and apart from any of this I, at least, would not get back to the job at Larry's house after all, meaning another day robbed of normality and a day's pay.

I headed over to the rectory on Salem Street to lay all of this on Loren and see if I could enlist him in going around town and talking to people too. To get there from Larry's the quickest route was down Main Street. On the corner of Main and Van Buren, there was a nineteenth-century brick building that had not been occupied for years. It had last been an art gallery, back in the old days when the chain stores were still going strong out in the strip malls and the only other commerce left down on Main Street was real estate offices. The art that the gallery had sold was embarrassing—pictures of covered bridges and other nostalgic scenes totally at odds with the reality of the time. Anyway, Brother Jobe was down there on Main and Van Buren this morning with a crew of New Faith men putting the finishing touches on a brand-new barbershop, of all things.

"Morning, Mr. Mayor," Jobe said. "Heck of a fandango last night, huh?"

"Mr. Bullock can put on the dog, all right."

"And very nice fiddling too, sir. How's your old noggin today?"

"Not a hundred percent," I said. "Yours?"

"Earlier on it felt like it was filled with weevils and hornets, but the good Lord has come through and blew them clean out and filled up the space with fresh air, sunshine, and love of fellow man."

"That's nice. I wish he'd do the same for me."

"Try prayer. It works."

"Maybe later. What's going on here?"

"What's it look like?"

"Looks like an old-fashioned barbershop."

"It ain't nothing old about it," he said. "It's the latest and most up-to-date."

"I hope you're not looking for a profit center here."

"More like a public service."

"You buy this building too?"

"Heck no. Renting it from Mr. Murray."

"Does he own it?"

"Holds it in receivership, I believe."

"That figures," I said. "Most folks get their hair cut at home these days."

"Well, that's *country*, don't you think? We aim to civilize them up. Get a *town* look going. Come on in. You can be our very first customer."

We stepped inside. They had done a nice job of cleaning it up. Two brothers were still painting the wainscot. Another brother painted black lettering backward on the window up in the shop front: FREE SHAVES AND HAIRCUTS. A fourth was sweeping the hardwood floor. The room seemed especially large because so little was in it: one authentic barber chair, a sink, a counter, a few old bentwood chairs for the theoretical customers to wait in, and a mirror on the wall in front of the barber seat. He even had a motley assortment of old magazines on hand: *National Geographic*s from the 1980s, a 1967 *Life,* a *Popular Science* with a cover story on—what else?—flying cars!

"Where'd you find these?"

"The high school basement," he said. "You wouldn't believe what's down there. The barber chair we got up in Fort Edward. Five hundred bucks. Cheap. Have a seat. Brother Judah, come hither and attend!"

A tall, funereal, wading bird of a young man with a beaklike nose leaned his broom against the wall and came over.

"Shave?" he said.

"Huh? No, I don't want to shave off my beard."

"Why not?" Brother Jobe said.

"I just don't. I'm used to it."

"Well, at least let Brother Judah trim it up."

"Okay. But just a trim."

"Do you object if he trims your hair as well?"

"He can trim my hair."

"Go to, son," Brother Jobe said.

Judah lit a double spirit lamp under a kind of oblong kettle on the shelf above the sink, apparently a small water heater. He tied a smock around my throat and began trimming my hair, which I admit had gotten shaggy. I watched him closely in the mirror. He had all the moves of an experienced barber.

"Where'd you get your training?" I said.

"New Faith," he said.

Stupid question on my part, I guess. Once in a while, Jane Ann cut my hair, but otherwise it was not something I put a lot of effort into. Judah trimmed around my ears and down around the back of my neck. By the time he was done with my hair, steam was coming out of the kettle. He adjusted the chair into a reclining position, put a stopper in the sink, poured some of the boiling water in, and tempered it off with a splash of cold from the tap. Then he dropped in a small white towel, wrung it out, and draped it over my face. The steamy towel felt absolutely wonderful. I closed my eyes and let the heat penetrate. Judah banged around for a minute, and then I heard the *whup, whup, whup* of him stropping a razor.

234 JAMES HOWARD KUNSTLER

He took the towel off, dropped it back in the sink. He had whipped up some fresh lather in a bowl and stood with a shaving brush in his left hand and a straight razor in his right.

"Can I trust you with that thing?" I said.

"I never seen a man killed yet with a shaving brush," Brother Jobe said.

"What are you aiming to do with that razor?" I said to Judah.

"I'm just gon' clean up the whiskers on your throat and cheek-bones," Judah said. His voice was almost comically high for such a tall, grave-looking fellow.

"Oh, all right," I said.

No one besides me had ever held a razor to my neck before. I didn't like the idea, but I let go of my petty fears and lay back. The warm lather felt comforting, and Judah had a sure hand with the razor. He scraped my neck clean and made a few passes along my upper cheeks. Then I heard him go to the beard itself with his scissors, *clickity-click*. Finally, he cleaned up the lather and whisker bits with another hot towel, jacked the chair back up, and stepped aside so I could admire myself in the mirror. I must say I looked polished up in a way I hadn't been for years. I saw a glimmer of the old corporate executive there. I couldn't help smiling.

"You see," Brother Jobe said. "What a salubrious effect it has."

"I feel improved, all right."

"And improved for the better! That's what New Faith is all about. You town folks have come to be a scrufty-looking bunch. It's demoralizing. You know, I'm thinking of opening up a men's haberdash right next door."

"Where would you get the goods?"

"Why, we'd turn 'em out ourself, just like we do now for our own."

"You want us all to dress up like you?"

"Well, what's wrong with that? The New Faith look is clean and upright."

"So, none of us townies would have to sign on with your out-fit officially. You just get us all looking the same and soon it's a fait accompli."

"What kind of fate is that?"

"Never mind."

"It don't sound like a bad fate," Brother Jobe said. "Anyways, I want to present you with this. Brother Judah, gimme that there razor."

Judah wiped it down and handed it to Brother Jobe.

"Im'a give this to you so you can tidy yourself up at home on the days that we closed down here," Brother Jobe said. "The mayor of a town ought to set the tone for others, don't you think? Here. We got a half a gross of 'em down in Pennsylvania. Good German steel. With my compliments."

He slapped the razor into my hand.

"Thanks."

"And lookit, the blade locks up just so, and then you can't hurt yourself."

"I always was a slow and careful shaver."

"Sure, but in a fight you want it so's you don't cut your own goshdurn fingers off."

"A fight! We don't have many razor fights up here."

"No? It's common practice down home."

"Can I have a word with you outside?" I said.

We stepped outside. The heat was rising again. Buddy Haseltine was washing the dust off Terry Einhorn's store window with a rag in an unsteady hand. A couple of women carrying baskets lingered outside Russo's bakery.

"Care for some instruction in the finer points of razor fighting, old son?"

"Can you be serious for a moment?"

"I'm always serious. Even my funnin' is serious. Don't you know that yet?"

"Well, that's good because I have a serious problem. Do you know who Wayne Karp is?"

"I haven't met the gentleman, but I'm aware of his, uh, position in the community."

"It appears he was down here burglarizing houses last night when all the people were over at Bullock's."

"You don't say. That ain't right."

"Anything turn up missing at the school?"

"Not so's I know. But we had five of the women watching all them kids and several brothers making reg'lar watch rounds."

"I'm going to have to go see him."

"I understand he's got some kind of village up there, near the old landfill."

"An old trailer park."

"Hmmph. Trailer trash. Ain't that old-timey! I gather you'd like some backup. You can have Joseph and them."

"For the moment I would like you to send a courier over to Bullock to get some warrants."

"Can do."

"Then, tomorrow the Reverend Holder and I will figure out how to proceed with this."

"Why him?"

"He's our constable now."

"He ain't exactly the rough and ready sort."

"I'm not looking to start a war."

# FORTY-NINE

There was no one at home in the rectory.

Katie Zucker, Todd's wife, was next door at the church in her capacity as deacon, up on a stepladder hanging the hymn numbers for Sunday's service on the hymn board beside the pulpit. She told me that Loren and Jane Ann had gone out berry picking.

"You've certainly come out of your shell lately, Robert."

"It's just circumstances," I said.

"I hear that Britney Watling has joined your household."

"That's more or less the truth, Katie," I said.

"Don't you think it looks funny?"

"I'm sure it does," I said. "But so does an American town with no cars or electric lights and people like us who don't have regular jobs to go to anymore, and folks dying before their time from all kinds of things."

Katie made a face up there on her ladder. At the University of Vermont in the old days, she was a nationally ranked speed skater who almost made the U.S. Olympic team. Afterward, before marrying Todd, she worked as a northeast regional sales rep for Nike, earning large commissions and bonuses. Now she was a farmer's wife and church caretaker. Her hair was turning silver though she still had an athlete's body, even after two children. We had a little bit of history. A year after Sandy passed away, Katie had too much to drink at the Harvest Ball up in Hebron and made a pass at me in a way that was a little too demonstrative. Todd was right across the room. It was embarrassing.

"Hey, did you lose weight or something?" she said, conspicuously changing the subject.

"I just got my hair cut."

"Oh? You look like one of those Civil War generals."

I knew where to find Loren and Jane Ann if they were picking wild blackberries. They'd be up on the railroad tracks along the Battenkill. A particular stretch where one side of the cut faced due south was especially rich with fruit, and I headed out that way. It was nice to be rambling out in the countryside by myself for a change, free of other people's demands. On the steel bridge where the tracks cross the river a half mile outside town, I stopped for a while to watch the river, knowing Loren and Jane Ann would have to come back that way. A few dun-colored caddis flies were coming off the water. I watched an osprey rise off the stream with a good twelve-inch trout in his talons. When he was gone with his prize, plenty more trout were visible finning in the feeding lanes in the shadow of the bridge's trusses and girders. I was sorry I hadn't brought a rod. I sat there with my legs dangling off the edge of the deck, feeling the guilty pleasure of letting my obligations slide for a while. I wasn't concerned about trains coming by, because they didn't run anymore. Perhaps a half hour later I heard human voices down the way and looked up to see Loren and Jane Ann at the far end of the bridge.

"That you, Robert?" Loren said.

"I'm looking for you," I said.

When they came up on me sitting there, Loren gave me a slight shove like he wanted to push me over the edge into the river. Of course, he was just clowning around. But it was enough to give my heart a flutter. The stream was a good forty feet down from the deck of the bridge, and the water probably wasn't more than four feet deep, so if you fell, you'd probably break your neck. Then Loren put his arm under my chin and held my head as he rubbed his knuckles into my scalp: a noogie. I endured it stoically until he stopped. Then they sat down next to me, Jane Ann on my left and Loren on my right. Each had a plastic pail half full of blackberries.

"Can I try some?" I said.

"No," Loren said. "Jane Ann's making jam for me."

"You can have some of mine," Jane Ann said.

"Don't give him any of yours either," Loren said.

"Here, just taste a couple," Jane Ann said.

"Hey, what'd I say?" Loren said. "Go pick your own."

"Okay, old Mr. Cranky Puss," Jane Ann said.

"Fuck you," Loren said to her.

"Nice talk—"

"And fuck you too," Loren said to me.

"—for a man of the cloth."

"And fuck the cloth, as a matter of fact."

We sat there, the three of us in a row, watching the swallows and the fish and the caddis flies and the yellow irises blooming along a sandbank below. Jane Ann said they had seen a bear up the tracks. It ran away when it saw them.

"Did you ever eat bear?" Loren said.

"No. You?" I said.

"Sure."

"What's it like?"

"It's not like chicken," Loren said. "More like pork meets roadkill."

"Don't see much roadkill anymore."

"Amen to that," Jane Ann said.

"Except for us," Loren said. "We're history's roadkill."

We fell into silence for another while.

"Looks like somebody gave you a haircut," Jane Ann said eventually. "Your new houseguest? Or should I say roommate?"

I wondered if my discomfort was visible. I hastened to explain how the New Faithers had opened the barbershop on Main.

"What's next?" Jane Ann said, "a salon for us ladies?"

"I don't know," I said. "Maybe if they're really ambitious they'll get the railroad going again."

"Don't hold your breath on that one," Loren said. "Did you come out here to show us your haircut? It's darn fetching. Don't you think Robert looks fetching, dear?"

Jane Ann didn't go for the bait.

"We've got a problem," I said and explained how Wayne Karp and his boys had been prowling around the night before while everyone was over at Bullock's, and how I wanted Loren, in his capacity as constable, to go around and help me ascertain if people discovered anything stolen from their houses and barns."

"And what if they did steal stuff?"

"Then we'll have to do something about it," I said. "If you want me to find another constable, I'd understand."

"You don't think I have what it takes?" Loren said.

"You're a clergyman."

"So was Savonarola."

"I don't see you leading a crusade."

"He didn't lead a crusade. He cleaned up a town."

"I don't see us cleaning up Karptown," I said.

"Whatever it is you intend to do, don't you dare count me out of it," Loren said.

"My hero," Jane Ann said. "This gives me goose bumps."

For a moment, Loren looked like he wanted to throw Jane Ann off the bridge. I was beginning to worry what he was capable of, what he might do.

# FIFTY

We waited until evening, when the men who worked on the surrounding farms and elsewhere would have returned home. At the first house we went to, Peter Wedekind's at the top of Bayard Street, we encountered yet another problem. Peter had gone by Einhorn's store to buy a few things on his way home from Deaver's farm and was enticed across the street for a look at the new barbershop, whereupon a bunch of New Faith men tossed him into a chair and held him down while they shaved off his beard. He was naturally very annoyed, he said, though his wife, Alma, said she liked his new look.

"But that's not right, is it?" Peter said. "Forced shaving?"

"It's certainly not," I said.

At the next house we went to, Bill and Aggie Schroeder's, they were missing a pair of sterling silver fluted candlesticks that were three hundred years old and glaringly absent from their dining room table when they returned from Bullock's levee, they said. Bill, who operated the creamery on the western edge of town, hadn't strayed downtown on his way home, and still had his beard. In all, six other men in the houses we visited had had their beards forcibly shaved off because they happened to pass by Main and Van Buren that afternoon. Some of these households also discovered valuables missing, once we'd inquired: silver, jewelry, tools. By now, the sun was going down. Loren and I split up, and went around town for another hour, and when we met up again at the rectory, the final tally was eleven men forcibly shaved (plus three voluntarily) and two substantial lists of items stolen from various homes. The townspeople were angry, confused, and puzzled about the connection between the burglaries and the forced shavings, even though it was obvious to me that two separate things were going on. Some of them apparently thought that New Faith had carried out the robberies.

Jane Ann was cooking off her blackberry jam in their summer kitchen as Loren and I compared notes and came to the inevitable conclusion that we'd have to arrest both Brother Jobe and Wayne Karp.

"How do you want to handle this?" Loren said.

"Well, that's going to take some thought, now, isn't it?"

# FIFTY-ONE

Britney was still up with Sarah when I returned home. They were both in the big stuffed chair, reading a book together by the light of a candle. It was *The Wind in the Willows*, which I had read to Daniel and then Genna years ago, the wonderful friendships of Rat, Mole, Badger, and Mr. Toad of Toad Hall. I closed the front door and stood there awkwardly, in my own house.

"Are you hungry?" Britney said.

"Yes, I am."

"Mr. Schmidt came by with a stewing hen. It's in the Dutch oven out there."

"How did he know you were here?"

"I don't know."

"Well, that was kind of him," I said. "I suppose you two have already eaten."

"Well, yes."

"Maybe I'll have a look, then."

"There's some beer too."

I went out to the summer kitchen and lit a candle. The beer was in a plastic gallon jug. We reused them endlessly. It was a pale ale, very hoppy and strong. I felt the glow in my stomach immediately. The Dutch oven still retained some warmth. I lifted the heavy cast-iron lid. Britney had deboned the meat. Plenty was left and it was swimming in a cream-thickened sauce with new onions and peas along with some cornmeal dumplings flecked with thyme. I spooned out a bowlful and brought it back inside the house along with a tumbler of beer.

"I hope you didn't wait up for me," I said.

"I feel safer if you're here."

"You could lock the door."

"But then you'd have to wake me up to get in," she said.

"Is the beer from Mr. Schmidt too?"

"Yes."

"This is delicious," I said, holding up my bowl. "You're a very good cook."

"Thank you."

"Mr. Toad got arrested and they put him in the jail," Sarah said.

"Don't worry," I said. "He'll get out before long."

"Did you have a motorcar in the old days?"

"I certainly did. We just called them cars, though."

"Do you think we'll ever have them again?"

I chewed for a minute and glugged down some beer.

"No, I don't think we'll have them again, Sarah," I said.

"Ever?"

"Probably not."

"Oh . . ." She seemed hugely disappointed.

"Do you know what happened to them?"

"Not really," Sarah said.

"Well, I'll try to explain. Here's what happened. Cars had engines, and the engines needed a certain kind of magic liquid to run on, and—"

"What's an engine?"

"It's a machine that makes things go. You put the magic liquid in it and then the engine can do work. It can turn wheels and make the car go."

"What's the magic liquid?"

"It's called fuel."

"What's fuel?"

"It's like . . . Do you see this chicken stew that I'm eating?"

"Yes."

"Well, this is fuel for my body. It gives me energy, makes me strong, powers my muscles and my brain, makes it possible for me to do things like saw wood and carry stuff from one place to another."

"Do you have an engine?"

"My whole body is a kind of engine. A living engine. And yours is too. We all need food and water to run our bodies. That's what food is for."

"It tastes good," Sarah said. "That's why I like food."

"That's true. It can taste very good if there is a good cook around."

"My favorite food is pudding. What's yours?"

"Right now, this is my favorite food."

"Did the motorcars run out of food?"

"The cars needed a very special kind of food to run in their engines. It was called gasoline. It was made of oil, which came out of the ground. We had a lot of oil in the old days, but then we used so much that we had a problem getting it. We had to get more and more of the stuff from faraway places across the ocean. And that led to a lot of trouble."

"What kind of trouble?"

"People in other countries like China and Japan and Germany needed oil too, and there wasn't enough to go around, so they fought over what was left. And soon, the fighting caused more problems with money and getting all the other things we needed to live, like steel and rubber. And there were such big problems with money that a lot of people couldn't buy cars, and even if they could, the gasoline was very expensive, or else sometimes you couldn't get it at all, even if you had enough money—"

"How come?"

"Because we couldn't get the oil to make the gasoline from those faraway lands anymore. So people had to stop using the cars."

"What happened to all the cars?"

"They were made from steel and people needed the steel for other things, so over the years they took the cars away and melted them down."

Sarah started rubbing her eyes.

"It's time for you to go to sleep," Britney said.

"But what about Rat, and Mole, and Mr. Toad?"

"They'll be here tomorrow," Britney said.

"What if people come and take all the books away and melt them like they did to the motorcars."

"Books don't melt," Britney said.

# FIFTY-TWO

I was reading in bed by candlelight later that night when I heard a light rapping on the door.

"Yes . . ."

Britney came in. She was barefoot and wearing an old green chenille bathrobe that had belonged to Sandy. She sat in a chair to my left that was the place I customarily tossed my clothes if they weren't too dirty to put on again the next day.

"What are you reading?"

"Albert Speer's memoirs."

"Who was he?"

"Hitler's pet architect."

"Hitler had an architect as a pet?"

I explained the Hitler-Speer thing to her as concisely as possible. The truth was my pulse had quickened just having her in my room, and though it was another warm evening, I began to shiver slightly.

"You're good at history," she said.

"I'm fascinated by it."

"How so?"

"Where we are now in relation to where we once were. It's quite a strange story."

"Oh. I don't miss the old days so much anymore."

"In the old days I used to fly across the country three, four times a month. Imagine that. Clear across North America and back. Boston to San Francisco, Boston to Las Vegas. Over and over."

"What was it like, being in an airplane?"

"Didn't you ever fly?"

"No."

"Really? Well, I was a nervous flyer at first. Being packed into an aluminum tube with a hundred other people. And the climb was so steep. It took ten minutes or so to get up to cruising altitude where the air is thinner and there was less drag on the body of the aircraft. Finally, they'd level off around forty thousand feet, about eight miles high."

"It makes me queasy just to hear you say that."

"I got to enjoy it. My company paid for business class seats. They gave you free drinks and nice things to eat and they played movies that were still showing in the cinemas. You forgot you were sitting in a metal tube eight miles up in the sky."

"I don't think I'll ever fly in an airplane."

"I think you're probably right about that."

"When I was a little girl, I rode the train a couple of times from Albany to New York City," she said. "You'd think they could get trains running again, at least. You don't need oil to run a train. Even I know that."

"Yeah, you'd think," I said. "Except I'm not sure there's any 'they' left out there to get them running. And I wonder where you'd go if 'they' did."

I told Britney about my side trip to the state capitol when we were in Albany, the lieutenant governor pretending to be still part of something that had obviously dissolved all around him.

"I wonder what New York City's like now," she said.

"I'm beginning to think we're lucky to be where we are."

"It's not wrong, me being here with you, is it?"

"I wouldn't want you to think so."

"I won't then," she said. "I'll think something else. I'll think its fortunate."

"That may be a good way to think about it. For both of us."

Britney sat quietly for a while, gazing into the braided rug between the chair and the bed. I could see a pulse beating in the pale skin at her right temple, next to where little wisps of light-colored hair curled above her ear.

"Oh, there's something else we were wondering about," she said eventually.

"What?"

"Sarah wonders if you can teach her how to play the fiddle."

"I can try."

"I would be very grateful if you would."

She continued to sit there in the chair. I didn't know what to say. I felt increasingly paralyzed by her presence. A little breeze blew through the open window and made the candle flame shudder. It also carried traces of her scent my way. Then Britney stood up, letting the bathrobe fall off her shoulders onto the floor as she did. Her nakedness was shocking. Though small, she was a perfectly formed woman.

"Can I lie beside you?" she said.

"Yes," I said, surrendering consciously.

She came around the bed and slipped in under the top sheet, which was all I used during the hot nights of the summer. She pressed against my side. I put Albert Speer down on the night table and extended an arm so she could nestle more closely under it. Her fragrance and the silkiness of her skin next to mine shredded what remained of my thoughts. What followed seemed driven by mindless instinct. Soon she was on top of me, all wetness, and youth, her breasts swaying in the candle light. She assisted me inside her, and I felt as though I was crossing a frontier into a dangerous wilderness where the animals would never learn to speak and might not be so friendly. When we finally subsided, she came back under my arm, and we lay there silently with the flickering candlelight playing on the ceiling. At some point, I blew it out. We fell asleep— at least I did—and woke up some time later—I have no idea how much later—and repeated our exertions slowly and deliberately the second time.

Before I fell back asleep, I thought I heard her say, "You have a family now. What do you think of that?"

"It could be I'm extremely fortunate."

# FIFTY-THREE

Loren and I went over to the high school in the morning. We just walked in the front door. Nobody asked what we were doing. I hadn't been inside the place since my boy Daniel was a student there. We had to shut it down after that. That was the year of the flu, which took so many young lives, and also there was no way to run the furnaces anymore. New Faith had done an impressive job of cleaning it up, though it was still recognizably institutional. The hallways were still lined with dreary sea-foam-colored ceramic tiles, but the lockers had been removed. The place was strikingly busy at that hour, men and women bustling around the corridors, here and there a few children scurrying along. They ignored us as if we were invisible, and it was only when Brother Elam happened by, and I hailed him, that anyone would pay attention to us.

Elam directed us to Brother Jobe's headquarters which, if I remembered correctly, had been the principal's office, a suite of several rooms, actually. He was working at a small round table in the outer office where the secretaries used to sit, scribbling furiously with a steel pen and an inkwell, blotting his lines with a rag as he scratched away on the paper. He sat in a pink upholstered chair under a slightly water-stained framed portrait of George Washington that must have been part of the original decor. But otherwise, he had transformed the rooms into something that resembled an Edwardian hotel suite. I could see that the inner office had been converted to a bedroom and that a woman was in there making the bed. When she went around to the far side of the bed, I saw that it was the same girl who had been sitting next to Brother Jobe the night we first met.

"What a surprise," he said without looking up. "Mornin,' Mr. Mayor, Parson Holder. Do you know what it means to be full of the Holy Ghost?" Without waiting for an answer, he continued. "How important is it for God's ministers to be continually at prayer? To know the power and the nature of God you got to partake of his inbreathed word. Morning and night, at every meal, at work, at bathing, whatever chance you got. The Psalmist said that he hid God's word in his heart, that he might not sin against him. And you will find that the more of God's word you hide in your heart, the easier it is to live a righteous life."

Brother Jobe looked up at us with an impressively toothy smile.

"Have you prepared your Sunday sermon yet, Parson?" he said to Loren.

"Not yet."

"You going to get around to it or speak extempore."

"I usually make some notes beforehand."

"Do you? Well, listen up to this here." He cleared his throat. "You people who are seeking the baptism are entering a realm of illumination by the power of the Holy Ghost. He reveals the preciousness and the power of the blood of Christ. I find by the revelation of the spirit that there is not one thing in me that the blood does not cleanse. I find that God sanctifies me by the blood and reveals his power in the work of the spirit. Oh, this life in the Holy Ghost! This life of grace growing and knowledge increasing in the power of the spirit, the life and the mind of Christ being renewed in you, and of constant revelations of the might of his power. It is the only kind of thing that lets folks stand."

He glanced up again.

"Ain't that some sermonizing?"

"It's very musical," Loren said.

"Well, if you don't mind talking shop a moment here, Parson, don't you find that to be effective—you got to connect with a different part of the congregation's brain? You're right, it is a kind of music. But is it an accident that the spirit finds our people most often in the act of singing?"

"No," Loren said.

"And wouldn't you say the singing region of the brain is different from the digging-a-ditch part?"

"Probably."

"One of these days I'll have to come by and listen to you hold forth," Brother Jobe said. "Would you mind?"

"Not in the least."

"And you can bring your whole dadblamed congregation to our Sunday service any old time—we got the whole goldurned auditorium and it must seat seven hundred."

"Thank you."

"Now what-all you boys come to see me about?"

"Actually, I'm here to place you under arrest," Loren said.

Brother Jobe's face registered shock at first, but slowly dissolved into a grin of even vaster amusement and satisfaction than the one he had shown at reading his own sermon.

"Ain't this one for the books," he said. "What's the charge going to be?"

"Either disturbing the peace or criminal mischief or battery, third degree," Loren said. "I haven't quite decided. Maybe we'll mix and match."

"Hey, that's good. Sounds like you been boning up. But what for exactly?"

"Cutting people's beards off against their will."

"I see. Okay, why don't you boys pull up a seat, let's powwow on this. First off: you got a jail?"

We did have a jail. It was on the second floor of the old town hall, and Loren and I had checked it out earlier that morning. I don't think it had been used in thirty, forty years. It was cluttered with old file cabinets and other junk. We would have to spend a couple of hours mucking it out and mopping it up, and we had no idea where the keys to the locks of the two cells might be found.

"Yes, we have a jail," I said. "Look, Brother Jobe, I'm not against you or your organization, and I appreciate what you've done for the town since you arrived. But you can't snatch people off the street and have your way with them—"

"Have my way with 'em! *Hooo-weee!*"

"You know what I mean."

"Looks to me like you all can't take a joke," he said, but he kept grinning as though his amusement knew no bounds.

"The people in town are pretty ticked off," Loren said.

"Maybe so," Brother Jobe said, "but at least now they look good being that way."

"If we don't make a public show of bringing you in," I said, "I'm afraid things could get ugly around here."

"Bottom line: you want me to work with you?"

"Yes. That's pretty much it."

"Heck, I'll work with you."

"Okay," I said. "What do you say we come get you around seven o'clock this evening? You meet us at the front door. We walk you through town so everybody can see, and lock you up."

"Fair enough. Then what happens."

"Somehow we get Wayne Karp down there with you."

"In the jail?"

"Yes."

"That trailer trash? I hope you've got two separate cells."

"We do," Loren said.

"Well then, I'll look forward to making his acquaintance. How do you propose to bring him in?"

"I don't know," Loren said.

"You can probably use these here," Brother Jobe said. He stepped across the room, fetched a wad of papers on top a bookshelf, and handed them to me. "Writs and such," he said. "Signed by Mr. Bullock, all properlike. I sent young Brother Minor over to fetch them. He helped remind Mr. Bullock of the service we rendered him. They come in late last night."

The wad included a warrant to search Karptown for stolen goods, a warrant for the arrest of Wayne Karp, a summons for

254 JAMES HOWARD KUNSTLER

Bunny Willman and Wayne Karp to appear before a grand jury two weeks hence, two blank arrest warrants to be used as we saw fit to bring in whoever had been with Wayne burgling houses the night of the levee.

"That's pretty comprehensive," I said. "How'd you get Mr. Bullock off square one, finally."

"We had a . . . a meeting of the minds, so to speak."

I handed the papers to Loren.

"We'll go up to Karptown later today," he said.

"You're a couple of brave boys."

"The object is to inform them that the law is back in business here," Loren said. "They got a lot to answer for."

"You know, I've offered my men to the mayor here."

"I'm aware of that," Loren said. "Thanks. If necessary, we'll take you up on that."

"Some of 'em have been to places and dealt with folks that even Mr. Wayne Karp wouldn't want to know about. You don't have to explain none of this to Mr. Karp, but we got your back. The welfare of this town is our business too. Maybe he'll understand that he can come in now walking upright or come in later by some other means of locomotion."

"We've got modest expectations," Loren said.

"Reach for the stars, I always say."

"We've got to start reaching for the lower branches before we get to the stars," I said.

"Some day I'm going to teach you to think big, old son," Brother Jobe said. "Tell you what, though: you bring the sumbitch in tonight, I'll have him converted into a Jesus-loving lamb of God quicker'n you can say Deuteronomy 32:35."

# FIFTY-FOUR

Loren left directly to prepare the jail. Brother Jobe said he was welcome to "borrow" Brother Judah from down at the barbershop if he needed any help with the task. He asked me to "stick around." There was something he wanted to show me, he said. He put his sermon aside and I followed him in his brisk, waddling walk deeper into the interior of the old school. The classrooms had been converted into workshops, several with walls knocked down between them to make larger spaces. There was a woodworking shop where a half-dozen brothers were using hand tools to fabricate what looked like window and door sashes. There was an equally large sewing shop where five sisters cut patterns on big tables and worked at ancient foot-powered sewing machines. There was a harness shop and a metal shop attached to a new forge built out from the exterior wall as an addition, but with a dirt floor. Two brothers were smithing horseshoes while a boy about fourteen worked a six-foot bellows by the hearth. The heat was unbearable.

At the end of the long hall was the old gymnasium. I was not quite prepared for what he was about to show me. Brother Jobe held the door open. Within, they had begun a colossal construction operation, framing the hundred-foot by seventy-five-foot room, with its fifty-foot-high ceiling, into a matrix of tiny rooms, deployed in three decks, with stairways zigzagging at diagonal corners.

"What do you think?" Brother Jobe said.

"What is this? A giant three-D tic-tac-toe stadium?"

"Naw. Heart of the hive, so to speak."

"Heart of the hive?"

I counted seven brothers working in there. The interior rang with
their hammer blows and the chuffing of handsaws as they completed
what was in effect a gigantic balloon frame. They were hanging joists
way up on the top deck that day. Hundreds of board feet of scavenged lumber stood neatly stacked in piles on the old hardwood gym
floor: two-by-fours, two-by-sixes, one-by in various widths.

"She look safe to you?" Brother Jobe said.

"I suppose."

"We don't have no master builder type among us."

"It looks like they've got it pinned into the walls and ceiling
trusses pretty well."

"Is that your seal of approval?"

"I don't know as it would pass code," I said, "but the good news
is there isn't anymore code enforcement."

That seemed to please him.

"Come here," he said. "Lookit: what I want to show you."

We went up one of the corner stairways. It felt solid enough.
At the absolute center of the whole structure, on the middle deck,
was a framed cube of a room that would have corridors on two sides
but apparently no windows opening to light. Nothing was up yet
but stud wall and a floor.

"This here's the royal chamber," Brother Jobe said.

"Is this where the queen bee lives?"

"She passes a great deal of time here, yes. In what will be her
winter quarters."

"Then you have a queen bee?"

"We got something like that," he said. "You want to meet her?"

I hesitated. It was hard with Brother Jobe to tell where meta-
phor left off and something uncomfortably like hyperreality began.

"She won't sting you to death," he said. "Don't worry."

"This is an actual person you're talking about?"

"Hell yes. Mary Beth Ivanhoe of Lynchburg, Virginia. That
actual enough for you?"

"I guess."

"Anyways, I was kind of hoping you'd help us out with this here room. It's a very special room. Mary Beth will be spending most of her time here, and she is not always feeling tip-top. She ain't sick, but she gets . . . indisposed. It has to be a very beautiful room, like a jewel box. I got in mind wood paneling, inlay and such. Nice woods, finished finely. It requires first-class workmanship, and I know you can do it. Course, I was thinking you could educate some of our brothers in the process. You'd have to work up a ventilation scheme because she generates a lot of heat. What do you say?"

"I may have to work it in around other commitments."

"Then you'll do it?"

"I can probably do it."

"That's good. Very good," he said fervidly. "However you can make it happen, you won't be sorry. I promise. Now let's go drop in on the old girl."

# FIFTY-FIVE

The original school building had been U-shaped, with a grassy courtyard inside the U that had never been actually used for much more than a place for a few redwood picnic tables under some scraggly trees, such was the thoughtlessness of the folks who commissioned these buildings. When we left the gymnasium, Brother Jobe took me back down the hall and through a new doorway that had been cut into a corridor that led into the courtyard. Unseen from the road these many weeks, the New Faith building crew had filled in the courtyard with another labyrinth of rooms, chambers, and corridors in wood construction. They'd used clerestory windows to get light inside, but these were as yet unglazed. It all had a raw finish, like a frontier outpost. The cell-like rooms within were unpainted, and there was no finished flooring besides the recycled planking. Each room contained a bed, so I figured that the whole thing was a kind of dormitory.

"Our women sleep here," Brother Jobe said. I didn't know whether he meant all the women, or just the unmarried ones, or what. I didn't really want to know. Maybe, I thought, they had some kind of thing going on like the Shakers of the nineteenth century, with men and women assigned to separate quarters. As we penetrated the complex I became aware of an odd sweet-sickly smell. It increased when we reached a doorway near what I sensed to be about the center of the filled-in courtyard.

Brother Jobe rapped carefully on the door. One of the sisters answered. The two of them exchanged whispers. A gust of warm air washed over us. It carried that same sweet funky odor, but more intensely, as if someone had baked fresh corn bread in an unwashed sock. I followed Brother Jobe inside. The room was round, or rather seemed so, because carpets had been hung over the walls in a way that rounded out the corners, as though we were in a yurt. Up above there was a cupola, but they had hung drapes from the openings so the light entering was reduced, and it was actually very dim in the room, which needed ventilation badly. The floor was covered with layers of carpets. At the center of the room stood a large, heavy canopied bed with gauzy mosquito netting hung off it, and on it an extremely fat woman reclined in a posture of oriental luxury, propped up by many pillows. Curiously, her head seemed tiny in relation to the rest of her body. Perhaps it was because she was wearing a tight black headdress or turban. Her skin was extremely pale, almost pearl-like. She wore a shiny yellow satin tunic embroidered with glittery things, rhinestones or sequins, I couldn't tell. It seemed to barely contain her waxy flesh, in particular her heaving, lumpy bosom. Her arms extruded from their short sleeves like a couple of country hams. Everything below her hips was concealed in a sacklike robe of yellow satin. Altogether she gave the impression of something not exactly human. The odors in the room seemed to emanate from her.

She was methodically eating little cakes off a silver tray, one after another, with machinelike regularity. Five sisters sat in a semicircle on the far side of her bed, softly singing, or rather chanting, a harmonic Appalachian-style round that repeated over and over hypnotically, like a kind of meditative prayer. Something about *a long time traveling*. Another sister prepared a fresh tray of cakes from a rolling cart that seemed well provisioned with many types of food, like in the *dim sum* restaurants of yesteryear. Yet another sister sat in a chair at the near side of the bed, waving a woven reed fan at the figure reclining there.

"Morning, precious mother," Brother Jobe called, rather musically, as one might address a longtime invalid on a routine visit. The figure ignored him, concentrating intensely on the food before her. The sister who let us in brought up a couple of chairs for us and set them beside the bed. Then she drew open one panel of the mosquito netting and tied it to the bedpost at the foot of the bed. "I brung a visitor, mother," Brother Jobe said.

She finally broke her concentration on the food and lifted her head in our direction. She seemed to have trouble focusing her vision. Some kind of mucousy goop had collected around her heavily lidded eyes, and one eyeball kept wandering off to the side, on its own, as though the owner could not control it, or perhaps she was undergoing some kind of neurological spasm.

"What you got to say for yourself, Robert?" she said in a voice that was strikingly harsh and nasal, as though she were speaking through a long brass tube from the next room. I was so transfixed by a kind of reflex disgust that it was another moment before I realized that nobody had introduced me to her by name.

"I don't know, ma'am," I said.

"You be nice to BJ here when you put him in the hoosegow."

"He won't be there long," I said, wondering how she knew about that too.

"That's for damn sure," she said, and gave out a harsh throaty laugh which seemed to pain her.

"You don't know the Lord, do you, Robert?" she said.

"Maybe not in the way you mean."

"But you walk with an upright spirit, don't you?"

"I don't know. I'm not the best judge. I get along okay."

"For an Israelite. Oh my . . ."

She seemed to undergo a minor paroxysm. Her wandering eye rolled up under the lid, which quivered, and a bit of masticated cake leaked out of her mouth. The others did not react, or at least not with alarm.

"Is she all right?" I said.

Brother Jobe just nodded and patted my arm. Then she came out of it. One of the sisters wiped the food off her chin, while another replaced the now empty tray of cakes with a freshly refilled one.

"Pardon me," she said, apparently coming back to herself. "I'm subject to fits. Did you know this old boy was a Jew, BJ?"

"He's a member in good standing at the Congregational, far as I know, mother," Brother Jobe said.

"Ain't it so, Robert?" she said. "Born Ear-lick or something like that."

"Ehrlich," I said.

"That a fact?" Brother Jobe said.

"What of it?"

"You're chosen," the fat woman said.

"I never felt special," I said.

"I'm anointing you, son, on behalf of you know who. Don't be thick. Take the responsibility, or be goddamned."

"May I ask what you're choosing me for?"

"To be a father," she said. "No, to be more than a father."

"I've already been one."

"Then you'll know what to do."

"I don't understand."

"You will. In all your trials. Oh . . ."

The fat lady appeared to hyperventilate. Her left eye rolled up again, and she fell into another spasm, more profound this time, like an epileptic seizure. In the process, she knocked the little tray of sweets off the bed. Her body went rigid and tremored. She spit up more food. If it had been up to me, I would have rushed to make sure her airway was clear, or to put something in between her teeth to keep her from biting her tongue, but the others went about their business as if they'd seen it happen a thousand times, and perhaps they had. The sister with the fan just fanned. The singers kept chanting. The fit lasted less than a minute. Then the fat woman subsided in place and seemed to fall instantly into a deep fathomless slumber, her aspirations noisy and full.

"You sleep now, precious mother," Brother Jobe said, while sort of lifting me by the elbow out of my seat, saying, "Let's go, old son."

I couldn't wait to get out of there. He took me back through the labyrinth of new construction to the lobby in the old part of the school. It was developing into yet another hot day, but nothing like the heat in that room. The sheer memory of that funky odor was still nauseating.

"How'd she know my name and all that," I said.

"Ain't it obvious?"

"Not to me."

"Mary Beth ain't like other people."

"What's her deal?"

"Look, old son. There's real strangeness in this world of ours. Back in the machine times, there was so much noise front and back, so to speak, it kept us from knowing what lies behind the surface of things. Now it stands out more."

"Am I ever going to understand what I just saw?"

"I don't know as I understand it all myself. She has powers. It's a dadblamed miracle. Probably a sort of curse too, for her."

"What am I supposed to do?"

"I don't know," Brother Jobe said. "Ride with it. The truth will be revealed by and by. Like the old song goes: farther along, we'll understand why."

"Are you going to cooperate and come in with Loren and me this evening?"

"Sure I am. Didn't I already say so? You just come by. I'll be ready. Now about this Karp fella. He won't let you search his premises for stolen goods. I ain't even met the sumbitch, and I can tell you that. When you decide you want to bring him in, you come here and apply to Brother Joseph for assistance. You hear? He'll know what to do."

"We have to give Karp a chance to come in peacefully with us, first."

"You ever study where God's law diverges from man's law?"

"No."

"Well, oddly enough, man's law ain't always grounded in human nature. Ain't that a funny paradox?"

"I'm just trying to avoid a war."

"If I didn't know better, I'd say you got too much Jesus in you."

# FIFTY-SIX

I struggled with whether to tell Loren about my audience with Mary Beth Ivanhoe, the "precious mother" of the New Faithers, and decided against it. I felt it would only make him turn more hostile toward them. Anyway, I had not digested the experience myself. He asked if Brother Jobe had showed me around the place, and I told him they were building a warren of rooms in the old gymnasium.

"Sounds like they're turning the place into a fucking termite mound," was all he said.

With the help of Brother Judah, we got the two jail cells cleaned up on the second floor of the old town hall. They were across a center aisle from each other in the rear behind the old police offices, which had been closed down when the town moved operations to the building out on Highway 29 in 1983. The old police offices had most recently served as the dressing rooms for our community theater productions. Props and scenery flats from *Guys and Dolls* were still scattered about in there. Then it dawned on us that we had to furnish the cells with at least a bed and a slop bucket each. Judah said they had extra beds at New Faith and he'd fetch some over in a wagon. Meanwhile, Loren and I went to scare up some padlocks, which was not such an easy task, since a lock without a key was useless. Loren found an old combination lock in a kitchen drawer in the rectory. He remembered the combination because it had been on his locker at the health club he belonged to in Glens Falls for fifteen years. The other padlock wasn't so easy. It took us a couple of hours. Finally we found one with a key in it in Claude Wormsley's desk at the old water treatment plant. Once we had the locks, we scrounged a couple of lengths of chain from

Tom Allison's livery. By this time, Judah had gotten two beds delivered and our jail was open for business.

At quarter to seven, when we were confident that most everyone in town had come home from their places of work, we returned to the school where Brother Jobe "surrendered" to Loren in the lobby. He was lovingly surrounded by a couple dozen of his followers, who seemed more entertained than worried. One of the sisters handed him a big picnic basket, but as Loren prepared to bind Brother Jobe's hands behind him with rope—we didn't have any handcuffs—he gave me the picnic basket to carry for him.

"You don't mind, do you?" Brother Jobe said, with a wink, as if this was all a show, which to some extent it was.

"Well it is supper time," I said. "And, frankly, with all the scrounging and cleaning, we hadn't made provision for meals yet."

"That's a heck of a way to run a penitentiary," Brother Jobe said.

Another sister handed me a leather briefcase.

"His books and papers and like that," she said.

"Might's well turn out a sermon or two in stir," Brother Jobe said.

He made his farewells and we paraded him all the way down Salem Street to the corner of Main Street and Academy, where the old town hall stood. Along the way, plenty of people sitting out on their porches or inside at their dining room tables saw us pass by with our "prisoner." A few children playing out in the streets followed behind us for a while, until they began taunting Brother Jobe and Loren barked at them to "get lost" or he'd "lock them up too." Robbie Furnival, one of the shaving victims, passed us by on his way home and volunteered to testify in any court proceedings. By the time we got Brother Jobe to the jail, we figured we'd made our point and word would get out around town that this dangerous character was in our custody, and there would be no more involuntary beard shaving or other affronts to civil liberties in Union Grove from the New Faith bunch.

Once up in the cell, though, Brother Jobe became irascible, letting his underlying annoyance show, and demanded various extra furnishings that perhaps we should have thought of ourselves but didn't: a table and chair, which we got from the old police office, a jug of drinking water, a blanket, and a couple of candles. That took another hour of scrounging. Finally, we secured the door to his cell with a sturdy length of chain and ran the padlock through it. By that time, he had a napkin tucked into his collar and seemed pleasantly preoccupied with the fried chicken, corn bread, pickled okra, and other delicacies that the sisters had packed for his supper, not to mention a quart of cider, all laid out nicely on the table before him.

"We'll come back later and tuck you in," Loren said.

Brother Jobe just snorted and waved goodbye.

# FIFTY-SEVEN

Jane Ann fixed us a quick supper of smoked trout with new potatoes and dill, and then we set off on foot for Karptown up the North Road, armed only with Bullock's writs. The sun still hung above Pumpkin Hill when we set out, and it was a warm evening. Deerflies hectored us along the way. It was the first appearance of the year for these hateful pests, who went into orbit around your head and nearly drove you crazy before they came in for the painful bite. Near the turnoff to the Schmidt farm, where I had met up with Shawn Watling on that fateful morning weeks ago, we watched a pack of coyotes skulk out of the woods and cross the road perhaps twenty yards ahead of us. Several of them stopped for a moment to regard us and bared their teeth, then continued on their way and vanished into the trees on the other side. They were impressive animals. Over the years, it was said, the coyotes had been mixing with the red wolves coming down from Canada to our part of the country, where there were fewer people than there used to be. Judging by their size, it seemed that they were becoming less coyote and more wolf now. After seeing them, Loren and I cut ourselves a couple of stout walking staffs before continuing on our way.

When we got there, Karptown seemed a festive place. Formerly the Hill n' Dale Mobile Home Park, it had taken on the flavor of something halfway between a frontier outpost and a medieval peasant village. For one thing, no cars or trucks were around. They'd all been sold for scrap during the Great Collection years ago. So the establishment was pleasantly inviting. The only motor vehicle on the premises was a Harley-Davidson motorcycle, a *Sportster* model, mounted totemically over the ceremonial entrance gate that they had constructed where the Hill n' Dale original driveway met the road. They had nailed up horizontal timbers between two oak trees on each side of the driveway about twenty feet above the ground. The Harley was up there in a wheelie pose. It was painted black, decorated all over with feathers, and had some small animal skulls dangling on rawhide strips from the ape-hanger handlebars.

Over the years, as the Hill n' Dale morphed into Karptown, it had expanded demographically in a way not unlike Bullock's plantation. Misfits, losers, and former motorheads from all around Washington County had drifted into Wayne's orbit and pledged their allegiance to him, the way that the failed dairymen, shop-keepers, and tradesmen with lost occupations had come under Bullock's wing. There may have been a hundred or so adults and children living in Karptown now. The original twenty trailers had been rearranged, added onto, and filled in considerably. Since Wayne ran the general supply and the old landfill along with it, and had his crews out in the county constantly disassembling va-cant buildings for their materials, his people could pretty much put up what they wanted to, and Karptown had evolved into a ramshackle masterpiece of twenty-first-century folk art. Wayne's own domicile, befitting the chieftain of a large clan, was com-posed of three conjoined trailers around a kind of great hall built of logs, with a thick fieldstone chimney at its center. This was where their wintertime communions took place—and they were said to be a very communal bunch. In behavior, they were less like their own parents and forbears and more like the Iroquois who had inhabited the same area four hundred years earlier. Wayne's Place, as this tribal headquarters was called unpretentiously, was renowned for its wild levees and holiday bashes. But Union Grove townies generally did not consort with them, and Karp's follow-ers were at this point, like Bullock's people, a social world unto themselves. I had never been inside Wayne's inner sanctum my-self. However, the front gate to Karptown had no doors on it, and I had often glimpsed the scene inside when walking past it on my way to the general supply, or beyond to Cossayuna and Hebron.

The other dwellings were fancifully cobbled out of all kinds of materials, from turquoise enameled metal panels off old highway strip office buildings, to cinder blocks, to plate glass, to rustic timber framing, with a lot of inventive, storybook-like bays, turrets, and balconies. The lack of county code enforcement had a positive effect on the creative side of things there. Many of the trailers and cottages had totem poles in front too. Totem pole carving was something that seemed to have taken the place of TV and motor sports for them.

The buildings were arrayed on a modest street-and-block pattern like a classical Roman castrum. Over the years, in their endless quest for firewood (and totem pole stock), Karp's people had pushed the forest back about two hundred yards from the periphery of the tight little village. In the zone of cleared land between the forest and the village, they grew mostly corn, which they roasted in great quantities in season. Their food growing efforts were otherwise rudimentary compared, say, to Bullock's. But Wayne Karp's position in the region was such that his operations enjoyed a substantial income in barter, and most of that was food, since he could scrounge everything else he needed on his own.

When we entered Karptown that evening, the sun was finally down but plenty of rosy light was left in the sky. It was a mild evening. At this time of year, a lot of their living took place outside, especially cooking. Dozens of smoke columns rose up in the breezeless air. The aroma of marijuana joined with that of grilling meat. Voices, laughter, and some shouting resounded around the village. No dogs barked. They didn't keep dogs. They didn't need them for work, and whatever meat they had, they wanted to eat themselves. Most of the villagers kept chickens, and they roamed freely pecking bugs out of the weeds. The horses they required for their daily endeavors were kept down the road on the grounds of the general supply. It was unnecessary for them to keep cows, since milk was the most abundant commodity in our corner of the world.

Inside the gate, as you first encountered the place, was something akin to a town square: a weedy quadrant with a wooden stage at center, sunken slightly, with split log seats rising in a semicircle of twelve rows above it—in essence, an amphitheater. When we came in, a man was onstage playing guitar and singing to an audience of a dozen others, who came and went languorously, some of them smoking their pipes. They ignored us.

"What's that song?" Loren said. "It sounds familiar but I don't remember the name."

"Me either. Are you ready for this?"

"Well, we're here," Loren said. He looked a little green.

"Okay, then, let's go."

Wayne's Place was on this square to the right. It occupied most of the north side. We stepped up to an elaborately carved door under a rustic wooden portico that had been appended to the central trailer of Wayne's complex. The door carvings depicted a lone tractor-trailer on a highway, with an eagle soaring above it. Between the truck and the eagle hung a brass door knocker in the shape of a clenched fist. I rapped on the door smartly with it. The door swung open right away, startling us. Inside stood a woman around forty, in a turquoise halter top and cutoff blue jeans. Her frizzy brown hair was bunched up on top and sprayed out as though she were some kind of tropical bird. She had wings tattooed above her eyebrows in the clan's customary way.

"Who're you?" she said.

"I'm the mayor from down in Union Grove and he's the constable."

That made her smile.

"This ain't the Grove," she said.

"We know," Loren said.

"What do you want, then?"

"We want to talk to Wayne. Is he here?"

"Oh, he's here all right."

She stood there giving us the hairy eyeball.

"Can you tell him we're here and we'd like to talk to him?"

She sort of stiffened her back and said, "Wait here."

After she closed the door, Loren said, "Where else would we wait?" He seemed to be growing grumpier by the minute.

"I think I know what that song is after all," I said.

"Are you going to tell me?"

"Smells Like Teen Spirit."

Loren turned to look at the guitar player, who was finishing his number with a flourish of strenuous arpeggios.

"I fucking hate that song," Loren said. "But his arrangement isn't bad. For a while there, I thought he was playing a folk song, you know, one of the old standards."

"It practically is, now, after all these years."

"Wouldn't it be wonderful if the world could just forget some of those really awful songs?"

"Apparently the oral tradition is still in force," I said as the door jerked open again.

"Come with me," the woman with the topknot said.

We followed her through a series of dimly lighted rooms full of velour furniture and bad art until we arrived at the back end and came outside again to a kind of broad patio facing the cornfields at the edge of the woods. A trellis overhead supported grape vines. The fruit was just forming in miniature bunches. Wayne was entertaining three other men and five women, arrayed over a full complement of rustic furniture. Chicken quarters sputtered over a grill on a halved fifty-five-gallon steel drum. A big waterpipe made out of a laboratory flask sat on a wooden side table, and the smell of marijuana lingered on the still air. It was like a scene out of the old days. Wayne was half supine in a rustic lounge chair. He had a slingshot, the powerful kind they used to sell in outdoor catalogs, and was firing at crows out in the corn. On the slate paving beside him was a plastic bucket full of pebbles. As we stepped out he let one fly. It missed.

"If that was a ball bearing, that crow there'd be a dead crow now," he said. Then he noticed us. "Well, got-damn. If it ain't Fiddler Joe. Been a while."

I could practically see the machinery in his brain working as he recognized who I was and what happened last time we met. He seemed to have a pretty good buzz on. There were jugs and pitchers on a long table and everyone held a glass of something.

"Which one of you is the mayor?" Wayne said.

"That would be me," I said.

"Since when."

"A few weeks ago."

"Well, if they had a got-damn newspaper around here, maybe some of us hillbillies would know what the hell is going on," Wayne said, before turning to Loren. "That'd make you the other one, I suppose."

"Right, I'm the constable."

"Wait a minute, wait a minute. I know you. You're the preacher down there to the Grove, right."

"I'm the minister of First Congregational."

"Since when you church types become law enforcement types?"

"It's the new thing," Loren said.

"You don't say? Like a fad?"

"Just around here."

"Oh? Well, come on in and take a load off your damn minds. Mi casa es su casa. Bodie! Tiffany! Let these fellas sit down. Come on! Move your asses. In fact, all you all git. The shooting gallery is temporarily closed. Go on, git."

The others downed their drinks, picked themselves up resentfully, and left, except the woman with the topknot.

"Brenda, why don't you give that chicken a turn and offer these boys something to drink?"

We declined.

"Aw for shit's sake, you must be thirsty," Wayne said. "It's a four-mile walk from the Grove, ain't it?"

"We got whiskey, cider, and beer," Brenda said, like a waitress in an old-time roadhouse.

"You want to shoot the shit with me," Wayne said, "you better be prepared to drink with me. Go on, sit down. I didn't pitch all that riffraff out for nothing."

Loren surprised me and asked for whiskey. I said I'd have a cider. We sat down.

"You know, I'm kind of getting to like it with the electric off," Wayne said expansively "We seen every got-damn DVD in the county and there ain't no more cable anyways, whether the 'lectric's on or off. I do miss my music, though. How are you all getting on down in town?"

"Mostly pretty well," Loren said. "Except when we get break-ins and crimes and stuff."

"We don't have any crime problem here."

"Why's that?"

"Because I rule with an iron got-damn fist," Wayne said, and then brayed energetically at his own joke.

Loren took some papers out of his shoulder bag. "I've got some warrants here."

"You don't say."

"I think this chicken's done," Brenda said.

"It ain't done until I say it's done."

"Come have a look at it."

"Just leave it and shut the fuck up."

Brenda now left the patio area in a bit of a huff.

"Lemme see those things," Wayne said. Loren got up and gave him the warrants. "Well, I got to hand it to Mr. Bullock in the penmanship department—no pun intended. Look at those *W*s and *G*s. These are as pretty as the got-damn Declaration of Independence. And the wax seal there, that's a nice touch. Almost enough for me to take seriously."

Wayne picked his slingshot off the slate floor and let fly at a crow perched on a cornstalk. To the amazement of us all, including Wayne, I think, the crow folded with the impact of the stone at the same time it emitted a particularly harsh and plaintive death cry and fell off its perch into the shadows.

"Score that Wayne one, crows zero," Wayne said. "Mind refreshing my glass? I'd ask Brenda, but she's not here."

"I think your chicken's getting away from you," I said.

"Well, don't just sit there. Get up and turn it."

I was nearest to the grill, so I got up and turned the chicken while Loren poured Wayne another whiskey—and another for himself.

"You fellas are good guests," he said. "Maybe you'll come back some night with your wives. And you," he said, meaning me, "you bring your damn fiddle. We'll have ourselves a time."

"What do you say about the warrants," Loren said.

"I admire them. They have the right look and all. Can I keep them? They'd make nice silveneers."

"Are you going to let us search for stolen goods?" Loren said.

"Of course not."

"Are you going to surrender and come on in with us?"

"Are you crazy?"

"Are you going to turn over Bunny Willman."

"Hell no."

"Then your position is that you're above the law?" Loren said.

"That ain't my position, it's my reality. How are you going to enforce this got-damn nonsense?"

"You'll be surprised," I said.

"Tell me. I really want to know."

"If I told you, it wouldn't be a surprise, would it."

"Got me on that one," Wayne said. He pointed my way and made a show of cracking up. "Well, as I see it, we got nothing further to discuss. But you did a nice job on the chicken there, Fiddler. If you want to run out into the corn and fetch that crow, I'd throw it on the grill for you."

"No thanks."

"Then I'll take over from here."

Wayne finally lifted himself out of the lounge chair and, in his catlike way, slunk over to relieve me of the grilling tongs.

"Oh, one other thing before you leave," he said.

"What's that?"

"Have another stiff drink on me for the road. Night's falling and you're going to need it."

# FIFTY-EIGHT

We hadn't gone a quarter mile down the road when we heard the footfalls behind us. Wayne's men captured us effortlessly. The gang of six he'd sent down included Bunny Willman. We didn't try to run. They tied our hands behind us, hobbled our ankles, and marched us back to Karptown—not without quite a few kicks in our asses along the way. Night had gathered by then. Stars blazed above the candlelit village and the moon was rising. The amphitheater on the village square was crowded with bodies. The same guitar player was still at it onstage, furiously scrubbing his strings, now in the glow of a dozen tin candle lamps arrayed around the lip of the stage.

A couple of wooden armchairs were set up at both extremes of the stage. They put Loren in the one on the left and me in the one on the right and bound us into them so we couldn't move. The haze of marijuana was so thick that I might have gotten high myself if I hadn't been so overwhelmed with dread. The audience was passing jugs around. They evinced the same chatty excitement that crowds always do before a public spectacle, whether it's a musical or a comedy show or a hanging. Of course, I worried about what part we were going to play in the evening's entertainment. Eventually Wayne emerged from the front door of his compound, along with several cohorts, and made his way down an aisle to the stage. He hopped up fluidly with a clipboard under his arm like the recreational director on a cruise ship. The guitar player stopped bashing his strings and ambled off stage. A hush fell over the audience as Wayne began to speak.

"Let's give Woody a big hand for putting out so much positive energy. Woody always brings a smile," he said, presumably referring to the guitar player. The crowd responded with some feeble clapping.

"As you can see—hey, pipe down out there—as you can see, we got some special guests for the main part of tonight's show." This provoked a mix of cheers, jeers, catcalls, whistles, and raspberries from the crowd. Someone threw a hunk of something—corn bread perhaps —at Loren. It bounced off his temple harmlessly. "Hey, watch out there, Mojo," Wayne said, wagging a finger. "It ain't up to you to start in on that." The audience laughed knowingly. "Before we get underway with the feature presentation, we have a couple of warm-up acts I hope you'll all enjoy, including our special guests." Wayne glanced at his clipboard. "First, we got Ricky Z, Potato, Tracy Ballard, Jesse, Pinky, and Little Eric doing highlights from episode sixty-six of *The Sopranos,* starring Potato as Tony. "Won't you please give them a big hand."

This mummery went on at considerable length. A few of the "actors" were good mimics. The story was incoherent. I barely remembered the TV series anyway. That I even got sucked into trying to follow it, though, was a testament to their earnestness. Their antics elicited a lot of laughs, though I don't think the dramatic events depicted were necessarily funny, since they mostly involved the characters abusing each other verbally, when someone was not getting shot or beaten up.

When the long piece concluded and the actors had taken their curtain calls, Wayne came back out. An insect changing of the guard had occurred with nightfall: deerflies back to headquarters, mosquitoes out in ravening swarms. With my hands bound to the chair, I could only endure their bites. My shoulders were killing me, and I had to pee so badly I was sure I'd have to go in my pants sooner or later. Loren looked like he was suffering too.

"Next up, give a nice welcome to Casey Zito, Torry Zito, Jarrod Zito, the fabulous Zito brothers, doing one of your old favorites, "Creeping Death" by Metallica. Give 'em a big hand."

Three teenage boys came out, bearing an obvious family resemblance, ranging from perhaps thirteen to eighteen. The oldest one wore a braided goatee and had the tribal tattoos over his eyes. He carried an acoustic guitar. The middle brother came out with what looked like a yard-square piece of aluminum roofing material, and the youngest had a big conga drum. They took an eternity setting up and tuning. The performance itself consisted of the middle brother making a thunderous racket by bending, warping, and banging the square of sheet metal while the youngest boy furiously slapped his drum. The guitar player thrashed his strings and struggled to be heard singing above the din his brothers made. I thought it would never end, and then I thought the audience would never stop clapping. The oldest boy said, "We'd sing another one, but we ain't practiced."

After they got off, a couple of men brought out a mattress and laid it in the middle of the stage. Then they brought out a sofa and put it behind the mattress. Wayne came back out, exhaling an impressive cloud of smoke in the footlights.

"Okay, okay, hush up, now," he said. "This next act, the last time we tried it, the man upstairs sent us a young one, and you know we need a little help that way lately, so give a big hand to Skooch and Melinda doing this scene from that old triple-X favorite, *Teacher's Pet*."

A nubile woman perhaps in her twenties came out and sat on the sofa. She was wearing a white blouse and a short plaid skirt with knee socks.

"I'm a schoolgirl," she said and giggled. Then she opened a big book, like an atlas, and pretended to study.

"Ding-dong," a voice cried offstage.

"Oh, gee, somebody's at the door," Melinda said. "I wonder who it is."

She got off the sofa and went to the side of the stage, right in front of me, actually.

"Why, Mr. Skooch. What are you doing here?"

Skooch entered, a powerful young man with his long black hair tied up in a ponytail, wing tattoos over his eyebrows in the

Karptown style, and braided beard too. He was costumed in a shiny old suit jacket and a necktie, but no shirt.

"Why, hello, Melinda," he said. "The principal, Mr. Dingus, has a new policy of sending us teachers out on house calls to our favorite students, and you're my special pet."

"Really? What a coincidence, Mr. Skooch, because you're my favorite teacher," Melinda said. "But it seems you forgot your shirt."

"No, this is our new official summer school attire."

"Gosh," Melinda said, "maybe I should get more comfortable too."

This launched the old scenario familiar to those of us who had lived through the age when recorded pornography was a bigger business than Hollywood proper. Except it was a live stage show, being played out about ten feet from my chair, not an image on a laptop computer or a hotel TV screen. Soon the two performers crossed the line beyond playacting into the realm of raw animal instinct. I watched the audience as they watched the show with uniformly rapt attention, including the five or six children present. Loren followed the action with an unreadable blank expression, though his face looked unnaturally flushed. As the tension mounted on stage, the audience members took up the chant, "Go, go, go, go . . ." and when Skooch concluded his exertions, a wave of sustained applause swept the amphitheater. Then it was over, though the odors of procreation lingered on stage in the still, moist air. The performers seemed to rapidly recover their decorum. They declined a curtain call and bustled efficiently off stage.

The stagehands struck the set. Wayne came back on.

"That was great, Melinda and Skooch. Just like the real thing—" Shouts from the audience. "Yeah, I guess you're right, Roy, that *was* the real thing. We sure hope that brings a little magic for you especially Melinda—that the man upstairs will smile on you and start baking a little bun in your oven. Thank you both. Now, onto tonight's feature. We have a couple of visitors on board

tonight. They came out here earlier to talk to me. I did my darndest
to be nice. Gave 'em drinks. Grilled up some pullets. And I got
to say, they were just rude. Sassy. Impolite. Served me with papers.
Imagine that! It's an old-time thing, for those of you too young
to remember. A government agent serves you with papers and—
I don't care which way you cut it—it comes down to this: they
want to take away your property or they want to take away your
freedom. No, don't argue."

Nobody was arguing, of course. Least of all me and Loren.
Nobody in the seats made a peep.

"That's how it is," Wayne said. "Always has been, always will
be. Anyway, these two come up from town. This one on my left
here, he says he's the new mayor down there in the Grove. That
right?" Wayne stepped my way, to see if I was paying attention, I
guess. "You hear me? I axed if that's how you represent yourself?"

I didn't answer.

"Whatever. I hope politics don't ruin him. I forget his name.
Fiddler Joe, I call him, because I seen him play once at a Harvest
Ball up to Hebron or White Creek or some damn place. I forget.
He's good. Got-damn good fiddler. You could use coaching on the
administration of justice end of things, though. You could study with
me at five hundred dollars the hour. Have your secretary call my
secretary and we'll see what we can get going. Anyway, this other
fella to my right. You going to tell me your name?"

Loren didn't speak either.

"All right. Well, I just call him Preacher Man. He's a minister
down at the main church there in town. He says he's the constable
now too. Can you imagine that? A man of God serving the very
ones that want to deprive somebody of his property and his freedom. It just don't add up. But I'm only a common man. What do
I know? I'm common as dirt, ain't I?" Wayne said and started cir-
cling around the stage toward Loren, for whom he now seemed to
have a special animus, judging by his increasingly loud voice. "And
if I'm common as dirt, you all out there must be dirt too, because,
after all, I am your chief, I am your fearless leader, I'm of you and

you're of me. So we must all be . . . dirt," Wayne said, spitting out that last word as his anger ratcheted higher. "What do you think, Preacher Man? Are we beneath you as the soil is beneath you?"

Loren remained silent.

"Well, I intend to show you what we're made of tonight by giving you a lesson. It ain't Sunday, so this won't be a Sunday school lesson, exactly. Maybe it's philosophy. There's some biology involved, so put in a bid for science too. I really don't know. Education was never my strong suit. Except for shop class. I got-damned excelled at taking things apart—though I didn't much care for putting them back together. Anyways, the aim here is to demonstrate what is in God's realm and what's in man's, and maybe how they shouldn't run together in one person 'cause you will only end up confusing people while coming to grief yourself. By the way, this lesson is free of charge. Before I'm done with you, I imagine you will be speaking to God in person. You might ax him how he came to put you in such a pickle."

Wayne stooped down and glared into Loren's eyes.

"How dare you serve me with papers? You nor nobody else down in that town will ever even think about doing it again." Then he stood back up. "Okay, boys. Bring out the glory wheel."

Four stagehands brought up some kind of hulking wooden apparatus from the rear, behind the stage. There was a steel pipe running into a hub at center that they fitted into a hole in the floor at center stage. The apparatus proved to be a plywood wheel about eight feet in diameter. Once they got it in place, they spun it around. It clattered noisily along the floorboards on casters. On the top surface of the wheel stood a simple wooden contraption that I quickly understood to be a set of stocks, with holes for the arms and one for the neck.

"There she is, friends," Wayne said. "The Round Widow, Proud Mary, the Devil's Dance Floor, the Prayer Stool, the Old Rugged Redeemer—we have lots of names for her. Some of the folks out in the cheap seats have rode on her, since this is the approved method for settling the accounts of misdoers hereabouts.

But you two are the first outsiders to get in on the action—except for a stray picker or two over the years, and they hardly qualified as people. Boys, help the Preacher Man up onto her and make sure he's comfortable."

Several of Wayne's men freed Loren from the chair that he was bound into and steered him onto the wheel. They had to shove him down to get him to kneel before the stocks, and he resisted as they forced his head and hands in the slots and bolted the top down.

"There's no point putting up a fight, Preacher Man. I guaran-got-damn-tee that this will go better if you just let go and relax. That tension works against you. Think happy thoughts. Like you just got a hand job from some parish lady in the—"

"Fuck you," Loren said.

"Huh?" Wayne said.

"You lowlife piece of shit."

"Ouch! My ears suddenly hurt," Wayne said. "What a way for a preacher man to talk. And there are children present." Wayne slunk catlike across the stage toward me and bent down close to my face. "Does he talk to your homefolks like that?"

I didn't say anything. I didn't want to say anything.

"Can't hear you, Fiddler," Wayne said. "Well if he don't talk that way to the homefolks then I suppose he saves it for the likes of us. That's interesting."

An indignant murmur ran through the crowd, then whistling and some shouts.

Wayne slithered back toward Loren in the stocks. He took something out of his pocket and stooped down to apply it to Loren's face. It turned out to be a florid red lipstick—whenever they took a house apart, they came up with all sorts of things—and he painted Loren's face with it, giving him a red clown nose, red lips, red eyebrows, and two red clown dots on his cheeks.

"Don't you look *purty* now?" Wayne said, standing aside for the audience to see. More whistles, cheers, and catcalls, and cries of "Get 'er done, Wayne-o!" Wayne kicked the edge of the wheel

into motion, shoving it round and round until it picked up speed.
Soon Loren became a blur. I stopped counting after fifty revolu-
tions. After quite a while, Wayne applied his foot as a brake to bring
the wheel to a stop. As he did, and then brought the stocks back
facing front, Loren could be seen vomiting.

"That's disgusting!" someone shouted from the audience.

Wayne seemed to inflate his chest, then leaned down to face
Loren.

"Look what you done now," Wayne said. "Goodness gracious
what a mess. Could we get a mop up here, please? I guess this explains
why you went the church route instead of astronaut training—"

That was the moment when Loren spit into Wayne's face.

The crowd howled. Whatever Wayne said was lost in the well-
ing noise. Meanwhile, he reared back and smacked Loren's head
with the back of his hand and must have whaled on him five times
more in each direction until blood the same color as the lipstick
ran out Loren's nose and mouth. One of Wayne's men came forward with a mop and pail and handed Wayne a wet rag to wipe
the vomit and spit off his face.

"Bring the got-damn instruments out here," Wayne shouted.
"Let's get this underway."

Another man brought up a canvas tarpaulin. He laid it on the
stage floor next to Wayne and opened it up. Inside was an array of
items that might be used to punish a captive human body.

"You know, when you spit in my face, you spit in the face of
everyone out there," Wayne said to Loren. "This isn't a democracy, exactly, but we do share the common burdens and enjoy the
common benefits of life. So, here's how we'll do it, Preacher Man.
I'm going to ask every one of my people to come up here and address your ass however they deem fitting, by whatever means they
like. That sound okay to you? No, don't answer, it doesn't matter
anymore what you think. Like I already said: try to relax, think
happy thoughts, and go with the flow."

Wayne bent down and rummaged among the various implements at his feet, picking them up one after the other.

"Listen up, people. What we got here: a nice ash broomstick, a horsewhip, a light carriage whip for you ladies, a brass curtain rod, a canoe paddle, a length of rubber hose with some fishing sinkers inside, and last but not least, a genuine Adirondak brand, official American League centennial-year fungo bat—this here's probably a collector's item. Now, those of you that want a turn, form a line on this side of the stage, and we'll get 'er done in a nice, orderly, systematic way. Just remember, only one stroke per customer allowed. No hogging the spotlight. We don't want to be here all got-damn night. I'm sure we'll get the point across, which is: if you come up this way trying serve any got-damn papers impinging on the personal or property rights of the sovereign individual, then your sovereign got-damn ass will be mine."

Wayne spun the wheel half a turn so that Loren was facing the rear of the stage with his rear end presented to the audience.

"Step right up," Wayne said. "The glory wheel is now open for business."

A line formed quickly leaving the seats about three-quarters empty. Most of those in line were men and boys, and those who remained in the seats mostly women and girls. The first to swing at Loren was the middle Zito boy, the one who had shaken a piece of sheet metal as a percussion instrument earlier in the evening. He chose the brass curtain rod and laid a stroke full force against Loren's behind. Loren endured it stoically, as well as the next several. But then the hulking Bunny Willman stepped up to the stage. He didn't pick up any of the arrayed implements. Instead he reared back and delivered a fierce kick, with a heavyweight workman's boot, right in the cleft below the cheeks where Loren's privy parts were tucked in. Loren gave out a bellow of a kind I don't think I'd ever heard come from a human being. And so it continued for a good twenty minutes. At some point about halfway through, a red stain appeared on Loren's pants. The blows from the last ones on line were as vicious as the early ones. As the line wound down, Loren had gone from emitting a shriek at every blow to issuing a barely audible grunt. The blood had spread across his behind and began seeping down the legs of his pants, on the inside of his thighs. The very last person on line, the woman named Brenda who had answered the door to Wayne's abode hours earlier, actually broke the ash broomstick, she swung so hard.

"Don't worry, I'll just deduct it from your pay, darlin'," Wayne said as he resumed his position front and center. "I was going to lay a stroke or two on you myself, maybe even ram the back end of that horsewhip up your bunghole for good measure, but my people have spoken so eloquently by their actions that I really don't think it's necessary. Anyway, it made me tired just watching all that." He kicked the wheel so that Loren came around frontwise again. His head hung limply in the stocks.

"I suppose you can guess whose turn it is now," Wayne said, stalking over my way. I was numb all over. I couldn't feel my hands or feet. My pulse pounded so loudly, I thought the top of my skull might blow off. "Yeah, that's the bad news," Wayne said. "It *is* your turn. The good news is, I ain't going to make you ride Old Mary. I thought to myself, maybe I should fetch a claw hammer and take it to his hands, you know, bust 'em up so bad he'd never hold a knife and fork again, let alone a freakin' musical instrument. But got-dammit, I like you too much. For all the got-damned trouble you cause me, Fiddler Joe, I like the way you play that thing and I don't want to hurt you because we need all the got-damn good music we have around here—and besides, you ain't as mouthy as your compadre here. So I'm not going to hurt you. Physically. But I do want to give you a lesson that you ain't likely to soon forget. And if I do see your ass up this way again, I promise I will ream it out good and got-damned well next time plus break every last one of your golden fingers. Let's see that bucket, boys."

Wayne's factotums brought up a big white joint-compound bucket and set it down between where Wayne stood and where I sat. It reeked.

"What I got here is a generous dip of outhouse slops," Wayne said. The crowd cheered and applauded. "You still have nice bathrooms down in the Grove, I hear. Town water an' all. Well, things are a little more nitty-gritty up here, you know. All that heat we've been getting has worked this stuff pretty ripe. I can hardly stand it myself. I thought this might be a nice way to make an impression on you about overstepping your jurisdictional lines and at the same time offer a little memento from us to take back home with you. Or all over you, I should say. Anyway, here she comes. I'm sorry we couldn't serve it up fresh and warm for you. Bodie, Pinky, get 'er done."

Wayne stepped back gingerly where nothing would splash on him and let the other two do the pouring. It took two of them to hoist the heavy bucket above my head.

"Take her nice and easy, boys. Let him enjoy the flow of it."

The stuff ran down into my shirt and pants and over my eyes and lips, liquids, solids, and all the stuff in between. After a while, it just felt cold splashing over me. Finally, the two men turned the bucket over my head and left it there. I could hear the crowd yell its approval before I shook it off and heard it bounce across the stage. I struggled not to inhale or ingest any of the filth that was dripping off my face.

"*Whooooo-weeeee*," if you aren't the very lily of the dell," Wayne said. "Okay, everybody, that's the end of tonight's feature presentation. The show's over. Thanks for coming and let's keep up that artistic community spirit. Anybody wants a musical instrument, we got all kinds over to the general. Guitars up the ying-yang. Tubas. Clarinet. Whatever. Just come by and put in for it. Those of you who would like to sign up to perform in next Tuesday night's show, go see Brenda at my place. She's always there at suppertime between sundown and full dark. For Pete's sake, you Zito boys, learn another song or two. And practice, practice, practice! Get some gotdamn discipline, why don't you. Goodnight everybody."

There was a final smattering of applause. The filth still dripped off my ears and chin. I tried to spit out what was on my lips without getting any inside my mouth. I barely noticed that Wayne had cut my bonds until he said, "Go help your compadre, Fiddler. Get him up and get gone before I change my mind and kill you both."

Once I realized my hands were free, I desperately tried to wipe the stuff off my face. By now, they opened the top of the stocks on the wheel and Loren had slumped off into a heap below. I knelt down beside him on the wheel.

"It's me, Loren. Can you hear me?"

He squeezed his eyes and nodded, and then yielded to a spasm.

"I think they're letting us go."

"It hurts real bad," Loren said. His voice was a croak.

"Try to get up. I'll take you back."

I reached under his armpits and jerked him to his feet as though he were a two-hundred-pound barbell.

"Oh, Jesus," he said.

"Can you walk?"

He limped two steps with my assistance.

"I . . . think something's . . . torn up inside," he said.

"Put more of your weight on me."

Wayne had left the amphitheater. A few of his people still milled around, both onstage and off in the seats. They simply ignored us. Several men were mopping up the spot where my chair had been. Loren took tiny shuffling steps, grimacing, and contorting his head to the side in pain.

We struggled down the three stage steps, then off to the side of the amphitheater, uphill through the dust and weeds toward the village gate. Stragglers stood still and stared as we passed by. A few registered looks of disgust. One of the few young children there spit at us. A woman stepped forward and held out a raggedy T-shirt full of holes. I took it and wiped as much of the filth off my face as possible, though my hair was still full of it. When we got up to the gate I had to stop and throw up. But then we passed under the rampant motorcycle and onto the road, and I actually believed they had let us go for real.

# FIFTY-NINE

Loren was in a lot of pain as we made our way down the road. He groaned continually and now and again cried out and cursed. I propped him up as best I could, but he stumbled several times. He said he could feel blood running down his legs. It seemed to take forever to get to the old bridge over Black Creek. We agreed to stop there. A path well trodden by fishermen led from the road down to the bank. The moon, now clear of the treetops, cast enough light to see by. I helped Loren down the path. The stream had a gravel bed, and there was a little beach beside a pool on the upstream side of the bridge. I left Loren there so he could drink some water while I went to wash the filth off myself downstream. The creek was no more than knee deep and quite chilly. I scrubbed as much as I could without soap and soaked my head, but the stench stayed with me. Then I went back to help Loren wash off. Finally I helped him struggle out of the water.

"I can't walk . . . the rest of the way," he said. He was breathing in gasps. "You're going to have to . . . send somebody up to get me in a . . . a wagon or something. Let's not even . . . argue about it."

"All right. Hold still a moment."

I hitched up a leg of his pants. The moonlight did not pick up color very well, but I could see a rivulet of something darker than water run down his leg.

"How am I . . . doing?"

"I think you're still bleeding some."

"I think so too. Before you go . . . get me a good stick. For the coyotes."

"All right."

I found him something like a war club. He said he didn't want
to sit, it hurt too much, so I helped him creep over to a clump of
alders he could hold onto and sort of lean on. I assured him I'd be
back soon and left him there by the bridge in the moonlight. I
doubted anyone from Karptown would come looking for us again.
They'd had all the fun and excitement they needed.

It had been a long time since I ran any distance, but I jogged
most of the way back to town. Much of it was downhill. I went
directly to the high school and banged on the door at the front
entrance, which was locked, naturally. I knew they ran regular
watches around the building. In a little while, one of the brothers
appeared. I didn't know this one's name, but he seemed to recognize me. He let me in. I asked him to get Joseph. He went directly.
Two minutes later, Joseph strode down the hallway, lifting a sus-
pender into place, with Elam right behind buttoning his shirt as he
walked. I told them what had happened to Loren and me up at
Karptown. Joseph said Brother Jobe had left him with instructions
to help if I called upon him. I told him to get somebody over to
Doctor Copeland's, tell him to have his wife prepare for surgery, have
her fetch Bobbie Deland over to assist, and for Jerry to report here
to the school with his wagon as soon as possible, to get Loren down.

Joseph turned to Elam. "Send Brother Jonah to get the doc,"
he said. "You go get Minor, Seth, Caleb, and Lazarus to tack up
all the horses that are fit to ride and harness a rig. I'll get the rest
of the men up. Let's all meet out front in half an hour."

Elam took off at a trot. I begged Joseph to take me to a shower
and bring me some fresh clothes, including a pair of size-ten boots,
if they could spare any. He showed me to the shower in the boys'
locker room and then went to get the clothes. I'd last been in the
locker room when Daniel was on the soccer team. Being there gave
me another reason to rue and wonder at the strangeness of how
our lives had gone in this century. The shower was warm but not
hot. They had a wood-burning boiler up on the roof rigged up to
the plumbing system. But they fired it only at breakfast and

suppertime. Anyway, it was good enough. They had plenty of sharp lye soap on hand. I scrubbed my scalp raw. Joseph soon returned with some clothing and a towel. Also a bottle of whiskey.

"I thought maybe you'd like to wash your mouth out," he said. "And knock some back to ease your mind."

"Most considerate of you," I said and did exactly that. He'd brought me a good muslin shirt and dark linen pants, a pair of suspenders. They fit well enough. The boots were nicely broken-in.

"They're Brother Jobe's boots," he said.

"Imagine that."

We talked over a plan as I dressed. The objective was simple: to extract Wayne Karp and bring him to jail. I described the layout of Karptown, the location of Wayne's place inside it, and so forth. I knew Joseph was capable of accomplishing this. But I was worried he might take things too far.

"You are not to kill this man," I said. "Whatever he has done, he is going to answer in a court of law."

"Eventually he'll answer to something higher."

"I'm just asking you not to hasten that moment."

"Okay, sir."

"Nor kill anyone else up there if you can avoid it."

"I'll take care."

"This can't turn into an Indian war kind of thing where one raid leads back and forth to another and another."

"I understand."

"And don't burn the place down, either. Most of the people up there aren't guilty of anything."

"Of course."

"I'll be going with you as far as the Black Creek Bridge. We'll stop there and get Reverend Holder into Doc Copeland's rig. I'll accompany them back to the doctor's place while you and your men get Karp. I will meet you back at the jail, with your prisoner, somewhere between three and four in the morning."

"Okay on that, sir."

"How many men in all are you going to take?"

"We have twenty horses all told. Minus the rig. Minus a horse for you. Minus any horses unfit to ride tonight. Maybe fifteen, seventeen men."

"Is it enough?"

"Any more than that, you just increase the chance for something to go wrong."

I followed Joseph to what proved to be the men's quarters, along the far wing of the school, away from the gym wing. The brothers slept five or more to the classroom there, like a dormitory. We went through them with a lantern as Joseph handpicked the brothers best suited to this venture, the most experienced, boldest.

In a little while, we all began to marshal out in front of the school. The moon was at its zenith and the clear sky blazed with stars. Minor, Elam, and the others led a string of horses down from the pasture, along with a utility cart. Minor seemed in especially high spirits.

"Good to see you again, sir," Minor said. "Tell me: how do you stop a rooster from crowing on Sunday?"

"I don't know. How?"

"Fricassee him on Saturday."

A moment later, Jerry Copeland pulled in the high school drive in his rig, a two-wheeled box cart behind a Morgan horse named Buddy, with Brother Jonah in the seat beside him. He trotted up past the gardens to the school's entrance. Jonah jumped out as I hurried over. In the box behind the seat was a stretcher on an old mattress.

"What's this all about, Robert," Jerry said.

I told him what happened to Loren up in Karptown. By the strenuous way Jerry rubbed his eyes I knew that he was extremely concerned.

"What are you thinking?" I said.

"I'm thinking I hope the bastards didn't rip anything up in the peritoneal cavity. I don't have any antibiotics, Robert. You get a bunch of shit in there it's not good news."

Just then, Elam came to notify me they were ready to ride and had my old mount, Cadmus, saddled up for me. I went with Elam and climbed aboard.

"I'm hereby deputizing all of you, limited to this operation tonight," I said and turned things over to Joseph to explain what I'd outlined previously to him about bringing Wayne Karp back alive and not harming any innocent people. Then we trotted off under the stars.

# SIXTY

Loren was on all fours in the cold, damp gravel beside Black Creek when we returned. He couldn't stand any longer, and he couldn't sit, he said, and it was too wet to lie down. He had been busy puking there on and off since I left. We brought the stretcher down for him and helped him aboard. Four of the strongest brothers hoisted him up the bank to Jerry's wagon and loaded him in the box. Jerry got him to lie on his stomach on the mattress and we backed the wagon around. Joseph and his men then continued on toward Karptown. I followed behind Jerry's wagon and we got back to town in half an hour.

Jeanette Copeland had prepared the room that Jerry used sometimes as a lab and sometimes for surgery. It was a far cry from the hospital operating rooms of the old days, but it was what we had. Bobbie Deland, a registered nurse—in the days when nurses were registered—was on hand along with Bonnie Sweetland who, as a midwife, had competence to assist. They had fired the boiler upstairs and had the room blazing with candles, several with reflector mirrors on adjustable wooden stands that could be moved as needed. Jerry also had an autoclave fitted over a small alcohol stove for sterilizing his surgical instruments. Steam curled out of it. In contrast to this makeshift equipment, the operating table was a fully articulated model that had come out of the Glens Falls hospital, complete with fixtures for placing a surgical patient in what Jerry called the lithotomy position. Altogether, the setup was a retreat from the heyday of high-tech medicine, but a lot better than nothing. At least we still understood the role of microorganisms and the need for cleanliness. Jerry had done a few surgical rotations as an intern years ago, but beyond that he had no formal training. The surgeries he did now took place in a gray area of expertise somewhere between what he had managed to learn on his own and what circumstances forced him to do. Sometimes he simply found himself in uncharted territory and did what he could.

As soon as we got there, Jerry gave Loren a morphine lozenge to place under his tongue. Jerry had been experimenting lately in refining cooked opium into a crude morphine alkaloid using slacked lime and sal ammoniac from soldering blocks to precipitate the morphine out of solution. It was a process not unlike what they used to do in the jungles of Indochina and the slums of Tijuana in the old days of the international drug trade, so it wasn't that difficult. He had managed to produce a few grams of the stuff so far. Loren began to feel relief from the pain in a little while, and not long after that he fell into a stuporous sleep. The five of us lifted him out of the cart on the stretcher, into the operating room, and into position on the table. Jerry scrubbed his hands, then drenched them and his arms clear up to the biceps in grain alcohol. Bobbie cut Loren's pants off with scissors. Bonnie swabbed the dried blood off his thighs. Jeanette laid a set of shiny steel surgical instruments on a clean towel on a rolling cart. They worked together with impressive efficiency. I searched Loren's pants pockets until I found what I was looking for: the key to the padlock on the other cell back at the jail. Otherwise, it was obvious that I was in the way. The room was barely large enough for the four of them and the patient, and besides I had other things to do, so I left and rode Cadmus over to the rectory.

Jane Ann was up reading by candlelight when I came in.

"Where is he?" she said with a strong note of accusation in her voice, as if she knew something bad had happened and I was naturally responsible.

"He's over at Jerry Copeland's."

"What happened?"

"Wayne Karp . . . did a job on him."

"What kind of job?"

"Jerry's checking him out right now."

Jane Ann got up and put her sandals on.

"If you go over there," I said, "you can't barge into the room. Jerry's got him on the table."

"The table?"

"The operating table."

She went white.

"I've got a horse outside," I said.

I rode her back over to Jerry's. She knocked on the door to his lab and called through to them inside. Jerry said not to come in. Jeanette said, "Go in the house, Jane Ann, and make some tea. We'll come and get you when we're done."

"Is he going to be all right?"

"We're stitching him up," Jerry said.

"Go in the house, Jane Ann," Jeanette said again.

"Will you stay here with me?" Jane Ann said to me.

"I can't. They're bringing Wayne to the jail. I have to be there."

Jane Ann broke down in tears and fell into my arms. She cried there for a while, then pushed herself away. Then she went inside the Copeland's house where a candle was burning in the kitchen. I could hear that she was still sobbing when I rode off on Cadmus.

I went to my own house next. It felt like a week since I had been there. The clock on the mantelpiece said it was three twenty in the morning. I found Britney upstairs in my bed. I had to wake her.

"Where have you been so long?" she said.

"We've had some trouble," I said.

"I thought it was something I did. I thought you were mad at me."

Moonlight streamed in the window. I was struck by how beautiful she looked in it, sitting there, naked from the waist up.

"I'm not mad at you," I said. "But I have to get something here and go."

"Go where?"

"They're bringing Wayne Karp to the jail. Can you move over to the other side of the bed for the moment, please? I have to get something from under the mattress."

Britney moved over. I reached down at the head of the bed to a place between the mattress and the box spring, where I felt around and pulled out the pistol that I took to Albany with me and killed a man with, the same pistol that had killed Shawn Watling.

"What is that?"

"Nothing," I said, as I tucked it behind my back in my waistband.

"It looked like a gun."

"Okay, it was a gun."

"What's going on?"

"Just a precaution."

"Will you come back?"

"Of course I'll come back."

"I'm sorry if I made you feel bad."

"You didn't make me feel bad," I said. "You made me feel whole."

I left her there in the moonlight.

# SIXTY-ONE

I waited outside on the front steps of the old town hall, there being no reason to disturb Brother Jobe's sleep until the others showed up. Cadmus seemed comfortable in front of Einhorn's store, up the block, where there was a picket post and a water trough. I finished the slab of corn bread that I had snatched on my way out of the house and wished I had more, or better still a square of ham and cheese pudding, or best of all, one of Bullock's hamburgers. The street was utterly still. With no electric lights functioning, only the moon lit the town. All around, in the houses up Academy Street, Van Buren, and Jackson, my friends and neighbors slept innocently as the earth turned them toward another day of hard work and summer heat. I wondered: if someone sat out there on the town hall steps of Union Grove long enough, night after night, would they eventually see a mountain lion walk casually down Main Street. The air was still caressingly mild. Exhaustion was creeping through my veins, my joints, and my spinal fluxes. When I blinked, my eyes did not want to open again.

I woke up sharply to the clip-clop of horses trotting down the street and the creak of harness leather. It was still fully dark, so I could have been asleep for only a few minutes. Brother Joseph had just rounded Van Buren onto Main at a trot on his big mount, Temperance. Behind him, Brother Jonah drove the utility cart. A hogtied figure occupied the box of the cart. Four other mounted New Faith men rode behind the cart. They slowed to a walk and then stopped in front of the town hall. Joseph dismounted. I went down to him. The whole group looked exceedingly grim.

"How did it go?" I said.

"We had some trouble."

"Where are the rest of your men?"

"They're back at the hermitage now."

"Huh?"

"What you call the old high school."

"Oh. What about that trouble?"

"There was some shooting."

"Did you kill anyone?"

"No."

"Did any of your own men get hurt?"

"We brought in your prisoner, sir."

"I see," I said, wondering why Joseph avoided answering my question. "Well, I'm ready to receive him."

"Yes, sir."

Seth and Caleb dragged Wayne to the edge of the box and made sure that he landed on his feet on the pavement. The way they had him tied up, he couldn't stand up straight. I went over to him. He craned his neck to look up at me.

"Hello there, Fiddler Joe," Wayne said.

"You're under arrest, Wayne."

"No shit. Hope your jail is fireproof?"

"Why? Your people planning to burn it down with you in it?"

"Now you're making me a little sorry that I didn't ram that fungo bat up your ass after all."

"That may end up being the least of your regrets," I said and pointed to the front stairs. "Bring him along now."

Inside the building, Jonah led the way up the stairway with a candle lamp. Brother Jobe was sitting up in his bed, wearing a nightshirt, when we entered the old jail room. He shaded his eyes against the lamp but didn't say anything. Wayne stopped a moment before Brother Jobe's cell, and the two stared at each other.

"What are you in here for, little buddy," Wayne said to Brother Jobe.

"I'm here to pray for your soul, old son," he replied.

Wayne cackled. I had the brothers put him in the cell we'd

prepared for him. I threw the length of chain around the bars and made sure the door was all snugged up with the padlock closed.

"Can I see you alone for a moment," Joseph said, when I was done.

I took him into the adjoining room, the old police office, and closed the door.

"We lost Minor," Joseph said.

"What!"

"You know how he was. Headstrong. He had to go in with the first bunch."

"In where?"

"Mr. Karp's domicile. Like I said, there were shots fired. Minor wasn't so lucky."

"Did Wayne shoot him?"

"Yes, sir, Mr. Karp himself."

"How come you didn't shoot Wayne?"

"You said not to."

I kicked one of the old stage flats from *Guys and Dolls*. My boot went clean through the canvas. "Goddammit all."

"We took Minor over to the doctor's, but it was too late."

"I'm very sorry. He was a fine young man."

"We're going to miss him," Joseph said. Tears welled up in his eyes, but he didn't lose his composure. "Are you going to let Brother Jobe out now?"

"I can't let him out. He hasn't been in here overnight yet."

"Don't tell him about Minor," Joseph said. "Not a word. We'll tell him about it in our own way when he's back with us. But don't you say anything."

"All right."

We returned to the jail room. Brother Jobe was now kneeling at his bed with his hands clasped on the mattress, his eyes closed, and his lips moving soundlessly, the way little children pray.

Joseph told the others to come along, leaving me alone with Wayne and Brother Jobe.

"Nice accommodations," Wayne said. "And real secure too."
He rattled the door to his cell.

I leaned against the wall beside his cell and drew the pistol out
from the back of my waistband.

"Remember this?" I said.

Wayne sauntered over. I retreated a step.

"Hey, I'm not going to bite you," he said. "Why, got-damn,
that's one of our old pieces. Ruger .41, right? I'm surprised you
didn't throw it in the crick or something."

"I thought I might actually need it some day."

"I bet it makes you feel real powerful."

"It kind of does. I shot a man with it."

"Really? That ain't like you."

"Shit happens."

"I'll say. Where'd you do that mighty deed?"

"It's not important."

"We didn't hear nothing about it up our way."

"It happened quite a ways from there."

"I suppose you'd like to kill me now."

"Yes. I sort of would."

"You going to think about it for a while or what?"

"I'm going see if the Reverend Holder survives what you did
to him."

"And if he don't, you going to kill me?"

"Pretty much, I'm thinking."

"And then I s'pose you'd say I was trying to break out or some
shit, right?"

"Something like that."

"And what if he pulls through?"

"Then we'll try you in a court of law and probably hang you."

"It don't look so good for me either way."

"Nope."

"Guess I'll just have to stand by then."

"I guess so."

"You think my people are going to sit still for this?"

"I don't know what they'll do. But the frame of mind I'm in right now, I'd send the cavalry back up there and burn your whole village down if they tried something."

"Union Grove would burn just as nice too?"

"You're wrong about that. All those trailers and shanties packed in so close together up there. I'm surprised you haven't burned it down accidentally yourself. Anyway, make yourself comfortable here. We'll get some breakfast over for you by and by. There's water in the pitcher and a pot for you to piss in. I'll be next door in the office if you need anything."

"Tell me one more thing, Fiddler Joe."

"What?"

"Who all is this wing nut across the way?"

"I guess you'd say he's another preacher man."

"What's he in for?"

"Cutting off beards without permission."

"Who the hell you got to get permission from around here to cut off a got-damn beard?"

"The owner of the beard," I said.

"Well, ain't that some shit," he said.

# Sixty-two

I left the two of them in the jail room and went next door where I was able to pile up a bunch of decrepit cushions, dusty stage drapes, and other material to sleep on. As I was doing that, the first pink-gray light of sunrise gathered in the grungy panes of the arched windows. It was sickening to realize I had been up all night long. I fell asleep immediately on becoming horizontal, despite the musty smell of all that rotting cloth.

When I woke up, the room was uncomfortably warm and sunlight streamed in the big window. My clothes were damp. It took a moment to remember what I was doing there. I had no idea what time it was. I felt hungover despite not having drunk anything, and I was hungry. I decided to go directly over to Einhorn's store, bring back some corn bread, cheese, hard-boiled eggs, and tea for the two prisoners and myself, and then go over to Jerry Copeland's to see about Loren. But first I went next door to the jail to check on everybody.

Brother Jobe's cell was empty. The combination lock was still in place, locked into the chain, but Brother Jobe was gone. He wasn't hiding under his bed either—I checked. Wayne, on the other hand, was asleep on his bed, or so I thought. As I looked more closely into his cell, I saw a dark red puddle on the floor underneath the bed. His torso seemed inert, as though he were not breathing.

"Wayne!" I shouted.

He just lay there. I went back into the police office and broke apart a scenery flat to get a length of one-by-three lumber. Then I returned to the jail room and stuck the wood through the bars of Wayne's cell to poke him. The end where I broke it was sharp. I poked his foot and called his name. He didn't respond. I inserted the stick at the cleft of the seat of his jeans and poked the point around there some. Either he possessed remarkable powers of self-control or he was unconscious.

I unlocked his cell and stepped in warily with the pistol drawn and the hammer on full cock. Wayne didn't move a muscle. I poked the end of the stick in his ear. Nothing. I released the hammer on the gun and stuck it back in my trousers. Then I reached down and carefully rolled him over. He fell off the bed as dully as a sash weight and landed faceup. There was a big hole in his skull where his right eye had been and another messy wound in his mouth. It seemed impossible that gunshots would have failed to wake me up. It was bewildering. Wayne was already stiff with rigor mortis. His arms remained in the same position, sort of clinched up and defensive, when his body lay supine on the floor, as they had been when he lay on his stomach on the bed. I stooped down and watched him carefully for a good while, eventually convinced he was definitely not breathing. Finally, I tried to find a pulse on the carotid artery in his neck. He had no pulse. Wayne Karp was dead.

I locked the body back in the cell and left the old town hall. Cadmus was gone from the picket. No doubt the New Faith brothers had taken him back to the high school. Terry Einhorn was behind the counter of his store, emptying a sack into a bin.

"What time is it, Terry?"

"Just before noon, I'd say. Hey, here's some good news: Mr. Bullock just got a boatload of trade goods up from Albany. I've got a hundred pounds of genuine whole wheat flour, three sacks of peanuts, and a half barrel of molasses. Also mouse traps—"

"I've got a dead body up in the jail, Terry."

"Huh?"

"I could really use your help—you and your boy—getting it over to the cooler at Doctor Copeland's."

"Don't tell me that Brother Whatsisname hung himself."

"No. It's Wayne Karp."

"How in hell did he get in there?"

I gave Terry a bare bones account of how Wayne ended up in our jail. I couldn't explain how he happened to turn up dead that morning, though, or account for how Brother Jobe got out, and I didn't want to spend any more time puzzling on it there in the store. Terry and his boy Teddy helped me, of course. We wrapped Wayne's body in theater drapes and took it to Jerry's in the handcart that Buddy Haseltine used to make deliveries. When we got there, Jeanette was coming down the outside staircase to the second-floor infirmary above Jerry's office carrying a bundle of cloth dressings stained with blood. Though the sight of all that blood was shocking, the fact that she was coming from up there suggested that Loren had made it through the surgery.

"How's is he?" I said.

"He had a significant tear inside," she said, "but it was at the rectum, which means less chance that anything got into the peritoneal cavity. You know, we don't have a sigmoidoscope with fiber optics anymore, so it's hard to see up in there. Anyway, we stitched him up. Now it's a matter of hoping his bloodstream didn't pick up anything."

"Is he awake?" I asked.

"No, Jerry's keeping him heavily sedated for now."

"Where's Jerry?"

"Asleep. He's exhausted."

"I have a body here."

Jeanette flinched.

"Over in that cart," I said. She glanced at Terry, who waved nervously.

"What the hell is going on around here?" she said.

I told her it was Wayne Karp and someone had killed him in his jail cell, and more than that I couldn't say, except we had to get him into the springhouse because it was getting hot out.

She said, go ahead, put him in there, if we could find room for him. She left us and went inside the house with the bloody dressings. Terry and his boy helped me carry Wayne inside the springhouse. Another body was in there, on a table, among the milk cans and other stuff of daily life. I assumed it was Minor's body, since Joseph had said they brought him to the doctor's. It was covered with a blue tarp. We made more room on the big table and put Wayne up there next to Minor, the two of them side by side, mutely, in death. It seemed unfair to Minor. Terry and his boy went back to their store on Main Street. I went upstairs to the infirmary to look in on Loren. I had to see for myself that he had made it through the surgery.

Loren was there, all right, in the clean, bright, austere room. He appeared to be sleeping peacefully, snoring even. Jane Ann sat in an armchair in the corner. Her eyes were red, from crying or sleeplessness. She shot a hostile glance at me when I stepped into the room. They'd rigged Loren up to an IV, with some kind of clear solution in a bottle on a drip valve through a rubber tube to a needle in the inside of his elbow. It was the only hint of modern medicine in the room.

"I ran into Jeanette," I said, trying to whisper. "She sounded optimistic."

Jane Ann nodded noncommittally.

"I'm sorry," I said.

Her shoulders bowed a moment, her body shuddered and she started to weep. I went to her and knelt down beside the chair, taking her hands in mine.

"He's going to recover," I said. "We'll get through this."

She cried some more. Eventually, she pulled her hands away, patted my shoulders, and ran her fingers through her hair.

"Can I get you anything?" I said.

She said no, she'd be all right, and I left her there. I dreaded what I had to do next.

# SIXTY-THREE

When I got to the old high school sometime later and asked to talk to Brother Jobe, one of the sisters, without hesitation, led me around the back of the building, around the north end of their big garden where the football field used to be, and pointed at the edge of the woods along an up-slope pasture. A distant figure dressed in black sat up there.

"Thank you," I said.

"I think he's been waiting for you."

I climbed over a stile into the pasture and made my way up the hill. Cadmus was among the horses there. A dozen of them were huddled in the shade of a large oak tree along the fence running up to the woods. At the top of the hill, Brother Jobe sat in an unpainted rough-sawn slat chair with a jug on the ground in the clover beside his chair. He was drinking whiskey from a jelly glass with cartoon characters embossed on it. Sweat beaded on his low forehead.

"Afternoon, old son. Have a drink?"

In fact, I was still intensely hungry, and I was not accustomed to drinking liquor in the middle of the day, but it suddenly seemed like a good idea.

"All right," I said.

"I only have but one glass," he said. "You're welcome to share or drink straight out of that there jug. I don't have no cooties."

I went for the jug. A stiff pull. It was good whiskey.

"Have a ding-dang seat, you're making me nervous."

I sat on the ground next to him.

"I love to watch the horses," he said. "You know, all those years back down home, my people were just crazy for the NASCAR.

They'd go out to some honking huge oval track at Darlington or
Daytona and watch those dadblamed machines go round and round
and round, making all that noise. A horrible din. For hours and
hours. If I knew how somebody could endure that, I'd die happy.
Not to mention calling it *recreation*! Heck, it'd be more interesting
to go out to the freeway overpass and watch traffic. At least the
goldurn cars'd go in different directions. Anyway, I'm glad that
foolishness is over. The car wrecked the southland. It wrecked
Atlanta worse than Sherman ever did. It paved over my Virginia.
They made themselves slaves to the car and everything connected
with it, and it destroyed them in the end. Well, here's to the New
South. May it rest in peace."

He raised his glass and took a good gulp. We had a nice view
from the top of the pasture. You could see clear over the school
into town, down Van Buren, the street trees all in a line, the jumble
of rooftops amid the billowing foliage, and a glimpse of Main Street
at the end of the vista.

"I can see how you could grow to love this little burg, though,"
Brother Jobe said. "It's a sweet corner of the country. Good fertile
land too. I wish the town wasn't so beat, but maybe we can bring
her back. You see down there where the school auditorium is?"

"Yeah . . ."

"We're going to build a pitched roof on her with a real steeple—
not one of those dumb-ass cartoon steeples like they did in the old
times on them churches that looked like goldurn muffler shops.
In a few years you won't recognize this place. It'll be like unto a
shining city set upon a hill."

"How'd you get out of your cell, Brother Jobe?" I said, the
whiskey finally driving some of the tension out of my skull.

"How do you suppose?"

"I can imagine you worked the combination lock open somehow."

"Yeah, well, that would be an obvious one."

"Is that what you did?"

Brother Jobe shrugged.

306 JAMES HOWARD KUNSTLER

"What I can't figure, though, is how you got into Karp's cell. That's a regular padlock, and I have the only key and the lock isn't broken. I don't see how you did it."

"What'd I tell you the other day about this being a world of strangeness? Science don't rule the roost no more."

"Did you kill him?"

"Was I supposed to know that he's dead?"

"I'd say so."

"Then I'd say he was struck down by the Lord's righteous wrath."

"Were you the instrument of it?"

"Look at that fine mare yonder, the big bay with the star blaze. I'm aiming to breed my jack to her and go into the mule business big time. You folks don't appreciate a mule. They ain't stubborn. They're sensible is all. You can't make them do some durn fool thing that'll endanger their lives or well-being. They're smart. But they'll gladly follow any reasonable command, and they're smoother riders than your horse. People feel it's demeaning to ride a mule, but I'll take a mule to a saddle horse any day. Plus, they can endure the heat where a horse can't."

"What am I going to say to those people up in Karptown when I bring the body back?"

"If it was me, I'd tell them to come down and fetch it themself."

"It looks like we lynched him."

"Maybe they'll have to suck it up."

"What if they don't."

"Then they're liable to see more of the Lord's justice."

"You were the one who was so hot for legitimate authority and due process around here."

"Still am. I want to live in a peaceful, orderly land. Nobody's sicker of strife than I am. Trouble is, some people and the things they do, there's no earthly legal remedy for. You gave it a good shot, though, old son. You're upright as all get out."

"He died in my charge."

"No one worth caring about will see it that way."

"What are you going to do? Cast a spell over everybody?"

"Have a little faith. I have faith in you," Brother Jobe said. He poured himself three fingers of whiskey in the glass and passed the jug to me. I was nearly brain-dead with fatigue and frustration, on top of the whiskey. I put the jug aside.

"What do you propose I say about how come you busted out of jail?"

"Say I was bonded out on my own recognizance and will appear in court to pay a substantial fine for my unseemly attempt at good-humored fun. Giving haircuts ain't a capital crime here is it?"

"You mind me asking you a personal question?" I said.

"I dunno. What?"

"What's your actual given name?"

"What's it matter?"

"Just curious."

"I was born Lyle Beecham Wilsey."

"You're a regular human being, right?"

"I like to think so," he said.

There was little more to say, except for one thing.

"I was shocked to hear about Brother Minor. We spent a week together riding down to Albany and back, you know."

"I know."

"He was considerate of us who rode with him. I was fond of him."

"Yes, he was a spirited young man," Brother Jobe said. "Brave, righteous. Helpful. Cheerful. I had high hopes for him. He was my son."

# Sixty-four

His words struck me like a blow with a shovel. Next thing I knew, I was blubbering into the clover, hardly on account of Minor alone, but because of my Daniel, and Genna, and Sandy, and all of us who had lost so much over a few years time, and the sheer accumulated discomfort of my senses. I know I was hardly in my right mind. No doubt my perceptions were off. But when at last I stopped weeping, and lifted my face back off the ground, and turned around to speak to Brother Jobe, I found nothing there but an empty chair and a hot wind blowing up the pasture, rattling the branches in the nearby trees. There wasn't even any sign of him walking down the pasture back to the school. It was like he'd simply vanished. I assumed he was using this opportunity to make yet another point—which he would later deny, of course—about exactly who and what he was. But for the moment I decided to simply accept the fact that, whatever else he might be, he was a father who had lost a son.

And when I returned to my little 1904 arts-and-crafts house on Linden Street, it was at last with nothing left to do, no onerous tasks or obligations ahead of me. Britney had left a note on the table out in the summer kitchen: *Dear Robert, I have heard much talk about your doings and all that went on. Not knowing when you might return, I took Sarah and we are out gathering wilds where Bright Creek meets the river. Corn bread and good cheese in the cupboard. Also some apple butter from Mr. Schmidt. In case you return before we do. We look forward to having you home. Love, Us.*

Bright Creek ran into the Battenkill a half mile west of the old railroad bridge. You could follow the tracks there because the tracks ran through the whole river valley. I spotted them just where she'd said they would be. Britney was standing thigh-deep upstream of the creek junction using my fly rod to work the pool where the two streams came together. Sarah was off wading a shallow side channel behind a gravel bar, picking watercress and stuffing it in a large creel that hung off her shoulder on a strap. I left the tracks and busted my way through a slough of bracken to the gravel bar by the river proper. As I got closer I could see that Britney was dapping with earthworms, letting the hook drift downstream in the current. The trout liked the pool there at the junction of the two streams because the spring-fed water of Bright Creek was a lot cooler than the river. It energized them and they fed more. I was impressed to discover that she knew this. I sat on a driftwood stump there on the gravel bar watching. She worked the pool with her back to me. Within a minute she had hooked a large, lively trout. She brought it in without any trouble and grasped it by its lower jaw, the way experienced anglers do, to get the hook out. Then, with the butt of the rod jammed under her arm, she took a paring knife out of her creel and slit the trout's belly from the anal vent to near its gills, like you're supposed to. She reached in and removed its guts and flung the guts out in the current. Then she ran her thumb down along the spine inside of the rib cavity to get out the congealed blood there that can make the meat taste off if you leave it in, especially on a hot day. Finally, she slipped the fish inside the creel and washed the slime and blood off her fingers in the current. I clapped my hands in appreciation. Hearing that, she finally turned around. What a sight she was in a wet cotton dress. I kicked off my boots and waded out in the water, scooped her into my arms, and carried her to the gravel bank.

A while later we were all back at the house. The three of us ate a fine supper of grilled trout with sorrel cream sauce, and red potatoes out of Britney's old garden behind the ruins of the Watling place, and watercress sautéed in butter for hardly a moment with a dash of vinegar, and cream custard with wild blackberries for dessert. Above all, I was starved for something I could think of only as *normality*, and felt I had begun to get a purchase on it as I settled down to read a chapter of *The Wind in the Willows* with Sarah, when there was a knock on the door. Britney answered it. Jerry Copeland was standing there, looking distracted and more morose than usual. For a moment I was seized again by the despairing nausea that had gripped me so many times in the days just passed.

"I hope it's not about Loren," I said.

"No, but you better come with me."

"What is it?"

"I think you better see for yourself," Jerry said.

We walked over to his place together. He said Loren appeared to be recovering. He didn't show signs of serious infection. His temperature was only slightly elevated. Jerry was going to taper him off of the morphine the next day. He would not say anything more about why we were going over to his place, though. It was getting on toward darkness in town, another warm night. The sun had sunk below the treetops and swallows were dipping for bugs in the dooryard gardens. People were out on their porches, and they shouted salutations as they saw us hurry by.

When we got to Jerry's, he led me into the springhouse out back. He lit a hanging candle lamp overhead and another plain stub in a brass saucer. The two bodies lay together side by side on the table, both now covered by the blue tarp. Jerry drew it back, exposing their heads and torsos. On the left lay Brother Minor, Wayne Karp to the right, their heads slightly elevated on wooden blocks.

"Have a look," Jerry said. "Tell me what you see."

I studied them a few minutes.

"Their wounds are similar," I said.

"Think so? Look closer."

Jerry held the candle just above their heads.

"They're extremely similar," I said.

"No," he said. "They're absolutely identical. See where the skin is split above each eye socket. Identical fractures across the supraorbital ridge and then diagonally down the malar bone. Same length of fracture to the millimeter. The eyeball itself is gone in both. Blown out or . . . something. Then, down below in the lower wound, see how the lip is split open with a fracture at the incisive fossa, below the nose. Same length of fracture to the millimeter. Now look here. Three teeth broken off: numbers two, three, and four. Upper lateral incisor, cuspid, first premolar. Same thing over here at this one."

"It's weird," I said.

"Look real close at the teeth. See where number two, the lateral incisor is diagonally sheared off on this fellow?" Jerry said, meaning Minor.

"Yeah?"

"Now look at Wayne."

He was right. They were absolutely identical.

"Very weird."

"I measured it with a micrometer, by the way," Jerry said. "I'll tell you something else: I pulled a .38-caliber wadcutter out of this young man's brain. And a second one down there in his neck."

"Yes . . . ?"

We stared at the two corpses another minute or so.

"The young man on the left there was brought in about three thirty in the morning," he said. "Wayne here—well you brought him in yourself at noon."

"That's right."

"You got any idea who killed him?"

I hesitated a moment as a whole catalog of scenarios, complications, explanations, and cockamamy stories scrolled through my imagination.

"I did," I said.

"How come?"

"He was trying to escape."

"What you kill him with?"

"Pistol."

"There aren't any bullets in Wayne's head. Whatever did this to him, it wasn't a bullet."

"Maybe they passed through."

"There aren't any exit wounds."

"Hmm. That's odd too."

"I'll say."

I glanced back and forth between the corpses and Jerry.

"Just thought you'd be interested," Jerry said after an awkward interval. "He was an arrogant prick, though, wasn't he, Wayne Karp?"

"He wasn't a model citizen," I said. "But he was a leader of men, in his own way."

We stood there and gazed at the bodies a while longer, and then Jerry drew the tarp back over their faces.

# Sixty-five

In the days that followed, stories circulated around town about Brother Minor and Wayne Karp coming to an eerily similar end. I doubt Jerry said anything to anyone, but Jeanette might have whispered it among her circle, or perhaps their boy Jasper told his friends, who might have told their parents. Anyway, the tale got around and was quickly conventionalized into an *eye-for-an-eye* legend which, in ten more years, would probably mutate into a classic ghost story of our region. I had to answer for Karp's death in an inquest, but the coroner was Jerry Copeland, and the matter was little more than a procedural formality, though my testimony was completely false. The truth would have been too incredible for the community to digest.

Not long after I had left Jerry in the springhouse that night, a New Faith delegation came by and took Minor's body away to prepare it for burial. Wayne's people got wind of his demise and sent a wagon down the following day to get him. Which is to say that nobody besides Jerry and me really examined the two bodies side by side, and nobody else knew how precisely their wounds compared, or what might have caused them—except for one other person, and I was not altogether sure anymore that he was exactly what you might call a person.

But the story was spooky enough to keep the superstitious denizens of Karptown from mounting revenge on Union Grove—that and perhaps their fear of the New Faith cavalry. We heard stories about them too, about how one would-be alpha male or another was jockeying for leadership of their community with Wayne gone, and factions had formed, and friction was leading to conflict among them. There was also talk of the New Faith bunch taking over the operation of the general supply and the old landfill with it, but we in town preferred the Karptowners to keep running it since it occupied the time of the more antisocial elements in Washington County and afforded them a means of support to keep them from banditry and other mischief. We didn't care, especially, who ruled their little world, though we preferred someone who might be reasoned with. And for all of their peculiarities and short-comings, the Karptown bunch had a system down for collecting a lot of useful materials that we depended on, and trading it more or less fairly.

I thought it was a good sign when Brother Jobe decided to bury Minor in the Union Grove cemetery, instead of somewhere on the grounds of the old high school. Minor was the first of their number to pass away since they came here. It made me wonder whether some of the New Faithers might begin drifting away from the core group and move in amongst us in town, rather than any of us going over to their side, which had been everyone's fear until then. There were plenty of empty houses around town.

As it became known that Brother Jobe's own son had been killed, much of the resentment against the sect, and him in particular, was put aside. Many Union Grove people attended Minor's funeral service at the high school and followed the coffin to the town cemetery afterward, and Brother Jobe gave a eulogy of exceptional eloquence—though he looked to me, at odd moments, strangely like a large insect in his black garb, with his arms waving this way and that way in fervid gesticulation so that there seemed to be many more than two of them.

Two weeks later, Brother Jobe went before Bullock on a first-degree battery complaint in the matter of cutting off the beards of nine individuals against their will. A guilty plea was entered and Brother Jobe was fined nine thousand dollars, about the price of a hundred-pound sack of buckwheat groats.

After Minor's funeral, the life of our town and the factions within it and around it seemed to settle into that fugitive condition I refer to as *normality*—which, I suppose, is a way of saying a merciful period of time in which nothing terrible happens. Though things did happen. Heath Rucker, the former constable, and even more distantly a State Farm Insurance claims adjuster, was found hanged in his kitchen from a length of cable, clearly a suicide. He had no family left. The temperature on July twentieth reached 107 degrees, the highest that any record existed for in our area. Della Laudermilk had a baby, the first one born in our community that year. Carl Weibel's son, Will, wed Felix Holyrood's sixteen-year-old daughter, Dawn, a marriage of consequence for two of the leading farm families of the region. Sister Annabelle of the New Faith came to preside over the new clothing store they opened next to the barbershop on Main. Brother Jobe was right about one thing: the New Faith look caught on because people in town started wearing the clothes they made. The secular look, composed of remnants of the old days or often clumsily sewn home-made clothes, seemed downright shabby in comparison.

By midsummer, Stephen Bullock resumed regular trade with Albany with a new, larger boat, though he eventually recovered the *Elizabeth* too. Among the interesting items that came our way from that trade via Einhorn's store was a sack of coffee beans (which lasted three days), some additional supplies of weevil-free true wheat flour, a hundred-weight of sea salt, fifty pounds of Dutch cocoa, and a crate of somewhat shriveled, leathery-skinned lemons. Bullock learned that the port of Albany was under new and more honest administration, and that the remainder of Dan Curry's bunch had been rooted out like rats.

Loren Holder recovered from his injuries and returned to his duties at the First Congregational, though he told me and several other close friends that he had "lost God." If so, then it might have been the conclusion of an older personal struggle that pre-dated his encounter with Wayne Karp. And anyway he seemed to hedge his bets by saying it was more possible that the human race possessed a spark of divinity that was worth cultivating than that a mysterious *being* was up there in the ether somewhere with anthropomorphic qualities of goodness and mercy running the whole show, and maybe it was the job of clergy to nurture that divine spark in us and make something of it. The word *worship* always rubbed him the wrong way, anyhow, Loren said. That summer, Loren also got the other project dear to his heart underway: conversion of the old Wayland-Union Mill building into a community laundry, with one Brother Shiloh, formerly a civil engineer for the Roanoke Water Authority, assigned by Brother Jobe to figure out a plumbing scheme.

The music circle resumed regular Christmas practice Monday nights, while the ever busy Andrew Pendergast organized auditions for a fall production of Rodgers and Hammerstein's 1940s musical, *Carousel*. The role of Julie Jordan went to Maggie Furnival. The story was set in a New England seacoast mill town in the nineteenth century, something more our speed lately than the Broadway hijinks of *Guys and Dolls*.

The electricity stayed off, without even a few more spasms. We got used to it. George Murdlow's candlemaking operation had to go further afield for supplies of beeswax, which was far superior to the abundant tallow in our neighborhood of Washington County. I got in four cords of stovewood working a no-title woodlot on the back side of Pumpkin Hill with the help of Tom Allison and his team of Haflingers.

A weird corn fungus appeared in mid-August, something nobody had seen before. We held an emergency meeting of the town trustees and passed an ordinance to send a team of inspectors around to every farm and compel the burning of all infected fields. It did not sweep the county, but it made us nervous since we had little to fall back on but buckwheat, Bullock's limited experiments with spelt, and whatever came up the river from Albany.

The fate of our nation remained shrouded in mystery. Without the occasional radio broadcast, we existed beyond the hypothetical doings of President Harvey Albright and his people in Minneapolis (or wherever), and their people, and their people's people. Printed broadsides out of Newburgh, Kingston, Poughkeepsie, and other towns down the Hudson Valley came to us via

Bullock's trade boats. They were full of religious hysteria with nuggets of news here and there. The hurricane that battered New England in June generated ocean surges that left parts of Manhattan, Brooklyn, and low-lying New Jersey uninhabitable. The immense overburden of skyscrapers in Manhattan had proven unusable without electric service. Long Island, a geographic dead end, had suffered terribly from the hurricane and a dengue fever epidemic, and now had a population equivalent to what it had been in the year 1800—with an immense surplus of free parking. Of the world beyond the Atlantic Ocean, we heard nothing at all. We were content to be undisturbed in our little backwater, Union Grove, Washington County, in a place once called the Empire State, where the Battenkill runs into the Hudson River.

Britney was right. I now had a family to look after. It made all the difference. She was tough and tender both and brought me home to myself after a long sojourn in a dark region of my heart. I still thought about Sandy, and mourned her and Genna, and often woke before dawn wondering if my Daniel was out there somewhere, still alive. But I had new responsibilities and new affections, and by the end of August, I had a little girl who was able to play "Old Joe Clark" on the fiddle. I resumed my regular labors, starting with the cupola of Larry Prager's barn, and enjoyed the benefit of using the donkey we had rescued in Albany. And that is the end of the story of that particular summer when we had so much trouble and so much good fortune in the world we were making by hand.